ISLAND REDEMPTION

Suzanne Cass

S C
STORM CLOUD
PRESS

Island Redemption

Storm Cloud Press, Perth Australia

Copyright © 2017 Suzanne Cass

All rights reserved.

ISBN: 978-0648266808

*To my husband, Gary, who endured watching all those
seasons of Survivor with me.*

CHAPTER ONE

A rivulet of sweat ran down between Cilla's breasts. It was hot. Searing hot, with not even a hint of breeze to cool the air.

Had she made a mistake coming here?

'Everyone, pick up your stuff and get ready to jump.' Cilla's heart rate skyrocketed at the sound of the host, JJ Hannah's, voice. Nervous flutters twisted her stomach into knots. It was time. The moment they'd all been waiting for. She rubbed her palms on the material of her shorts, her hands suddenly slick. The water looked deep, but when JJ told them to go, she knew she'd do it without a moment's hesitation.

Lining up with the other contestants along the edge of the boat, she looked down into the crystal blue ocean, watching flashes of silver as schools of tiny fish darted away.

'Jump,' JJ said, his voice loud and clear. Cilla jumped.

The water was smooth and deliciously cool against her hot skin. Adjusting the small backpack to sit up high behind the nape of her neck, she started to breaststroke toward the island. Others were doing the same around her with varying degrees of success. Two stronger guys were stroking out in front of her, halfway there already. A girl to her left spluttered and floundered, her large bag weighing her down. One man still stood on the edge of the sailboat, agitatedly muttering to himself that he wasn't good at this kind of thing.

Twenty meters off to their right, another wooden fishing boat—an exact replica of the one she'd sat upon—rose and fell in sync with the ocean swell. Each craft held nine contestants, and now Cilla could see they were also fighting their way toward shore.

Directly in front of them lay a large island, with a wide sweep of pure white sand shaped in a crooked imitation of a smile. Coconut palms stood tall, hovering at the back of the beach, casting their pom-pom shadows on the sand. A small range of mountains covered in a blanket of dark green towered behind the shore. Soft wavelets broke musically with an easy swish.

Paradise found.

Now she was in the water, her nervousness had all but disappeared. It was good to be doing something at long last. All that sitting and waiting had worn her nerves raw with an impatient need to get this game started. She was a powerful swimmer—it came with the territory when you lived and worked around boats—and Cilla knew her body would do the job for her. So she let her concentration slide to the beach and what might lie ahead.

She was about to be marooned on a deserted island with seventeen other people. As a young girl, Cilla had always dreamt of doing exactly this; a childhood fantasy. She knew many others had the same idealistic vision, but that was as far as most people took it. Now the reality-show, Sea-Quest, was about to make her dream come true.

But it wasn't just her desire to attest to her survival skills bringing her here. It was the prize money that drew her, as it had so surely attracted all the other candidates. The winner would have a chance to dig for a treasure chest holding a one million dollar prize. And she needed that money. Desperately. For both herself and her grandmother.

There was a prize for the runner-up of two hundred thousand, but second place had never entered her mind. She was here to win. At all costs.

A resolute scowl settled over her features as she continued to swim toward the beach. Her grandmother had always told her determination was one of her strong suits, she'd never given up on anything, even as a little girl. And she was determined not to give up on this. Determined to succeed.

* * *

'We'll just wait for the stragglers.' JJ flashed his perfect teeth. Most of the group were now standing in a sodden semi-circle on a large blue mat spread beneath the shade of a coconut tree. Cilla studied JJ from under the brim of her baseball cap while they waited for the three remaining contestants to drag themselves up the shore.

JJ was everything she'd been expecting; everything she'd seen on TV. Ruggedly handsome, with perceptive brown eyes and sleek ebony skin. The black muscle-shirt stretched over his torso highlighted his impossibly square shoulders, with designer jeans covering his impressive thighs like a sheath. A black fedora hat sat at a jaunty angle on top of his immaculately shaved head. JJ might look like the epitome of a well-dressed rock star, but she knew better than to draw assumptions from his appearance. He had a razor sharp intelligence, tempered with a self-effacing humor that made him the perfect host for this reality-show.

This man would be their lifeline to the outside for the next month; the chieftain of the teams. He would be there as an impartial observer, but was he really friend or executioner? She'd love to know what thoughts he kept so artfully hidden from the world behind his dimple encrusted grin and unshakable manner.

'Right, we're all here now. Let's make a start,' JJ said, making a pretence of counting heads. 'Welcome to Thailand. This is Ko Mae Ko Island and it'll be your home —for some of you at least—for the next thirty-five days.' He opened his arms in an expansive gesture. 'First, we need to introduce ourselves. You, down the end, why don't you begin? Tell us your name and what you do for a living.' JJ indicated a tall Asian man with a gap-toothed smile who stood next to Cilla.

'Uh… Okay…' The man cleared his throat and started again. 'Hi, I'm Chongan Long. Cho for short. I'm a financial advisor and I'm here to win.'

Cilla groaned under her breath. Arrogance would get you voted out of this game pretty quick; she knew that much from watching all the previous seasons on TV.

Cilla wasn't sure exactly how she was going to play this game yet, she needed to get a better handle on everyone else's tactics first. But one thing was for sure, it wasn't in her nature to be egotistical or to throw her weight around. There were other ways to get people to do what you wanted. She was more likely to make friends and keep a low profile. Her job included sailing boats for a living and it meant she was physically fit and strong, giving her a awareness of the ocean few other people had. But because of her petite size, most people were prone to disregard her, and that was the way she wanted to keep it.

'Great to meet you, Cho, and I'm sure there are seventeen other contestants here who might want to argue that point.' JJ's smile didn't quite reach the corners of his eyes.

Then he looked at Cilla with a nod of his head. Straightening her spine, she drew in a deep breath and painted on her brightest smile. 'Hi everyone.' Making eye contact with a few people in the circle, she said, 'I'm Cilla Parsons and I work for a sailboat charter company.' Her statement made a few give a quiet gasp.

'Interesting,' replied JJ. 'It sounds like you enjoy what you do.'

'Yes, I do,' she answered. Sailing was her passion and there was no use hiding the fact she got to do the one thing she loved every single day.

'A knowledge of the sea is probably a skill that'll come in handy for some of the knockout battles, don't you think?' he said, an amused glint in his eye. Trust JJ to hold nothing back.

'Perhaps,' she answered coyly.

JJ pointed to the next person in line, the plumpish lady who'd struggled to get her large bag to shore. Everyone's gaze moved away from Cilla. She took a slow, deep breath. That hadn't been as hard as she anticipated, but she still had to force her shoulders to loosen up.

She tried to focus on everybody's names as they went around the circle. The girl next to her was called Phoebe, and then there was an African American woman called

Alisha, but long before they reached the other end of the line she'd lost track of people's names and what they did. All the faces blurred together, her mind a whirl of what was to come, her edginess returning tenfold. A lot of these people were much bigger than her, and she could see the glint of staunch ambition in more than one person's eyes too. Would her determination and sheer will to win be enough? She'd have to try even harder than anyone else. *Between deception and survival lies redemption*; that was the show's motto, and somehow she'd have to find a way to be the last contestant standing, so she might indeed find redemption. In the form of one million dollars.

The sound of JJ's voice broke through her musing and stopped the quiet whispering going on in the background. 'Before we get started on dividing into teams, I have a minor task for you to complete. There are certain items you'll need to make your stay on this island easier. Some of them are essential, others more of a luxury.' He paused and lifted a hand. 'If you look over there, you'll see a large wooden corral.' Cilla followed JJ's pointed finger to a deeply shaded area at the back of the beach where there was a fence-like structure.

'On my go, you'll all race in and collect as many items as you can in the allotted time of one minute.' It all sounded fairly straightforward. 'There is a twist, however.' Cilla held her breath. Of course there was a twist, how could it be Sea-Quest without a twist? 'The items you obtain remain your property and yours alone. Even after you've been divided into your teams, you don't have to share your treasure. Is that clear?'

The consequences of JJ's statement made Cilla's head spin. It seemed it was never too early to start the game of strategy. Her feet itched with the need to sprint over to the corral.

'Everyone line up behind the groove in the sand over here,' JJ said, pointing toward the ocean side of the beach. Cilla was jostled and bumped as she moved, trying to find the best position for her start. She was squashed between a small overweight man who was already pink in the face from the heat, and a lithe blonde-haired girl with hard-edged eyes. The fat guy didn't look hard to beat, but then again looks could be deceiving, especially out here. All these people had been chosen because they possessed something special, excelled at something, be it mental strength or physical toughness.

'Get ready. You'll go on my count of three.' JJ raised his enormous arm like someone from an old-time movie about to start a car race. 'One. Two. Three.' JJ dropped his hand and Cilla went. Her bare toes dug deep into the sand, her quad muscles working overtime as her legs pumped and she sped over the beach. Inside that enclosure were items that would give an advantage to whoever grabbed them, and she desired an edge. She needed the upper hand.

But once inside, the heavy shade made everything appear gloomy and unclear, and much as she hated to, Cilla had to pause for precious seconds to let her eyes adjust.

Then she saw what she wanted, over in the far corner, laid out on a rickety table. The sharp glint of a metal edge gleamed in a stray beam of sunlight. A machete. A fundamental item for survival on this island. As she bounded forward, already breathing heavily from her run up the beach, she felt another body running alongside her in the same direction. Not daring to look over, she put on an extra spurt of speed.

Her hand landed on the wooden shaft of the machete a millisecond before the other person's.

It was a man, tall and broad, his long tanned fingers lying next to hers on the handle. Touching hers. Cilla stood frozen. Would he use his obvious strength to wrench the large knife away from her? Technically, they weren't allowed to do that, but with such a melee going on in the rest of the arena, no one would notice who really got to the knife first.

She lifted her gaze to search his features, trying to discover whether it held threat or surrender. It contained neither. The only thing registering in his honey-colored eyes was surprise. He had an open friendly face, with an aquiline nose, topped with short dark hair, mostly hidden by a black cap. He must've been on the other boat, she'd have remembered if someone with his good looks had been sitting in her group. And her mind had been in such a mess when they'd been giving their names, she must've missed him at the introduction.

He seemed to take equal notice of her. Shaking her head, she gritted her teeth. It didn't matter who he was, or why he was here, at this particular moment he was her sworn enemy.

His fingers still rested on hers as they both held onto the machete, warm and supple. He could easily tug the blade out of her hand, but he didn't, and they stood there in mute stalemate.

Cilla narrowed her eyes and glared at him. She wasn't letting this go freely. Sure, she was a fair bit smaller than him, her slim form no match for his height or nicely muscled arms flexing beneath his T-shirt. But she knew things, knew how to protect herself. Knew how to get out of trouble.

Tensing her shoulders, she tightened her grip on the handle; her knuckles going white. Maybe it was this slight movement that made him let go, or maybe it was the belligerent look in her eye, but the blade suddenly became hers. The man with the honey-brown eyes took a step back, his gaze fixed and steady on her face.

Without hesitating, she turned and raced away. She'd spied a snorkel and goggle set over on a large pile of straw when she'd first come in, and that became her next single-minded objective.

* * *

'Bloody hell!' Why had he let that woman have the machete? It'd been his for the taking if he wanted it. Just because she had the greenest eyes he'd ever seen shouldn't have swayed him in the slightest. Emerald green if he had to pick a color.

Tam Connor ran a hand through his cropped hair in exasperation as he watched the back of the woman who'd just stolen his prime piece of property retreat to the other side of the corral.

Get moving, you idiot.

Tam darted sideways and grabbed the last remaining tool lying on the wooden bench. It was a small trowel. Not nearly in the league of the machete, but at least it was something. Then he turned, looking for anything else he might grab. A low growl emanated from between his teeth. How could he have let that woman get to him? She'd taken all the wind out of his sails and left him standing there like a stunned child. He squeezed his eyes shut, trying to pull himself together.

That was the first and last time he was going to let anyone take advantage of him in the game. Next time he'd hang on for dear life and he wouldn't care whether it was a man or a woman he was competing against either. If nothing else, this first confrontation had shown him how much he needed to put that chivalrous side of himself away. After all, there was a lot riding on the outcome of this game. A million dollars would change his life.

An idea occurred to him, and he dropped to his hands and knees and peered under the table. Not caring that small sticks and leaves stuck into his skin, he shuffled forward to stare deeper into the gloom.

Yes. There was something there, shoved way up the back and almost out of sight. Reaching in, he tried to lift it. The item was heavy and his biceps tensed as he dragged it out. A cooking pot, a large one too. Now that was more like it. This might give him more of the clout he needed, after all it was hard to eat uncooked beans or rice.

'You've twenty seconds remaining,' JJ's disembodied voice echoed around the enclosure and Tam swore again. He had time to grab one more item, but there wasn't much left. Everyone else seemed to have their arms full. He spotted shapes hanging on the nearby fence and dragged the massive pot in that direction. He could see a long coiled rope and a heavy-looking sack, both tied at shoulder height to a fence post. Make a choice. Quick. He dived toward the bag, hoping it had something edible inside. The knot was tight and his fingers fumbled with the coarse string.

'Time's up. Everyone back onto the blue mat with your goodies.'

'Woo hoo,' Tam yelled with glee. He had the bag and

judging by the weight and consistency, it felt like it contained rice. He shoved it into the cauldron and dragged them both toward the mat, leaving a smooth trail in the sand behind him.

'So, let's see what you got,' said JJ as they all jostled for a spot on the mat. Tam took a surreptitious glance around. There she was, standing in front and just to the left of him, close enough to touch. Her auburn ponytail bobbed at a jaunty angle as she tossed her head to clear wayward strands of hair away from her face. Was that a nose stud he'd glimpsed back in the corral? It wasn't uncommon nowadays for girls to have all kinds of piercings. That got him to wondering if there were any more hidden on her body. There was some kind of word tattooed in the bend in her arm, as well. What did it say? He was surprised by the thrum of anticipation humming through him at the idea of discovering the answer to that question.

There was no hint of remorse or guilt in her features; she probably hadn't thought twice about the machete incident. She'd also scored a snorkel and goggle kit, a small bag which might've held fishing gear and a large water canteen. Impressive haul. She'd bring some very helpful items to whichever team she joined. She was very petite. He was tall enough to see clearly over the top of her head. He couldn't see how she could possibly hope to win any of the physical knockouts battles. But then again, she'd just secured her first victory of the game, and over him no less. There were other ways to guarantee success rather than brute strength. He'd need to watch her carefully.

'So, as many of you may have guessed, these pieces you've collected may be worth a lot or a little to you in this game.' JJ fixed them all with his famous stare, his eyes so dark they were almost black in the dim light beneath the trees. 'These items will become very important to you in the next step of the game, which is sorting out our two teams.' There were murmurs from behind Tam, but he ignored them. 'With age comes wisdom and so I'll be choosing the two eldest contestants to become our temporary team leaders.' The murmurs became loud exclamations, some of disgust, some of admiration.

'Hands up who thinks they're the oldest here?' Four hands went up and JJ sorted out ages and then made two contestants stand on two separate mats off to the right of the group.

'This is Jason Paige.' JJ pointed to the sturdy, gray-haired man with one of the best handlebar mustaches Tam had ever seen standing on the red mat. 'And this is Alisha Jackson.' He pointed to a large African-American lady on the purple mat. 'We're now going to do a school-yard pick to choose teams, taking turns to choose one team member at a time. This choice is going to be made doubly interesting because you can either pick a person for their perceived strength, stamina, good looks or whatever other physical attributes they might have. Or you can pick for the items they'll bring to the team. But remember, it's up to you which items—if any—you share with the team. The leader will pick the first person, then the second person will pick a third and so on until you have nine members on each team.'

The connotations of what Tam had just heard were enormous. Now they could be chosen on the merits of their treasure as much as any perceived physical advantages. Of course everyone would share their items. Wouldn't they? He eyed the three things at his feet. Would

CHAPTER TWO

'Welcome to camp Dawnbreakers,' Cilla heard Alisha shout, waving her ample arms to encompass the wide swathe of shoreline. Cilla, still a distance behind the main group, dumped her backpack on the sand and stopped to take it all in. It was perfect, picturesque. The deserted island beach dreams were made of, and she was going to be fortunate enough to call this home for the next little while. Hopefully weeks and not just days, as long as she could keep from being voted out of the game.

Simon, the man Cilla had chosen for their team during the schoolyard pick, stopped to join in her admiration, dropping a heavy-looking sack down next to her. His bare arm brushed against hers, and she had to resist the urge to step away. Didn't this guy know what personal space was?

'Home sweet home, huh?' He grinned down at her with an expectant air. She'd chosen him because of his build, he looked strong, with well-defined biceps and broad shoulders. Cilla hoped he'd come through in the knockouts and use those muscles to the team's advantage. He had army regulation short hair beneath his Boston Red

Sock's hat, and a large roman nose that dwarfed the rest of his face. Cilla also noticed the tail end of a dragon tattoo heading across his chest beneath his tight singlet. Worn in an obvious attempt to show off as much of his bulging torso as possible.

'Yup, we should be quite comfortable here.' Returning her gaze to the beach, she cast an expert eye over the gentle slope, noting a large flat area just inside the tree line that might make a suitable spot to build a shelter.

'I hope our team has someone who's good at building. I don't do well in the cold or the wet.'

'Oh, really?' she said, her reply faint, barely disguising her amusement.

'No, I don't,' he reiterated. 'It plays havoc with my metabolism. And I'll need to find some protein quickly. I need lots of protein. I eat at least every three hours.'

'Um…' He did realize he'd just signed up for Sea-Quest, right?

Shaking his head, presumably at some internal considerations over how he was going to continue his strict regime, he said, 'I guess, I'd better get over there and give them a hand then. They're going to need the use of these babies if they want to build any kind of shelter soon.' He lifted an arm and flexed one of his biceps alarmingly close to her nose as he spoke, smiling at her as if she'd just been awarded some great honour. Was this guy for real? She was feeling just a tad sorry she'd picked him. She half expected him to lean in and kiss his own bicep. He'd better not, she wouldn't be responsible for her actions if he did.

Just as he was about to step away, he turned and said casually, 'You are going to share those goggles around, aren't you, Cilla? Or are you aiming to be the hero and catch all the fish yourself?' He laughed as if to lighten the question, but Cilla was taken aback at his astute directness. And at the rapacious gleam she caught in his eye. It seemed that his vain, dim-witted persona was more of a veneer than she'd first been led to believe.

'Of course you can try them if you want. Whoever thinks they can catch dinner is more than welcome.' Cilla kept her tone as even as possible, hiding her surprise. Let him try if he liked, but she'd be shocked if he caught anything. She'd grabbed the snorkel and goggles because she knew they'd help locate fish and other sea-creatures, but they were missing the most important component, a spear. She hoped they might get a chance later on at one of the knockouts to win it. Spear-fishing was something she was very good at, but for now she'd keep that information under wraps. Knowledge was power in this game, and she wasn't about to let out too many of her secrets. Not yet.

'What about you? Hopefully, you're going to share some of that sack of beans around too?'

He gave her a winning playboy-model smile, showing off teeth that were just a little too straight and said, 'Of course I am, Cilla. A person would have to be plain stupid if they didn't put the team before themselves out here, wouldn't they?'

Yep, she'd definitely underestimated him. She made a mental note not to do that with anyone else in this game.

Simon picked up the bag as if it weighed nothing and marched off toward the others. Picking up her backpack and grabbing the machete from where she'd stuck it into the sand, she wandered after him. Heading toward their team flag, she could see the word DAWNBREAKERS written in heavy black letters across a purple background.

The color matched the bandanas they'd been given, which they must wear at all times to distinguish their side. JJ had told them Dawnbreaker was a name of a famous pirate ship. The teams on Sea-Quest were always named after pirate ships, it was just another part to the kitschy theme pitched at the reality TV fans. The other team were to be called the Nightramblers. Just as lame a name, if you asked Cilla, but then who was she to pass comment on trashy TV. She'd just sold her soul to become part of that same empire. She was here to compete for and win one million dollars. The idea still sat uncomfortably on her shoulders, but she'd have to get used to it, and fast. This would be her truth for the next month or so.

'Give us a hand, will you?' a voice drifted to her on the sea breeze. She turned and saw the guy with the cauldron, Tam, rounding the headland behind her, dragging the heavy pot. Cilla hid a smile. He'd made such a big commotion about not needing any help back at the beach. She still hadn't figured out exactly how she felt about this man. Unsure if she was angry or grateful for *letting* her have the machete.

Walking back to where he was struggling with the pot, she looked him up and down. He was a lot taller than her, but that wouldn't have been hard given her five foot three frame. That made him at least six foot one or two, she guessed. He looked to be of a similar age to her. She'd packed an awful lot of living into her twenty-six years, her face shaped by the sun and wind and her outdoor lifestyle, and it always surprised her when people with bland, wrinkle free features who'd lived most of their lives inside turned out to be much older than she was.

One thing she'd noticed about him when they both

reached for the machete was his hands were smooth and well-manicured; definitely a city boy. And those amazing colored eyes. They were such a pale hazel. Reminding her of butterscotch candy or honey on toast. He wore a black cap turned backward, a Mickey Mouse emblem on the front.

Drawing closer, she noticed his white T-shirt moulding nicely to his shoulders as they flexed with the weight of the massive pot; the way it drew tight across his flat, masculine chest. Physically the man was the complete package, taut and attractive. In any other situation Cilla would've been interested, but not this time. She was here for one reason only.

'Come on, we can carry it between us,' she said, bending down and grabbing the handle of the cauldron.

'Thanks.' He gave a smile of appreciation. She took the weight in her left hand and balanced herself by holding the machete in her right. It was heavy. Very heavy, especially with the bag of rice inside as well. They could barely keep it an inch off the ground between them. Respect bloomed for how far he'd dragged it on his own. He'd not done such a bad job after all.

'There might be some good caves over there,' Tam puffed. When she raised an inquiring eyebrow at him, he nodded toward the end of the beach where tall limestone cliffs reared up. 'Good for hiding in if our shelter's not up to scratch,' he said with an amused tilt of his chin. He had a point. Some shelters she'd seen built on the television series hadn't been very weatherproof, especially in a violent monsoon downpour. They stopped to stare at the cliffs, dropping the heavy cauldron in the sand.

'You're right, this area is supposed to be renowned for

its caves. Maybe we should do some scouting later,' she replied.

'Did your research, I see.'

'A little.' She shrugged. 'Didn't you?' He nodded his agreement, still out of breath from lugging the heavy vessel. Exactly how far did his knowledge extended? She wouldn't tell him she'd done much more than just research online or in books. She'd sailed these waters and explored many of the nearby islands. Never actually been on this island before, mind you.

'Have you been to Thailand before?' She kept her tone light and friendly.

'Nah, this is the first time I've been out of the good old US of A. This is all new to me.' He gave a boyish grin that made her stomach do a strange little flip-flop at the easy-going warmth in his expression. She quashed the feeling straightaway. She wasn't here to find a relationship, she reminded herself ruthlessly. She was here to save her grandmother from being thrown out on the street.

'But I've watched a lot of these shows on TV and made sure I read up on my survival techniques before I came out here. I don't like to be unprepared for anything,' he said, narrowing his eyes as he focussed on the cliffs. He was an avid fan then, that was good to know. And methodical too, by the sounds of it. That was also good to know. She liked logical people, they were easier to understand. Unlike those who were unpredictable and unstable. Such as her father.

'Shall we keep going?' He indicated the group ahead, and they bent to retrieve the pot, letting it hang, heavy and solid between them as they walked.

'I hear there's some kind of hidden lake or lagoon in the

middle of this island,' she said conversationally.

'Really?' he grunted, swivelling his head to look at her. 'We should definitely explore that.' Eagerness lit up his face at the idea. Again her stomach reacted, giving a delighted surge because he also seemed to share her sense of adventure. 'How far is it? Could we walk there?'

'I'm pretty sure we could get there if we tried,' she replied. A sudden image of her and Tam walking up a narrow trail, talking and joking, appeared in her mind's eye. It'd be just the two of them, encompassed by the jungle, alone together, intimate. She'd say something witty to him, perhaps turn to catch his eye. He might reach down to touch her face, brush away a stray strand of hair as they laughed. *Whoa.* What was going on with her today? She had to stop her mind wandering off on its own tangent. His close presence was doing odd things to her hormones… or something. Reigning in her rabid imagination, she tamped a secure lid down on those emotions.

Drawing in a sharp breath, she said, 'But then again, it depends where on the island our beach is situated.' She pursed her lips, as if in deep thought, buying time. Then they reached the rest of the gathered team, and she was saved from having to answer him. They dropped the pot onto the sand with a satisfying thud.

'So what do we do first?' The question came from Glen, a lumpy man in his mid-forties who was permanently pink in the face. He'd been the last person picked for their team. Cilla couldn't help feeling a tiny bit sorry for him. Then again, she'd do well to remember he was her adversary. 'Should we start building a shelter? Who knows anything about woodwork or carpentry?' Glen asked.

A heated discussion between a few members of the team started, but no decision was forthcoming. She exchanged a glance with Tam, but his expression was closed, giving away nothing.

Taking the opportunity, she did a mental tour of the others in her team, putting names to faces. There was Cho, the one who'd broadcast his intention to win Sea-Quest this year. On the walk to their beach, Cilla had overheard him telling Alisha he was of Chinese heritage, but born and bred in the US. Not bad looking, in a softish, geeky kind of way. Then there was Madison, with long blonde hair and sapphire blue eyes. She would've been extremely beautiful if it hadn't been for the permanent sneer on her face, or the fact she was now yelling at the rest of them.

'What do you mean, build the shelter on the beach? Of course we have to establish it under the cover of the trees. Are you all imbeciles?' Madison said loudly, cutting a Latino lady off mid-sentence.

'There's no need to call people names,' replied the Latino woman, gesticulating with her hands to bring her point home. Cilla remembered her name was Paloma. She had gorgeous olive-colored skin and carried a few extra pounds on her chunky frame. Cilla could tell by the way she was waving her arms around and not backing away from Madison's scorn that she had a fair amount of fire to her personality too. 'I just thought it'd be safer to be out from underneath the trees, so we don't get a large branch landing on our roof in the middle of a storm,' Paloma continued. The woman had a point. But the beach was way too exposed, they might get washed away if a big tide combined with a storm. Cilla kept her comments to herself, preferring to watch and listen.

'Look, you both have valid points, so perhaps we should take a vote on it.' This remark came from a short, stocky woman with a boyish haircut who'd stepped between the two women. Cilla couldn't remember her name. Was it something like Margaret? Miriam?

Then there were Simon and Tam, both standing in the background, not saying much. And finally there was Alisha, the provisional leader of their team. Nine in all.

Who could she trust out of all these people? Should she start making alliances yet? Alliances were a must in this game. You didn't get far without someone else guarding your back. Should she wait for someone to approach her, or should she take the initiative? It was all a lot harder than it'd seemed watching from home. She was usually good at being decisive, but out here it was difficult to separate reality from the game. Her instinct was screaming not to go near Madison or Paloma, they'd be nothing but trouble. But they were also tough players, out here to win at all costs. They might be good people to align with. It was all so confusing.

'I'm going to make an executive decision,' Alisha's voice broke through the arguments. 'I for one don't want to get wet tonight.' She cast a meaningful glance at the clouds gathering off to the north. It often rained at night in the tropics and judging by the glowering clouds sulking closer and closer to them, tonight might be one of those nights.

'Look, they've given us some timber and posts and other stuff,' said Alisha, pointing at a pile of hardwood dropped haphazardly next to a cleared area. 'We're going to put the shelter up here, under this gigantic tree.' Alisha pointed to the flat area that Cilla had already pinpointed in her head as a suitable spot.

'I'm good at digging holes, do you want me to start for the posts?' Simon spoke up at last.

'Good, I'll help you,' said Tam, stepping toward the big man.

They were of a similar height, Tam just pipping Simon out by an inch or so. They were both attractive, very easy on the eye, and Cilla was looking forward to watching them throw themselves into the work ahead. Simon definitely had more impressive muscles, arms, legs, chest all buffed and bulging. While Tam was longer, leaner, less bulky. But the difference was more than just physical, it was in their demeanour. Simon's gaze was constantly darting, checking to see who was watching him. Tam, on the other hand, stood relaxed and easy, observing everyone, taking in the situation.

'I'll sort out the largest poles for the foundations and bring them over,' Cilla said, heading toward the large pile of rough timber. A shelter was definitely a good start. It'd be nice to spend their first night warm and dry.

* * *

Tiny shivers racked her body. She couldn't stop them and couldn't control them. Cilla was soaked to the bone and freezing cold. Even though she clamped her jaw shut, she still couldn't stop her teeth from trying to rattle free from her head. She never been this cold before. Ever. Of course she'd been caught out in her fair share of wild storms while out sailing aboard her boat, but then she'd had the luxury of wet weather gear and the promise of dry clothes and a hot drink down below in the cabin when the time came. Now there was no end in sight to this storm, and dawn was a long, long way off.

The team hadn't been successful in their first attempt at

building a a house, as just as Alisha had predicted, tropical rain was now coming down in buckets. The torrent had started as the last vestiges of grey light fled, taking the day with it and plunging the island into pitch darkness. They had no flint, and therefore no fire. So they'd all agreed the only course of action left was to huddle in the half-built shelter and try to get some sleep. Somehow Cilla drew the short straw and had been relegated to lie right at the very end of the row of people now all crammed together like a bunch of bedraggled kittens on the too-small platform.

Rain dripped incessantly onto her face, running in rivulets down her cheeks and forming a tiny waterfall off her chin. She was wearing every piece of clothing they had allowed her to bring to the island, but it made no difference. She wished whole-heartedly she'd followed her instinct this afternoon and snuck off to scout out some of the caves that were sure to be bisecting the cliffs only a few hundred feet away. Instead, she'd stayed and tried to help create the pitiful lean-to they were now all trying to sleep under.

Moving slowly, so as not to wake the person she was lying next to, Cilla inched in closer, flattening her body next to theirs to see if she could glean just a tiny bit more body heat. She had no idea who she was next to. It'd been too dark, and they all had to feel their way to a spot. It was a man, she could tell by the hard planes of his back, but that was all.

'Oh God, move over will you,' a voice whispered out of the darkness.

'Wh-what? Wh-what do you m-m-mean?' she replied through chattering teeth.

'I can't stand you shivering all night next to me. Move in

closer and I'll swap spots with you.'

'No, I-I'm f-fine, really.'

'Don't be a hero, move over.' She felt him leave the space in front of her and then she could feel hands pushing on her back, forcing her into the spot he'd just vacated. Who was it? She didn't know them all well enough yet to pick out individual voices. She tried to filter the few words he'd said, but her numb mind wouldn't give her the answer she needed. Whoever it was had left a spot that was warm and almost dry, and she snuggled into the sleeping body on the other side, not caring who that was either.

Great. After only one night, she already had no dignity left.

The man lay down next to her, shuffled himself in tight up against her back and then draped a long arm over her shoulder, covering the top half of her torso and tucking her in against his chest.

Ever so slowly, her shivers subsided. She wasn't warm by any stretch of the imagination, but she didn't feel like she was about to freeze from the inside out anymore. The rain tapered off and now only came down in smatterings of small wet drops, instead of the deluge it'd been before.

The body crushed against hers was definitely male, she could feel the outline of his quad muscles pushed into the back of her thighs. At least that ruled out Glen. She was sure his protruding stomach would've felt like being squashed up against a goose-down pillow. She was pressed so hard up against the stranger's chest that she could feel the solid thud of his heartbeat through her shoulder blades. Strong and warm. His breath came as hot pulses of air in her ear as he breathed slowly in and out.

With his breath brushing over her, so intimate, so close, a curl of tension writhed through her abdomen. A pleasant feeling spread down her legs, right to the ends of her toes. Suddenly it hit her. It wasn't just his warmth she was responding to. It was something else altogether.

She tensed, no longer comfortable with her position. What had she been thinking, allowing this kind of intimacy? Should she move back to the end of the line, back to her freezing huddle on the outskirts of the group?

No, she refused to do that.

She'd just need to calm herself down and appreciate what she had. Enjoy the heat and try to overlook the other feelings.

Who was it? Simon? Cho? Or Tam? They were the only three candidates. What did it really matter? She was warmer, drier, and almost drowsy now. She'd face the reality of whoever was causing her body's cravings in the cold, hard light of day. Not tonight.

It'd been a long time since she'd felt sheltered by someone. By her own choice, she reminded herself. Her last relationship had ended badly, and she'd consciously steered away from men ever since. Had it really been over a year since a man had held her? She counted back to the date of her breakup with Marco. Yep. One year and two months. Maybe that was why her body was having this strange reaction to the man behind her. She hadn't been this close to anyone in a long time, that was all. Her body was just responding to the virulent male shoved up against her.

Thoughts of her ex, Marco, brought back memories of her boat. He'd lived with her for a while on *Halcyon*, before she'd kicked him off. How she loved sleeping on board, listening to the quiet slap of the waves against the outside of the hull, lulling her to sleep. If she didn't win this money, she'd lose *Halcyon*. Her mind flashed back to the day, eight weeks ago, when two debt collectors had shown up on her jetty in the Whitsunday's.

The day her life had been turned upside down.

'Are you Pricilla Parsons?' She'd been careful to lay the paintbrush on the top of the varnish tin before she got up from where she was kneeling on the deck. Turning around, it surprised her to see two men, both dressed in drab suits and ties, standing on the jetty next to her boat. One had bands of grey in his immaculate hair, matching the color of his suit. The other one was much younger and quite good looking.

'Yes.' She didn't see any harm in owning up to who she was. 'Who are you?' Something about the smirk that crept onto the younger man's face stopped her from stepping forward to greet them. Instead, she leant casually against the mast.

'My name is Andrew Barnes,' replied the older man, gesturing toward his companion. 'And this is Ben Somers.' The smirk on Ben's face turned decidedly predatory as the younger man watched her. 'We're employed by the Dominion Bank of West Wyoming.'

'Mmm hmm.' Cilla didn't speak. But the cogs were whirling in her head. Had something happened to her money? She had to make a conscious effort to stop her hands from twisting together with worry.

'May I come aboard your boat?' Andrew put one foot on the gunwale and took a firm hold of the rigging before Cilla even had time to react.

'I guess so.' She couldn't come up with a valid reason

why not, but was strangely hesitant to let him on board. In the next instant he stepped over the safety rail and was standing next to her on the foredeck, much too close for comfort. She wanted to take a step backward, but managed to quell the urge. Andrew reached inside his grey jacket, pulled out a white envelope and handed it to her.

Instinct made her reach out and take the envelope from him.

'Pricilla Parsons, you've just been served with a default notice.'

'What?' She turned the letter over in her hands, unable to make any sense of what the man had just said. 'What do you mean?'

'You must talk to your bank about that, Miss Parsons.' Andrew turned and made his way off her boat, giving Ben a signal to get moving.

'I don't understand. What's this all about?' she called after them. 'Has the bank gone broke or something?' She tried to stop the desperation from entering her voice, but failed.

'No, Miss Parsons, the bank has not gone broke. If you cannot pay on your default notice in thirty days, The Dominion Bank will commence legal proceedings against you, and they will repossess both your house and your boat.' Andrew had now regained the wooden jetty and with a satisfied smile he and his companion turned on their heels and strode back toward the clubhouse and dry land.

Lost for words she watched them go.

Hanging up her cell phone half an hour later, she had to sit down at a nearby picnic table. She was shaking all over, and tears felt imminent. The manager at the bank had just told her that unless she could come up with nearly three hundred thousand dollars, they were taking her to court and repossess all her assets. At first she'd thought it was all a huge joke, until the deadpan voice of the man on the other end of the phone had assured her he was extremely serious. Not only were they going to take her boat, but they were also going to foreclose on her grandmother's house in Wyoming. Evict her and sell it out from underneath her. Because the house was in Cilla's name. The bank manager wouldn't answer any of her questions as to how or why this had happened, just told her in a polite voice to get a good lawyer and let them sort it out.

Taking his advice, she got a lawyer the very next day. It took a few more days to get to the bottom of why she owed so much money. It seemed her father had set up another loan in her name, using the boat and house as collateral, and over the past two years had racked up hundreds of thousands of dollars in debt, with no plans for repayment. He'd committed identity fraud. He was the one owing all the money, but her lawyer told her it would be mighty hard to prove. It could take months or even years to clear her name, and in the meantime all her possessions and bank accounts were frozen.

Cilla was at a loss as to how easy it'd been for her father to do this to them. Her grandmother had signed the deed to the house over to Cilla so it'd be in safe hands. The house was going to be hers anyway when her grandmother passed away. And now it was no longer safe, and no longer in her hands. She'd told her near-hysterical grandmother that everything would be all right over the phone, that she would think of something and put it all to rights.

That's when the chance to become a contestant on Sea-Quest had come up, and she'd grasped at the idea like a drowning woman seizing a life raft. The prize money represented a light at the end of a very dark tunnel for Cilla. She had to win. It was the only way she could see out of this financial hole her deadbeat father had landed her in.

And now here she was, not even able to get through the first night without having to rely on the human decency of the guy behind her, whoever he was. A man who caused her body to react in ways she'd not thought possible while she was cold and wet and crammed in next to eight other sleeping people. Closing her eyes, she tried to ignore her body's persistent nagging and find sleep.

* * *

Weak sunlight filtered through the thatch of the partly made roof, playing across Tam's eyelids until he was forced to open them. The wooden platform beneath him was hard and unforgiving and all his muscles stiffened up in protest at having to rough it. But at least he was warm and dry now. Unlike last night. That was the first time he'd ever had to endure nature in all her unleashed glory. The island had thrown them a hard lesson in survival for their first night out. He'd been bitterly cold and wetter than a soggy sheet on wash day. Hopefully, there wouldn't be too many more nights like that one.

Something moved beneath his arm, startling him until he remembered where he was; what he'd done last night. The woman curled in front of him was stirring, a slim arm thrown above her head in a stretch. It was Cilla, and she felt disturbingly good tucked against his chest, small and warm, and a streak of protectiveness ran through him. *Don't be an idiot.* He shouldn't want to be protecting anyone. All these people were his competition, his opposition. He'd be voting one of them out—possibly Cilla—eventually, and he'd do well to remember that.

'Morning, Cilla,' he whispered into her ear, sleep making his voice husky. He felt her start of surprise, then she turned slowly toward him, craning her neck to get a glimpse of who it was behind her.

'Tam?' He heard her stifle a small groan. Was that regret in her tone? Was it possible she hadn't been sure who he was when he'd played the hero last night? There was definitely an element of surprise in her eyes when she saw who he was.

'Morning,' she replied with a yawn. 'Thanks for... you know.' This time there was more of the sincere gratitude in her voice. Oh well, even if she hadn't known who her savior had been, she at least had the decency to thank him.

'Not a problem.' And it wasn't. He was truly okay with giving up his spot for her. And therein lay the dilemma. He'd done the very thing he'd vowed not to do just as recently as yesterday afternoon, when he'd let her have the machete. God, was he always destined to be the honourable fool? Around this woman it seemed the answer might be a resounding yes. Cilla snuggled her head back down on the bamboo and closed her eyes.

Grunting with ill-concealed annoyance at his own lack of fortitude, he rolled over and got up, any idea that he might catch a few more minutes sleep now gone. No one else was up yet, but there was no way he could continue to lie here pretending to doze.

Leaving Cilla and the rest of them lying together in the

shelter, looking for all the world like sardines stacked in a tin, he padded on bare feet out onto the sand. The beach looked washed clean from the downpour. Their footprints had almost faded from existence, now merely muted shadows of themselves. It was cool under the shade, so he walked forward into the sun and dabbled his feet in the shallow water at the margin of the beach. It looked like it was going to be a glorious day; hot, but with a sea breeze already on its way.

First things first. Nature called. He made his way into the jungle toward the makeshift toilet the team had constructed. Passing close by the pallet, he could see some of the others finally starting to stir.

'Hey, wait up.' Tam turned in time to see the muscular woman with short-cropped hair wave at him from the edge of the shelter. He waited for her to join him, and they headed down a fresh trail Simon had cut through the undergrowth yesterday.

'Thanks for waiting. I'm busting to go.' The woman hustled off down the trail in front of Tam. 'I'm Margaux, by the way, but you can just call me Marg. You're Thomas, right?'

'Yes, that's right, but I prefer Tam.'

'Righto, Tam it is. I'm pretty good with names and faces, I'm sure I've got everyone in our team down already, eh? What about you, are you good with names?'

'Um, I guess so,' Tam replied, a little bewildered by the barrage of conversation this early in the morning.

'I'm from Toronto, French-Canadian, you can probably tell by the accent, eh? What about you?'

'I was born and raised in LA.'

'LA, huh? I've never been there, mind you, but I'd love

to go sometime. It must've been awesome living there, nice and warm, I bet. Not like the ice and snow of Toronto. At least you'll be used to all these beaches and oceans and stuff. We've got nothing like this in Canada.'

Well, he wouldn't have put it quite like that, but there wasn't a chance for him to reply. The woman could surely talk and continued to dominate the discussion all the way down the path. Despite her penchant for hogging the conversation, Tam liked Marg. She had a ready smile that crinkled the corners of her eyes and an open, easy manner. Her figure hugging T-shirt and tiny little shorts showing off her well-defined body. This lady had muscles bigger than a lot of men Tam knew. As long as she lived up to her appearance, she'd be a great help for the team in all the physical knockouts.

'Cool hat.' It didn't feel like Marg had even drawn breath between one topic of conversation and the next. 'What is that on the front, Mickey Mouse? Did you steal it from your nephew or something? Oh, or maybe you have a kid of your own. Have you been to Disneyland before?'

Which question did he answer first? Tam reached up and ran a finger lightly over the Mickey emblem. Yes, this hat meant a lot to him, in ways he wasn't sure how to explain to Marg. But in the time it took to consider how best to answer the myriad of questions, Marg had dropped that subject and was onto the next one.

'You don't mind if I go first, do you? I'm bursting!' Without even waiting for a reply, Marg popped behind the screening bushes they'd left around the toilet for privacy, leaving Tam feeling more than a little uncomfortable standing on the other side.

The incongruity of the situation didn't stop Marg from

talking, however. 'My partner would die if she saw me now, peeing in a hole in the middle of the jungle.' Marg let out a hearty laugh of self-deprecation. 'Lucy didn't want me to come on this show. She's more timid than I am, there's no way she could do this. She won't even go camping with me. I was saying to her, just before I left—ARGHHH!'

Tam rushed forward at the ear-splitting scream.

'What is that goddamn thing?' Marg dashed around the bush, still pulling her shorts up and pointing back toward the ground. Tam cautiously stepped toward the spot Marg was pointing at. There was huge, alien-looking bug, crouched in amongst the leaf litter.

'Jesus,' he replied in disgust. Then taking a closer look he said, 'I think it might be something called a cicada.' He didn't let the relief show on his face, not wanting to humiliate her. He'd been expecting some gigantic spider or scorpion, or another of the deadly insects that lived on the island he'd read up on in the past month. 'They're harmless, although this one is quite large.' He let it crawl on his hand and held it up for Marg to see. 'These are the things that make that incessant noise all night, like a loud, broken orchestra.'

'Awesome.' Marg came up to have a closer look. 'Don't get many bugs in Canada either,' she admitted with a wide smile.

Tam put the large cicada onto the trunk of a tree and went around the bush to relieve himself. When he emerged again, he found Marg staring thoughtfully up into the branches of a coconut palm.

'We need to learn how to climb these, so we can get us some coconuts,' she said, running a hand through her cropped hair. 'Have you got any ideas?'

'I think it's better if you have a rope. We should probably wait until we get back to camp.'

'Awesome. Well, you can show me how to do it. I've always wanted to get my own coconuts, you know, like Gilligan on Gilligan's Island.'

Tam laughed along with the blond woman. He'd loved that show, too.

'Shall we go back and see what's for breakfast?' Marg turned her sandalled feet back toward the path. Tam watched Marg's impressive thighs flex while she walked. He almost had to break into a jog to keep up with her.

As they walked, his mind roamed back to last night, when Cilla had lain at his back, cold, wet, and shaking like a leaf. When he could no longer put up with listening to her chattering teeth, he'd pushed her over and taken her spot. He'd been cold out on the edge, but hadn't suffered nearly as much as she'd seemed to. Common sense dictated he should've left her out there. But he was beginning to see it wasn't so easy to separate the game from decent human morals and emotions. The last thing he wanted was to get entangled with the people he was competing against. But that might be harder than he first anticipated. If it came down to the crunch though, he hoped he could put his need to win over any need to be popular or liked.

CHAPTER THREE

'Everyone come in and line up on your mats.' JJ beckoned both teams down onto the beach. Cilla followed the rest of Dawnbreakers out from underneath the shade of a coconut palm into the blistering sunlight. She had to squint; the light and heat reflecting from the white sand was so fierce she couldn't see a thing. Sunglasses were a must for any sailor to protect their eyes from the sea, sun and sand. But they were considered a luxury on Sea-Quest and therefore not allowed.

Standing in the burning rays, she was grateful she'd worn a white T-shirt over her bikini. At least the capped sleeves would cover her shoulders to stop sunburn. Her gaze fell on two of the other women, Madison and Paloma, both wearing skimpy bikinis. Even with sunscreen on, they'd suffer later. Although Cilla's bright orange swimsuit might rival theirs for color, they were much more practical, in the form of a sports crop-top and cut-off shorts. Cilla felt safe, knowing her choice of swimwear, while not sexy or seductive, would see her through any knockout battle JJ might throw at them.

The four men had removed their shirts, exposing bare torsos. She guessed they would also learn the hard way, especially Glen, whose lily-white skin would soon go as red as a beetroot. Simon might fare a little better. He already had a golden glow to his skin. The tan looked so even, Cilla was tempted to believe it may not all be a product of natural sunlight. Tam had tan-lines on his arms and neck, as if he spent time out in the sun but with a shirt on. Although his chest and back were pale, she was impressed by the definition in his shoulders and the way his pecs flexed as he gestured to Glen during their discussion. Yep, she could definitely spend a lot more time looking at him.

'Welcome to your first knockout battle.' Cilla's heart skipped a beat at JJ's words. Anticipation had tied her stomach in knots all morning. This was it, their team's reputation was about to be put on the line. They needed to win this knockout. She needed them to win this knockout.

'I hope your swimming skills are all up to scratch, as well as your skills of deduction, because you're going to need both of them for this knockout.'

Cilla surveyed JJ's face as he spoke. There were no telltale signs, nothing to show what he thought of each team's abilities. His gaze measured them both with the same equanimity, his arresting brown eyes sparkling from beneath his fedora. The dimple in his left cheek was on full display today, dark skin accentuating his white teeth. Was he a nice guy, or not? The verdict still wasn't in as far as Cilla was concerned.

'Six members from each team will race over a series of obstacles out to that boat.' Everyone's gaze followed JJ's pointing finger; to a tiny canoe that sat over one hundred meters, bobbing out in the ocean.

'You'll untie the boat and paddle it back to shore, bringing the bags of puzzle pieces you've collected on the way. Your three remaining members will use those puzzle pieces to assemble a well-known saying. The first team to construct their puzzle and use it to raise their flag gets an exemption.' JJ made it sound easy. Cilla knew it would be far from that. They needed that exemption. It meant they wouldn't have to go to the conclave tonight, where someone would be the first person to be voted out of the game.

'I'll give you a few minutes to strategise,' said JJ. That was their cue to decide who was going to do what. Cilla thought she knew her own strengths and weaknesses, but would the rest of her companions acknowledge theirs?

'So Dawnbreakers, you have fire, is that right?' JJ's question caught them all off-guard and the entire team stopped talking at once. The Nightrebels went still as statues too, waiting for their answer. Fire was a tremendous advantage this early in the game.

Alisha answered for them, 'Yes, that's right, JJ.' She shot a triumphant glance over at the other team. 'Cho was able to help us with that.' Alisha didn't elaborate, and Cilla was glad she hadn't given away their methods. Cho started a fire this morning, using Glen's reading glasses as a magnifying glass, concentrating a spot of sunlight onto a handful of dry coconut husk. After many false starts and much frustration—the wood was still damp because of the continuous rain—they finally had a blazing fire. It was well banked and should be smoldering when they returned to camp.

Cho didn't know it yet, but she was indebted to him.

She'd been debating whether to show them how to light a fire her way. Using two dry pieces of wood and lots of friction. Her lifestyle, living on-board her yacht, often dropping anchor in any bay or harbor that took her fancy, had helped provide her with much of the knowledge for this game. But she'd be keeping that titbit to herself for as long as possible.

* * *

'Come on Paloma, you can do it,' Tam shouted, encouraging the struggling Latino woman. 'That's right, climb up like it was a stepladder. Make sure your hands have a good hold first, before you move your feet.' He kept his voice steady, but inside he was seething and he had to resist the growing urge to yell at her. This was only the first obstacle, and Paloma couldn't seem to get her body over it. Her fists were all tangled in the heavy ropes of the net and she hung like a limp jellyfish, as if there was no strength in her muscles.

The other four team members chosen to do the swimming option had gone on ahead, helping Glen swim the distance to the next obstacle. Glen was their weakest swimmer, and they'd all thought he'd be the one slowing them down. They might've been wrong on that count. Tam had told them he'd stay with Paloma. Now he was standing in chest deep water on the other side of the ten-foot high net barrier, his stomach churning with impatience.

Alisha, Cho, and Madison stood on the beach yelling at Paloma; most of the comments were encouraging, but Tam could hear Madison's remarks becoming less helpful by the second. They'd volunteered themselves to do the puzzle section of the knockout. He hoped they were as good as they purported themselves to be. These knockouts were often won or lost in the final few seconds.

Paloma hauled herself the last few rungs up the net and flung her body over the top of the metal bar.

'Well done, Paloma. You can let go now and jump into the water.' Tam thought he heard her mutter something in Spanish under her breath as she continued her painstaking climb down the other side. Probably cursing, but whether it was directed at him or the teammates on the beach, he had no way of knowing. He had to restrain himself from jumping up and pulling the woman into the water. Then he remembered she had four kids and a husband waiting for her at home. The thought should've made him more solicitous toward her, but she was definitely trying all of his patience right now.

As soon as she lowered herself down, Tam started swimming toward the next obstacle—two pontoons connected by a narrow plank. He could see Glen inching his way across, one foot in front of the other, arms windmilling out to the sides. Marg and Simon were already across to the other side, cheering him on. Cilla trod water near the first platform, waiting, her water-dark head bobbing with the rise and fall of the waves.

'Try not to touch the platform until Glen gets to the other side,' Cilla said as he was about to reach up and hang off the ropes. 'It makes it harder to balance on the plank,' she added with an apologetic lift to the corner of her mouth. Tam trod water and waited his turn. At least Paloma was an excellent swimmer. She'd made up a little time. The Nightrebels weren't having nearly as much trouble. They were already halfway to the third obstacle, swimming as a group and looking strong together.

Suzanne Cass

Glen made it to the other pontoon and turned back to give them a gleeful wave.

'Right, you go next, Paloma,' Tam directed. He gave her a push up to help her onto the pontoon, his hand placed firmly on her backside. Tam was surprised when Paloma made the crossing in record time. Paloma was excellent at balancing it seemed.

He floated with Cilla in the aquamarine water while they waited for Paloma to make the crossing.

'You can go now, I'll come over last,' he said.

'Oh, really?' There was an edge to her question he didn't quite understand, making him hesitate a fraction before answering. He wasn't about to start ordering her around, but they needed to work together as a team to get through this.

'I just want to make sure the whole team gets there as soon as possible.'

She didn't answer, but her narrowed eyes suggested she thought she'd be the judge of that. Was she going to argue with him? Perhaps she hadn't really forgiven him for the machete incident after all. He thought he'd more than redeemed himself the other night when he'd kept her warm. But who knew what went on in women's minds.

Paloma was nearly across, so Cilla hauled herself up onto the platform, giving one final glance in his direction. The urge to put his hand on her backside and give her a push was considerable, but he stopped himself just in time. If she didn't appreciate being told what to do, how would she take having his hand on her ass?

He watched Cilla as she made her way over the beam, using her arms to help her balance, her bare feet feeling their way along. She'd said she was a sailor. He could imagine her doing the same on the plunging deck of a yacht at sea. This was probably an easy hurdle for her.

Watching her making the crossing, Tam found himself considering Cilla's legs. She had wonderful legs. Not long, but definitely toned and well-proportioned, leading up to a very fine ass. That thought made him remember how her extremely nice rear-end had felt jammed up against his thighs in the shelter, when he'd swapped places with her. It'd made it damn near impossible to sleep. Every time she'd twitched or shuffled, he'd become hyperaware of her all over again.

Yep, she was more than a little mesmerizing. He'd have to watch himself, take care this... thing he had for her didn't overwhelm him. Keep in mind the one reason, the only reason he was here.

She was a tad intriguing though, self-sufficient and down to earth. A no-nonsense type of person. What would her life be like living on a boat, always transient, moving from place to place, harbor to harbor on a whim? Ephemeral. Free. Not a life for him, that was for certain. He needed the grounding of somewhere permanent to live, and he liked the noise and bustle of the city. He'd only been on the island for three days, but the quiet, slow rotation of time out here, although soothing, would eventually stifle him with its sheer simplicity.

Raising his awareness from his inner musings, he saw Cilla was nearing the end of the beam and he readied himself to go.

The next obstacle was easy in theory, but not so in practice. Each of them had to duck-dive along a rope held in place by a red buoy and retrieve a bag of puzzle pieces. Some bags were deeper than others, but the rules stipulated they all had to grab one bag each. And Glen was struggling with that. He wasn't a great swimmer in the first place, so diving and holding his breath while untying a fiddly knot was almost beyond him. Tam ground his teeth together, keeping control of his temper.

'You're nearly there Glen, come on, one more dive and you've got this. The knot is just hanging there now.' Cilla used a calm tone to keep Glen focussed. Tam felt anything but calm. She was doing a much better job than he was. She had her hand under his armpit, half-supporting him as he wallowed in the water. The man was almost hyperventilating, dragging in huge gasps of air. A twinge of compassion went through Tam. Even though the guy was practically useless, he seemed to be trying as hard as he could.

Tam swum up and lent his support to Glen's other arm.

'Take a few seconds, get your breath back, you won't do us any good if you pass out.' Tam tried to make his words sound sympathetic. Cilla threw him a grateful glance. The sparkling light reflected off the water, making her green eyes seem to glow even more like emeralds.

'I'm good now,' Glen said, his plump cheeks wobbling as he nodded his head. 'I'll give it another go.' He sucked in a huge gulp of air and disappeared beneath the waves. Tam and Cilla floated together, waiting for the second time that day. A long silence stretched between them. As a rule, Tam never found it hard to start a conversation with a woman. He always had something witty or intelligent to say. But out here, the woman with brilliant green eyes seemed to erase all thoughts from his mind. She must think he was an imbecile, or rude, or both.

'Got it!' Glen's triumphant face emerged, streaming

water, the bag held high.

'Great work, let's go then.' Tam turned Glen toward the small canoe, another twenty meters further out and started for it. The other three had already clambered into the boat, but they weren't allowed to start paddling until all six of them were in. Nightrebels were three quarters of the way back to the beach in their canoe. Dammit. They were going to lose this knockout.

'Come on, Glen, we have to pick up the pace. Give me your bag so you can use both arms for swimming.' Tam's movement through the water slowed now Glen's heavy bag of puzzle pieces hampered him. But he still wasn't as slow as Glen. 'Try turning on your back and sculling backward,' he suggested. Glen reminded him of a big, white whale as he did a slow ponderous turn onto his back. Their pace increased, but not as much as he'd hoped.

Cilla swam on the other side of Glen, breast stroking slow and steady, not out of breath in the slightest. She was an excellent swimmer. She appeared to glide through the water with no effort, even impeded as she was by her heavy puzzle bag. Tam would have to remember that bit of information. It might come in handy when they were competing one on one.

Everything about Cilla seemed to be pragmatic. Even her bikini looked more like sports-wear than swimwear, a sensible Lycra crop-top and little shorts. She looked better in that functional swimsuit than either Madison or Paloma did in their ridiculously tiny bikinis. Now she was wearing a white T-shirt over her bathers, but Tam could still remember the sight of her strolling down the beach this morning, legs striding out, tight swim shorts highlighting her pert bottom, showing off her flat, toned stomach to best advantage.

Concentrate on swimming, idiot.

Sooner than he thought, they reached the boat and the other three were hauling Glen in and taking the bags from Tam. Pulling himself into the small canoe which rocked precariously as he swung his leg over the side, he took his seat in the bow. Shaking water from his hair, he tried to slow his breathing. The swim, laden with two bags, had been more taxing than he imagined. Cilla landed on the seat beside him, water flowing from her hair and clothes.

Marg handed them both an oar. 'Get rowing guys, we need to catch the other team.'

Tam followed her discouraged gaze and saw the other boat riding a last wave that would take them onto the beach.

'Shit. Shit,' he swore.

'Yep,' Cilla replied as she dug the oar deep into the water. He did the same on his side and they cut a swathe through the aqua water.

The seat was only just wide enough for them both to fit on, and the left side of Cilla's body was jammed tight up against him. Every time she pulled the blade through the water, her bare leg brushed up against his. Her skin was cool from their swim, but smooth and soft against his. He could feel the ripple of her thigh muscle as she worked to keep herself on the seat and lift the heavy oar.

Get a grip. Now was not the time to be having fantasies. He'd made a promise to himself he wouldn't get caught up with anyone during this game. Throwing all his weight into rowing, he made the boat leap forward with a surge.

They weren't far behind the other team by the time they crashed onto the beach. Between himself and Simon, they'd made the little canoe fairly fly. Cho, Alisha, and Madison ran into the water to help drag the boat up the beach.

'Give me the bags,' Madison demanded. She tore three bags out of Simon's hands and ran up toward the table where the puzzle was to be completed. 'Hurry up and bring the other bags. Quickly,' she practically screamed. The bossy diva side of Madison didn't impress Tam at all. Alisha and Cho ran after her with the remaining bags.

Cilla dropped her oar on the sand and leant forward in the boat, resting her elbows on her knees, head hung low.

'You okay?' She looked exhausted, but she turned her face up to him and gave a tired smile.

'Yeah. That was pretty tough, huh?'

Tam rolled his shoulders, feeling his muscles protesting, his chest still heaving from the exertion. For all of her slight form and petite stature, she'd done well, hadn't given up rowing even once for the entire ride in. She was certainly made of sterner stuff than first impressions implied.

'At least we've finished our part. Now it's up to those other three,' he replied.

'Amen to that. I guess we'd better head up there and lend our support. There's a lot riding on the outcome of this.' She got to her feet, and half clambered, half staggered out of her side of the boat.

He agreed. No one wanted to be the first person voted out of the game. Ever.

Tam didn't like the look of their odds when he saw how far behind his team was compared to the Nightrebels. They had to use their large puzzle pieces to build a life-size version of a ship's wheel; the kind used to steer the huge wooden pirate ships in all those tacky B-grade movies.

Madison was trying to take over the puzzle, domineering and bullying Alisha and Cho. However, Cho was standing up to her. His nimble hands took away a few of the pieces Madison had put in the wrong place and started methodically placing one puzzle piece after another. Madison didn't like being usurped, flicking her blond ponytail in annoyance, her perfect mouth forming into a childish pout. Good. Tam was glad Cho was using some initiative; it looked like he'd be a valuable member to the team.

Tam glanced down at Cilla standing next to him and saw her throw an agitated gaze toward the other team. His gaze traced her profile, following the soft curve of her high cheekbones down to those full pink lips. A smattering of freckles covered her fine nose. She was beautiful, if you liked your women a little on the wild, untamed side. He watched as her expression changed from despair to surprise, the corners of her mouth lifting into a half-smile. He snapped his gaze away from her face.

The Nightrebels had fallen behind. They'd done an entire section of the puzzle upside down and now had to pull it apart. There was a lot of yelling and arm waving going on, but would it be enough?

* * *

'Dawnbreakers win exemption from the conclave.' They were the sweetest words Cilla had ever heard. She watched JJ hold a statue aloft and couldn't wipe the grin off her face. A body crashed into her and she felt her feet leave the ground as Simon lifted her up in a huge bear-hug, swinging her around in a circle.

'We won. We won,' he chanted, and for once in his life he was actually not annoying. She laughed along with him and then Alisha, Marg and Tam joined in the embrace, a mutual outpouring of ecstasy mixed with complete disbelief.

'Come and get it, Dawnbreakers,' JJ boomed over their loud whoops of joy. Cho went out to grab the figurine and brought it back to the team, triumphant. It was a life-size replica of some kind of rainbow-colored parrot, looking like it'd been seized straight off the set of the movie Treasure Island. But right now Cilla didn't care what it looked like; it was what it symbolized that was important. Freedom from the vote tonight.

The Nightrebels stood subdued and glowering on their mat. Cilla thought she might've even seen one of the older ladies in the group shedding a few tears. It'd been so close. It could just as easily have been them crying at the thought of having to go to the conclave tonight. But they were safe. She was safe, for another couple of days at least. Until the next knockout battle. Thanks mainly to the efforts of Tam and Simon's rowing prowess. Simon had definitely put his impressive biceps to good use today. And Tam, with his muscular arms and tall stature, had done more than his fair share of the work too. Tiny goose bumps raised up all over her body when she thought about how it'd felt, Tam's bicep bumping into her shoulder, his long leg pressed up against hers as they both struggled to keep the boat moving forward. It'd been difficult to keep her concentration on the paddle, and the beach in front of them.

'There are a couple of little extra rewards involved in this knockout, that I didn't mention earlier.' JJ waited until the noise from the victory celebration had died down. It was hot out here in the blazing sun, and Cilla could feel sweat trickling between her shoulder blades. But she could see no evidence of perspiration touching JJ's skin. His black T-shirt—his signature apparel—was well chosen, hiding any telltale sweat marks, making him seem immune to the heat. It made Cilla feel grubby and second-rate, just looking at his crisp cleanliness.

'Not only were you playing for exemption from the conclave, you were also playing for fire.' He held up a flint for them all to see. Cilla noticed how his hands were neatly manicured. Blunt fingers, manly and thick, the lighter shade of his fingernails obvious against the darkness of the skin on the backs of his hands. 'But Dawnbreakers don't really need it now, do you?'

'We'll have it anyway thanks, JJ,' said Alisha, walking up and taking the proffered item. 'A flint will still come in handy.' Cilla watched the Nightrebels out of the corner of her eye as they frowned in Alisha's direction. No flint meant no fire for them tonight, and worse than having no heat, it meant they'd go hungry, with no way to cook their rice. This wasn't a good omen for the Nightrebels.

'But because we cannot have our contestants dropping like flies due to dehydration or starvation, we'll be giving the Nightrebels a flint as well,' said JJ. Damn, they'd just lost any advantage they might have had over the other team. Her gut roiled with the unfairness of it all.

'Second, will a member from each team come out and get this clue.' JJ held up a small rolled parchment in each hand. Madison was the first off the mark, rushing out to snatch the proffered paper from his hand. 'You're required to share this information between all team members. It's a clue to the whereabouts of a special golden doubloon that'll give the person who finds it a single exemption.' There were a couple of low, appreciative whistles from Simon and Glen. This could bestow great power in the game. Cilla could see all her team member's eyes light up with the possibilities.

As soon as they were out of ear-shot of the other team, Cho said, 'Come on, Madison, let's see it then.' There was a slight hitch to his voice as he wasn't quite able to contain his excitement.

They all stood in a circle around Madison and watched her fingers strip away the twine holding it together and unroll the handmade parchment. She read it out, her voice slow and measured. 'Decipher these clues to find the hidden doubloon.' Stretching out the parchment so they could all see it, she continued, 'It's a series of pictures. Does anyone know what they mean?'

Cilla crammed in as tight as she could next to Alisha, peering over her shoulder to get a good look at the symbols; just a couple of stylized drawings, really. The first one was a picture of a large wave curling toward the shore. Did that mean the doubloon was somewhere near the water? The second picture was of a large tree towering over a stick-figure standing beneath it. That could represent any number of large trees near their beach, and Cilla was no closer to understanding that clue. The third picture was of a shovel next to a hole in the ground. Well, at least she knew it meant she'd be digging for the doubloon, but how deep? And the fourth looked like it might've been meant to represent a cave, but it had a big red cross through it. Did that mean they shouldn't be looking in any of the myriad of caves or crevices in the cliff faces surrounding their beach?

It was all so confusing.

Cilla spent the rest of the walk back to their camp turning the images over and over in her mind, trying to come up with an exact spot to look for the doubloon. She was sure everyone else was doing exactly the same thing. As usual, the game of Sea-Quest excelled at giving with one hand and taking away with the other. The clues were vague and cryptic. The person who found this exemption doubloon would have to be either very clever, or very lucky. Dammit, she needed to be that person.

* * *

'I'd kill for a coffee right now, eh?' The sigh Marg brought forth said it all, and Tam had to sympathise with her. 'One little sip, that's all I need. If I concentrate hard enough, I can almost taste it.' Marg closed her eyes, the tip of her tongue darting out to lick the imaginary foam from her lips. Firelight played over her features, casting shadows that highlighted her square jaw. 'There's an awesome café half a block from my place, where the barista roasts his own beans. The coffee is so dark and strong and earthy. It's to die for.' This time her sigh came out more like a groan.

'Why bother tormenting yourself?' Simon asked, his mouth cocked in a derisive smirk. 'Look at me, I'm fading away before my very own eyes. I need my daily protein to keep this body going.' He flexed his pecs at her. 'But I've decided not even to think about what I'm missing out on. That way it won't distract me from what I came here to do. To win this game.' His smirk turned into a sly grin.

'Oh, go away, Simon.' Marg shuffled her backside around in the sand and turned her back on Simon to face Cilla. 'He's so annoying,' she whispered in a conciliatory tone, making Tam want to laugh out loud.

'I'm right here, I can still hear you,' Simon replied. Marg ignored him. They were all sitting around the campfire, digesting their meagre meal of boiled rice and seaweed, with a little coconut milk to add a hint of flavour.

'What food do you miss the most, Cilla?' Marg asked. Tam's gaze slipped toward Cilla, noticing her give a shrug and then wince, as if her shoulders ached. Which they probably did if they felt anything like his after the effort they'd put into paddling that canoe today.

'I miss a lot of things,' he heard her say. Tam returned his gaze to the sun-bright coals of the fire. He liked the sound of her voice in the dark. It was light and serene, like a gentle sea breeze flowing over him. 'I do love Jelly Babies though. I always have a packet or a jar of them around somewhere when I'm on my boat.'

'Hmm, they're okay, I guess,' said Marg, not sounding overly impressed. She leant over so she could peer past Cilla, trying to make out Tam's form in the firelight. 'What about you, Tam? What's your favorite food, eh?'

Uh oh, now Marg had him fixed in her sharp gaze, catching him unaware. 'Hmm, that's a harder question to answer than you might think,' he replied. 'I have quite a few favorites, coffee being one of my top ten, same as you.' Cilla canted her head on to the side, watching him, curiosity in her gaze as she rested her chin on the top of her knees. In the orange glow of the fire, her eyes were dark and unreadable, her steady stare unnerving, making him lose his train of thought.

'Um, I ah...' he stumbled over his words. Godammit, this was an easy question, he'd been day-dreaming about the foods he missed just this morning. It was her eyes.

That's what was making him fumble. Drawing in a deep breath, he started again. 'I really love a good turkey leg, or even a humble corn dog.' There were groans of approval from the others sitting around the fire. 'But if I had to pin it down to one thing, and because I work with the kids at Disneyland, it would be… a Peanut Butter Heaven.'

'What's that?' asked Marg. No one else said a word as they waited to hear what this delight entailed.

'It's a peanut butter sandwich, dipped in chocolate. The kids absolutely love it, and it really is one-hundred times better than just a peanut butter sandwich on its own.'

'Do you mean completely covered in chocolate?' asked Paloma in a breathy murmur, her eyes pinpoints of light in the dark.

'It sounds awesome,' chimed in Marg, in equal awe.

'Hang on, did you say you work at Disneyland?' Cilla turned to face him. 'I've never been to Disneyland.' Of course she would be the one to pick up on the hint he'd just given. Everyone else was still drooling over peanut butter and chocolate, but she was staring at him with open-mouthed incredulity. He lifted his left eyebrow in wry amusement. 'Do normal people work at Disneyland, really?' she asked, and he could tell she was intrigued.

'Yes, I do. Does that surprise you?'

'I guess it does,' she admitted.

'I'm a child clinical psychologist,' he said. 'I do most of my work with disadvantaged kids.'

'Really?' Simon let out a snort of disbelief.

Ignoring Simon, Cilla said, 'Doing what?' That slightly surprised tone was still there, giving away the fact she found it hard to reconcile him, the big brawny guy, dealing with the serious business of helping children.

'I spend a lot of time running around Disneyland, eating Peanut Butter Heavens and flying around on the Dumbo ride, chaperoning groups of kids. Giving them a good time. Something most of them have never experienced before. But I'm also trying to help them deal with the blows life might've dealt them. There is a method to my madness. A proven theory behind the way we use fun to help the kids open up.'

'Wow, peel back the layers and it's amazing what you find,' said Marg. 'You're an interesting man, Tam Connor.' The tone of Marg's voice was soft, evaluating, weighing up this additional information about him. He saw the same sentiments echoed in Cilla's gaze.

Maybe he'd said too much, given away more info than he should. But then, working with disadvantaged kids was a fulfilling job, one he was proud of. The long slog to get through his Degree to become a child psychologist had definitely been worth it, and he couldn't wait to see those excited little faces again, watch their eyes light up as he told them all about his escapades on a deserted island. He was determined to make it as far as possible in this game, so he could go back home with his head held high and tell them he'd done it all for them. He'd tell them that whenever he'd felt like giving in, he would think about them all; about Tommy who was abandoned on the street by his mother when he was only two, or Angel who was seven and lived in a one-room hovel with her drunken father. Their fortitude spurred him on.

'That's one reason I came on Sea-Quest. To collect stories to tell the kids when I get back home.' Tam kept his tone light, deflecting Marg's newfound respect.

'Yeah, give over, Tam. You're here for the money, just

like the rest of us. Tell us your secret, the real reason you're here,' said Simon, his voice rough with disdain. Tam curled his fists together in front of him, holding back the sudden hot surge of anger at Simon's tactless comment. He saw Cilla shoot a glare of dislike at Simon through the dark.

Swallowing the resentful words on the tip of his tongue, Tam managed to control himself, saying instead, 'Of course I'm here for the money.' He kept his voice smooth, showing no outward sign of chagrin. 'I want to use it to build a bigger clinic. There are so many other kids out there who need our help.'

Cilla twitched next to him on the sand, and he decided it was time to change the subject.

'As long as we're giving up some of our secrets, tell me exactly what you do, Cilla? I know you said you sail boats for a living, but that's quite a broad spectrum,' he said, smoothly deflecting further questions away from himself.

Starting, as if caught off-guard, she mumbled, 'Well... I do just about anything that encompasses sailing a boat.' Raising her hands, palm upward, she seemed to grapple for the words to explain her gypsy lifestyle. 'I do things like skipper a charter boat for people who can't sail it themselves.'

'Give us an example,' Marg encouraged from Cilla's other side.

'Okay. I've spent the last year working in the Whitsunday Islands, off the Queensland coast of Australia, for a charter boat company. People want an idyllic holiday, floating around on a yacht, drifting from island to island. But a lot of them have no idea how to actually sail. That's where I come in. My official title is Sailguide, but I also sometimes double up as a kind of hostess, cooking their food, cleaning the boat, that kind of thing.'

'What size boats are we talking?' Tam asked. She sure lived differently from anybody else he knew.

'Anything from a thirty-one footer right up to a luxury fifty-foot catamaran.'

Glen, who'd been silent until now, uttered a face-shattering yawn. He got up from his spot on the opposite side of the fire and started a slow shuffle toward their shelter. 'I don't know about you guys, but that knockout today wrecked me.' Typical Glen, he was making a habit of going to bed early so he could nab the best spot, right in the middle of the platform. Tam watched his bulky form as it slowly morphed into the darkness and disappeared. He could hear Glen feeling around, making himself comfortable.

'Have you ever sailed on the really big ones, like an ocean racer?' Tam asked. He'd only seen those types of boats on the TV, and he'd love to hear about how it actually felt to sail them.

Cho, Madison, Alisha, and Paloma started up their own quiet conversation, as usual, picking apart what they'd done wrong in today's knockout, Madison dominating the discussion.

'I'm off as well, I need to get my beauty sleep.' Simon stood up and looked down on them from. 'Come on, Marg, let's go grab some Z's. You can sandwich in between me and fat—' he stopped in the middle of what he was about to say. '—Glen,' he continued. 'Then I won't have to lie next to him, or touch him, or anything like that.'

'You big baby.' Marg didn't make a move to get up. 'What's wrong with you? Are you homophobic? Because I might take offense if I thought you were.'

'No, I'm not.' His words were vehement. 'I...don't need to be lying next to other men. Especially flabby men,' he finished lamely.

'You really are a chauvinist, aren't you?' Marg sighed. But she got to her feet. 'Come on then, I need some sleep too and I'm not so choosy about who keeps me warm at night. At least if I'm sandwiched in between two males, Lucy can't accuse me of cheating, eh?'

Tam watched the unlikely allies stumble off over the sand, then returned his gaze back to Cilla. She was rubbing her eyes and an enormous yawn split her face.

'I was going to ask you about racing yachts, but it seems that might be a good topic for another night,' he said.

'Yeah, I'm shattered. You probably don't feel a thing after all that rowing, but I'm aching all over.' She rolled her shoulders and gave an ironic laugh as she pushed herself up. But she only got halfway up before she fell back down and he found himself reaching for her.

Standing up, Tam offered her a hand. For a second she hesitated, then reached up and grabbed it. Her palm was small and cool against his, her petite fingers wrapped around his wrist.

'You did an outstanding job today.' He hadn't let go of her hand and now they were standing together, much too close, on the sand. She was warm and inviting, mere inches away, her proximity making his chest expand. He'd almost forgotten how his body had reacted to hers on the first night on the island. Now, a craving, quick as lightning, flashed through him.

This wouldn't do. It was one thing to admit he was attracted to this woman, but he needed to control his body's appetites. He couldn't let her distract him from his goal.

But before he could react, she took a step backward, unfastening her hand from his and moving away from his encompassing awareness.

'Goodnight, Tam.' She turned her back and walked away from him.

CHAPTER FOUR

Cilla bobbed in the water off the rocky outcrop, holding her prize aloft.

'You got one!' Alisha's voice was shrill with delight. 'Ooh, it's a lobster. We'll eat like kings tonight. Wait till my husband hears about this,' she crowed, clapping her hands with glee. Cilla pushed the goggles onto her forehead and swam the short distance to the limestone headland.

This was the first time they'd tried their hand at diving for seafood using the goggles. Simon had fashioned a crude knife from pieces of metal and some driftwood washed up on the beach. It was by no means a proper spear gun and far from the diving knife Cilla was used to, but it was quite effective. Their fishing attempts at using the hook and line off the end of the headland had so far been unsuccessful. At least they wouldn't be coming back totally empty-handed this morning. Cilla threw the crustacean at Alisha's feet—making her squeal like a delighted child—then hauled herself out of the water.

'You kill it. I'm no good at that sort of thing.' Alisha kicked the writhing lobster with her toe and then shied away as it turned on her, claws raised. Cilla gripped the knife, her knuckles turning white around the handle. She thrust it through the middle of the lobster's head. The lobster didn't even twitch, it died instantly. It was the most humane way to kill them, but Cilla didn't take any joy in killing. She dropped it into the small rock pool containing the rest of her haul—two large crabs and three sea urchins. At least she could take heart from the fact they'd lived free and happy right until the second they died. Back in the real world, she didn't eat meat. But out here, with debilitating hunger pangs cramping through her belly, she was willing to eat this fresh shellfish at least. After all, it was a matter of survival. And she needed to survive, be strong and capable if she was to win. Eating fish and shellfish was a small compromise, compared to the reality of her grandmother being evicted from her own house. Would she be prepared to eat real meat, strips of pig or cow flesh, if it came down to it? Her mind skipped away from that question.

'It's my turn now. Come on, give up those goggles.'

'Are you sure you don't want to try the fishing lines again? We could use the sea urchins for bait this time and dangle them off the point, where the water is deeper.' Cilla cast a meaningful look toward the edge of the outcrop. 'There're definitely fish hiding in the crevices and shady spots, I saw lots of them.' She was hesitant about Alisha duck-diving with goggles if she'd never done it before, but she didn't want to sound like she doubted her. After all, she'd been more than adept at everything else she'd turned her hand to so far. Only problem was, she'd be the one who'd have to dive in and rescue the rather large woman if she got into difficulty.

'No, I want to try diving first. If I catch nothing this way, then we can do the boring old fishing thing.'

'Fair enough,' Cilla capitulated, not wanting to labour the point with Alisha. 'Here you go. Just remember not to get too close to the rock wall, or brush against anything. There're definitely things that *are* poisonous down there,' Cilla replied. And that was the truth. She wasn't trying to scare the woman, just get her to take a bit of care. 'I'm not kidding, Alisha. Don't touch anything unless you're completely sure what it is. And don't walk over the coral, you might step on something nasty.'

'You make it sound positively spooky,' trilled Alisha, her wide confident smile putting Cilla more at ease. 'I mightn't have snorkelled for dinner before, but I swim a lot in the ocean back home.' She sat on the edge of the rock, re-adjusting the goggles and snorkel, her black skin gleaming in the sun. She had on a one-piece bathing suit, which did nothing to hide the rolls of fat wobbling around her belly.

It was true, Alisha was a strong swimmer. But Cilla would keep an eagle eye on her, just in case. She watched as the other woman swam about twenty meters out and inspected the water, trying to see what lay below her in the clear, deep blue.

Cilla cast her gaze out over the sparkling sea. It was early—she and Alisha had decided to try their hand at ocean foraging straight after breakfast—but the day was warming up in rapid degrees. Cilla loved the heat; she could bask on these rocks like a stranded seal all day. Her skin was already going a darker color with all the time spent in the sun. A delicate breeze rippled across the ocean, spritzing it into tiny waves, which danced with light. Dawnbreakers' beach lay behind and to her left, curving away in a swathe of white sand. Small puffs of clouds clumped on the horizon, but the sky above stretched away, blue as a forget-me-not flower.

Cilla licked the salt from her lips and relaxed back on her elbows, soaking up the sun. Right at this moment, it was indeed paradise.

A shadow hovered over the rocks beside her, blocking out her sunlight.

'Can I join in the sun-baking?' Cilla looked up, blinking the bright light out of her eyes.

Tam.

Her peaceful bubble evaporated. Why did his presence put her on edge? She tried not to begrudge his company. It wasn't his fault she had mixed feelings toward the man.

'Sure, grab a rock.'

Tam waved to Alisha out in the blue before he sat down next to Cilla, dangling his feet into the water. A little closer than she would've liked.

'Have you caught anything yet?'

'Yes, we have.' She pointed to the rock pool a few meters away.

'Wow, that's great. A bit of protein to go with our rice and beans, huh?'

'Yep. We need to supplement our meals, or we're all going to fade away to nothing by the end of this game.'

'Some of us more than others,' he countered with a sly lift of his eyebrow.

'I certainly packed on the pounds before I came out here, though. Didn't you?' Cilla asked, remembering how much junk food she'd eaten over the past few weeks to try to get some padding onto her naturally slender frame.

'Really, it doesn't show. You're in great shape. And no, not especially. I always eat a lot, anyway. Maybe I squeezed in a few extra Peanut Butter Heavens here and there.' He gave her a cheeky grin, and it made her grin right back.

Hang on. Had he given her a compliment?

He took off his baseball cap and then, much to her surprise, stripped off his blue singlet as well. She'd seen him shirtless a few times, but from this vantage point— lying right beside him—she got an extra up-close and personal view. His back and shoulders were tanning up from their exposure to the sun, almost matching the bronze on his arms now. He was perfectly proportioned, broad shoulders fanning down to a lean waist, the bulk of his well-defined musculature obvious underneath the layer of smooth skin. He must've worked hard to get that physique.

'Do you go to the gym a lot?' The words blurted out of Cilla's mouth before she could think to stop them.

Honey-colored eyes turned toward her. 'Every now and then. Why?'

'Oh, no reason, I was just wondering,' she mumbled, feeling the blood rise in her neck.

'There's a big gym at Disney. The staff are encouraged to use it,' he continued. She silently thanked him as he pretended not to notice her blushing. 'It's good to stay fit. I believe a healthy body helps maintain a healthy mind. And I've got my hands full keeping up with lots of very energetic kids every day.' The corner of his mouth twitched when he talked about the children. It was cute. Endearing, even.

Tam lay back on his elbows next to her, eyes fixed on her

face. *God, he was good-looking.*

'What about you? Do you spend much time in the gym?'

'What?' Her mind wouldn't work properly, entangled as it was in the contemplation of his handsome face. 'Um... no, I get little time, what with living on a boat and all.' She finally managed to get her tongue working. 'I prefer to keep fit just by being alive. You know, walking on the beach, swimming in the ocean, winding the winch to trim a sail. That kind of thing.' She'd have to remember not to look directly at him too often. She didn't need to be losing her wits because a gorgeous man looked her way. *Remember why you're here, Cilla.*

'Well, it suits you. You look great.'

There it was again. This time a definite compliment, one she couldn't ignore.

'Thanks.' His bare arm brushed against her shoulder as he turned back to face the ocean. She had to resist the urge to reach up and rub her bicep, to wipe away the burning sensation where his skin had come into contact with hers. A low thrum of energy ran through her body, pooling in her abdomen. She wasn't normally one to swoon over a man, any man, no matter how good-looking they were. But the heat was still there between her thighs, and every time he grazed her arm it got a little warmer. She needed to get her self-control back.

Letting out a grunt of frustration, Cilla sat up, pretending to check on Alisha's progress. Her mind skipped back to her response to Tam on their very first night on the island. And then to the other night by the campfire, when he'd held her hand and stood so close to her, making a burning hunger fizz through her body. At last she had to admit it. *Lust*. Pure, unadulterated lust. That's what she was feeling. There, she'd acknowledged it. She was in lust with Tam. It'd been quite a while since she'd felt sexually attracted to a man. But that would not change one damn thing. She was out here with only one objective and she would *not* let one tall, charming man get in her way.

'I got something!' Tam and Cilla both swiveled their heads in Alisha's direction. She was holding something up in her hand in a triumphant salute. Alisha swam in and threw her treasure up onto the ledge. It was a crab, about half the size of the two Cilla had caught.

'I know it's small, but it's a good start,' Alisha said, as she tried to climb up the slippery rock face.

'Definitely.' Tam leant down and grabbed her hand, pulling her up as if she weighed nothing. Then he took the crab from her and deposited it in the rock pool.

'All that diving and holding your breath is hard work. I might take a break for a second,' Alisha puffed, dragging the goggles off her head.

'Do you girls mind if I have a go then?'

'Knock yourself out,' Alisha replied, patting her wet curls down and fluttering her eyelashes in pretend flirtation.

Both women stood on the rim of the limestone and watched Tam take a few powerful strokes to get him out above the coral outcrop a few feet below the water. He took two quick breaths and then his head disappeared beneath the surface.

'I think we should form an alliance. Don't you?'

'Pardon me?' Cilla was taken aback by Alisha's question that seemed to come out of nowhere.

'Oh, don't act all coy, girl. You know how these things work.' Alisha let herself down to sit on the rock, eliciting a grunt as her amble bottom hit the rock. Cilla did the same, watching Alisha out of the corner of her eye.

'Me, you, and that big hunk of a man could make a good alliance. I also think we have a good chance of making it to the final three.'

'That's a very interesting idea.' It wasn't as if Cilla hadn't thought about forming alliances over the previous few days. It happened a lot in the game of Sea-Quest. But it was a minefield of pros and cons. Cilla had watched alliances work extremely well occasionally, when the people stuck together as they promised they would. But she'd also seen some fail in a spectacular fashion as well. Was she ready to do this? She could see Alisha would be a powerful ally, but Tam?

'Are you sure we can trust Tam?'

'Yes, I am. Look at him. He's physically strong, which will help us in the knockouts. But he's also hardworking, with good morals,' Alisha replied.

'Do you believe his story about wanting to win the money to help the kids?' Cilla's gut had told her that Tam's narrative the other night at the campfire didn't ring one-hundred percent true. There was something missing, but Cilla couldn't put a finger on what exactly.

Alisha didn't answer straight away, instead she fluffed out her hair to dry and repositioned her backside onto a more comfortable rocky perch. 'I'm not sure,' she said with a contemplative grimace. Good, at least Alisha was on the same page.

The grimace remained on Alisha's face as she continued, 'He told me he grew up in Carson, and I think there might be more to his background than he's letting on.'

'Why?' Cilla was intrigued.

'Because Carson is not a nice place. You don't live there unless you've got nowhere else to go. It's definitely the wrong side of the tracks in Los Angeles, full of poverty and gangs and violence.'

'Really. I didn't know that.' Having grown up in Wyoming, and fleeing to Australia as soon as she was able, Cilla had never been to LA.

'Don't get me wrong.' Alisha held her hands up in appeal. 'I'm sure not every single person who grows up in that area deals drugs for a gang, but something is missing from what he's told us. He has a core of steel, a determination to win at all costs he keeps very well hidden from everybody. I've noticed it a few times when he gets carried away at knockouts. That inner fortitude isn't something you learn by counseling kids at Disney.'

Now that Alisha mentioned it, Cilla had to agree. It was concealed beneath the layers of his pleasant veneer, but it was there. A warrior mentality. She knew he wasn't one to back away from a fight, no matter how large the opposition.

'And you still want him in an alliance with us?'

'Of course I do. I believe if he makes a decision he'll stick by it, no matter what. Just because he hasn't told us the complete truth doesn't make any of the other things I said about him incorrect.' Alisha turned her dark gaze onto Cilla, an unsettling light of perception in her eyes. 'After all, I know you're holding back stuff. About your reasons for being here. But I don't judge you. I believe I can trust you to make a great alliance.' Cilla had thought the story she'd spun so far had been foolproof. Most of it had been the truth. She could definitely use the money to buy a bigger boat. And the part where she said she wanted to help her grandmother out of financial bother was also true. She just hadn't elaborated on how much trouble it really was.

The fact that her father had a huge gambling problem and had used her grandmother's house as collateral—and lost—she kept to herself. If she was completely honest, she had to concede she didn't want anyone to know that her father, Wayde, was a narcissistic arsehole. Always had been and always would be. She had a deadbeat for a father, and she was ashamed of the fact.

The misappropriation of her grandmother's home was the last straw on an enormous pile of hurt Wayde had inflicted on his small family over the years. Cilla had often wondered how she could possibly have been born of his flesh and blood. They had nothing in common. He'd always had a problem with alcohol, spending most of the meagre money he earned on booze. That's why Cilla had spent her early years living with her grandmother; Wayde had palmed her off when he could no longer afford to buy her the most basic of commodities, such as food, or even clothing. He seemed to keep one step away from living on the street though, instead crashing on a couch at a friend's house, or renting a tiny room in some dingy dive of a house where drugs and drinking were part of the nightly ritual. At some stage his drinking had slowly but surely escalated to include high-stakes gambling.

If only her mother were still alive, maybe she might've been able to pull him into line. According to her grandmother, Cilla's mother, Lily, was the only woman Wayde had ever listened to. But Lily died giving birth to

Cilla. And from that moment on, Wayde started down the slippery slope of booze and gambling. In his drunken rages he'd often become violent, and Cilla learned very quickly how to avoid him, keeping out of reach of his unsteady punches and kicks.

Even so, it was a tremendous blow to find out the extent of his deviousness, and a small part of her still wondered how he could do that to his own family?

Keeping her stare out on the ocean, she didn't answer Alisha, only waited for Tam to resurface.

Alisha gave her a shrewd glance, and said, 'Some others have already started making their alliances. It's obvious Simon and Madison have been talking to each other. And if two people were ever made for each other, it's those two.' She let out a most unladylike snort. Cilla had noticed that they'd been giving each other furtive glances across the campfire the other night, and she agreed with the older woman's observations.

'And I'll admit that I've already been approached by Glen and Paloma on different occasions, but both of them make my blood run cold.' Now that was a surprising bit of information. But when Cilla thought about it, Alisha would be most people's first choice. She was mothering, loyal, but still ultra tough.

'But you two, well I think I can trust you. As far as you can trust anyone in this game anyhow.'

'Thank you, Alisha. And I feel I can trust you, too,' Cilla replied. 'What about Marg? Should we include her?'

'Mmm, I've thought of that too. We'd be better off with a small core of three to start with. We could always bring Marg in later.' Again, what Alisha said was spot-on, but Cilla hesitated. When it came to Tam, her emotions were conflicted. If she admitted what she'd felt only minutes ago was real, then could she form an alliance with someone she was attracted to? Would that be fair to either of them, and would it alter her ability to think logically?

Then again, she was a strong-willed, determined woman who could control a few simple hormonal urges. What did she have to lose?

'Okay, let's do it,' Cilla said. Alisha's face split with a grin and she stuck out her hand to shake on the agreement.

As if on cue, Tam surfaced close to the rock and gave a shout of glee. 'Another lobster.' He shook his head like a dog, water droplets splashing all over them. His dark hair stood up in spikes, a smile of pure pleasure making him seem more carefree than she'd ever seen before.

'You did well for a first timer,' said Cilla.

'Thanks,' he acknowledged as he hauled himself up onto the rock.

'Tam, we have a question for you.' Alisha cocked her head to one side, staring at him. 'We want to know if you'd like to join our alliance?'

The beaming smile vanished from Tam's face.

* * *

'I'm sorry, JJ, I can't do it,' Cilla said, placing the offending item with great care back on the table. Tam was dumfounded. She couldn't really mean that, she never gave up. Did she?

'Come on, Cilla, you can do this. Don't think about it, just close your eyes and chew,' Marg shouted encouragement. Tam wanted to shout a similar reinforcement, but something in Cilla's haunted eyes made him stop.

'You'll lose a point for Dawnbreakers if you don't eat this, Cilla,' JJ said with quiet authority. There was no pity on his face, just certainty.

'I know, JJ. I... I can't do it, I'm sorry.'

'No need to apologize. You did your best. If Jason from Nightrebels can eat the chicken, then they'll be ahead by one point.' JJ pointed to Jason, who was chomping his way through this so-called *island epicurean* knockout battle. Tam couldn't tear his gaze from Cilla, who stood staring at the ground, shoulders hunched. He knew by the cheering that Jason had completed his round successfully.

Cilla walked away from the table in the centre of the clearing to join the rest of them on the mat. Alisha gave her a quick hug, and said, 'Don't worry girl, look at them.' She gestured toward the other team. 'There's no way that geeky bald guy with the glasses is going to finish this round. Then we'll be tied again.' Alisha awarded her a huge grin, but Cilla didn't smile back. Tam could hear other muttered comments that weren't nearly as helpful as Alisha's and he saw Cilla flinch at their unkind observations. She was taking this hard. Until now, she'd seemed almost unbreakable. Her skills, knowledge of survival and resilience under pressure were worn like a coat of armor. But this knockout had cracked her thick fortification wide open.

At least this knockout was for prize and plunder and not an exemption battle. Still, it'd be nice to be the proud owners of the large tarpaulin, four blankets and four cushions on display off to the side of the clearing.

In this Sea-Quest island epicurean knockout, the meals on offer were supposed to comprise certain island delicacies, but in reality the food was plain disgusting.

Designed to make them retch and heave and refuse to eat it. Each Dawnbreakers team member was paired off against a Nightrebels member, and if they ate their repulsive food item, then they received a point. The team with the most points at the end of eight rounds was the winner.

Tam's food had been some kind of fermented fish. Supposedly a local delicacy, but in truth it'd been ghastly. He'd held his nose and tipped the slimy, stinking mess down his gullet in one quick gulp, swilling a whole canteen of water down afterwards to wash away the taste. At least he'd kept his fish down, just. But so had his counterpart.

So far, Cilla was the only person not to complete her round. Her gross food had been a twenty-one-day old chick, cooked while still in the egg. She had to peel the shell off and then eat the thing whole, beak, feet, head, everything. Tam had watched her raise it to her mouth, and even put it to her lips, but then she'd dry retched so violently he thought she might actually vomit.

Looking around, he saw Cilla was no longer standing on the mat. She was sitting on the ground under some shrubs a few meters away, hugging her knees to her chest. He couldn't leave her there, looking so tortured, so isolated. After all, they were in an alliance now.

'You okay?'

'Leave me alone, Tam. I'm sure you hate me as much as the rest of the team.'

'We don't hate you, Cilla. I don't hate you. Everyone is human after all.'

'Not in this game. You have to be more than human if you want to win.' It sounded like a mantra. He ignored the venom in her voice, understanding it was directed inwards at herself, not at him.

'What happened? Why couldn't you eat it?'

I'm a vegetarian,' Cilla said, her words slow and grim. She was licking her lips, as if she could still taste the tiny feathers in her mouth.

'But you ate the lobsters and crabs we caught this morning, didn't you?' Tam was confused.

'Yes, but *I* caught those, and *I* killed them. I know how they lived and how they died.'

'So you don't eat meat for moral reasons. Okay, I get it.'

'Oh God. What if I lost the knockout for us?' Her face was a picture of misery.

'Cilla, it's okay, I'm sure everyone will—'

'You stupid bitch, what the hell do you think you were up to?' Madison's face was nearly purple with rage, her blue eyes screwed-up and piggish. Tam was instantly on guard, moving to intercept her before she got too close to where Cilla sat, huddled on the ground.

'Hang on a minute, Madison, you don't know the entire story,' he said, shooting a quick glance back at Cilla to make sure she was okay.

'Oh, I see how it is now. Are you actually going to defend her? All she had to do was eat one stupid little chicken. It was dead. It would've been some much needed protein for her.' Madison pushed Tam backward, trying to get at Cilla. His protective instinct kicked up a notch, and he stood his ground, squaring off against Madison.

'Shit, if only I'd been chosen to eat that one. I would've gobbled it up and asked for more.' Madison's beautiful face contorted with fury. Tam heard Cilla dry retch behind him, the thought of having to eat that baby chicken whole still tormenting her. He didn't turn around, keeping Madison firmly in his sights. 'Everyone else ate whatever was given to them. I ate those disgusting cockroaches, even though those bloody things terrify the hell out of me.' She peered around Tam, trying to spear Cilla with her words. 'We lost a point because of you. You failed the team, you loser.' Madison spat the last words through clenched teeth and stormed off to join the team who were all cheering on Cho. It looked like he had to drink a glass of animal's blood. Every time he took a swig, he was almost heaving the whole thing back up again.

Tam sent him a silent entreaty. *Just keep it down, Cho. Whatever you do, don't throw it up.*

He unclenched his fists. He wouldn't have hit Madison, even though she deserved it.

In the end, he coaxed Cilla back to where the rest of the team were yelling for Cho to scull the last bit of blood in the bottom of his glass. Cho succeeded, although his face was going a rather interesting shade of green. Tam gave Cilla an encouraging squeeze on the shoulder, and she offered him a weak smile.

This alliance thing had him a little rattled, and when Alisha first suggested it, he'd been lost for words. It was a logical proposition, however, and when he'd gathered his wits, he'd agreed. He wished he knew for sure whether it was logic that drove the choice, or the chance to get closer to Cilla. He knew romances weren't a good idea out here. But it wouldn't hurt to have some strong, loyal friends around, would it? Even if he was incredibly drawn to one of those friends, he was mentally tough enough not to act on his urges.

'Cho wins this round,' JJ yelled, his animated voice

bringing Tam back from his thoughts. 'Sally-Anne you didn't keep your drink down long enough before you threw it back up. That gives Dawnbreakers and Nightrebels seven points each.' They were back to a tie. *Thank God.* Tam looked over toward the knockout table. Sally-Anne looked like a Barbie Doll wannabe. Fortyish, long blonde hair and tight clothes. Her face was smeared with blood. It dripped down her chin where she'd vomited it all over the sand. Poor woman. He didn't envy her one bit. Just looking at her was making Cho's face go greener.

This was the first time they'd seen team Nightrebels since they'd been to the conclave the other night. Tam didn't remember the names of all the other people, but JJ told them, as they'd come in for the knockout this morning, that team Nightrebels had voted out someone called Phoebe. He thought he could recall a plump girl who spoke very loudly. The loss didn't affect him; he felt not the slightest pang of guilt or dismay at her being the first person voted out of this season's Sea-Quest. Better her than one of their team. He hoped their luck continued to hold, and they kept winning.

* * *

White sand crunched beneath her bare feet. Footprints fanned out behind Cilla in a wandering line, following the crash and roll of the waves as they broke on the shoreline. She was a long way from the camp now. Experience told her it wasn't good to isolate yourself, even for small amounts of time, in this game. But she had to have this precious half hour to herself.

A deep frown creased her forehead. They were probably all talking about her right now back at camp, but it couldn't be helped. She needed time to regroup and readjust to the new paradigm in the team. One where she was found wanting by the other team members. What hurt even more was the fact their disappointment was warranted.

She'd let them all down.

They'd lost the prize and plunder knockout. Nightrebels got to take home the blankets and the tarp, which would keep them warmer and a heck of a lot drier. Dawnbreakers would have to cope with their leaking roof and use each other to keep warm at night. And Cilla was partly to blame for their loss. Paloma had also failed to eat her disgusting dish of fish eyes, which had been crawling with flies. But everyone seemed to blame Cilla.

It wasn't like she'd been physically unable to complete the knockout. It was definitely a mind-over-matter thing. But when she'd seen that poor little chick, all curled up, fully formed, her heart had lurched into her mouth. Anguish, disgust and rage had warred equally in her chest. But in the end, anguish won. Tears had sprung, uncalled for as she'd stared at the tiny thing in her hands, feathers folded neatly down over its body and eyes closed, as if merely asleep, awaiting the right time to hatch out into the world. She'd squeezed the tears away, closing her eyes, as if shutting out the sight of the poor thing would help. But nothing was going to make her force that baby animal through her lips. Not even the thought of losing one million dollars.

The revelation shocked her.

She wasn't used to failing. She'd made damn sure she was always self-reliant, strong and capable. Her ex, Marco, had once called her the ice-queen, but he'd been drunk when he said it. At the time, his comment had stung.

Maybe that was how other people perceived her. Part of it was a veneer she put up to protect herself. Marco had never bothered to try and break through that veneer, he'd never truly understood her. Marco had been drunk nearly every night toward the end, just before she left him. Drunk and mean, just like her dad. How had she fallen for a guy so similar to her father? She still wasn't sure. But at least she had the guts to leave him in the end. She'd abandoned him in Townsville, sailed her boat out of the harbor while he'd been ashore one morning, and never looked back.

She hadn't figured on this exact knockout catching her out, though. The game was throwing her a curve ball, and somehow she had to recover. Sea-Quest was renowned for placing twists and turns in contestants' paths to keep everyone guessing, but she'd been sure her survival skills and knowledge of the islands would get her through. At least this had only been a plunder knockout for reward, and they were not now heading off to the conclave to vote someone out.

She blew a breath out between pursed lips. It was time to turn around and go back to camp. Time to put on the brave face again and act as if Madison's taunts didn't cut her to the bone.

As she turned around, she brought her head up for the first time since she'd left camp. The curve of a small beach stretched before her, cut by the blunt edges of a limestone cliff, forcing its way out to sea and forming a narrow headland. The beach was pristine. Pure white sand, surrounded by the halo of green fringing the back edge and crystalline aqua blue water on the other. A bird calling from within the depths of the jungle competed with the sound of gently breaking waves to form a natural symphony.

The late afternoon was peaceful and serene. Some of the tranquillity pierced her soul, and it was easier to shake off a little of her self-recrimination.

She should search underneath some of those larger trees looming over the edges of the headland. The elusive doubloon could be hidden in their crevices or buried beneath their roots. If she found it, then destiny would definitely weigh a lot lighter.

Her feet found the flat spots between the rocks as she worked her way up a small sloping rock face. A cliff of at least thirty feet high reared upwards further back, but the rocks around the foot of the cliff were low, scoured by the pounding surf. In these flat spaces, trees had found a root-hold in the sparse sand. She made her way into the shade of the cliff, poking around underneath the draping branches and wide, spreading roots of a large fig tree. It'd be a good place to hide a doubloon, well away from the rising tide.

Cilla backed out onto the rocks a few minutes later. Nothing. She'd found nothing in there.

'Hi, Cilla, whatcha doing?' Cilla jerked her head around. It was Paloma. What was she doing so far down the beach? Paloma had a friendly grin plastered on her face, but there was a certain tightness around her eyes, putting Cilla on edge.

'Just poking around, checking for crabs, you know.' The lie didn't come easily to Cilla's lips.

'Huh? You were looking for the doubloon, weren't you?'

'Um…' Cilla didn't know what to say. She hadn't expected such a direct question, especially from Paloma, who was always smiling and talking about her four kids.

This was a different Paloma, one who was suddenly centered on the game. Paloma ran an impatient hand over her dark hair.

'Of course you were. We all are, we just don't want to admit it,' Paloma replied. Uncomfortable, Cilla remained silent. 'I've been searching for it.' Paloma's Latino accent became more pronounced with the anxiety of the admission. 'And if I've been searching, then so has everyone else.'

The unanswered question hung between them. Had either of them found it?

'It'd be a significant advantage to have, if we ever go to the conclave. No?'

'Yes, it would,' Cilla admitted. 'Shall we head back now?' She started walking toward camp, not waiting to see if Paloma followed her. The frankness of the conversation had rattled her. Until now, the specter of the hidden doubloon hadn't figured too much in her plans. But now the idea Paloma was searching for it—and perhaps had already found it—changed everything. Cilla needed to get her head back into the game and start looking for the doubloon in earnest. It could be the difference between staying here and going home.

CHAPTER FIVE

'The Nightrebels win exemption.' Those four little words hovered in the air, mocking Cilla. Her arms, already sore from the knockout, hung by her sides, heavy as lead. They'd lost the latest challenge, and now as punishment they'd have to vote one member of their team off the island. Cilla let her chin fall onto her chest, staring at the ground without really seeing it. This wasn't good. Not good for her team, and especially not good for her. If the last prize and plunder knockout was anything to go by, Madison was going to blame Cilla for their loss.

She drew in a deep breath. It was an effort, but she straightened her spine, one vertebra at a time. She needed to get her game face on and make sure she wasn't the one on the chopping block tonight. Not let any of her desperation or apprehension show. Keep her wits about her and her senses sharp. Now wasn't the time to fall to pieces.

'See you at the conclave, Dawnbreakers,' said JJ, sending them one of his intense stares from beneath the brim of his black fedora.

'Not looking forward to that, JJ,' Glen replied, the extra skin underneath his chin wobbling as he spoke.

'Me either,' echoed Simon. For once he seemed to have lost his jaunty strut. They all turned and trudged single file down the path to their campsite. Cilla's mind was buzzing with what-ifs.

The knockout had been a game of ten-pin bowling. Simple in theory. Except this was Sea-Quest, and of course it had to have a pirate bent to it. So the balls were made from coconuts, but they weren't bowled in the traditional manner. No, in true Sea-Quest fashion they had to be shot out of *cannons*; rudely fashioned hollow logs, which the coconuts were fired through using a sling-shot contraption. The ten-pins were also wooden caricatures of a normal pin, twice the size and three times as heavy. The bowling alley had been made of rough wooden planks nailed together, with huge gaps between them, some of the planks tilted on crazy angles. Not in the slightest bit conducive to bowling with any degree of accuracy.

The stronger men had fared fairly well with this contraption, mainly because they'd been able to wrangle the coconut and shoot it using sheer brute strength. Most of the women had fared much worse, however. Cilla and another dark-haired elfin girl from the Nightrebels team were clearly the worst bowlers of the bunch.

Cilla ground her teeth and muttered under her breath, frustration oozing from every pore. She'd never be able to look at another coconut the same way again. She'd tried her hardest to wrestle that stupid ball into submission, but every time she shot it down the cannon, instead of hurtling down the makeshift bowling alley like it should, it trickled down, always just missing the pins at the other end. The most she ever knocked over was four pins. She couldn't have chosen a worse time to fail. Not right after her loss at the food-eating knockout. People would see her as the weakest link.

'Cheer up, Cilla, we knew we couldn't escape the conclave forever,' Alisha said, her voice drifting up from behind. 'And stop taking the blame for this loss. I've been watching you stomp up this path like you want to pound everything in sight to dust. So, stop it.'

'I might be in trouble tonight, Alisha,' Cilla whispered back over her shoulder. 'I don't want to be the first Dawnbreakers member voted out.'

'Baloney, we all played a part in that loss. It was much harder than it looked. We all need to watch our backs.'

'I think Madison is gunning for me, though. Did you hear her? She saved her worst insults for me. And I'm sure that's exactly what she's whispering in Paloma's ear right now.' Cilla indicated to Madison and Paloma, walking with heads tipped together up the front of the line.

'Maybe you're right.' Alisha's frank admission sent chills running up her spine. She threw a stricken gaze at the woman pacing quietly along behind her. Alisha gave her a quick wink in return. 'But I'll be damned if that nasty piece of work is going to get her way tonight. We have an alliance, Cilla, and we're going to use it.' Her tough words helped ease some of the panic fluttering inside Cilla's rib cage. Facing forward again, her tread became more determined, and she raised her chin to glare in Madison's direction. Alisha was right, she wouldn't let horrible Madison have her way.

They arrived back at their campsite half an hour later, none of them with much to say. It was only mid-afternoon, the sun still hot enough to make the sweat run down between Cilla's shoulder blades. Swarms of small midges did lazy circles above the camp, making the air feel thick and claustrophobic. They had many hours left to do their maneuverings. It was going to be a long afternoon.

Cilla thought she would've looked forward to this part of the game; the mental manipulation of other people. But now she was feeling she may have misjudged how much the fear of being the one voted out would affect her intellectually. She was emotionally exhausted already just thinking about all the options on the walk to camp. She watched Simon heading down the beach for a cooling swim, with Glen hot on his heels. The jostling to be heard had begun. Who did they want to vote out?

Those perplexing questions must've been showing on Cilla's face, because Marg said, 'Don't go worrying yourself too much, eh.' She plonked herself down on the edge of the platform next to Cilla. When Cilla raised a disconcerted eyebrow, Marg laughed and said, 'You're as easy to read as an open book when you're mad.'

'Really, I didn't realize.' She'd have to remember to keep her feelings a lot more guarded from now on.

'Well, you are. I could see you hitting out at every poor unsuspecting shrub we walked past. Taking out your anger on the foliage, eh? At least that's better than taking it out on other people, unlike some others who I won't mention.' Marg gave a slight tilt of her head Madison's way. 'I'm a fairly tolerant person, but she's really starting to aggravate me. She needs to watch what she says.' Marg whispered the last few words, but it did little to conceal the spite in her tone.

Wanting to move away from prying ears, Cilla said,

'Come on, let's go for a swim, the ocean looks amazing.' Marg nodded in agreement.

The water was silky and wonderfully cool. She and Marg sat in the calm shallows, the waves lapping at her collarbone. Grabbing handfuls of sand, she scoured her skin. Sand was the only option for keeping themselves clean out here. Without the luxury of real soap, they had to make do. Sand washed the dirt off and left her skin feeling buffed and smooth. Although it didn't make her smell any better.

'This is nice, eh? I can think clearer with a cool head.' Marg dunked her head and then shook it, spraying water off her short hair, all over Cilla. She took a scoop of sand and rubbed it vigorously through her hair. Cilla followed suit.

'What I wouldn't give to have some shampoo right now,' Cilla moaned. 'Sea water always leaves my hair so salty and tangled.'

'I know, that's why I had mine cut extra short before I came out here. It used to come right down to my ass. Lucy doesn't like it short. But I told her she wasn't the one who had to live with it, so she'd have to learn to like it!'

'Well, it suits you,' Cilla replied, meaning it.

'Thanks.' Marg gave her a cheeky grin. 'Now, we need to decide who—' Marg broke off and glared over Cilla's left shoulder. 'Simon and Glen are coming over. Follow my lead,' she hissed out of the side of her mouth, and then plastered a welcoming smile onto her face.

'Hiya girls.' Simon splashed water over them in what she guessed was supposed to be a playful interaction. It just annoyed her. 'So, who are you girls voting out tonight?' he asked.

'Straight to the point. No beating around the bush with you, eh?' Marg's voice was cool.

'Oh, come on, admit it, that must've been what you were discussing before we came over.'

'No, we weren't, actually. We were talking about hair,' Cilla replied, taking Marg's cue and keeping her voice steady.

'Typical,' said Glen, rolling his eyes. But when Marg turned her inscrutable gaze on him, he seemed to regret his outburst. 'I mean, of course you were talking about hair, but would you like to entertain a conversation about the conclave tonight with us instead?' Try as hard as he could, Glen would never be able to redeem himself in Cilla's eyes. He was a greasy little man who didn't mind fawning over all the stronger players, worming his way into their hearts and minds by bowing and scraping to their every whim. Back home she would've had nothing to do with him, probably even going as far as to tell him to piss off. But out here she'd have to tolerate him. It made her insides crawl with dislike, that this game would reduce her to betraying her better instincts. But it was part of playing Sea-Quest, and she knew everyone else was doing much the same thing.

Giving him a fake smile, she said, 'We'd like to hear what you have to say.' She watched the two men settle themselves into the water next to them, Simon flexing his large biceps, the dragon tattoo seeming to come to life as he rippled his chest muscles. Simon sat a tad too close, and Cilla had to use the excuse of reaching for another handful of sand to ease herself a few inches away from him. It was amusing that he was still trying to ingratiate himself with her. She didn't want to antagonize him, so she hadn't told him to leave her alone, but she'd done nothing to encourage him either.

Cilla's gaze drifted over Simon's shoulder to where Tam and Cho were sitting in the shade on the beach, chatting. Tam had removed his hat, and was running his hand through his dark hair, causing it to stand up in an unruly fashion. Funny, but his disorderly hair made him seem even more endearing. Even more gorgeous. Unconsciously, her eyes traced the line of Tam's broad shoulders, taking in the glorious curvature of his bare chest, sweeping down over his six-pack stomach. What would it feel like to run her hands over them, have those muscles flex beneath her fingertips?

Sucking in air over her teeth, she forced her gaze back to the people in front of her. Grabbing another handful of sand, she scrubbed it over her thighs with more force than was completely necessary. It'd do her no good daydreaming about Tam. She'd never allow herself to do the things she wanted to do to him. Not when he stood between her and the million dollars. It'd be too risky for her to let him gain a foothold in her emotions. She couldn't tolerate even one tiny chink to open up in her armor. She must keep her mind focussed on the game.

'What're your feelings about voting Paloma off?' Cilla was dragged back to the present by Marg's out-of-the-blue question. Keeping her surprise in check, she nodded in acceptance when Glen threw her a quizzical glance. Whatever Marg was up to, Cilla was prepared to go along with it, as long as it meant she wasn't on the chopping block.

'What if Paloma has found the golden doubloon?' Glen asked the question that'd hovered in Cilla's mind for days.

'Don't be silly, we would've heard if anyone had found that old thing,' Marg replied with a wink and a cocky shake of her head. Cilla wasn't so sure. Memories of her conversation with Paloma on the beach the other day clawed through her mind, sending a shiver of panic down into her belly.

* * *

'Welcome to your first conclave.' Tam mounted the last few steps to the raised platform as JJ spoke. 'Behind you, you will find a firebrand. Each of you take one and light it from the fire.' He pointed to the massive steel fire-pit in the middle of the floor. Tam picked up the large stick, with some kind of dirty rag wrapped around the top, and dipped it toward the flames.

'This is part of the ritual of Sea-Quest. The only way to avoid the hangman's noose is to keep your firebrand burning bright.' Tam knew JJ was referring to the ceremonial dousing of each contestant's firebrand when they were voted off. They then had to walk through the noose—a stylized rope loop as broad as a doorway, hanging from a beam suspended over the conclave— before they were ejected from the island. The comment made the hairs on the back of his neck stand to attention.

'Take a seat everyone.' Tam placed his now lit firebrand in one of the slots built specially into the platform behind a row of wooden benches. Then he crammed himself onto the end of the last bench. There was only just enough room for all nine of them to sit down. He was packed up against Marg, and he could feel the nervousness thrumming through her. She was twitching like a bird on a wire. He was surprised when her thigh rubbed up against his to find her muscles were iron bound. She was tauter than most men he knew. A solid, compact woman. She obviously worked hard on the weights to get this fit.

The same uneasy tension ran through him as well, and he was finding it hard to stop his knee from jerking up and down. Taking a calming breath, he let his gaze roam over their surroundings, wanting to drink the whole experience in. They were on a huge wooden platform, built at tree-top height. During the day the view would've been spectacular, but tonight inky blackness engulfed them on all sides. There was a fence guarding the edge and giant metal pots scattered in the corners, set with fires deep in their bellies acting as an eerie light-source. There were sets of odd-sized wooden chests, all with gold coins and jewelry spilling out of them. Jolly Roger flags flew from poles and other pirate totems, cutlasses, tricorn hats and even a tall mast with square sails, were set haphazardly around the fringes of the platform. Very rustic and *Pirates of the Caribbean*.

JJ sat to the left of the group on the stump of an old tree, observing them silently. Tonight he was wearing a black, skin-tight hoodie, zipped all the way up, the silver zip shining in the firelight. He'd swapped his fedora hat for a stylish black flat-cap that made him look even more suave, if that was indeed possible. The man was a mass of contradictions. Smooth and well-dressed on the surface, with his hundred mega-watt smile. But there was a dangerous undercurrent running beneath all that sophistication. Tam wouldn't want to come upon JJ alone in a dark alley, that much was for sure. There'd been hints in the press that their host had some dark past he preferred not to talk about, but so far nothing concrete had come to light. Now that Tam had met the man in the flesh, he was still no closer to understanding him.

JJ started talking once they were all settled on the benches. 'Of course, as always in Sea-Quest, there'll be a spin on the game this time around. This season there is to be a Deception Cove.' JJ hardly paused at the audible intake of breath from all nine players. 'Those of you who're voted off will not automatically be sent out of the game. Instead, you will go to Deception Cove. There you'll compete with the other contestants who've been voted out to see who remains on Deception. At some stage one of you will be allowed back into the game.'

A collective sigh rose from everyone, as they all let go of the breath they'd been holding. 'Team members will not get to see what's going on at Deception Cove, or who's left after each knockout. It'll remain a secret until such a stage that we decide to return the champion and re-instate them into the game. This could happen at any point, and with no warning.' JJ watched them as he delivered the news, the twinkle in his eye the only give-away he was enjoying their reactions perhaps more than he should. 'This'll also impact on who'll come back as panel members later in the game, so we're going to keep the panel's identity hidden from you all until the last conclave as well. But...' JJ paused for two long, drawn out seconds, 'the panel members will still see all the clever antics you get up to at the conclave, because we'll be streaming it live to them every night. So, remember, everything you do and say impacts on your chance in this game.'

Holy heck, another twist to the game. Tam allowed himself a tiny smile. Where some people might find this news intimidating, he found it invigorating. This'd put a lot of people on edge, but not him. He'd take much interest in watching how this twist affected other people. That was part of his job as a psychologist, to watch and observe, take notes and make judgments on people's mental state. That knowledge would help him on this island; any edge he could gain over the others gave him power.

The news shocked Marg; it was as plain as day on her face. 'This could be a good thing,' she whispered to him out of the side of her mouth. He nodded his head a fraction. How would the others in his team cope?

He searched the semi-circle of faces until he found Cilla's slight form, right down the other end of the line. Her face was tight and drawn. The upward curve of her lips, which normally hinted at her ever-ready smile, wasn't in evidence. She was unhappy with the news. It'd upset some pre-determined plan by the looks of the deep frown lines crossing her forehead. But even with the frown and sour turn of her mouth, she was still strikingly beautiful. Her dark auburn hair was pulled into a plait, a few wayward tendrils escaping and floating down around her cheeks, softening her features. Firelight flickered orange, casting a warm glow over her features. The stud in her nose sparkled and flickered along with the reflection in her eyes. An impulse to go over and smooth the frown lines from her face overwhelmed him. It was an unconscious instinct, but the strength of the sentiment came as a shock.

He shook his head. He needed to get his mind concentrating on the game. She was intruding too often into his thoughts. Just this-morning after the bowling knockout, he'd noticed the way her shoulders had hunched in defense at Madison's taunts and a quick anger had risen inside, making him react without thinking, directing a scathing comment toward Madison. At the time, he'd told himself he was only looking out for the people in his alliance. But the way Marg and Cho had looked at him—with a sideways glance, awareness flickering in their eyes—had made him take a mental step backward. He didn't want to make it too obvious he was in an alliance with Cilla, and he definitely didn't want anyone thinking he cared about her. But it was obvious she was taking this to heart. Combining that with the loss at the food knockout, he guessed she'd be fighting back the guilt and humiliation of it all. If only she'd talk to him. It wasn't healthy to pretend to be as self-reliant as she wanted them to believe she was.

'So, Madison, tell me what you're thinking about your first time at conclave.' Tam's head snapped up, breaking his contemplation. JJ had pounced on their one weak link, like a bloodhound following a trail. JJ knew Madison was causing waves in the camp.

'Well, JJ, as you can see, we lost at the knockout today. And I believe that was because some people pulling their weight more than others.' And there it was. Madison had driven straight to the heart of the sore point. Tam hoped others didn't blindly react to her accusations and give away their plan tonight. He checked Alisha's face for signs of irritation, but was surprised to find her smiling quietly. At least she would not be baited by Madison's childish attempts to drag them all into a war of words.

Cilla's face was expressionless. She was doing a superb job at hiding the hurt and anger she must be feeling at Madison's criticisms. Good, both of them were sticking to the plan. If only Simon and Marg did what they'd said, then they'd all be safe for at least three more days.

He couldn't help it, he had to sneak another glance at Cilla. She was watching JJ with a scary intensity as he asked Glen a pointed question about team moral. Her posture was overly straight, her lips pulled together in a purposeful guise of calm. Looking as if this wasn't affecting her at all. There was a slight tinge of pink high on her cheekbones. He watched the spots darken as Madison spoke. Then he saw her balled up fists shoved behind her back and wondered how he could've fallen for her ruse. Her knuckles were white with the strain of keeping her thoughts to herself and again he found a pang of desire to go up and loosen her fists, finger by finger, stroking her hand until the tension left them.

Dammit, there he went again. His fascination with her had to stop. He gritted his teeth, determined not to look at her for the rest of the evening.

* * *

'Glen, it seems as if there's a division in this team. Can you tell me about that?' Cilla swiveled her head to stare at Glen. He looked taken aback at the fact JJ had directed the question toward him.

'Um, I'm not really sure what you mean, JJ.' Glen feigned ignorance, his round face going slack with false surprise. Of course, he knew all about the accusations Madison had been making toward her. He'd sat and listened to her rant about it for long enough. It irritated her immensely that Glen was one of the people Cilla was relying on tonight. He and Simon had agreed in principle to Marg and Alisha's plan. Would he keep his promise, though? Promises held little weight out here. Not in the game of Sea-Quest.

'Are you trying to tell me you haven't noticed that

Madison is blaming certain people for losing today's knockout? Come on man, you can't be that oblivious to what's going on at camp.' JJ was really egging Glen on tonight, going for the jugular.

'Well, yes, of course I heard her saying things. But I tried to stay out of it. I think we have a great team and I'm quite happy with how we played in the knockout.' Glen was hedging his bets, trying to keep everyone happy. The same way he always did. Sneaky and slimy. He wasn't about to reveal how he was going to vote.

'Even though you lost? Come on, Glen, don't tell me everything is completely rosy back at camp. You must've noticed some kind of tension.'

'We were going to end up at conclave some time or other, weren't we?' Glen was a slippery one, using his salesmanship skills to his advantage. He was a medical drug rep, and in Cilla's mind they rated right up there with used car salesmen for smarmy deceit. She hadn't trusted him from the first time she'd seen him on the boat. And now here she was, hoping he'd save her neck from the noose that was tightening around it.

She listened to Glen and JJ spar with words, back and forth, Glen giving nothing of consequence away.

'Cilla.' She jumped at the sound of her name. 'What's your take on today's knockout? Could you have done better at the cannon bowling? Do you think it was your fault the team lost?' JJ didn't pull any punches. She looked at him properly for the first time that night. Friend or foe? She'd asked herself the same question back on the initial day when they landed on the island. He certainly liked to unearth the truth, or at the absolute least hoped to stir up a hornet's nest with his direct questions.

'No, JJ, this wasn't my fault. I did the best I could,' she replied, voice cool.

'Fair enough. What about a division in the team, what do you have to say about that?'

'There'll always be personality clashes whenever you get nine people together. But I don't think it's anything we can't overcome with a little compassion and discussion. And anyway, it's not all about who wins or loses at knockouts. There's also camp life to be considered.'

'What, you think a couple of measly old fish and some crabs are going to redeem you in the minds of the team?' Madison's snort of condemnation echoed around the platform.

'Anything to say to that allegation, Cilla?' JJ's eyes were bright with anticipation.

'Not really.' Cilla didn't elaborate, glaring at JJ for uncounted moments until his gaze finally shifted.

'Anyone else care to comment on that?' Nobody answered, and no one dared look in JJ's direction. Even Madison held her tongue.

'Right.' JJ's curt tone told Cilla he wasn't thrilled with their answers. 'It appears although there are problems in this team, not one person is willing to own up to them, except for Madison. I wonder, does that make her a purveyor of the truth, or a target?' There was silence. No one was prepared to answer JJ on that question either.

'It's time to vote then. Cilla, you can go first,' JJ said as he gestured to the narrow wooden bridge leading to a separate, smaller basket-shaped platform, which looked incredibly like the crows-nest lookout found at the top of a ship's mast. Tucked into the small space was a rickety table covered in writing implements. Her legs jerked in reflex and she found herself walking toward the voting platform before her mind could react. *Here goes nothing*. Or maybe she should say, *here goes everything*. Because to win this game meant everything to her. The money meant everything. It took most of her concentration to negotiate the slats slung between the two thick ropes. Her hands fumbled with the rope rails and her feet felt as if there were great stones tied to the ends of her legs. Finally she made it across and found the ridiculous oversized pen in her hand, a blank piece of parchment in front of her. She had to steady her hand against the edge of the table so she could write down a name. The name of the person she was hoping to vote out tonight. Madison.

What they were planning was risky, and if anyone changed their vote at the last second, she could very well be the one walking through that damned noose. Closing her eyes for the briefest of moments, she hoped Simon, Glen, Cho and Marg all voted the way they'd promised this afternoon. She knew she could trust Alisha and Tam to follow the plan.

Cilla sat down and regarded Glen as he trudged over to vote, his stomach swaying in time with the movement of the bridge. Her heartbeat wouldn't return to normal, even now. Everyone else had their turn at walking over the slender bridge and writing down a name. Nobody smiled; it was a solemn business. She watched with foreboding as JJ went to retrieve all the votes. He came back carrying a small metal trunk, engraved with filigree symbols. With an air of pomp and ceremony, JJ placed the chest onto a tree-stump table and lifted the lid.

'Before I read the votes, I have to ask, does anyone have the golden doubloon, and would they like to play tonight?

If so, please bring it forward now.' Cilla held her breath. Had anyone found it yet?

Then, as if watching everything in a slow-motion replay, Cilla saw Paloma stand up and pace quietly over to where JJ stood with the trunk. Cilla hissed with surprise. She heard a few other low mutters of disbelief, but didn't dare look at anyone else. One of the legs had just fallen off Marg's plan. She wanted to moan with despair, but instead clasped her hands, slick with sweat, in her lap.

'I found it,' Paloma said with a grin. 'And I ain't stupid enough not to play it tonight. I heard the rumors.'

'Really,' JJ replied as he held his hand out for the doubloon. Examining it closely, he raised an eyebrow as he looked at Paloma. 'This is a genuine doubloon. Any votes cast for Paloma don't count,' he intoned in a hollow voice. Cilla took a deep breath, but it did nothing to lessen the heaviness cramping her breastbone.

'I'll read out the votes,' said JJ. Cilla watched the compares' hand as it snaked into the chest and came up, triumphant, holding a piece of parchment. He then unfolded it with exaggerated care.

'The first vote goes to, Madison,' he said, waving the parchment up for them all to view.

Yes! Cilla's heart leapt inside her ribcage. It was what she'd hoped for, but even so it was a little unnerving to see the name in black print, naked upon the creamy page for all to see. Would they really be able to get rid of her?

Madison's eyes narrowed to mere slits, and she cast a withering glance toward Cilla's end of the bench, her lip curling in a snarl. But her shoulders remained arrogantly straight and the tilt of her head suggested she didn't entertain, even for a moment, the thought there might be more votes with her name on them.

'The second vote goes to, Paloma. But because she has the doubloon, this vote doesn't count.' And there it was, the partial unravelling of their well thought out plan. JJ's hand reached into the jar again. 'The third vote goes to… Madison. That's two votes to Madison.'

'The fourth vote is for…' JJ paused as he unfolded the parchment. 'Cilla.'

Oh God! It was to be expected. She knew there might be a couple of votes for her from Madison and Paloma, but she hadn't anticipated the wall of despair and doubt…and was that anger? The emotions hit her like a runaway locomotive, bands of fear constricting her torso so it became hard to breathe. She needed to see Madison's name up there, or at the very least, Paloma's. Not hers. The urge to hide her face in her hands was great, but she managed to defeat it—just. Gritting her teeth together, she set her jaw at a haughty angle. If Madison could do it, so could she. She wouldn't let anyone else see her fear. Glen was sitting next to her, and he turned and lifted a sympathetic eyebrow. She hoped like hell that he didn't take it into his head to give her a mollifying hug. She might have to punch him if he did that.

JJ's hand snaked toward the jar again. The suspense was killing her. She wanted to jump out of her seat and scream at him to hurry.

'This vote is for, Cilla.' He held the paper up for all to see, and Cilla thought she recognized Glen's curling script. Her heart sank. They might not have fallen for Marg's ruse after all. She moved a few inches away from Glen, not wanting that sniveling traitorous bastard anywhere near her. She watched his face for the slightest hint of unfaithfulness. But Glen was deadpan, not even a twitch of an eye or the quirk of his mouth to give him away.

Marg's plan had been to pretend to vote Paloma out, but then actually vote Madison instead. She'd told Simon and Glen that Paloma did nothing around camp, and was getting on Marg's nerves something atrocious. Alisha had suggested—and they all agreed—that Simon was in an alliance with Madison, and possibly Glen as well. No one admitted it outright in front of the two men. Instead, Marg played an admirable game of pretending that although Madison annoyed them, she was much too valuable in knockouts to get rid of so soon. They needed the strongest team possible to keep winning; to keep away from the conclave. Cilla learned a lot about the art of being manipulative, sitting in the water, watching Marg weave her words of deceit.

It seemed, however, Marg's words hadn't been enough.

'That's two votes for Cilla and two for Madison,' JJ said, narrating the score, as if the numbers weren't burned indelibly into her brain.

'The sixth vote is for… Cilla. Another vote takes you to three, and leaves Madison at two.' If Glen and Simon had voted for Paloma, like they'd agreed, then her name should have come up by now. Three votes were too many for them to be still following the plan.

Her hands went cold and clammy. JJ's long fingers reached into the chest again. This time she found she didn't want to know what name he was going to pull out.

'This next vote is for Cilla as well.' Was that a flash of sympathy she saw in JJ's gaze? 'That's four votes for Cilla and two for Madison,' JJ crooned politely.

Cilla did the mental calculations in her head. One more

vote and she was out. Sweat started to run down between her breasts. This was so much harder than she'd ever dreamed it would be. Her gaze flickered across the group of people arrayed to her left. There was pity or concern on some faces, and mere indifference to actual animosity on others. How had she got to this point, where someone actually hated her? The thought made her take a step backward in her head. She knew this game wasn't real, but some people didn't understand that division as easily. She could see for Madison, the hatred was undeniable.

Her gaze fell on Tam, and his lips curved upwards in a reassuring smile. His eyes were the color of burnished gold in the firelight, reminding her of a lion in all its bright and powerful glory. She stared at him, needing the encouragement apparent in his steady gaze.

'This vote goes to…' Cilla's attention snapped back to JJ, and she held her breath. '… Madison.' The breath whooshed out of her in a torrent. Reprieve. If only for a few seconds.

'Cilla, you still have four votes, Madison, you have three.' JJ waggled the paper in front of them and then placed it on the growing pile next to him. Paloma let out a tiny giggle of glee. Cilla was glad at least one of them could see the funny side of things.

'And the last vote goes to…' This time JJ paused so long that Cilla longed to snatch the paper out of his hands and read it aloud herself. '… Madison.' There was a small sound from the vicinity of where Madison sat in the middle of the group. It could've been a muffled scream of defiance, but Cilla dared not look.

Thank God.

'That means you both have four votes each and we have

a tie.'

CHAPTER SIX

'We have a tie.' Tam's stomach clenched. JJ sounded so rational, as if it didn't really matter that one of their team was about to have their dreams crushed. 'In the case of a draw, the rules state that you'll both compete in another knockout. The loser of this knockout will be the person going to Deception Cove tonight.'

Shit, Tam swore under his breath. This was going from bad to worse. A second knockout? It could be anything. And goddammit, Madison was pretty good at most things regarding survival—when she wasn't mouthing off. Tam's mind raced with plans and wild ideas, but none of them would help Cilla now. From the side of the stage he noticed movement in the shadows as two crew members started pushing out a pair of enormous steel bowls in the shape of a ship's hull, with a rope strung across the top of each.

JJ pointed at the metal ships with his index finger, putting a stop to the wave of whispers hissing through the team. 'Fire was every pirate's secret fear. If a ship caught fire, it was usually the end of everyone on board. But in this knockout fire is your friend. You'll need to build a fire that'll blaze long enough and high enough to burn through this rigging rope at the top,' he said, walking to a spot equidistant between the two cauldrons and placing a hand on the ropes suspended two feet above each fire pit.

'The first person to burn through the rigging and raise their Jolly Roger flag is the winner.'

Tam didn't trust himself to look at Cilla. He knew her well enough now to realize if she were to go tonight, she'd hold her head high, pretend it didn't matter, and walk down those stairs with her back straight and chin up. She wouldn't let any tears fall. Not in front of everyone, at least.

But it would matter. Terribly. Now he was seeing little pieces of her true self revealed in those moments when she let down that tough exterior, he knew it'd shatter her heart.

And there was something else, something she wasn't letting on. This money meant a lot more to her than she was making out. She tried to hide the desperation, but he'd caught glimpses of it in her eyes the day she'd refused to eat the chicken. This was more than just a game for Cilla, it was almost as if her life depended on winning this prize.

Out of the corner of his eye, he saw Cilla's slender form move toward one of the steel bowls. There was silence in the group. The dark seemed to press in around them. This was intense. He'd not dreamed the conclave would ever matter this much to him.

It's only a game.

The words pounded in his head.

It surprised him at how quickly his team-members had

come to mean something to him. The authenticity of the experience, of the game, was sucking him in. As a psychologist he could understand why the enforced intimacy of the group, along with the passion bred from the large reward at the end, would impact on his sense of reality. But he'd been sure he'd be able to withhold at least a part of his true self, keep aloof from the personalities and politics and neediness of the other players. This was all becoming much, much trickier than he'd expected.

And hardest of all was admitting to himself that the one person he really didn't want to lose from this game was Cilla. He was starting to care for her, against all reason and against his express promises to himself.

'We have given you everything you'll need to complete this knockout,' JJ said. 'There's a flint, coconut husks and plenty of kindling, as well as larger chunks of wood.' Tam watched Cilla pick up the flint and striker and turn them over in her hands.

'On my count of three, you'll begin your battle. One. Two. Three.' JJ stepped away from the two women hunched over their piles of wood, a predatory gleam in his eye.

'This is easy, you can do this in your sleep,' Madison muttered. She was chucking mounds of dry husks into the bottom of the steel basin, piling handfuls of kindling and small sticks on top. She struck the flint violently, sending sparks flying. A few caught in the husks and tiny flames licked upward, mushrooming into a hungry conflagration. Madison blew on the fire, making it leap skyward. She started placing some larger sticks on top.

Cilla was taking a different tack, and Tam was concerned to see her fire wasn't nearly as big as Madison's.

She held a wispy nest of husks cupped in her hands. A tiny spark glowed within and she blew on it gently, coaxing it to a larger flame. When it was well caught, she placed it in the cauldron and layered more and more husk on top. A healthy orange blaze sprang into life, the glow reflecting off the steely determination in her eyes. Kindling was added next, slow and measured, not thrown haphazardly like Madison was doing. Cilla built a small tepee with the kindling, directing the flames to rise higher and higher. Instead of loading on the larger pieces, she kept piling on the smaller sticks, the bright flames crackling and snapping with glee at the dry tinder.

Madison's fire was traditional, burning exactly like it was supposed to, smaller sticks first and then larger pieces to shore up the flames. It'd definitely burn through the rope when the larger pieces of wood caught properly.

Cilla's fire was a wild creature, untamed and unpredictable, but larger and brighter. And hungrier. Would it sustain the heat long enough to eat through the rope? The flames surged upwards.

'Come on, Cilla, you can do it,' Tam shouted. He couldn't help it. He didn't care now if everyone knew where his alliance lay. He wanted her to win. Needed her to win.

Her rope turned black as the flames licked the underside. She kept feeding the beast more and more kindling. But then it was all gone, there were no more small twigs to feed the hungry fire. Sparks flew upwards and drifted down like tiny fireworks, covering the stage with ash and burnt confetti.

Then, finally, the rope started to burn for real, one of the smaller bits of twine flamed and snapped with a pop.

Madison glanced over at Cilla and swore. She blew on her fire and then shoved a handful of kindling on top.

But it was too late; the second piece of plaited twine making up Cilla's rope snapped in a shower of black soot. Then the third and final piece, unable to hold the strain on its own, gave way, sending the small skull and crossbones flag racing for the sky.

She'd won! Cilla had done it. There was hushed silence as everyone digested the fact that Cilla was staying and Madison was gone.

'Cilla, wins the knockout,' JJ said in a loud voice. 'Bring me your firebrand, Madison.'

Madison threw down a handful of sticks, stubborn disbelief etched on her face.

'No, this can't be,' she shouted, stamping her feet like a child. 'I can't have lost. She's the one who's supposed to be going tonight.' Madison pointed at Cilla, her lips drawing back in a venomous snarl. JJ stepped between the two women, his large, muscled form dwarfing them both. 'The team has spoken, Madison. Bring me your firebrand. You'll have a chance to get back into this game. Off you go to Deception Cove.'

* * *

Firebrands wavered ahead of her, lighting the sandy path with their weak, fluttering gleam. Cilla followed the bobbing lights, her feet moving automatically, but her mind refused to focus. She'd come so close to being sent to Deception Cove tonight. The repercussions of that fate rolled around and around in her head like a murky fog.

Hulking shapes morphed out of the darkness and then a pale strip of sand, lit by the fragile moonlight, told her they'd reached their campsite. They were home. Safe for now.

'Wow, that was awesome,' Marg said, her voice resounded through the night air from somewhere behind Cilla.

'I'm not sure I'd use the word awesome, Marg.' Cilla could hear the reproach in Tam's tone.

'I don't mean awesome that Cilla nearly got voted out, dufus. I mean the whole thing. Our first conclave. I never thought it'd be so powerful. But you're okay, aren't you, Cilla? At least you're still here, eh?' Marg asked, contrite now.

'Mmm hmm.' Cilla didn't trust herself to speak. The rest of the team busied themselves putting away their meagre belongings, relighting the fire and standing their firebrands all in a row along the back of the beach. She dumped her bag beneath the sleeping platform. In the darting shadows and deep patches of darkness, it'd be easy enough for her to slip away unnoticed. She needed some time alone. Time to put her façade back together. A façade that'd been temporarily destroyed by the wounded betrayal she was feeling right now. Half an hour should do. They wouldn't miss her for that short time.

Slipping into the gloom of the coconut trees at the rear of the beach, she used the tall trunks as cover. Treading with care and working her way parallel to the ocean, she threaded through the fallen leaves and dead branches. The voices faded behind her, replaced by the loud hum of cicadas singing their nightly chorus.

She emerged a couple of hundred yards from the campsite, near the wall of limestone that partitioned their beach from the next cove. The sound of gently lapping waves called her toward the ocean. Dipping her toes in the tepid water, she stood on the surf's edge, staring out to sea. The horizon was hard to discern, the ocean's inky blackness blended almost seamlessly with the deepest indigo of the heavens. Two elements, water and sky, held against each other in the softness of the night. Stars spiraled in their nightly dance, bright and stark in their multitudes of pinprick lights. The quarter moon was now hidden by the low clouds circling the skyline, setting them alight with an eerie glow. Cilla drew in a deep breath of salty air. And then another. The air was cool and soothing, and she felt the ache in her shoulders subside.

Her muscles may have relaxed, but her mind was still whirling. Simon and Glen must've voted for her. She knew there'd been a very real chance they'd vote with Madison. But it was different when fact became reality. It hurt. Worse than she could've imagined.

Having your name read out on a piece of parchment changed everything about the game. Cilla's insides churned with the nastiness of it all.

'Can I join you?' She jumped and a small scream escaped her lips before she could stifle it.

'Shit. Tam,' she said, lowering her fists from where they'd raised up of their own accord.

'That's some attitude.' He motioned to her still-clenched fists. 'Looks like you're ready to take me on.'

'Well, don't sneak up on people.' She glowered at him. Yes, she was used to protecting herself, but she'd told no one else why. Her reaction was bred from many nights spent lying in fear, waiting for her father's homecoming. Wondering how drunk he'd be, whether he was in a rare sanguine mood, or in his usual violent temper.

Tam stood next to her, his toes dug deep into the wet

sand, saying nothing.

'I guess you're staying, whether or not I want you to?' she said, her tone unfriendly. What she really needed was to be alone. She needed time to sort through what'd happened tonight. Sift the feelings of duplicity and hurt out from the other emotions of reprieve and triumph at her victory over Madison. But this was something she was used to doing alone. She didn't need or want anyone else's help.

'I'm sorry you had to go through that second knockout tonight,' he said in a soft voice, barely audible above the swish of the waves. 'It wasn't supposed to be you up there. You know that, right?'

'Of course I know that,' she snapped. 'I'm very aware of how this game works, Tam. And equally aware of how fickle and untrustworthy people's promises can be.' She turned to stare at him, but his gaze remained on the rolling waves. How much could she trust Tam? The thought spun round and round her head as she continued to stare at him, daring him to meet her eyes. Which he did, finally. Starlight reflected in his pupils, the rest of his face held in deep shadow, the planes of his cheekbones and square jawbone only hinted at by the barest of margins against the black night. He took a step closer to her. The tiny hairs on her forearms rose to attention.

'I'm glad to hear that. Keep remembering, this is a game and people aren't always what they seem out here. At least you're not blaming yourself, which is good.' Her body's proximity warning bells were telling her to take a step backward, to get away from the aura of sanctuary he was projecting.

'Of course I'm not blaming myself.' As if she'd ever

reveal it to him, even if she did. Who'd he think he was, trying to sooth her suffering like she was one of his child patients who needed a shoulder to cry on?

'I'm quite capable, you know, Tam. You don't need to feel sorry for me just because we're in some alliance together,' she said, her voice getting louder by the second. Her throat tightened and her breath started to come in fast gasps. Bubbles of anger surged upwards through her stomach. She drew closer. They were mere inches apart now.

'And while we're on that subject, I'm not sure I want to be part of this little alliance you and Alisha have going. It didn't seem to do me any good tonight. I would've been just as well off on my own, the amount of help you two gave me.' Her arms hung stiff by her sides, her hands again balled into fists.

'Itching for a fight, I see, Cilla. Go on, yell and scream. Get it out of your system. It'll do you good.' His assertion surprised her. Had he called her bluff? Was he really prepared to stand there while she railed at him? Let her vent her anger and frustration without fighting back? The concept was new to her.

All her anger evaporated in a puff of cool night air. God, she was a bitch. She'd wanted to hit out at him, hurt him, make him feel a little of what she'd been feeling. But he'd seen through her bluster and stood firm, ready to take whatever she dished out.

'You need to remember one thing though, Cilla. I'm not the enemy.'

'I know you're not,' she mumbled, lowering her head and covering her eyes with her hands. 'God, I'm so sorry.' The backs of her eyelids prickled. Oh no, please don't let her cry now. She never cried. She'd not cried since she was sixteen, on the day her father had hit her for the last time. After that her tears had dried up, nothing else had ever been bad enough to warrant them. But this game was turning everything she'd ever known to be true on its head. Tam's hand came to rest lightly on her bare shoulder. His grip was firm and warm on her cool skin. The contact made her aware of how close they were. His touch bringing all her senses to full alert.

'Sorry,' she said again. 'I didn't really mean all that.'

'I know.' His hand remained feather light on her shoulder. The moon chose that instant to escape from the clasps of the vaporous clouds, and in the pale light she could see his T-shirt stretched across the muscles of his shoulders, giving the impression of masculine energy tightly controlled. Could she trust him? She wasn't sure. Especially not when the man stirred her emotions as much as he did.

'I really am okay about the whole conclave thing, honest.' She tried to raise a smile, but all she could manage was a small shrug. What could she say that'd convince him she was fine? To make him move away from her. She raised her chin, trying to gauge his features. But Tam's face was cast in shadow, and she couldn't tell what sentiments were hiding behind those hooded eyes.

It was his unwavering touch that was her final undoing. It seemed to offer shelter and kindness, things she'd been sorely lacking in recent times.

A big, fat tear escaped, tracing a wet trail down her cheek. His left hand came up to grab her by the other shoulder.

'Cilla?'

Another traitorous tear rolled, hot and heavy, down her face, and tiny shudders coursed through her.

Before she knew how it happened, Tam enfolded her in his embrace, her cheekbone pressed hard against his warm chest.

Then the dam burst and she started to cry properly, sobbing as the tears streamed down her face. He never said a word, just held her, waiting out the tempest.

Well, if she was going to let herself collapse into a puddle of tears just this once, then she may as well bask in the extravagance of doing it in Tam's well-built arms. She could feel the slow thudding of his heart beneath her ear. The short stubble from his week spent without shaving roughened the top of her forehead.

His fingers brushed across the bare skin of her neck. The light touch sent a frisson of sensation down her spine, bringing with it an unmistakable flare of heat. Her pulse reacted by becoming erratic and her breathing was suddenly shallow. Her sobs abated. Her body became acutely aware of his male physicality, so close. All she had to do was tip her head up a little...

His lips met hers as if he'd been waiting for this moment. For her to let go.

* * *

Her mouth was supple and filled him with wanting. All of Tam's resolve to make this kiss one of compassion—a soothing kiss, one that'd last only fleeting seconds—dissolved the moment he touched Cilla. She tasted sweet and rich and the desire to keep savoring her ripped through him. Her tongue met his, dancing around his mouth, her teeth grazing his lips, nibbling and sucking. He deepened the kiss, wanting to draw all of her into him. He wanted more. More of her. She was intoxicating. All logic flew out the window. The fact her response was as unrestrained as his, had his senses reeling.

She pushed up against his chest and he could feel the roundness of her breasts through the fabric of his shirt. Instinct made him draw his hand up along the side of her ribs and cup her breast. It was the perfect size; small, but with just enough weight to fill his fingers. The feel of her, a mixture of curves and softness, taught muscles and heat sent a wave of fire straight to his gut. He became burning awareness and raw pleasure intermingled.

He dropped both hands and clutched her buttocks, lifting her even closer into him. Her arms came around his neck, her fingers in his hair, pulling his mouth down onto hers. All reasoning gone in a desire so hot and intense it charred him from the inside out. She was a dangerous, heady combination.

'Cilla, where are you?'

He tore his mouth away from hers and sucked in several deep breaths. It was Marg, come looking for her down on the beach. Holding Cilla by the shoulders, he pushed her away. Distance, he needed some distance between them so he could regain his equilibrium. The fact that her swollen lips were shining in the moonlight and her breathing was coming in ragged little hitches did nothing to help.

He drew himself upright and concentrated on conquering his desire. God, what would've happened if Marg hadn't intervened?

What'd he been thinking? He'd no right to take advantage of her like this. And taking advantage of her was exactly what he'd been doing. She wouldn't have kissed him like that if she'd not been so overwrought, so charged with emotion. What he'd done to Cilla was unfair, and shame writhed within at the thought.

If she'd been in her right mind, she would've been laughing in his face right now. Telling him to leave her alone and asking him who he thought he was to take advantage of her like that? He had no right. He was a loser. The words echoed around his head, the memory of them jolting him back to the day Julia had thrown him out of their apartment. The words she hurled after him as he stumbled down the street. *"You were never good enough for me, Tam. You'll never be good enough for anyone. You're a loser."*

Why did he think it'd be any different with Cilla?

He took a step back, letting her go. Lifting his gaze, he found her staring at him, weighing, considering.

'We'd better go.' He couldn't hide the rasp in his voice. Cilla raised an eyebrow, awareness of his shuttered features replacing the rosy hue of desire on her face.

'Yes, I think we'd better,' she replied.

CHAPTER SEVEN

Hefting the hessian bags and goggles into the crook of his arm, Tam tugged his cap down low and headed toward the rear of the beach.

He wouldn't say he was avoiding Cilla exactly. More like keeping his own council. It'd been two full days since that kiss, and it was still affecting him. It was part of the decree of his job not to take advantage of people in emotional pain. And what'd he done? Precisely that. A large part of him felt ashamed at his slip-up. But another— equally large part—was also undone when he remembered Cilla's response. She'd been burning with passion, opening to him like a flower to the sun. She'd wanted that kiss as much as he had.

There was also that dratted internal voice telling him a woman such as Cilla wouldn't want a man like him, anyway. Not if she knew the truth about him, about his past. It might be easy for people to admire the man he'd become on the surface, confident and likable—altruistic even, in his work with the kids. And maybe that persona was actual, but Tam knew the veracity of what lay beneath, and he wasn't ready to deal anyone into the reality of his childhood. The stigma of growing up on the wrong side of town. The deprivation and humiliation poverty brought with it. What he'd been forced to do to help his family survive.

He'd been about to reveal it all to Julia. He'd even been fixing to ask her to marry him. Until she'd blindsided him. She'd kicked him out of the apartment they'd shared for nearly two years, telling him she was in love with someone else, someone who was perfect for her. She'd only been biding her time with Tam.

That'd been three years ago. Since then, he'd only managed a few hook-ups. One-night stands. Or relationships only lasting a few weeks at most. It was better that way. His love-affair with Julia showed him how unwise it was to trust anyone with such complete and utter naivety. Thank God he hadn't told her about his past, she would've only used it to hurt him. He wouldn't be stupid enough to do that again.

Only his family knew about his dubious history. Because all his petty crimes of theft and robbery had been committed while he was a juvenile, he hadn't been required to make his record public, even when he became a counsellor. He was a different person now. Always striving to do the right thing, to be an upstanding citizen. His past was well behind him and he needed to keep looking to the future.

'Where you off to?' Simon's question broke into his thoughts. His quiet retreat from camp hadn't gone as completely unnoticed as he'd hoped. Tam turned to face Simon.

'Thought I might try my luck crabbing in that little bay

we found the other day.' He kept his face blank, but inwardly he seethed. He didn't want company, and certainly not Simon's. He was grumpy, tired and hungry, and Simon was possibly the last person he wanted to talk to.

'Cool, I'll come with you. That crabbing looks pretty easy. I wouldn't mind having a go at it.'

'Great,' Tam ground out between clenched teeth. 'Here, you carry the bags then.' He threw the hessian bags in Simon's direction and led the way onto the tiny track that ran north, following the boundary of the coastline. The little bay was a good twenty-minute walk away. He'd chosen it because it was isolated and well away from camp. And it was in the opposite direction Cilla had taken. He'd watched her surreptitiously as she gathered up the fishing lines, slung a water canteen over one shoulder, and headed off on the jungle track that led south; toward the long headland jutting out at the far end of their beach. That'd been nearly an hour ago.

Tam readjusted the flippers and goggles so he could carry them under one arm and pulled his cap down further over his eyes. It looked like it was going to be a long morning after all. At least there was no knockout today. They had a reprieve until tomorrow. He'd been going to spend the next few hours by himself, thinking.

Their shoes made little sound as they walked along the trail, the deep layer of rotting leaves muffling all sound. The vegetation was sparse at the edge of the jungle, but there was enough shade to make the morning seem almost pleasant. The tropical sun would warm up the island all too soon until the heat became virtually unbearable.

'So, I've got a question for you. Who do you think eats

more rice? Alisha or Marg?' Simon punctuated his query with a snort. The inane questions had started already, and the worst part was Simon actually thought he was funny. 'No, really, I mean it,' Simon continued. 'Because that rice bag is getting awfully empty and none of it seems to be going into my mouth.'

Tam bit back a retort, instead lengthening his stride, putting his head down. Setting out with the one purpose of making Simon so breathless he could no longer speak.

They managed to walk the track in a little under fifteen minutes. They were almost there. A sharp bend in the trail loomed ahead and Tam kept his gaze down, negotiating the sprawling tree roots that buckled the ground in front of him. He rounded the corner and came out at the margin of the foliage skimming the rear of the tiny beach. Just as his shoes hit the sand, he raised his head and stopped dead in his tracks.

Cilla was standing there, thigh deep in the water, her face in profile, staring out to sea. Completely naked.

Tam had stopped without warning, and Simon ran into the back of him with a grunt.

'What the...'

Tam was frozen to the spot.

'Quick, get down, before she sees us,' Simon said in a fierce whisper. At the same moment, he tugged on Tam's arm, pulling him toward the cover of two large boulders clustered a few feet away. Tam was too shocked to argue. He ducked down behind the boulder before he could clear his mind to think properly.

'Oh. My. God. I never expected to see that,' Simon said, voice high-pitched and dripping with innuendo. He poked his head above the slab of rock and ogled Cilla. 'Look at that ass. Perfect and round and tight. Mmm hmm, wouldn't you love to tap that one?'

Yes, Cilla's ass was perfect and round and tight. The image was seared into Tam's brain. He wished he hadn't just seen what he had. Like some kind of disgusting voyeur. He was almost glad he was crouching behind the rock, where she couldn't see his reaction. That one brief glimpse of her lithe figure had sent his pulse skipping through his veins and he could feel his body responding automatically, the growing bulge in his pants highlighting how much he was attracted to her. His body hummed with awareness at the remembered image of her smooth soft skin, of the curve of her hips, the side-on view of the slight swell of her breast seen right before he ducked behind the boulder. Sweat prickled his skin, and he knew it wasn't caused by the tropical sun.

It wouldn't do to let Simon see how she affected him. Simon had just shown his true colors, and Tam didn't appreciate this new version one bit. Something had always felt a little off with Simon, but up until right this very second Tam had never been able to put his finger on exactly what. Now, more than ever, he shouldn't show any kind of weakness around the man. He'd surely use it against him somehow. It'd been on impulse he'd followed Simon's lead, but now he felt an unsavory gall rise at the back of his throat. What they were doing was wrong on so many levels.

He would not squat here, a party to Simon's adolescent gawping.

Drawing breath, he tensed, ready to rise up and reveal himself. He wasn't sure what he was going to say, but he couldn't leave Cilla unaware of their presence any longer.

'Don't even think about it, mate,' Simon said. 'What's the harm in having a look? Let's keep it our little secret, hey?' A slightly amused expression filtered across his face.

'No.' Tam's reply was final. He surged upwards, but a heavy pull on his T-shirt stopped him. Simon dragged him back down to a crouching position, staring him straight in the face.

'She won't appreciate your gallantry one bit, you know.' Simon's eyes were cold, his face no longer genial, had turned stark and detached. 'She'll blame you, say you were intentionally spying on her. That you enjoyed watching. Women twist facts around to suit themselves.'

Tam was staggered at this unexpected change in Simon, at the bitterness dripping from his every word. This was so unlike the easy-going persona he'd seen so far on the island. Admittedly Simon was a vain man, but this transformation in his attitude was a whole new level. Whatever kind of terrible experiences Simon had encountered to give him this view, Tam didn't care to know. Now wasn't the time to delve into the depths of Simon's warped mind. He needed to act before it all became too late.

'I don't agree, Simon. An intelligent woman like Cilla will accept our apology.' He stared at the man hunkered down next to him, dead in the eye. A sly smile spread across Simon's square face.

'I'll tell her it was all your idea to spy. Even if she acts like she doesn't believe me, it'll have planted the seed of doubt in her mind. Your shiny coat of amour suddenly won't be so bright, will it, mate?' Simon's crafty smile faded, replaced by a steely gaze. It felt like Simon had twisted a knife into Tam's guts. How could he have gotten so close to the truth in that one lazily veiled threat? And he was right. Tam didn't want Cilla to think any less of him. If she thought he'd been spying on her, all sorts of walls would go up around that mind of hers. And around her heart as well.

He hesitated.

He hated himself for that hesitation.

Simon pounced. 'Please don't tell her. For my sake.'

There was desperation in Simon's tone, but Tam wasn't fooled. He already knew Simon was dangerous, but he went up a further couple of notches in Tam's estimation of exactly how intelligent and manipulative the man could be.

Simon took another peek over the top of the boulder. 'She's gone further out for a swim. If we leave now, she won't see us. Come on, mate, let's go.' He backed carefully away from the beach, keeping the rocks between himself and the view of the little bay. Tam shot him a sideways glance. Every second Tam hesitated, took Simon further into the jungle. If Tam stood up and revealed himself, he'd be on his own. He could see the bare truth written in Simon's determined frown.

Tam nearly gave voice to an oath, his whole body tingled with tension. It went against every human trait he valued to run away. Unable to speak, his fingers shook as he loosened his stranglehold on the flippers and swapped them over to his other hand.

'Fuck.' He still hesitated. Simon had disappeared completely, but his threat continued to hang in the air. Simon would tell Cilla if he didn't follow, of that Tam had no doubt. He'd lie, twist the facts to use against him. Simon may indeed get enough people to believe him, it might well be Tam's head on the chopping block next time they went to the conclave. If he went after Simon, maybe he could make him change his mind. Moving away from the sheltering boulders at a crouch, Tam re-traced Simon's footsteps.

* * *

'Hey, Tam, where're Alisha and Cilla? Simon's just come back with mail from Davy Jones' Locker, he wants everyone around so he can read it.' Glen came over to where Tam was prodding the fire.

'I think I saw them walking to the headland about an hour ago to catch some more crabs,' Tam replied. Glen stopped sucking on his coconut long enough to glance over in that direction, his florid face conveying a look of disinterest.

'Looks like they'll miss out then.'

'I'll go and get them,' Tam said with a sigh.

'Thanks.' Tam watched as Glen ambled over to the shelter. He was such a lazy bastard. It surprised him Glen had lasted this long out here. But he had Simon's ear, and that seemed to be his saving grace at the moment.

Tam's lengthy strides carried him over the sand at a quick rate and he was already halfway to the headland when a flash of orange caught his eye and he saw Cilla and Alisha making their way down the low rocky ledge, coming back to camp. Alisha raised a hand in acknowledgment. He watched the two women walk toward him, Alisha as wide as she was tall, her black hair standing out in a frizzy mess, and Cilla tall and trim, her orange bathers highlighting her slender shoulders. The sun was glinting off Cilla's olive skin, wet from swimming. A jolt of appreciation hit his stomach as he watched Cilla walk. He couldn't get over how she affected him physically every time he laid eyes on her. Especially now he knew what she looked like without clothes on. It'd been four days now since the voyeur moment when he'd seen her nude, and his pulse still went up a few notches at the mere thought. Whether his gut-reaction was from guilt or from a much baser instinct, Tam wasn't sure.

For a few days after he and Simon had seen Cilla in the bay, he'd wanted to blurt out the truth every time she came near. But on each occasion he was about to say something, a glance from Simon had stopped him. He was yet unsure why he was keeping the secret. Was it for Simon's sake, or his own?

Tucking his hands into his pockets, he stood and waited for them to approach. They were talking, heads together and arms flying with their animated conversation. He picked up their discussion as they came closer.

'Sneaky little cow, finding that doubloon so quick,' Alisha said.

'And stupid to use it at the first conclave,' Cilla replied with conviction. 'Paloma should've kept it.'

'She must've thought she was on the chopping block to use it, though.' Alisha's plump features crumpled into a deep frown. 'And she might well have been a goner too, if bloody Simon and Glen hadn't changed their votes at the last minute.'

'Yeah, underhanded bastards,' Cilla added thoughtfully.

There was a definite rift forming in the camp. Tam had noticed it after the first conclave, when Simon and Glen had changed their votes and Cilla was nearly voted out. But now it was obvious to everyone in the camp. There were two distinct sides. Simon, Paloma and Glen on one,

Marg, Alisha, Cilla and himself on the other. Cho seemed content to be a drifter, a swing vote, not cementing a bond with either side, trying to keep everyone happy. Tam was secretly worried Cho was leaning more toward siding with Simon. Tam still had the numbers on his side at the moment, but as he knew only too well, anything could happen in this game.

'Hopefully we win the knockout battle today,' Tam added, falling into step with the two women. 'And then we won't need to worry about doubloons, or Marg's elaborate plans.'

'Hi Tam, were you coming to find us?' Alisha asked with a grin.

He nodded. 'Simon has got some mail.' He lifted his head and found Cilla staring at him with those emerald eyes. He smiled, and she returned his smile, but it was a puzzled grin. She knew he'd been avoiding her, it was clear in the question mark of her raised eyebrow. But she hadn't pushed the subject, not once questioning his standoffishness over the past couple of days, letting him have the breathing room he desired. He hoped she thought he remained conflicted over their kiss. She'd never have guessed the true reason. That thought brought on another spasm of guilt. It was time to forget what he'd seen and move on. They were about to go into another knockout battle and he needed to get his mind back into the game, and stop obsessing over what-ifs and maybes.

Drawing a deep breath, he forced himself to hold her gaze for a few seconds longer than necessary, sending a silent entreaty for her to forgive him. His intestines flickered when he saw her give an almost imperceptible nod. He was forgiven.

'Look what I caught today.' Alisha held up three large crabs by the pincers, right in front of his face, breaking his gaze with Cilla. 'I'm getting better at this hunting and gathering thing,' she crowed, delighted at her haul. 'If only we didn't have to share them with everyone else.'

'Yes. Some people deserve to share more than others,' said Cilla.

'Yeah, that bloody Glen does nothing around the campsite, he just simpers and smirks and brown-noses up Simon's bum.' Alisha capered on the sand, giving a more-than-accurate impression of how Glen acted. Tam laughed out loud at her audacity.

'I wonder how Madison's going out on Deception? Do you think she's still there?' asked Cilla once their mirth had died down.

'It's hard to guess. We don't know who got voted off from the Nightrebels at the last conclave, so we don't know who she would've been up against. And we don't even know how many people they're going to keep at Deception at one time. Will they make the people at Deception battle every time a new person is voted out? Or will they keep them all together and do one big knockout right at the end?' said Alisha.

Neither Tam nor Cilla had an answer to Alisha's question. They'd been told a girl called Phoebe was voted out of team Nightrebels at their first conclave, but apart from her name they knew nothing else about her. Madison was a tough competitor, and Tam was pretty sure Phoebe wouldn't have stood much of a chance against her. It all depended on who'd been voted out of Nightrebels at the conclave three days ago. The only thing Tam could be absolutely sure of was that whoever and whenever the person returned from Deception, it would be timed to wreak the most havoc in the game.

'God, I'd love to know what goes on over there,' Cilla said.

'Well, I for one hope I never find out,' he replied.

'Hey guys, hurry up,' Simon yelled across the beach, beckoning them with an imperative wave of his hand. The rest of the team already stood around the fire, waiting.

Dumping her catch of seafood on the sand by the fire, Alisha said, 'Go on then, read it out.'

Simon cleared his throat and intoned in a low voice,

'For both plunder and protection.'
'Teamwork and strategy are worth a mention.'
'Roll with the bumps and go along the way.'
'To keep you safe from a double dose of Deception.'

'Sounds like this one is for both a prize and for exemption,' said Marg. 'I wonder what the prize will be?' They all did. Tam could hear his own stomach rumbling loudly at the mere thought of a food reward. It's what they all needed. Desperately. Alisha's and Cilla's seafood would only go so far.

'I'm worried about that *double dose of Deception* bit. What does that mean?' Marg ran a hand through her short hair, but no one had an answer to her question. 'Oh well, we sent Nightrebels to the conclave at the last knockout, we can do it again.'

* * *

'The team has spoken,' JJ said.

Cilla watched as JJ extinguished Paloma's flaming firebrand and the woman turned to head through the hangman's noose and down the stairs, her shoulders hunched and footsteps heavy. She didn't look back at the team who'd voted her out. A pang of guilt snaked through Cilla. It hurt to vote someone out, no matter who it was.

At their camp they'd become pretty much a family unit, albeit one with all the failings and mistakes and bickering that went along with being part of a true family. Surviving on the island had helped mould them as a team. Fighting the elements and lack of food together brought them closer. Paloma had her faults, but so did they all. There were probably others in the team who were equally deserving of going home tonight. But tonight Cilla had followed Alisha's wishes and voted Paloma off. She knew without a doubt the voting was going to get tougher and tougher to get right.

Today's knockout challenge had been for both plunder and exemption. As the winning team, they'd gained the prize of an all-you-can-eat smorgasbord of hamburgers and bottles of soda pop. And they got to eat the meal while watching the losing team vote out someone at the conclave. Giving them a distinct advantage. They'd get to see how the other team voted and watch all the power plays—who was an asset and who was an underdog. It'd be valuable information when they came to the merge.

But there'd been a twist. They had to vote one member out of their own team first. A double hanging.

'Okay guys, the hard part's over. The winners can go and claim your prize.' JJ gestured toward the row of tiered benches set up in the right-hand corner of the stage, covered by a rudimentary roof of thatched grass. Coils of rope were arranged along the benches and large wooden beer kegs guarded the edges of the pews, a menacing-looking cutlass resting across each one. A large table made of dark wood towered behind the seats, laden with food.

No one had to be told twice, they all surged forward, jostling and shoving good naturedly for the best spot. The aroma was heavenly, and Cilla's stomach rumbled like a herd of stampeding elephants. She couldn't pile the food quickly enough onto her plate. There were meat patties, and chicken patties and tomato and lettuce and pickles and sauce and mustard and enough buns to feed twenty people. There were even vegie patties, just for her. Plate piled high, she carefully negotiated her way through the benches to find a seat.

Simon was the only one already seated, and she hesitated for the briefest second before plonking herself on the rope cushion next to him. It wouldn't do to look as if she was shunning him. Tam manoeuvred along the row and sat next to her. His plate had twice as much food as hers. She lifted an eyebrow at him, but her mouth was too full of food for her to form any coherent words.

The food was so good it almost distracted her when Tam's knee accidentally bumped against hers as he sat down, along with the ensuing sizzle of heat that soared up her thigh. Almost, but not quite.

It'd been a long week. Tam had been avoiding her after their kiss on the beach. But she wasn't sure why. Did he regret it? Did he think it showed a moment of weakness, presenting his tender side? Did he think she might use that flaw against him? Who knew? In this game, every move a person made was scrutinised for strategy. Dissected to see if it could be manipulated in some way. It was nearly impossible to trust anyone out here. On the surface she'd forged a powerful bond with Alisha, Tam and Marg, but underneath she wondered if she could truly rely on them. And she knew they were thinking the same thing of her. It was a slippery slope they were negotiating. She did hope, however, they might remain friends outside the game.

Did she want to stay friends with Tam afterwards? Now that was a tricky one. And *friend* wasn't quite the correct word. She knew, given half a chance, her heart would want a lot more than *just friends* from Tam. Could she be sure what kind of person Tam really was though? He seemed solid and compassionate enough, but in her experience men changed once they had you hooked. They all seemed to have the ability to morph into reproductions of her father. Especially Marco.

She'd fallen in love with Marco because of his zest for life and his enjoyment of excellent food. Unfortunately, his love for food had gone hand in hand with his love for drink, which at first hadn't bothered Cilla. But after two years of his laid back persona, she started to see him more as a lazy bum rather than easygoing, and his drinking escalated until she was reminded more and more of her father. When she tried to tell Marco she wasn't happy with their relationship, he'd become violent and smacked her around. Exactly like her father.

She was understanding her interactions with her father had left her damaged in many ways. She found it hard to show affection. Marco had called her *the ice queen* toward the end of their relationship. She wondered if it were true. Whatever the case, it was tough to trust anyone, to let them in. It was all too hard.

'Nightrebels come on in,' JJ spoke, loud enough to be heard over the hubbub of the Dawnbreakers people finding their seats. A hush fell as they watched Nightrebels enter the stage. A line of glowing firebrands wound up the stairs, announcing the team one by one. It was hard to make out individual faces, hidden in the shadows cast by the flickering flames.

Some individuals from the Nightrebels cast envious glances toward the Dawnbreakers and their food, but most kept their heads down, ignoring the gluttony going on in the face of their own malnourishment.

As the other team took their places on the benches on the other side of the fire pit, rain started to fall in big soaking drops. It seemed nature was going to have her own vote in tonight's conclave. At least the small area where the Dawnbreakers were eating was covered, even if the thatched roof leaked in spots. Cilla crouched over her plate, protecting it from most of the wet drips escaping from the underside of the wooden beams above.

Even JJ wasn't safe from the ravages of the storm as it lashed the tribal platform. His tree-trunk chair was just as unprotected as the Nightrebels' team benches, and he was soon soaked to the skin. His expensive shirt plastered to his chest and his flat-cap drooping over his forehead. Somehow he still managed to remain poised and confidant and Cilla's respect for their host grew. He must be feeling at least a little vulnerable, his egalitarian well-dressed persona stripped bare by the rain. But his professionalism kept him out there in the pouring rain, doing his job, hammering team Nightrebels with his rigorous questioning.

The storm seemed to have an effect on the minds of Nightrebels. They looked like a string of lost children sitting in front of an angry principal. Their protective veneers were dropped, and while some sat hunched and sorry-looking, trying to stay warm in the chilly rain, others —the ones who felt most susceptible—started pleading for their lives.

'I wish I could've done more to help carry those boxes today. I really do.' A man called Ben scrubbed the rain from his bald head with his red bandana. 'But I'm sure the upcoming knockouts are going to require more mental skills than physical skills, and that's when you'll need my ability. I'll be able to win those knockouts for you, hands down.'

Ben looked to be of Korean descent, around mid-forties in age. Water ran down his face in rivulets, accentuating the obvious despair in his eyes.

'I agree with Ben, I don't reckon people should vote because of someone's physical ability. Just because I'm not the fittest woman on this team doesn't mean I should be a target,' said a younger woman from the middle row. 'I mean, there're a lot of other people in this team who don't do nearly as much around the campsite as I do. I'm good at keeping the fire going and I do the cooking most days. You guys would be lost without me.' She gave a nervous glance to her left, looking for support from the other women in the team.

Cilla studied the woman between large bites of her vegie-burger and decided that fitness probably wasn't why people wanted to vote her out tonight. She had mousey brown hair, a long nose, and a rotund belly. She was constantly preening, stroking her wet hair and wiping the rain from her face. Her whining was getting on Cilla's nerves, and she'd only been listening to her for a few minutes. She could imagine having to put up with it for weeks on end. That woman would be high maintenance.

'Sorry, Susan, you'll have to speak up,' said JJ. The wind was starting to howl now, and he had to lean forward to catch what she was saying.

The mousey woman continued to whine and Cilla tuned her out as she picked the last of the crumbs from her plate and considered returning to the table for another plateful.

'Learning anything?' Tam whispered into her ear.

'Yes.' She grinned at him. 'Our team isn't nearly as bad as I thought.' He swept his amber gaze over her and laughed along with her.

Then she sobered. 'It's a little sad as well.'

'What do you mean?' His breath tickled the side of her face as he leaned in closer. He smelled good, a mixture of spicy hamburger and fresh salty skin. As they spoke, he unconsciously licked sauce from his fingertips, one by one. She became mesmerised by this action, watching as he put each finger into his mouth and releasing it again with a smack of his lips. Tam had beautiful hands. Long-fingered, tanned and graceful. Oh, what he might do to her with those hands. What he *had* done to her with those hands the other night. When he'd kissed her. She remembered how he'd cupped her breast, hefted it in his hand, branding her with the heat of his fingers. Warmth flushed up her chest at the memories of the encounter. She almost moaned with frustration as she recalled how their kiss had ended. Very unsatisfactorily.

'What do you mean, Cilla?' Tam prompted her again. Averting her eyes, she drew in a sharp breath.

'Oh... I feel a little uncomfortable, I guess,' she mumbled. With a supreme effort, she regained her previous train of thought. Managing to shut down her body's response to him, she forced an ironic smile to her lips. 'Here we are watching their every move, assessing their weaknesses as if we're the predator and they're the prey. It's a bit morbid, actually.'

'Yep, I know. It's hard to watch…but fascinating at the same time.' Tam's voice wavered—was it with empathy or curiosity? 'I guess we have to remember we're all here to play the game.'

She nodded. 'Yes, we are.'

That night they watched as the Korean man, Ben, was voted off by Nightrebels. He trudged down the same stairs Paloma had vanished down only half an hour before, despair evident in his every step. Cilla felt a little sorry for him. There but for the grace of God went she.

As they all slogged through the damp darkness, bloated and weary, back to their camp, Cilla's thoughts were occupied not with the precious information she'd learned about team Nightrebels, but by the image of Tam's hands curled around her breast. *Lust*, she reminded herself. That was all this was. Lust and nothing more. And she'd always been able to control her own desire. She'd never let it consume her before, and it'd be no different out here.

CHAPTER EIGHT

'You must sit two players out of this knockout, Dawnbreakers. Who'll it be?' JJ asked. Glen was the first to put his hand up, which surprised Cilla. Perhaps he'd got wind of the pseudo plan to vote him out if they lost, and knowing how weak he was in knockouts, he'd chosen to take himself out of the equation.

Marg floated the idea that they throw this knockout; intentionally lose it, just so they could vote Glen off. She and Alisha talked about it briefly, but in the end they decided—even though they detested the mere sight of Glen—for the sake of a strong team, they needed to win every knockout possible. It wasn't good for team moral to lose a knockout on purpose.

At the moment they were streaking ahead of Nightrebels on the knockout tally board. Since the double elimination six days ago, Nightrebels had lost another knockout and voted another team member out. They'd lost four members, while Dawnbreakers had only lost two. A prominent position to be in if they could just hold on to this lead. Any advantage when the two teams finally joined would help her advance further in the game.

'I'll go as well,' said Marg. 'I haven't sat one out yet, and it's probably time.'

They chose Simon to be the caller because of his loud penetrating tone, and Cho and Alisha put their hands up to do the puzzle. Leaving Tam and Cilla paired together to do the obstacle course. Which would've been all good and well, except they had to do it blindfolded and tied together, relying on Simon's voice commands to guide them through a maze.

Cilla inspected the maze while JJ explained the rules. It was hard to see exactly what lay on the furthest edges of the maze from the ground, only Simon would be able to see what was out there from his vantage point atop the calling platform. She could make out piles of wooden beer kegs thrown haphazardly together, some kind of slalom course created out of large empty whisky bottles, and a roughly constructed long table with benches down both sides. Then it hit her. This maze was supposed to resemble the inside of a seedy whisky bar. The tackiness of this show never failed to surprise her.

'You ready for this?' Tam sent her a quick glance and then went back to tying the rope around her waist.

'Course I am.' If only she felt as sure as she sounded. They were about to be tied closely together, then blindfolded. Having to rely on their senses of sound and touch to find their way through. The hardest part of this whole thing wouldn't be the bumped elbows and scraped knees, it'd be Tam's enforced proximity. Cilla was able to control her body's cravings around him, as long as he didn't touch her. And this knockout called for their bodily contact to win this challenge.

Since their kiss on the beach over a week and a half ago, Cilla had toyed with the idea of seducing Tam, of using their obvious attraction as a tool to advance herself in the game. If she let things go further, he might well become putty in her hands, willing to do just about anything she asked. She'd seen it happen before. A lot of men tended to think with their dicks and not their heads, even when there was a million dollars at stake.

However, after laying awake most of one night, sorting through various scenarios, she found that she couldn't do it. Allure and captivation came so easily to some women, but not to her. She'd no doubt that if she exploited this visceral attraction, she'd be able to draw Tam in, make him a partner in crime—albeit perhaps an unwilling one. But there was something more to this attraction, a deeper connection, which, given time, Cilla would've liked to explore. And much as she hated to admit it, she was loath to do anything to destroy that connection. And using him as a sexual pawn in her game would surely do that.

When she was with Tam, there was a degree of heightened awareness, as if the very hairs on her body knew he was close and rose up to point in his direction, making her skin tingle with an undercurrent of mindfulness centred on him.

But it wasn't merely the physical effect he had on her body. He was affecting her mind as well. Their many conversations over the past week revealed he had an uncanny knack of stripping away the shield with which she normally protected her true self, driving straight to the heart of her doubts about her own capabilities and flaws. He prodded her with questions and scenarios for which she had no immediate answer, but in thinking about her answers she found herself opening up. She didn't mean to tell him the things she did. Small things she'd told no one else. Things such as how she kept a perfectly round, perfectly smooth stone she'd found on the beach in her pocket, so she was always reminded how lucky she was to live in the most beautiful place in the world. His calming presence seemed to draw her out of herself, almost like drawing poison from a wound. It was a vicious circle; the more he stripped away the safeguard she kept around her heart, the more sensitive she became to his attentions. It scared her; how he affected her. It was dangerous.

Concentrate. Her self-control needed to be rock solid today. She needed to ignore her body's blatant alertness to the fact his face hovered mere inches from her own as he checked on the knot tying them together. Or the fact his broad male shoulders loomed over her, making her hands itch to reach out and run over his powerful physique.

Realising she'd been holding her breath in an attempt to keep from inhaling Tam's scent, Cilla drew in air sharply and at the same time took a step backward.

'That rope must be tight enough now,' she said, a little more sharply than was perhaps necessary.

There was surprise in his glance, but he said nothing as he took his place beside her on the starting line.

Then JJ placed two eye patches over her eyes and tied them tightly at the rear of her head. The world went black. Other senses started to heighten, to make up for her lack of sight. A breath of wind tickled her cheek in passing. She could hear JJ's heavy footsteps crunching over the sand as he walked toward the next pair with their eye patches. The midday rays were hotter on her skin and she could smell the peppery mixture of sunshine and sweat that was Tam, standing so close beside her.

Tam grabbed her hand. It was large and warm and rough. Callouses on his palm, formed by his hard work on the island, abraded her skin, each movement of his fingers making her ultra-aware of their contact. Flame-like sensations licked from her fingers up her arm, setting the nerve ends in her palm tingling with anticipation. She stifled a grating intake of breath, which threatened to give her away.

'Contestants ready?' JJ said, his voice sounding clearly over the battleground. Tam's arm tensed next to hers, muscles at the ready. She tightened her grip on his hand. Their connection was the anchor to which she clung. Could she use her hyper-awareness of Tam's every move to her advantage? With this tension fizzing between them, she could follow him with a precision the other team might lack. If only she stopped fighting it, perhaps there was a benefit to be found and used in this attraction between them.

Cilla had already made a mental map of the maze before they were blindfolded and she tried to bring that image back to the forefront of her memory, shaking loose her mind's preoccupation with the purely physical sensations Tam was creating. Then she too tensed, ready to go.

'Go.' The word was a whiplash to her finely tuned ears, and they surged forward together at a near run, both going on instinct toward the first obstacle; three piles of wooden kegs directly across their path.

Simon's voice reached them, booming above the cacophony of the other team's caller yelling instructions. They'd chosen well, Simon's voice was deep and controlled, easy to hear.

'Keep going straight. You're on the right heading. Slow down, you're going too fast.' Cilla felt the tug of Tam's hand and she slowed to a walk, waving her free hand out in front, searching for any impediment. 'In two more paces you are going to hit the barrels, you need to take three paces to the left.' They did as they were told and with the brush of wood beneath her hand, Cilla knew they were round the first obstacle.

'Right, keep walking in the direction you're going. There'll be two benches coming up in about ten paces.' Simon was amazingly cool and calm and talked them through each obstacle as it came until they finally reached a pole where a bag of puzzle pieces hung.

'Tam, you need to reach up to your right, as high as you can. You'll need to let go of Cilla's hand.' His warm hand left hers. She smothered a silly feeling of deprivation. He was still standing there right next to her, he hadn't left her out here on her own. She made a determined effort not to reach out and make sure he was really there.

Then he bumped against her as he reached up high, feeling for the bag.

She was standing too close, so she stepped back to get out of his way. As she stepped backward, her heel caught on a stone behind her and because she was already unsteady without his hand keeping her firm, she overbalanced. There was nothing she could do. She knew she was going to fall. She prayed she wasn't going to land on anything hard. Or, God forbid, break her arm in the fall. At the last second, Tam's fingers scrabbled to grab her arm or clothes, something, feeling her falling. His forearm half-caught around her waist.

'Cilla—'

Then she felt him topple as well.

And they both crashed to the ground.

Somehow Tam managed to swing them around in mid-air so she landed on top of him. She heard the air whoosh out of his lungs as he hit the ground. Felt the firm planes of his chest break her fall.

The shock of finding herself lying on top of Tam, being cradled by his large body, paralysed her for uncounted seconds. The fact she couldn't see him only seemed to heighten the terrifying perception of his strong thighs beneath hers, his steely abs supporting her hips.

'You okay?' His stubble rasped along the side of her cheek. She could feel his breath warm across her lips and knew his mouth was within reach; if she wanted to take it.

'Yes, thanks to you.' Her voice was a hoarse croak. She gave a little cough and tried again. 'How about you?'

'My elbow hurts. But otherwise I think we landed on soft sand,' he replied, practical and coherent, not sounding the least bit affected by their proximity. It was the question in his tone that made her finally come to her senses and move.

As she gathered her shaky limbs together, Simon's voice eventually broke through her trance and she realized he was shouting, 'What are you doing? Get up! Get up!' His voice was no longer controlled and calm, but had taken on a slightly hysterical edge. 'You have to get moving, the others are ahead of us.'

It took them many more seconds to get off the ground and untangle themselves, with Simon still shouting instructions. The pole they'd been standing right next to now seemed suddenly impossible to find as they both swung their arms around wildly, hoping to hit it. Cilla felt a mixture of shame and anger color her face. How stupid of her to allow them to lose their lead.

They managed to make up for lost time and brought in their two bags of puzzle pieces only seconds after the Nightrebels team crossed the line. It took a while to remove their eye patches and the rope tying them together, so when Cilla finally raised her head, the spectacle greeting her wasn't what she was hoping for. Alisha and Cho had puzzle pieces scattered everywhere, trying to build what looked like an ancient version of a map of the world. But none of the sections seemed to slot together.

On the other hand, the oldest man of the other team, Jason, and a small dark-haired lady had their puzzle half-complete. Jason's fingers were flying, positioning pieces almost as if he'd done this before, his moustache twitching with glee, the small woman pointing or directing if he got confused.

Not one to believe in superstition, Cilla hoped that her and Tam's lapse in concentration hadn't jinxed the team. It'd be hard not to accept the blame if they lost.

Which they did.

Only a minute later, JJ announced, 'Nightrebels win exemption. Dawnbreakers you'll be going to the conclave tonight.'

Dejected, they formed into a single file and made their way along the track to their campsite. The only one who seemed even slightly upbeat was Marg, who gave a secret smile to Alisha and Cilla and inclined her head toward Glen.

* * *

Tam stumbled, catching his foot on a root in the dark, and he swore. They were on their way back to camp from the

141

conclave, after losing yet another knockout. Holding his flickering firebrand further out in front, he tried to get the glow to light his path, with little success. It didn't matter; they were practically at the campsite, anyway.

Three nights ago, they'd returned almost jubilant after voting Glen out. Tonight the mood was much more sombre. Poor Cho, he felt sorry for him. At least he'd kept his head high, leaving with a dignified nod to them all as he descended the stairs after the vote.

Tam was unsure if they'd done the wrong thing by voting Cho out tonight. He and Cilla had wanted to vote out Simon. But Alisha was adamant that Simon had found another one of those hidden doubloons and would play it if he caught wind of a plan to oust him.

They'd received another clue to a second doubloon after one of their prize and plunder knockouts. The clue had been just as vague as the original one, and although Tam searched, like everyone else, he had a feeling he'd been way off. But if Paloma had found the first one, seemingly without too much trouble, then he wouldn't put it past Simon to have found the second one.

They'd all noticed an immediate change in Simon since Glen had gone three days ago. He'd become a little more likable, less abrasive. Perhaps starting to understand he wasn't as invulnerable as he'd thought.

'Cho was too smart for his own good,' Alisha said, as they headed toward to the bubble of orange heat surrounding the fire.

'Yep, we don't need to be going up against that kind of smarts when the two teams join,' Simon agreed. 'Did you see how quick he finished that number puzzle today? He almost won us the knockout.'

'Almost.' Tam sat down between Cilla and Marg on the sand. 'But not quite.'

'Yeah, but he was crap at the physical knockouts. We could've beaten him easy if it was all up to physical knockouts. Unlike me, of course.' Simon raised his arm and flexed his enormous bicep to make his point. Tam kept his face impassive, but inside he seethed at the man's sheer vanity and arrogance. 'Cho was a dead weight when it came to physical knockouts. We were just pulling him along by the scruff of the neck. Hell, he probably would've been more use to us if he'd been in a wheelchair. Would've been easier to push.' Simon laughed at his own witticism. No one else did. Tam's gut clenched at the reference. Simon was such an ignorant dick. He often spoke without thinking.

'My father's in a wheelchair.' Tam gave into the urge to make Simon feel bad. But as soon as he said the words, he instantly regretted them. His announcement fell into the silence ensuing like a lead weight. No one said anything for seconds that stretched out long and unbroken. Cilla reached out and placed a light hand on his arm. Not conciliatory, merely supportive. *Shit.* He hadn't meant to reveal that information; had blurted it without thinking. He gave an easy smile and a shrug, pretending his words hadn't really mattered.

'Goddammit, I'm sorry man, I didn't mean to be so insensitive.' Simon seemed genuinely remorseful, the first time Tam thought he'd ever seen it. Finally, the guy realized he *was* a schmuck, for once.

'I'm sorry too, Tam, that must be hard for you, eh?' Marg leaned around Cilla and gave him a sympathetic pat on the knee.

He shrugged again. They were all looking at him expectantly. Shit, now what did he say? He guessed he may as well spill the rest of the beans.

'Maybe at first it was. But I'm used to it now. Dad was hurt at work. I was about nine years old. He was lucky though, the doctors claimed it could've been a lot worse. Me and my brothers and my mum, we all pulled together to help him. Now he's pretty much self-sufficient.' His sentences came out stilted. He wasn't used to talking about this.

'Well, at least you still have a father. Mine walked out on me and my mom when I was three, and I haven't seen hide or hair of the bastard since. And I reckon that's bloody awesome,' said Marg. Thank God for Marg, breaking through the awkwardness of the moment with her cutting humour, distracting everyone from his own sad tale.

'Yeah, well, I've got a father, but to him it's as if I don't exist. Nothing I do is ever good enough for him. That's why I came out here. To show him!' Simon said. Tam contemplated him. A few of the outrageous things Simon did now didn't seem so crazy in this new light. He had his own demons to battle.

Alisha and Marg started a conversation about their families and what constituted good parenting. The rest of them joined in, discussing how their fathers—or the lack of them—had affected them. Releasing a quiet breath, Tam relaxed. Talk was no longer concentrating on him. And surprisingly, he considered he'd come through relatively unscathed. Talking about his father hadn't been as painful as he'd imagined.

Tam reached up and scratched at the stubble covering

his face, only half-listening to the rest of the conversation. Now he knew why he'd never bothered to grow a beard before. The damn thing itched like crazy. After two-and-a-half weeks on the island, the growth—it couldn't really be called a beard yet—was softening from the bristling stubble of the early days. It would've been nice to have a mirror, to see exactly what effect the facial hair was having on his appearance. Would he look older, more mature? Or plain scruffy? Probably the latter, if any of the other guys were anything to go by. They were turning into a motley crew of castaways.

Tam's gaze drifted over to watch a play of emotions flicker across Cilla's face as she listened to Alisha and Marg's conversation.

She had a very expressive mouth. It quirked upward when Alisha spoke about the hard work she put into making sure her kids' needs were always met. Then her lips pulled down in a semi-pout when Simon rebutted the fact that her children probably had it too easy. Cilla's lips. They were becoming very familiar to him. He often found himself watching them with fascination. Luscious and appetising, especially when the tip of her tongue darted out in an unconscious display of irritation. He'd been so close to them the other morning, when she'd landed on top of him during the maze knockout. Even blindfolded he'd known how close they were, within kissing distance if he'd wanted to reach up and take them. The feel of her lithe body lying on top of his for those endless seconds still stayed bright in his memory. He had to quell a surge of heat as he thought of that moment. It'd felt right somehow, and he knew he wanted more. More of her body, more of her mind.

She confused him every time she opened her mouth. The tattoo on her arm said it all; Cilla was all about freedom. But freedom from what? Freedom from social pressures? Cilla didn't strike him as the pot-smoking hippy type. Freedom from personal ties; she lived on a boat and moved around a lot. Did that mean she wasn't into long-term relationships either? She'd no other tattoos on her body; the view of her naked at the beach had proved that once and for all. So this one was evidently special to her. He'd love to solve that riddle. It was obvious she was brave and resourceful, determinedly able to take care of herself. Just the fact she dared to come out to this island showed how much of a strong woman she knew herself to be. But there was also a fragile vulnerability within, he'd noticed it the night they kissed.

On that night, even though she'd responded to him with intense passion and flaring desire, he'd thought she was holding back as well, not allowing herself to fall completely. There was a wall, a very high wall, surrounding Cilla's heart and soul. This woman didn't give love easily. That was the chilling beauty of it, her mystery made him want her even more.

He also noticed how she'd conveniently not shared her family story when everyone else had been venting. Ah yes, mysterious, indeed.

* * *

Cilla listened as the small group talked about their aberrant families, but she kept her mouth shut tight. There was no way she was going to share her father's tortuous treachery. She'd tell an abridged version if they forced her to participate, but it'd be nowhere near the truth.

As she observed and sympathized with the others,

another part of her mind whirled with all the additional information. Did it perhaps explain some things about Tam? Like how he was so doggedly determined to help people—the kids in Disneyland being the most obvious case—as a means of making up for the fact he couldn't help when it came to his father. She cast a sidelong glance at him as Simon continued to talk about how many things he'd done to please his dad. Tam seemed to listen like everyone else, intent on Simon's pain. She could tell how much it'd cost; the agony it gave him to think about his father. It was in the way he clenched his teeth, even through his smile. The way he held his fists, close to his body, tight and tense, and the deep lines forming around his mouth, drawing it down in a grimace.

It did matter to him. A great deal.

An urge to cradle his head between her hands and smooth away those lines, kiss away the pain in his honey eyes took hold of her. She controlled it by wrapping her arms tight around her knees and burying her toes in the sand.

Tearing her gaze away from him, she stared into the blazing fire, letting them sear away the image of his face etched into her mind. Without noticing exactly how it'd happened, she'd allowed his pain to become her own.

The flames flickered and jumped, reminding her how this game was heating up. Her thoughts turned inwards. The possibility of the two teams joining was becoming stronger every day, as their numbers dwindled. Now, more than ever, she'd need a strong alliance to see her through. And she'd need to keep her wits about her. She couldn't be letting her emotions get the better of her.

The soft contours of her grandmother's rounded cheeks

developed within the dancing flames. Lines surrounded her crumpled lips, which were pursed in an accusing pout. Pale grey eyes stared at her from that face, silently entreating. The image was so clear it was all Cilla could do to stop herself reaching out to take her grandmother into her arms. An icy hand clutched at Cilla's heart. Her grandmother would be fraught with fear and anxiety, waiting back at home, hoping for Cilla to perform a miracle. To save her from destitution. Save her from losing the only house she'd ever known. Tears formed in Cilla's eyes at the thought of her grandmother, of how much she was relying on her.

She had to win.

How could she have allowed herself to forget why she was here so easily? Swayed by an attraction to a man, she'd been diverted for a while. Screwing her eyes shut against the fire's bright flames, she shoved the thoughts of Tam deep down into the recesses of her head, letting determination replace them. Determination to win this game. Win at all costs.

CHAPTER NINE

'Drop you bandanas, everyone, it's time for your teams to join.'

There were yells and whoops from both teams as JJ started throwing out the new bandanas. The wind was picking up and Cilla nearly missed hers as a fierce gust tried to carry it over her head. But she snatched it out of the air and tied it round her neck to wear as a scarf. She loved the bright grass-green color of the new bandanas. They heralded a new stage of the game, and she was ready to seize it with both hands. Thank God she'd made it this far. *Thank God Tam had made it as well.* What? Where'd that thought come from? Before she had time to analyze it, the two teams came together in a tangle of hugs and handshakes and introductions.

'The name of your new team is Moonrakers,' JJ said, raising his voice to be heard over the hubbub of learning names and congratulations. No one said the words, but Cilla knew everyone was thinking the same thing. Dawnbreakers had the advantage with five people left in their team to Nightrebels' four. She shook hands with the pseudo leader of Nightrebels, the one with the impressive handlebar moustache. He was early fiftyish with grey hair and kind eyes.

'Hello, I'm Jason Paige. Great to meet you.' Against her better judgement, she liked him at once. There was firmness to his handshake, but the laugh lines around his eyes were deep and he bathed her in the warmth of his smile.

'I'm Cilla Parsons. Great to meet you too.'

Then she found herself gathered up into another stranger's arms for a bear hug. 'Hi there, I'm Hayden.' She laughed at the enthusiasm of this man. He wasn't big like Jason, only half a head taller than her, but he too had a huge grin on his face and he hugged her with what seemed to be genuine delight. Cilla liked him immediately, too. Fresh people were always a danger to the equilibrium, but if first impressions were anything to go on, then this new team would be an interesting change to their last one.

Out of the corner of her eye she watched Tam receive Jason's handshake, his familiar wide grin spreading over his face as he welcomed the older man to the new team. But below Tam's genial smile, she could tell he was sizing the Jason up, deciding how much of a threat he might be.

The game had just stepped up a notch. It was all about individuals rather than teams now.

'Your new campsite will be in the old Nightrebels area. Their shelter is solid and they have a tarpaulin, which will keep you much drier,' JJ said. His voice was almost lost in the gusts of wind that were now whipping in off the ocean. A couple of the Dawnbreakers team cheered out loud. Cilla would be the first to admit it'd be no loss to leave their campsite behind.

'All your belongings have been transferred across, Dawnbreakers. And you'll also find a surprise waiting for you when you return.'

'Food?' squealed a small pixie-like woman Cilla had yet to meet.

'Yes, Rosa, food.' JJ had to use one hand to hold on to his hat as a particularly strong gust of wind hit them. 'There's a pirate's feast waiting for you back at camp.' JJ actually broke a smile at the pixie lady's antics, as she jumped with excitement. 'But you should probably hurry back to camp and make the most of the food while you can. It's about to get very wet around here.'

'What do you mean?' Tam cast a worried frown at JJ. Everyone else stopped talking and also looked in his direction.

'There's a big storm on the way.' Cilla glanced up. There were ominous clouds forming on the horizon, dark grey and puffed with moisture, lots of smaller clouds scudding across the sky below them. The wind was building in intensity, but the sun was still shining. This weather didn't look too different from anything else they'd experienced so far. After all, it was always raining here, it was the tropics.

'The Bureau of Meteorology has assured us that this is merely a bad storm and not a cyclone.' They all knew nature could be unpredictable. 'We've never had to evacuate anyone from a season because of foul weather,' JJ continued. 'Your safety is of paramount importance, of course.' But as Cilla watched JJ tip his gaze toward the sky, a thoughtful frown replacing his usual dimpled smile, she decided he was perhaps more worried than he liked to say.

'We should all get going then,' said Jason. 'Is there any

advice you can give us?'

'Not really.' JJ had the grace to grimace. 'We'll monitor the situation and you'll be given a two-way radio so you can contact us. If need be, we will evacuate you. But the best counsel I can give is if the wind picks up too much, you'll be safer away from the trees. Just in case they come down in the gale.'

'Right-oh then.' Jason's lips thinned, his quick glance at the looming clouds saying it all.

* * *

The giant food chest was visible even from this distance down the beach. Tam's stomach cramped at the mere sight of it. He'd never known hunger such as this. Sometimes he was sure his belly was so empty it dangled inside him like a deflated balloon, limp and lifeless.

Tam often fantasised about food. Most of the time it was the small things he missed. The smell of frying onions. The crisp, clean taste of a fresh apple. Or the cool slide of milk straight from the refrigerator running down the back of his throat. Food sometimes invaded his dreams. Cakes the size of beds and marshmallows the size of pillows became his nightly companions. At least, this living on rations of rice and beans had taught him a valuable lesson. Food—good food—was a luxury he wouldn't take for granted ever again.

'There it is,' yelled Jason, and he ran over the sand toward the campsite. 'Come on everyone, let's eat.' He didn't have to tell Tam twice; he jogged down the beach as well.

The rest of the newly joined team didn't take long to catch up. Tam slowed a little and ran next to Alisha. She wasn't a pretty sight when she ran. Today she was running so hard she had to hang on to her enormous breasts so they didn't hit her in the chin. Tam stifled a laugh at the sight. She'd lost a significant amount of weight while on the island—they all had—but she was always going to be a large woman. Tam didn't mind, her body was a suitable match to her equally large personality.

The others surged ahead, eager to be with Jason when he opened the food chest. Tam stayed with Alisha. It was a slow jog for him, however Alisha was puffing hard.

'What do you think about this new team, Alisha?'

'I think we've an excellent chance,' she panted between steps. 'And I already like the two guys, they might make valuable allies.' She was hard to understand as she pounded up the sand. 'Can't talk now. Running.' She gave him a grimace and grabbed her breasts tighter.

'Right,' he said through a grin. He let his gaze travel over the beach—their new home. The beach itself was smaller than their old campsite. Tam noticed there were three huge boulder-like islands nestled together off the headland, protecting it from the rough ocean outside. The enormous boulders seemed to almost float above the water, creating a safe haven within their arms. They were fascinating. He'd love to swim out and explore them later on, after this storm had passed.

JJ had been right in his prediction. The storm was coming up fast. Fronds on the coconut trees at the back of the shore were laid flat like streamers in the rising wind. Twigs and leaves were being thrown about, and he could see the waves building outside the haven of the boulders. They were in for a wild night.

He and Alisha reached the group around the food chest as they lifted the lid. Some girls actually screamed in delight at the sight. There were plates of cheese, fruit, bread, and best of all a huge tray of meat. There were even some bottles of beer tucked neatly in the corners.

'We should get that meat cooking before this wind makes it impossible to get near the fire,' said Jason. A man after his own heart. The barbecue was his number one priority too. They needed as much protein as they could cram into their bodies tonight. It might be weeks before they saw any more.

Tam helped Jason and Simon lift out the two big trays of meat and carried them over to the cooking fire. It'd been well banked and wouldn't take too much effort to get back up and burning bright. There was even a steel grill in the food chest. He and Simon found some stones to stand the grill on while Hayden got the fire blazing again and Jason got some good cooking sticks. The wind was starting to whip up the sand and Tam could feel it stinging the backs of his legs as he positioned the makeshift barbecue.

From what Tam could make out, the layout of the camp was neat and orderly. A sturdy hut hunkered down beneath a tropical coral tree. The limbs were low and broad and should help shelter them from the coming storm. Unlike Dawnbreakers' rather rudimentary shelter, this hut had three sides with a tarp stretched over the top to give added waterproofing. It wasn't large though, and they'd be all crammed in like sardines. He stupidly hoped that one of the bodies he was crammed up against would be Cilla's.

He could see her, over with the other the women, ferrying the rest of the food into the relative protection of the hut. Cilla glanced up and saw him watching her. A wonderful smile lit up her face. She moved toward him with a plate of cheese held high.

'Grab a hunk, Tam. It's delicious.' His hands were full, balancing the grill so that Simon could tuck another stone under one corner. She broke him off a bit and placed it in his mouth. Her fingers grazed his lips as he took the cheese. He nearly choked. Was it his imagination, or had she done that intentionally?

'Thanks,' he said around his mouthful, trying without much luck to swallow the cheese that was now sticking in his throat. It was probably delicious, but his mind wasn't focussing on his tastebuds anymore.

'Do you want some more?' Her fingers held another chunk close to his mouth.

'Yeah, sure.' This time her fingers did more than just graze the side of his lips; he was certain they lingered there. Tantalising. Teasing him, a slow smile spread over her face, leaving his whole body tingling. A flash of heat reached out from his lower abdomen at the hinted suggestion in her gaze.

'Cheese has never tasted so perfect.' She popped a piece into her mouth and closed her eyes to savour the creamy taste. He watched, fascinated by the way her dark lashes lay, child-like against her smooth cheekbones. When she opened her eyes again, she fixed him with an audacious smile. 'Don't you think?' Was she flirting with him? Maybe it was the heady rush of having proper food to eat. Whatever it was, he liked the way she'd become more animated, more alive.

'Yes. Best cheese ever,' he replied, locking gazes with her. He wanted to ask her for more, just to feel the feather-light slide of her fingertips again. Her emerald eyes widened a fraction as he continued to hold her stare. The heat turned from a slow burn to a rapidly growing fire licking through his groin.

This wouldn't do. He bent over to hide the bulge developing in his shorts. He'd have to remember to keep his reaction to her under wraps. But it was hard. Almost bloody impossible when she was looking at him that way.

'Oi, what about me then?' Simon called from over the other side of the fire. 'Do I get to taste this wonderful cheese as well?'

'Yes. Of course.' Her eyelids drooped, hooding the bright green irises, the teasing light dying as fast as it had appeared. She stepped away from him and the moment was gone.

Goddamn you, Simon.

'I think it's right now, guys. Let's get this meat cooking.' Jason started throwing raw hunks onto the grill, with Hayden pushing them into position with a pointed stick. The smell of the frying meat made Tam's mouth water. He'd forgotten how good that aroma was. Trying to put aside the strangely intimate moment he'd shared with Cilla, he concentrated on cooking instead.

'All we need now is a few onions, and it'd be the perfect barbecue.' Hayden gave a wistful smile.

'Amen to that one,' Tam replied.

A large, wet drop landed on the metal cooktop, making it sizzle and spit. Then another drop hit the fire with a hiss. The rain was falling in vast, singular drops the size of acorns. It wasn't heavy yet, the early warning drops of what was to come. He looked out toward the sea and was surprised to see both ocean and sky turning black, even though it was only noon. Sheets of lightning hurled their way from one side of the horizon to the other. Weather had a lethal beauty out here on the island. He could see rain squalls swallowing islands further out beyond the calm waters of their bay. It reminded him they were mere specks on another insignificant speck, lost out on an enormous ocean. It was both humbling and fortifying. They were out here to survive and their courage would be put to the test tonight.

'Here comes the rain,' yelled Tam. 'Looks like we got the meat on just in time.' He saw the women hurrying to get the last of the food out of the oncoming storm. He watched one of the new women—Rosa?—as she balanced a tray of fruit in each hand, making her way over the sand with sure-footed steps. She was petite, almost elf-like, with dark curly hair framing her face. She was perhaps a few years older than him and very pretty.

The second woman had introduced herself as Susan when they'd first met at the merge. She had mousey brown hair tied up in a ponytail away from her face. Her eyes lit up when she came over to shake hands with him, her plump cheeks trembling with delight as she held his hand. The merge was going to shake the dynamics of the Dawnbreakers up significantly. It was going to be an interesting few days as they figured each other out, testing their personalities, strengths and limitations. Would old friendships stay strong? He rolled that tricky problem over in silent contemplation as he watched the meat turn black on the grill.

* * *

The wind howled, a marauding animal prowling around the outside of their hut. Lightning was striking down repeatedly, followed by the loud booms of thunder. Cilla imagined bombs exploding nearby might sound much the same. The lightning was more frightening than the thunder, because it lit up the beach with its brilliance, and in that light the destruction the storm was wreaking was obvious. Enormous waves rose up right outside the shelter of their bay, throwing themselves at the rocky reefs and hurtling enormous plumes of spray into the air. As fast as the gale could throw massive branches and even entire tree trunks down the beach toward the ocean, the waves would push them back up onto the sand, creating a wall of flotsam that heaved and surged with each roll of the swell. Sand and leaves were flying through the air, turning into mini-missiles, filtering into their shelter through any nook and cranny.

Cilla had lived through her fair share of storms before, even having to ride out a cyclone on a forty-five foot yacht at sea once. But this was the scariest thing she'd ever encountered. Perhaps it had something to do with the fact that there were only flimsy coconut fronds protecting her from the fury of the wind outside. Or that, despite the tarp, water was streaming down in rivers through the roof. They'd tried to cover the front entrance with more coconut fronds, but the wind had already ripped most of those away. Everyone in team Moonrakers was soaking wet, miserable and afraid. They huddled together for warmth. No one spoke; it would've been futile against the noise of the wind, anyway.

Cilla was sandwiched between one of the new girls, Rosa, and Alisha. For once she was thankful for Alisha's spare padding. It felt like she was being squished against an extra-large pillow. She was in the centre of the clump of huddled human beings, so at least she was relatively warm. Cilla tried to tune out the destruction that was going on outside the shelter, concentrating instead on the relative safety inside. Tam and Hayden were bunched in behind her. Tam's strong bicep curled against her back. He must've had his chin resting on his arm, tucked up next to her shoulder blade, because she could feel the course of his breath as he blew warm air over the side of her face. It was a very curious sensation; despite all these people crammed in next to her, she found the only thing she could think about was his breathing. Familiar yet illuminating. Her mind was carried away by that thought.

Earlier today she'd taken the opportunity to run her fingertips over his lips under the pretence of placing a cube of cheese in his mouth. It was a move designed to tease and provoke, just having fun. But the way he'd looked at her had drawn her up short. His eyes had fixed her with that butter-scotch stare, the flare of desire unmistakable. But it'd been the ripple of nervous anticipation that surged through her in reply to his obvious hunger, which had been the ultimate surprise for her. It brought back the urgency with how she'd responded to his kiss on the beach, the way he'd taken ownership of her mouth and the way she'd wanted him to take more, had been willing to give him more and more. And the way her brain had subconsciously recalled every curve and dip of the hardened muscles of his stomach as she lay on top of him during the blind maze knockout. Never had she experienced such an immediate response to a man before. Sure, she'd wanted men, desired them, and definitely enjoyed the sex. But this slow burning ardour banked within her veins, ready to explode into flesh-eating flames every time Tam looked at her was completely new.

The sound of the wind changed, becoming louder, if

that was possible. The howl turning into a full-blown roar of rage, breaking off her fantasy about Tam.

There was an ominous rumble and crashing streaks of lightning flashed right over the top of their shelter. Suddenly there was a loud splintering sound and a booming crash that shook Cilla to the core as something heavy hit the tiny hut, knocking her sideways. Rain and wind lashed at her face.

Screams of fright and confusion filled the air.

In the pitch black it was hard to tell exactly what'd happened, but Cilla sensed rather than saw rain was now pouring in through a gaping hole in one side of the shelter.

A tree had fallen on the roof.

The shelter was destroyed.

Time seemed to slow as Cilla scrabbled for purchase, trying to sit upright. Her breath came in panicked little pants. She needed to get out of here. Quick!

'Cilla, are you alright?' Tam's voice finally broke through her fear. His mouth was right next to her ear, but he had to shout to be heard. Her head hurt. She raised a hand to her forehead and her fingers came away warm and sticky. Blood.

'I don't know, I think I might've cut my head.' She found she was struggling to sit until she felt Tam heave something heavy out of the way. At least now she could get to her feet.

Belatedly she remembered to ask, 'How about you? Are you hurt?'

'I'm fine,' his disembodied voice came out of the blackness. 'Let's get out of here.' He grabbed her under the arms and virtually lifted her up, steering her over the debris of the shelter and down onto the relative safety of the sand. It was pitch dark, but once on the beach she could just make out the ruined form of the hut against the shadowy grey of the scudding clouds. Darker forms moved through her line of sight as other team members clambered out of the wreckage. She sensed other bodies milling around her in the dark. But apart from Tam, who kept a tight hold of her hand, she couldn't tell who was who.

'What about Alisha? Where's Alisha?' Cilla found she was screaming now, but didn't care, shock and a need to be heard over the wind lending her voice a hysterical note.

'It's okay girl, I'm right here.' Cilla felt a hand on her shoulder and gathered the other woman in for a shaky hug. They kept hold of each other, afraid they'd lose one another. Cilla felt Tam's hand in hers, rock-steady, encircling her own. Her head was pounding, and she was glad of his calming touch. A warm trickle ran down the side of her temple. Blood must be flowing freely from the cut in her head. Her stomach turned over at the thought.

'Everyone who can walk, make their way over to me.' Cilla nearly didn't hear Jason over the roar of the gale. The three of them walked tentatively to where Jason stood in a clear patch of sand, out from underneath the boughs of the tree. Reaching in front of her until she felt fabric beneath her fingers, she held tight to Jason's jacket. She was glad it was dark so the others couldn't see how much she was shaking.

'Who's this,' Jason asked.

'Tam, Alisha and Cilla,' she yelled back.

'Good. We need to get everyone out here and accounted for.' He was only a shadowy presence in the blackness, but the sound of his voice and the fact he was taking control comforted her, and a little of the panic ebbed away.

'Everyone, over here, follow the sound of my voice,' Jason shouted again. Tam joined in, yelling directions to the spectral forms coming closer.

Soon there was a close-packed bunch of people crowding around Jason.

'Is everybody here now?' Jason did a roll call, and Cilla heard with relief people answer to their name.

'Is anyone hurt?' It crossed her mind not to own up to the cut on her head, but Tam would dob her in if she didn't confess. He had his hand wrapped tightly around hers, strong fingers threaded through hers. She hadn't had the courage to feel for damage again; there was quite a gash up there.

'I got hit on the head,' she admitted.

'Is that you, Cilla? How bad is it?'

'Yes, it's me. And… I don't know how bad it is. I think it'll probably need stitches.' She kept her voice steady, although the thought made her cringe inside. It wasn't the pain she was afraid of. She just wasn't good with anything to do with needles or hospitals. They brought back childhood memories she'd rather keep locked away. Of the abuse she'd suffered at her father's hand. The dark threats he'd made if she ever dared to reveal how she'd actually received her various injuries had caused her to be wary of all things medical.

'Shit,' Jason swore loudly. 'Can you get someone to help you staunch the bleeding?'

'Yep, Alisha, and I'll help her, Jason, you check if everyone else is okay,' Tam called from behind her. 'Cilla sit down.' She felt a gentle pressure on her shoulders and lowered herself slowly onto the sand. The wind was still howling, whipping sand up into her face.

She heard Jason say, 'Anyone else hurt?' then Tam knelt down in front of her, shielding her from the worst of the flying sand with his body. He was fumbling with something, but in the dark she couldn't see what he was doing. It wasn't until she heard a ripping sound that she realized he was tearing up his T-shirt. Alisha plumped down next to Cilla, close and reassuring.

'Cilla, give me your hand.' He found her hand and closed her fingers around a wad of cloth—the T-shirt he'd just ripped up. 'Place this over the cut and keep pressure on it, try to stop any bleeding.' She did as she was told, having to hold back a groan as the cloth touched her mangled forehead. He kept his fingers lightly pressed over hers. 'How does that feel?'

'It hurts,' she ground out between gritted teeth.

'Alisha, can you help Cilla keep pressure on that, I'm going to help Jason and the others. I think they're trying to build a sand wall to give us a bit of shelter from the wind.' His hand lifted, and he started to move away. 'I'll be back as soon as I can, Cilla.' Then his warm protection was gone, and she was left to be buffeted by the wind and sand. Alisha moved in closer and they huddled together.

Sooner than she might've imagined, Tam was back again. 'We've built a wall. Come this way. We're all going to gather behind it. It should offer some defence from the worst of the weather.' They shuffled along behind him through the driving sand and rain and eventually found the rest of the team. Lowering down to sit next to Marg and the others, Cilla found she was suddenly out of the full force of the wind. Wild gusts were still eddying around them, but the sand wall was taking the brunt of the pressure. It was amazing how much better it felt not having to force her body to stand against the battering gale. The rain had even eased up a little.

Tam sat down next to her and pulled her in close, tucking her in under his arm, trying to shelter her as much as he could from the elements.

'I think there's only an hour or so before dawn, we'll be safe here until then,' he said into her ear. 'Jason says the wind is dropping already, and I think he might be right. That big gust that blew the tree over was probably the storm's last hurrah before it went on its way.'

Nodding her agreement, she curled tighter into his chest, glad of the warmth from his body. Her head still throbbed painfully, but she drew in a calming breath and let the sense of security Tam offered seep into her soul. She couldn't believe how close to giving into a full-blown panic attack she'd been tonight. It wasn't like her to give in to fear. She prided herself on her practical handling of all situations. She didn't like that this island was forcing her to extremes, making her re-evaluate her own character. It was a tough pill to swallow, to find out she wasn't as infallible as she thought. First the inability to eat the baby chick episode and now her near-hysteria in this storm.

Just this once she'd take Tam's proffered comfort, let herself feel safe in his arms, even if it was for only a few scant hours.

* * *

Dawn stole up on them, silent and grey. One minute Cilla could see nothing except a few stars, which had evaded the scudding clouds, and the next minute black edges became grey, shapes morphing out of the gloom became trees. She could even make out the features on Tam's sleeping face, so close to her own.

Colour washed into the murky landscape as light climbed over the horizon.

Looking around, she took in the tangle of bodies clumped together on the wet sand. Everyone else looked to be asleep. Cilla watched as the encroaching light revealed the storm's destruction.

The beach was strewn with branches, large and small, and foliage of every kind. Tree trunks the size of missiles littered the sand, washed ashore from the storm-ravaged coast. Other trees were lying flat on the edge of the jungle, or leaning at odd angles where the wind had tried to blow them over, but failed. A lot of the softer leafed trees were stripped of their greenery, leaving bare sticks raising their fingers to the sky. At least the beach had remained fairly much intact, thanks to the large boulders sheltering the bay, but a sizeable hunk looked like it had been clawed out of the sand by some enormous wild animal near the other end, not shielded by the rocks.

Their hut was a write-off. Two of the sides were completely smashed to smithereens, the shredded tarp flapping angrily in the breeze. A large coconut palm lay on the ground next to the shelter—the tree responsible for doing all the damage. Thank God that hadn't landed right in the middle, merely glanced off the side as it fell.

The storm had blown itself out, only a weak breeze and a few clouds limping across the horizon remained.

A sound caught her attention, and turning her head she saw a boat swing into the bay, JJ's worried face at the bow. The vessel hardly even slowed as it sped in and crunched straight into the sand. Two crew members vaulted out to steady it with JJ hot on their heels, running up the beach toward them, not caring his designer jeans and expensive shoes were saturated in the rolling waves.

'Is everyone alright?' he shouted as he skidded to a stop next to their huddle of humanity. It was the first time she thought she'd ever seen naked fear on his face. 'We tried contacting you on the two-way, but we couldn't raise you.' Tam woke at the sound of JJ's voice and sat up with a start, blinking like an owl. Cilla sat up too, the effort causing her head to throb.

'Yes, we're all safe and accounted for. I think the two-way got smashed when the tree came down on our shelter,' Jason replied, sleep making his voice thick.

'Let's get the medics up here right away and get you all checked out.' JJ gestured for the two crew doctors who were disembarking the boat to come quickly. He swept an assessing gaze over the motley crew, taking in their condition and cataloguing any injuries. Taking two strides over to where Cilla was sitting on the sand, he knelt down next to her. She felt Tam lay a protective hand on her back.

'Cilla, you look like you got hit in the head. Let's get the medics to look at you first, okay?' She nodded and then regretted the movement.

As the female medic dropped her first aid bag in the sand next to her and asked her if it was alright if she lifted the blood-stained rag away so she could have a look, Cilla heard JJ ask, 'How about everyone else? Is anyone else injured?'

It turned out Marg had some bruising on her back and shoulders where some of the shelter had collapsed on top of her, and Susan had sprained her ankle when she'd jumped down onto the sand from the devastated shelter. They'd escaped remarkably unscathed, considering the state of their hut.

'Looks like you guys might've been saved by the lower branches of that coral tree you were camped under. That large bough directly above the roof of your hut took the brunt of the weight of the falling tree. Deflected it away from the centre, so it only gave a glancing blow,' JJ said. Cilla shuddered to think what might've happened if the tree had landed where it was supposed to. And she knew JJ would've been thinking the same thing. He was probably praising the Lord right now at how things had turned out. Things wouldn't have looked good for him, or the show, if someone had been badly injured or killed.

'Ow.' Cilla had been gritting her teeth and trying to stay still while the medic performed her ministrations, but the sting of antiseptic was too much.

'Sorry, Cilla.' The woman looked contrite, at least. 'But this needs to be cleaned so I can gauge the damage.'

'I know,' she replied, trying to raise a smile which quickly turned into a grimace.

'How does it look, doc? Is she going to live?' Tam had stayed by her side, holding her hand while the medic poked and prodded.

'It'll need stitches,' she said, her gaze pensive. Cilla's heart sank. She knew it'd been a possibility. She wondered how much that'd slow her down in the knockouts.

'She'll be good as new once you've fixed her up though,' said Tam, in a bright voice.

'Yes, she will. In a few weeks' time you'll hardly know it was there,' agreed the medic. 'But you won't be able to continue on Sea-Quest I'm afraid, it'd be too risky.'

Cilla reared back from the woman's touch. 'What did you just say?'

Chapter Ten

'You can't be serious! You're not taking me out of the game!' Cilla's heart was pounding, her voice loud and strained. They couldn't do this to her. She needed to stay.

'Tam, don't let them take me out.' She turned to him, desperate.

'Surely things aren't that bad, are they? It's just a scratch.' Tam looked to the medic, but couldn't hide the worried frown hovering on his brows. She'd been so angry at the thought a simple cut could remove her from the game, but seeing the unease in Tam, her anger turned quickly into fear. Fear she would be eliminated.

'It mightn't look all that bad, but out here in the tropics, things can become infected fast if you aren't careful.' The female medic kept her face implacable, but Cilla heard the truth behind her words. Bubbles of alarm rose up from her gut. For the second time in only a few brief hours, Cilla felt powerless and afraid. But she would not be meekly led away like some woolly headed lamb. Panic turned to stubbornness.

'I'm not going anywhere.' She knew she sounded like a

querulous child, but she no longer cared. 'It's my decision, isn't it? And I decide I'm staying.'

Cilla saw JJ's head appear above a group of team members who were sitting in a semicircle debriefing from the night's events. It was obvious he'd heard the altercation. Other heads turned as well, curiosity and surprise on their faces. Alisha's anxious face appeared beside JJ's and she made as if to get up, before JJ shook his head. She sat back down and JJ marched over.

'What's up, Cilla?'

'This medic of yours says I'm not fit to play the game anymore. That isn't true. I know you can't force me to leave,' her voice got louder, despite her efforts to keep it under control.

'Okay, Cilla, calm down.' JJ laid a placating hand on her shoulder. 'Let's talk this through. The medics aren't your enemies, they're here to help and give advice.' She clenched her jaw, wanting to pull away from his solicitous touch, his cool logic making her angrier.

'Fine, talk then. But you're not forcing me to go,' she muttered.

'Sorry, Helen,' JJ said to the female physician. 'What's your opinion on this one?'

'She's going to need twelve to fourteen stitches, which I can do out here in the field, but it won't be as pretty as a surgeon could do back on the mainland.' Cilla gave a snort of contempt. As if she cared about being pretty. A million dollars was more important than a little scar on her forehead.

'My main worry,' continued Helen, ignoring her snort, 'is infection afterwards. We can inject a big dose of antibiotics, but with the dirt and humidity and poor living conditions out here, I can't assure you it won't go septic.' Cilla snorted again.

'Don't take this lightly, Cilla,' JJ interrupted. 'An infection can turn into blood poisoning real quick out here. I've seen it happen before.'

'You need to at least hear her out,' Tam chipped in, and then raised his hands in surrender when she threw him an irritated glance. Even Tam was telling her to listen now. Whose side was he on?

She glared up into Tam's troubled face, until he leant forward and touched her leg, entreaty and something else unfathomable in his eyes. 'I don't want you to go either, Cilla, but I'd hate to see you take a stupid risk and end up really sick. Or worse.'

As Tam leant in to talk to her, she noticed what remained of his shirt flapping around his stomach. Then she remembered he'd torn it to pieces to help stop her bleeding. The tattered shirt and the fledgling beard made him look more like a Robin Caruso castaway than ever before. Her anger diminished at the memory of how he'd protected her last night, and she drew in a calming breath. Of course he wasn't trying to get rid of her; the pain in her head and fear of being sent home were making her paranoid, that was all.

'Fine, tell me what the risks are then.' She sat back, leaning on her hands, pretending for all the world this was just a precaution and she didn't care what they said.

'Sepsis is when an infection enters you blood stream. In this humidity, if you don't look after that cut and keep it as dry as possible, it could become infected. It also needs to be kept clean.' Helen gave a pointed glance toward the camp. Cilla knew living on the island in these very basic conditions, without hot running water or soap, wasn't ideal. 'Most infections are easy to treat with oral antibiotics, but in people who are perhaps compromised in some way, such as lacking food and clean water, then you can become more susceptible,' Helen said, explaining the obstacles with cool calculation. If only Cilla could feel that composed about the whole thing.

'So if she starts to get an infection, there must be some sort of signs we can look out for,' said Tam. She hated his matter-of-fact tone nearly as much as the smug look on Helen's face.

'Yep, the wound will probably go an angry red color and may even start oozing puss.'

'Lovely,' replied Cilla.

'Other signs that an infection may have turned septic are fever, and an increased heart rate.'

'Well, that shouldn't be too hard to spot, should it? If we keep a close eye on her,' said Tam. He gave her an encouraging wink and a little of the tension eased from her shoulders. How could she ever have doubted him?

'And what's the worst-case scenario?' JJ interceded. 'Cilla needs to weigh up all the odds, so she may as well know what the ultimate risk could be.'

'In rare cases this can lead to septic shock, and if it's not treated right away, you may die.' Helen sounded so practical she could've been talking about the results of a spelling test rather than the ultimate hazard. Death.

Tam let out a low whistle. 'That's a pretty big risk, Cilla.'

'Well, it's one I'm willing to take,' she snapped. Damn right she was willing to take it. She was strong and healthy, and she'd make sure she kept the wound clean and dry. She wouldn't let one minor scratch beat her. Not when her grandmother's house and her beautiful boat were on the line.

'The choice is yours, for now, Cilla.' JJ stared at her with those dark brown eyes, evaluating her determination to see this out. 'But we can veto your decision at any time if the medic thinks it's necessary, so please promise me if you feel sick, you'll let us know. I really don't want any of our contestants dying out here.'

Relief surged through her like a breaking wave. JJ was going to let her stay.

'Don't worry, JJ, I'm going to watch her like a hawk,' Tam growled. His gaze locked with hers and she was trapped by the resolve in his tortoiseshell eyes, daring her to argue. 'The whole team will watch over her. Any signs of fever or any kind of malaise and you'll be the first to know.'

* * *

Cilla was glowering at him. Why was it that every woman possessed a certain look calculated to cut a man down, let him know just how much he'd offended her in one single glance? Let her glower. She needed to appreciate the full risks of staying in the game with her injury and if he had to play the bad cop to make her see the implications, then so be it.

Apart from that, she was also damn cute when she was angry. Her cheeks were flushed pink and her eyes reminded him of flinty emeralds. It was a relief to see her face take on a healthy glow again, definitely a step up from the pale, drawn Cilla he'd woken up to this morning. That vulnerable Cilla had scared him, this irritable version he could cope with.

'You can watch me like a hawk from over there, Tam

Connor.' She left off the implied *I don't need your help*, but it was more than plain in the defiant tilt of her chin. He lifted an eyebrow in a smirk, but the gesture only made her scowl even harder. Fine, he'd sit over here in the shade of a coconut tree and feign indifference if it helped her win back a little of her self-respect.

Helen, the female medic, returned from the boat, carrying a large black case. He watched as she knelt down next to Cilla on the sand and spread out clean white sheets for her to lie on. Then she got out a rather large looking syringe and filled it from a small bottle.

Cilla's gaze flickered between him and Helen, the sight of the syringe seeming to distract her from her attempt to send him to the fires of hell with her stare. Then Helen got out some more medical implements, tweezers, a curved needle, a scalpel blade and some blue thread, laying them out neatly on a steel tray. The sparks of anger glinting in Cilla's eyes went out, replaced by doubt. Cilla stopped glaring at him altogether when latex gloves came out. It was as if he became invisible in the blink of an eye. She fixated on what Helen was doing, scrutinising every move she made with the wariness of prey watching a hunter.

Cilla's eyes got rounder and rounder as she watched Helen's preparations and she pulled her knees up to hug them into her chest, looking more like a worried child than the angry, indignant woman he'd been watching only seconds before. The transformation astounded him.

Was it just his imagination, or was Cilla's joking statement that she didn't like needles actually true? There seemed to be more than just simple apprehension in the way she clamped hold of her knees, her knuckles turning white with the pressure, as if willing herself not to stand up and run away.

Helen was unaware of the change in Cilla as she finished her arrangements. Ready to start, she leaned toward Cilla, syringe in hand.

'This is a local anaesthetic, to numb the area before I start stitching,' Helen said, all cool efficiency.

Cilla veered backward, and her hand gave a twitch as if to ward off an attack. She blinked and was again in control; the reaction shuttered behind hooded eyelids. But Tam had seen it. She was terrified. Most people didn't like injections, but what he saw in her face wasn't just an aversion to needles, it was naked fear. The knowledge hit Tam like a punch to the gut. What'd make her that afraid of a mere needle? An unpleasant experience with a doctor? Whatever the cause, he knew it wasn't just an insignificant once-off with a nurse who was too rough. Cilla was too capable, too strong-willed to be put off by a trifle such as a syringe.

Instinct kicked in and with a grunt he levered himself off the sand and walked over to her.

'Give me your hand,' he said gently.

'No.' She practically bared her teeth at him. 'I'm not one of your kids that needs their hand held because they have an ouch.' He had to stifle a laugh. Even when she was thoroughly pissed off and terrified, she was still gorgeous.

'Well, unless you stop acting in that manner, I'll think you are. Now lie down and stay still.' He placed his palms on her shoulders and pushed her gradually down onto the sheets. Then he captured both her hands in his and nodded to Helen. Cilla's gaze swung between the two of them, eyes narrowed and brows drawn down, shooting daggers.

'This'll sting a little.'

'I know, I've had a local before,' she snapped. As Helen leant over her head to administer the injection, Cilla's gaze locked onto Tam's, filled once more with fire and outrage, flecks of amber dancing through the emerald green. Good, at least she was distracted from her fear by her reignited fury at him.

He knew the exact instant the needle went in. Her pupils dilated and her grip on his hands became iron clad, but she didn't break their stare, or utter a sound.

'All done.' Helen drew back and released a breath. 'We'll leave it for a few minutes until it gets nice and numb.' Cilla closed her eyes, but it was a few seconds before she'd let go of his hands.

'Sorry,' she murmured.

Sorry for what? For showing an ounce of vulnerability?

'Not a problem. I love holding your hands.' She levered herself up, but ignored his remark. They sat in silence, side by side, she with her chin on her knees. He silently wondered whether he could ask her about what'd just happened. She might tell him, but then again, she was more likely just to spit in his eye.

For a moment Tam allowed himself to remember the warmth of Cilla as she sheltered in his arms last night. In the dark and the wind, she'd let herself trust him. But in the cold light of day, that trust was gone. Would it ever come back?

She was so still and quiet next to him.

'You okay?'

'Yep.' He thought that was the only reply he was going to get, but then she said, 'Why?'

'You looked a little freaked out by the whole thing. I

take it you aren't good with doctors.' A strange mixture of emotions fluttered across her face, but none of them made any sense. Resentment, desperation, and finally shame. What'd happened to make her ashamed?

'I don't like needles, or doctors, or anything to do with hospitals. I had a…couple of bad experiences as a kid, that's all.' She wouldn't look at him, instead staring out at the ocean. She looked so lost and alone. He wanted to put an arm around her slim shoulders and pull her in tight. Protect her from whatever demons were troubling her. He wanted to hold her until she confided it all to him, until she told him all her secrets. She was so tough and resilient on the outside, but he could feel there was some great internal injury she was hiding from the world. He was adept at reading people, it was part of what made him a good psychologist. He'd be able to help her, tease out those raw, damaging emotions and get her to accept them, even embrace them. If only she'd let him.

He wanted to help her.

The thought brought him up sharp. What was he thinking? He shouldn't be getting involved. Why was he letting her get under his skin?

Because her green eyes haunted him when he slept. And he was fascinated by the way the corners of her mouth curled upwards, even before she served up that killer smile. He loved to watch her sinuous walk as she prowled down the beach searching for crabs. And he wanted to know what it'd be like to trap a fistful of that gorgeous auburn hair and drag her face up to his so he could kiss her until she could no longer breathe.

Am I falling for this woman?

No.

That was ridiculous. Okay, he'd admit she was beautiful, and he was seriously attracted to her. That was all right, he was allowed to be enticed by women.

The problem was, he'd often find his gaze wandering to wherever she was in the camp, as if some internal compass was constantly pointing toward her. She had an aura, a presence that just couldn't be ignored. But they'd only known each other for a few weeks, it was far too quick to be falling for anyone. Yes, they'd been thrown together into much closer quarters than most people would normally encounter. Forced to work and eat and sleep right next to each other.

And yet...honesty made him admit there *was* a connection between them. He'd felt that sharp tug of recognition on the first day, when she'd stolen his machete. Should he explore that connection? Did he want to find out if she felt the same?

He had a sense she'd run at any hint, if he ever tried to reveal his feelings. He knew she'd needed him last night, had trusted him enough to let herself feel safe and protected, if only for a few hours. But she'd probably deny everything if he ever pushed the matter.

And if she ever found out he'd spied on her naked, she'd turn against him in an instant, of that much he was completely sure. She'd hate his duplicity in keeping the act a secret; view it as an ultimate betrayal. And why shouldn't she; he knew he'd see it the same way if the tables were turned. He should've told her, but now it was too late. She wouldn't welcome his advances, and he'd be a fool to cultivate his feelings for her any further.

But...

No, there was no attachment, it was just his

imagination, that was all. Lust for a gorgeous woman, mistaken for something more. He clamped his fists tightly into balls, determined to beat this mood. Love and trust were for fools. Julia had taught him that lesson well. He was here for the money, not to make friends. They'd only be on this island for another few weeks, and then they'd go their own separate ways. Forever.

Helen's shadow loomed over them, and he stiffened with surprise. 'Let's have a look, it should be numb enough by now.' He stood up and put out a hand to help Cilla back to her feet. She declined, making her own way to the temporary surgery Helen had set up in the shade of the coral tree. Bloody stubborn woman!

He helped Helen as she operated on Cilla's forehead; handing her implements when she needed them. He also took up Cilla's hand again, and surprisingly she didn't argue this time. The anaesthetic had done its job, Cilla didn't blanch even once as Helen put in fourteen stitches, but his hand was sore from the fierce grip she kept on his fingers throughout the whole procedure.

Watching her trying to ignore her fear, he made a decision. He'd said he'd help her through this hard time, and he'd stick to that promise. Once her head healed and there was no danger of infection, he'd distance himself. It had to be done. If he wanted to win that million dollars, he couldn't let himself get sucked into her needs. It'd make him weak and vulnerable, both things he couldn't afford on this island.

He needed to win that money. Money gave you power, protected you from the feelings of despair and ineptitude that poverty shackled you with. That money would save him.

Belatedly he remembered it would save the kids too. Help them break out of the cycle of deprivation in which they were trapped. He could relate to their fear and anguish, he knew how it felt to not have enough.

Yes, he was ashamed of what he'd done, and although those days of being an underprivileged kid were long gone, he still found it hard to banish the idea that with just one misstep he could end up down at the bottom of the heap again. He'd never admit it to another soul, but this million-dollar prize was his ticket to lifelong security. The prize for being runner-up was also enticing. Two hundred thousand dollars would go a long way, but no one ever really wanted to come in second. In Tam's mind, it was the million or nothing.

He couldn't let this woman's vulnerability get to him. If he did, she might ruin all his plans.

CHAPTER ELEVEN

The sound of soft giggling filled the night air, blending with the hum of cicadas.

Cilla raised a bottle of beer to her lips and took a swig, then passed it onto Hayden. She dug her toes deeper into the sand and revelled in the cool damp against her feet. A welcome relief to the claustrophobic humidity that still surrounded them, even this late at night. The sand tickled the soles of her feet and she couldn't help but giggle as well.

She was a little drunk, but what did it matter. They all were. Alisha had uncovered the bottles of beer they'd not got round to drinking the other night because of the storm. Thankfully, all the bottles had survived the shelter's destruction. The members of Moonrakers sat on the water's edge and drink them, watching the night devour the stars, getting tipsy and telling bad jokes.

They were only now climbing out of the funk of having to vote Jason off last night. The tension at camp after the last conclave had been palpable. The remaining members of the old Nightrebels team had been sullen and wary, not talking much as they hiked back to camp. Even Marg hadn't been her chipper self, staying stubbornly silent most of the night. Only Simon was his normal loud, annoying character. Everyone liked Jason. And that was why he had to go.

It'd been Simon who'd instigated the vote. Cilla hated to agree with Simon on anything. But his determination that Jason should be the first person from the Moonrakers team to go was right on target. With Jason on the team, they all stood less of a chance at winning the million.

The celebration tonight was a release from the tension and regret of yesterday. It felt good not to be thinking about the game for a while. Cilla took another swig of beer as it was passed back from Alisha.

Alisha laid her hand on Cilla's arm and cast a quick glance in Tam's direction before saying in quiet undertones, 'He's worried about you.'

Cilla snorted in a most unladylike manner, knowing exactly where Alisha was going with this.

'Yeah, well, he needs to stop treating me like an invalid. He's been hovering over me like a mother hen for the past few days. It's driving me crazy.'

'We all want to make sure you're okay,' Alisha whispered. 'How's your head today?'

'It probably looks worse than it feels.' The truth was it constantly throbbed, and every time she bent over or shook her head it felt like the branch was gouging the gash on her skull all over again. But she'd never own up to the fact. Not in a million years was she going to give anyone the slightest excuse to see her as weak or vulnerable and vote her off.

Especially not in front of Tam. The man had been

rubbing on her nerves with his constant ministrations. Just this morning he'd made her sit under the coral tree for half an hour while they all got breakfast ready, because he said, *she was looking pale.* She'd sat and stewed in her own thoughts, getting crosser and crosser by the second. And then he'd brought the bottle of antiseptic over and prodded and dabbed for what'd felt like hours until he was happy. The entire process had put her completely on edge. Not because he was hurting her, but because he was so damn close to her the whole time. To make matters worse, this morning he'd not even been wearing a shirt. Tam had knelt down next to where she was sitting and leaned in to inspect her head, affording her a perfect close-up view of his bare chest. She'd tried to stop breathing as he came in nearer. He smelled wonderful, salty from the ocean, musky and warm and...alive. It was intoxicating and erotic.

But what'd made her maddest was the fact he seemed to be enjoying the whole thing way too much. As he'd pulled away from her this morning, she was sure she caught the hint of a quixotic grin on his face.

Cilla grunted again and then conceded, 'It *was* a little sore yesterday. But it's much better today. Nothing for you to worry about. But thanks anyway, *Mom!*'

'All right, all right, no need to get rude. I'm just looking out for you. Because God knows, you don't seem to want to do it for yourself.' Alisha bumped her well-cushioned hip into Cilla's to lighten her words. 'But you might want to thank Tam next time you're talking to him.'

'What for? Making me dread the smell of Iodine?' Cilla laughed.

Alisha kept a straight face. 'No, for keeping you in the

game.'

'What do you mean?'

'He doesn't know this, but I overheard him arguing with JJ after the medic stitched you up. JJ still wasn't convinced you'd be all right. He was going to get you medevac'd out whether you liked it or not. Tam persuaded him not to. He promised JJ he'd look after you, make sure you didn't get sick.'

Cilla sighed. Dammit. Now she owed him again. Big time.

Hayden interrupted their quiet conversation as he said, 'I'm off to bed, otherwise I'm going to have one sore head in the morning. I'll leave you young ones to it.'

Tam snorted. 'You're not that much older than us.'

Hayden's teeth gleamed pale in the starlight. 'See you guys later.'

Cilla heard the soft scrunch of his feet in the sand as he walked up to the shelter. That left only the four of them. Tam, Marg, Alisha and herself. All the others had drifted off over the last hour to find the best spot in the shelter and let sleep claim them.

It'd been a good night. The two joined teams had bonded over the bottles of beer and gossip. There'd been lots of talk about home, the small details people missed, and the loved ones who were waiting for them. All talk of strategy and the game had been forgotten for a short while.

'I think I'm going to hit the hay too,' said Marg, through an enormous yawn.

Cilla leaned forward so she could look past Tam and directly at the other woman. 'No, Marg. Stay with us,' she pleaded. She'd been having so much fun. She was feeling mellow and happy and wanted this night to last a little longer.

'Wait for me,' said Alisha, also rising to her feet.

Cilla let out another disappointed noise, and Alisha replied, 'I'm sure Tam will be only too happy to keep you company.' Cilla didn't miss the insinuation in her tone, but for once she was too relaxed by the alcohol to bridle at the suggestion.

'Goodnight, Marg. Alisha,' said Tam, his masculine voice breaking through the fabric of the night. Cilla hadn't noticed how profoundly deep his voice really was until that exact minute. There was an unfathomable, gravelly quality to it that touched a chord inside her. And sent shivers of expectation down her spine.

Marg swayed on her feet as she stood up. 'It really is so beautiful here, isn't it?' Slowly turning, she wended her way up the beach, followed by Alisha.

Tam and Cilla were alone.

Tam shuffled closer to her. Cilla could feel the thrill of possibility fizzing between the bare skin of their nearly touching shoulders. A flush heated her chest and flamed in her face. She was thankful for the cover of night hiding her pink cheeks.

Cilla risked a glance at Tam. He sat staring out to sea, his camaraderie at bidding Marg and Alisha goodnight had faded, replaced by a pensive gaze. The line of his shoulders sharpened, and he wouldn't look at her. Why this sudden shift in his mood?

'Cilla, there's something I need to tell you.'

Uh oh, that sounded serious. Whatever he had to say, she didn't want to hear it. Not now. She didn't want to ruin this perfect evening by talking about solemn matters.

The sky was alight with billions of winking stars, the soft night air warm and encompassing. An easy breeze tickled her nose, and the beer was giving her a warm buzzing sensation in her stomach. What was he so desperate to tell her? Whatever it was, she knew it might have to power to destroy her feelings of contentment.

'I should've told you this days ago, but I didn't want you to…think any less of me.'

Whoa, this conversation seemed to be headed for the profound area; one she wanted to steer clear of tonight.

With a squeak, she stood up. 'Let's go for a swim.' It was a crude but effective ploy.

Distraction.

'Actually, let's go for a skinny-dip.' She stripped off her clothes, leaving them lying in a pile on the sand. That *had* to be the liquor talking.

'What the—'

She laughed out loud at the shock and surprise in his exclamation. She wasn't averse to swimming nude in the ocean with friends. She'd done it before. A tiny voice of reason was telling her skinny-dipping on this island with Tam was tantamount to idiocy. But the alcoholic haze made it easy to ignore. Just for tonight, she was going to throw caution to the wind.

'Come on, Tam. Are you a scaredy cat?' she taunted.

'Oh, really!' He surged up in one fluid movement, his T-shirt already up over his head.

She couldn't help but watch as he shucked his shorts and underclothes and stood in front of her. Daring her to look. With starlight as her only illumination, the details were a bit sketchy, but she got enough of an impression of his solid maleness to make a small tremor run through her body.

Laughing, she ran down into the ocean. She could hear him splashing through the shallow water behind her. Running out far enough for the water to swallow her hips, she waded into the dark sea, careful not to get her head wet. Her skin pebbled at the cool relief and she dropped the rest of her body into the water and swam for some lengths, enjoying the feel of her movement through the silky liquid.

Something touched her feet. Then she was suddenly dragged backward as two large hands grabbed her by the ankles. His hands slithered up to her waist and then easily lifted her so she was standing in front of him; the water still only waist deep.

He smiled. 'Caught you.'

'Yes, you did.' He was so close, his hands still resting lightly on her hips. His gaze flickered downwards, his smile confirming he liked what he saw.

She placed her hands on his chest. In a heartbeat the look in his eyes went from awareness of her body to smoldering heat, igniting an answering flame inside her.

Trailing her fingers over his chest, she felt the tickle of curling hairs and then the hard planes of unyielding muscle. She found his nipple and teased it ever so gently with her thumb. He gave a sharp inhalation at her touch. The sound excited her, emboldened her even more. Tracing the curve of his stomach downwards, over the ridges of his six-pack, she followed a line of hair lower and lower.

'Cilla, what are you doing?' She put a finger to his lips to stop him talking. What was she doing? She didn't rightly know. But she'd wanted to do it ever since she'd looked into those honey-colored eyes the very first day on this island. She might blame the alcohol for her wanton behavior, but that wouldn't be completely correct. Tam's mere presence sent an undercurrent through her, and now with her hands upon his body that undercurrent had turned into a surging tide, insistent and hard to defy, pulling her along against her will. It was unlike any temptation she'd ever encountered before.

'Do you want me to stop?'

'No,' his answer came from between gritted teeth.

Leaning in closer, she let her breasts graze his chest, delighting in the sensation it caused to ripple through her. His torso was warm in comparison to the cold water lapping at her thighs. Standing on tiptoe, she reached up to trail her lips down the side of his neck. He swallowed a groan as she found his ear with her mouth. They were cheek to cheek, and she could feel his jaw flexing.

He slid one hand from her hip across her bare back, gliding over the contours of her wet skin. Over the arc of her bottom, his fingers slithered until they came to rest in the crease of her buttock. With a grunt, he pulled her toward him and their bodies connected in a hot, wet sheet of warm skin. His touch flamed the desire that settled scorching and solid in her stomach.

Her hand reached down between them, under the water to cup him, her breath catching in her throat as she felt him harden beneath her touch. His whole body stilled. She stoked the span of him. He was smooth, velvet steel. He shuddered, and she gave a small smile.

'Do you like me touching you?'

His breathing was shallow and fast, his eyes fixed on hers. By way of an answer, he lowered his head and pressed his lips to hers. This kiss was more passionate and unrestrained than their first. This kiss was all raw sensuality. She opened her mouth to him and he tasted her with a forceful stroke of his tongue. She swept her tongue over his bottom lip, liking the way his growing stubble tickled her nose. A beard on a man had never bothered her before, but it'd never really enticed her either; until tonight. She felt the pulse in his throat quicken beneath her fingertips as she nipped his mouth with her teeth. The tension coiled tighter in her abdomen. She wanted him with an urgency that was frightening. It'd been a long time since she'd allowed herself the simple pleasure of enjoying a man's body. Maybe it was completely the wrong time and wrong place for that need to surface, but she was willing to face those demons later. For over a year she'd ignored her need, left it festering, painful and unfulfilled. Tonight she was would take that risk. Tam lured her in like no other man before.

He tore his mouth away from hers and drew in large breaths of air.

'God, you taste good. One kiss and I'm…'

She didn't let him finish. Threading her fingers through his wet hair, she drew his lips down to hers.

* * *

Tam couldn't think straight anymore. All conscious thought fled with the feel of Cilla's hand as she stroked him under the water. The pleasure of her touch swirled through him like a whirlwind, obliterating everything else before it. Every hope of staying away from Cilla was annihilated by this all-consuming fire of need. He'd pay whatever price this might cost his humanity tomorrow. Tonight he wanted to be with her, feel her move beneath him and consume her body and soul.

The dim light from the stars overhead turned her skin a powdery grey. But the outline of her shape was stark against the dark lapping waves and he took advantage of the view, drinking in the curve of her pert breasts, her lean abdomen. Her fingers were still exploring the contours of his body, kindling a fast-burning blaze wherever they touched. Her teeth scraped his shoulder, spreading the hunger even faster, making his erection pound.

Was he really going to do this?

He knelt down on the sand, the water now lapping at his throat. Lifting her onto his lap, he fought the urge to let out an animal growl as her heated centre pressed up against him. The contrast of her warm flesh to the cold liquid surrounding them was sharp.

She straddled him, her gaze fixing on his face. The hunger in her eyes excited him more than anything else.

A thought pierced his erotic haze, and he blanched, staring up into Cilla's face. 'What about... I mean, I don't have a condom.'

'I have an implant. We're safe, don't worry,' she answered, a sensuous smile warming her face.

Thank God. He would've stopped this if he had to, but holy hell, it would've been one of the hardest things he'd ever done. Keeping her eyes fixed on him, she slowly lowered herself down. His entire body flared with molten heat. The feeling was so intense he couldn't move for uncounted seconds. Then Cilla rotated her hips in a slow hypnotic rhythm. Fighting the impulse to rush, he wrapped his hands around her back and mirrored her actions, his strokes strong and controlled. He wanted to make this last.

Suzanne Cass

Her thighs grasped his hips tighter, her movements becoming more urgent.

'Tam…' her words came out as a husky moan. She tilted her head backward and whispered something unintelligible, her muscles contracting around him, burying him deep inside her.

Every nerve was alight with fire. He couldn't breathe. *Don't let this be over too soon.* Her ankles locked around his waist, driving him in even deeper, her fingernails digging into the flesh of his back as she clung to him. He tried to think about anything but the sensations overwhelming him, but he was becoming consumed with the need to release.

Cilla's breathing became more ragged with every thrust, her mounting pleasure threatening his slim hold on self-control.

A sound ripped from her throat, primal and triumphant. That sound drove him over the edge. Light, heat, sensation, movement all cleaved in one colossal rush and he was swept away on wave after wave.

He didn't know how long it lasted, but he found he was shaking from head to toe, his muscles so drained he struggled to hold Cilla's weight. Her head leant into the crook of his shoulder, her breath coming in great gasps.

This woman was wild.

'I've never done it in the ocean before,' he whispered into the tangle of her hair.

She raised her head and her eyelashes fluttered open, her eyes still with that glazed look which filled him with satisfaction. Lifting his hands to cup her face, he stared at her in the moonlight. Running his thumbs over her cheeks, he revelled in the softness of her skin. An edge of one thumb ran over the top of her nose-stud and for a moment he was surprised, having forgotten it was there. The metallic sharpness was a contrast to her smooth complexion. It was as much a part of her as her emerald eyes, her tattoo, her fierce determination. All blending together to form one perfect woman. Perfect for him.

'Me either,' she said, flashing a playful grin.

'I hope we haven't just given everyone in the shelter something interesting to watch.'

'Hmm, that's true.' She gave a giggle, but this time it was accompanied by the light of reason returning to her eyes. Sliding from his lap, she stood up, water cascading from her breasts. 'We should probably go, before someone comes looking for us.'

She grabbed his hand and towed him toward the beach, his feet dragging through the cool water.

Damn, their moment together was ending way too soon. So fleeting. His ardour was drifting away on the swell of the waves. And tomorrow it'd be time to pay the price of allowing himself this indulgence. How'd things be between him and Cilla now? Would he end up cursing that bottle of beer and his lack of self-control?

CHAPTER TWELVE

Jade-green liquid surrounded Cilla. Her body glided effortless and insubstantial through the crystal clear water. Small fish darted in front of her face, silver flashes of mercury leading her deeper into the lagoon.

Finally, her lungful of air ran out, and she turned upwards, water streaming from her hair as she popped through the surface like a cork breaking away from a bottle. It was absolute heaven to swim in fresh water, to wash away the sweat and grime and salty residue that'd lingered on her skin for the past few weeks.

This was Emerald Lagoon, a hidden lake of fresh water in the centre of the island, encircled on all sides by limestone cliffs and dense jungle greenery.

She was here because Simon had won the first individual plunder knockout today. The prize comprised of an overnight stay in a specially built retreat next to the lagoon, eating as much seafood as possible, and sleeping in a king-sized bed.

The strangest part of the whole reward had come when JJ told Simon to pick not one, but two people to share the prize with him. At first Cilla thought she hadn't heard right when Simon called her name. She was the last person he should be taking. Surely it should be one of the people who were in his alliance, like Hayden or Rosa. She stood next to him while he determined who else to take, and couldn't decide whether to be flattered or afraid.

But when Simon had chosen Tam as the second person, Cilla was more than a little taken aback. It was no secret Tam and Simon weren't the best of friends. What was Simon up to?

That thought had quickly been overshadowed when the idea of spending time alone with Tam at the lagoon made her heart do an uncharacteristic flip in her chest. Even Cilla didn't fail to see the romance of a luxury retreat in the middle of a tropical island. Would she and Tam be able to find time to slip away together? To be alone. Did she even want that?

The other night in the ocean was an aberration, the effect of a little too much alcohol and the sheer beauty of a starlit sultry evening. She'd made up her mind things were going to stay platonic between them now. But her body seemed to have a will of its own, humming with a vibration low down in her abdomen at the mere thought of being alone with Tam again. Of him running his hands over her hips, pulling her in to his... *Stop it.* She shook her head to rid herself of the image.

'I think I saw a sting ray,' Simon's excited shout broke her internal musings. 'You guys have to come over here and see this.' Cilla paddled over to where he thrashed about in the water near the beach. She followed his pointed finger and did indeed see a dark shape drifting over the sandy bottom.

Looking around, she located Tam's head, bobbing in the middle of the lagoon. He waved and gave her a dreamy smile. She left him to his swimming and turned onto her back, gliding toward the cliffs, letting the shadows from the jungle leaves kiss her face as she floated beneath them.

'I just saw another one,' Simon said, his raised voice snapping her out of her reverie. 'This place is amazing!' Cilla thought it might be the first time she'd ever seen a genuine smile of delight on his face. And then the gratuitous part of her brain kicked in. What better time to get to know Simon than out here, the three of them, away from the edgy tension of the campsite. And she needed Simon on her side. She needed as many people on her side as she could get, if she were to win this game. The question of why Simon had invited them also needed an answer. It was obvious there was some kind of strategy Simon was hoping to lay in place by inviting both of them along, and Cilla needed to find out what that was. If she could just mask her dislike for him enough to seem interested, she might find out something important.

'Yes it is, Simon. It's beautiful.' She started swimming toward him, painting on her best smile. 'And I want to thank you again for bringing me along on your prize.' Her feet touched the sandy bottom, and she walked over in the chest deep water to stand next to him. Smoothing her water-dark hair away from her face, she kept her gaze fixed on him. 'I have to admit, the part I'm looking forward to most is the seafood banquet.' She tilted her head sideways and dropped her gaze, so she was looking at him through lowered eyelashes. 'Well that, and getting to know you better as well. You know, without the rest of the team...around.' She tried to make her smile inviting as she spoke. God, she wished she was better at the flattery thing. It seemed to come as second nature to some women, the easy banter and the seductive come-to-bed eyes. Why did she find it so hard to master?

'Yep, me too. I'm so hungry I could eat the crutch out of a low-flying dove.'

Her smile faded. He hadn't got the hint at all. She sucked at the seduction thing alright.

'And I'm also looking forward to some…intimate conversation, Cilla.' He brushed her arm with a cool wet finger and then leaped off in pursuit of another fleeting sting ray shape, leaving her blinking in disbelief.

Maybe she wasn't as bad at the sweet talk thing as she thought after all.

Glancing quickly over her shoulder, she saw Tam was floating on his back some distance away. Had he seen their interaction?

Cilla was suddenly annoyed at herself. What did it matter if Tam had seen her talking to Simon, anyway? She was her own woman, able to talk to whoever she wanted, whenever she wanted. Just because they had sex in the ocean didn't mean she owed him anything. Even if it'd been so hot and fervent that the mere thought of it now still doubled her heart rate. Even if she now had to constantly fight the urge to lean in and gently nip his neck, to see if he'd react with the same soft growl as he had the other night.

In the two days since they'd made love in the ocean, there hadn't been a chance for Cilla and Tam to be alone together. They were always either doing something as a team or Marg or Alisha would tag along with them to the water-well, or to go fishing. She hadn't engineered it that way, but a small part of her was grateful, anyway. Their friendship remained open and easy, even if he exasperated her sometimes with his continued overprotectiveness. And she made a point of keeping the banter and camaraderie flowing, to stop anyone else from being suspicious. She was determined not to mention that night again. It was fraught with too many connotations and questions, most of which she wasn't ready to find the answers to.

She wasn't here to find love. She was here to win one million dollars.

It was time to shore up her alliances, open herself up to new tactics to ensure her survival. And if that meant creating a bond with Simon—faking it even—then that's what she was going to do.

* * *

Tam stuffed two more prawns into his mouth, reaching for another spoonful of yellow rice at the same time. The food would probably be delicious, if he actually took the chance to taste it. As it was, the food wasn't even touching the sides the way he was wolfing it down. He'd have to slow down soon, or he'd make himself sick.

'Oh, my stomach is aching, it's so full,' groaned Cilla. 'But I can't stop eating, this is all so wonderful.' And she crammed another huge piece of fish into her mouth, dripping with red curry sauce. Tam gave her a wink, but couldn't reply, his mouth was too jam-packed.

It was fifteen minutes later when he at last admitted defeat. There was still food piled high on his plate, but he knew he couldn't eat another bite. He sat back and took in the details of their feasting.

Darkness had fallen while they'd stuffed themselves silly. One of the four exquisitely dressed waitresses had lit the multitude of hanging lanterns positioned around the outside of the hut, so it was now lit with a warm orange light. They were seated at a low table beneath a large wooden gazebo, open to the jungle on all sides. The table was decorated with rattan placemats, with pirate flags tied to the wooden poles, skull and crossbones glaring down at them from all angles.

An inordinate amount of food was laid out for only three people. There were huge piles of rice and noodles heaped onto banana leaves, satay sticks, bowls of seafood curries, each steaming in their own heavenly aroma of Thai spices, tiny bowls containing all kinds of sweet and savoury dipping sauces, even a whole barbecued fish sat in the middle of the table.

'Are we allowed to take any of this food home to the team?' Cilla asked.

'You just read my mind,' Tam admitted, focussing on her face for the first time since they'd sat down.

'No, we're not. You heard what JJ said before we left. Do you want to get us disqualified or something?' It seemed this wonderful meal hadn't softened Simon's belligerent side then. Tam frowned at him over the table and didn't answer. Simon was correct, but Tam didn't like how he was so downright arrogant about it. Simon always thought he was right, and Tam was tiring of the man. Fast. He tolerated him publicly, but inside he often found himself having to keep a sincere urge to punch him in the face in check. He hoped he'd be able to hold his tongue during the imposed closeness of this prize, keep a cool head for the next twenty-four hours at least.

To take his mind off his dark thoughts, he forced his gaze over to Cilla. She looked good tonight. No, better than good; she looked great. Her clean hair was now drying and forming a nimbus of chestnut strands around her face. Her slim form was engulfed by the large white bathrobe they'd all been given to wear once they came out of the water. The stark white of the material highlighted the glowing olive skin of her shoulders and face. There was a soft, contented smile lingering on her mouth, her eyes half closed as she leaned back into her chair. She gave a groan and rubbed her belly, moistening her partly open lips at the same time. It was an unconscious act, but Tam felt his pulse give a few erratic beats at the thought of kissing those rosy lips. She'd tasted so perfect the other night. Her body felt so honest in his arms. Cilla had felt it too, he knew she had. The way her mouth opened before his lips had even touched hers, the urgent dart of her tongue unmistakable. The way she'd pressed her breasts hard into his chest and her fingernails had run ragged down his spine, revealed to him what her words couldn't. She wanted him as much as he wanted her.

So much for his resolve to stay away from her after her head was healed. Instead of remaining detached, he'd done the exact opposite; he'd allowed her to burrow even deeper under his skin.

They still continued their easy friendship; as if nothing had happened. They seemed to have both silently agreed to shut that memory away, walled it into a neat little box, not referring to it even once in the days afterwards. He'd do well to remember that Cilla had put it behind her. It was essential for him to do the same, get his head back into the game.

The problem was, he couldn't. Couldn't ignore the feel of her reacting to his touch, the manner in which she'd allowed him a glimpse at her true nature, her raw emotions.

He was a goner. He'd fallen for this intelligent, surprising, strong-willed woman. But what was he to do with that knowledge?

She'd run a mile if she ever found out how deeply he was beginning to care for her.

The sound of Cilla's voice withdrew him from his contemplations and he managed to plaster a grim half-smile on his face.

'You're right, Simon. Of course you're right,' Cilla said in a placating tone. She glanced over at Simon and gave him a knowing smile. Had her gaze lingered just a little too long? Of course not, he knew Cilla found Simon as insufferable as he did. She was just making him feel at ease. Maybe in the hopes he'd reveal something about his plans for the rest of the game. He should join in her act, start being nicer to Simon.

'But I keep thinking of poor Alisha and Marg and Hayden and Rosa, all at camp starving. Well, maybe not Hayden and Rosa,' she amended with a smile. Cilla held Simon's gaze for longer than necessary, it was unquestionable this time. Tam's gut clenched in a surprising reaction. He didn't like her looking at Simon that way, not one little bit.

Drawing in a calmative breath, he said, 'I agree, it seems a shame that everyone else is missing out on this wonderful food. But then I guess that's why a plunder knockout is such a big boon. We get the advantage of having eaten an enormous meal and slept peacefully in a soft bed, while the rest of them get nothing.'

'Got that correct, big boy.' Simon grinned across the

table at him and Tam had to grit his teeth together. Now wasn't the time to take offence at Simon's manner, even if it felt like a sly put down.

'Thanks for bringing us both along today, Simon. It was big of you.' The words almost stuck in Tam's throat.

'Not a problem, bro.' Simon flicked his fingers in a gesture of indifference.

'Yeah, thanks, Simon,' Cilla said, echoing his sentiments.

'We may as well make the most of the time we've got cooped up here together,' said Simon, putting his feet up on a nearby chair and stretching his arms behind his head. 'How about we all get to know each other a little better? That kind of knowledge could be gold in this game, you know.' Again, Simon was right. The more they knew about each other, the better. Everyone knew at some stage of the game they would play the knockout called, *how much do you know about your team members*. Tonight was all about more leverage in the game.

'Let's start with you, Cilla. Tell us why you came on Sea-Quest?' Simon speared Cilla with a sharp gaze, at odds to the sleepy grin he fired in her direction.

'Oh, okay then.' It was obvious Cilla had been caught off guard, but she gathered her thoughts and said, 'It was actually my boss, Brad Dursley, who got me to audition. He owns a charter boat business, Whitsunday Yacht Escapes, renting out luxury yachts. He's the one who hired me as a Sailguide.'

'Sounds kinda like a rich dick to me,' said Simon with contempt.

'Well, he is a multi-millionaire, but he's also a great down-to-earth guy. I love working for him,' she continued, unfazed by Simon's comments. 'Anyway, he called me into his office one day, to look at the website for Sea-Quest. Told me they were looking for contestants for their next game and asked if I thought he'd make a good competitor?' Tam could see that thoughts of Brad brought a faraway smile to Cilla's face. It seemed she truly did like her boss.

'So he gave you the idea to audition then?' asked Tam, wanting her to continue with the story.

'Yeah. He joked to me it wouldn't be the money he was playing for. Rather for the glory and prestige. That's when I realized another million wouldn't change Brad's life much. But it might change mine.'

'Ain't that the truth,' growled Simon in agreement.

'Pity Brad didn't make it on to Sea-Quest too,' she continued. 'But I think he might secretly enjoy it more sitting at home dissecting the show from the comfort of his expensive condo than actually playing the game.'

'Cool,' said Simon, 'but you didn't—'

'Hey, Simon, I'd love to hear about your childhood. I bet you were a wild and cheeky kid,' Cilla interrupted. She was almost cooing at the man, leaning her elbows on the table and gazing at him with soft, expectant eyes.

Simon hesitated before giving a shrug. 'Sure, doll, anything you want.' He launched into a spiel about his early life, but Tam couldn't concentrate. It was more than obvious Cilla hadn't wanted to talk about why she'd entered Sea-Quest, so she'd neatly deflected Simon from his conversation by playing up to the man's colossal ego.

Simon was really getting on his nerves. But Tam was determined he'd keep his temper. He had to if he was going to gain anything from this reward. Apart from everything else, it wouldn't do for Cilla to see how much

Simon got him riled up. And the last thing she needed to know was how jealous he was getting watching this little scene unfold before him.

Tam tuned out the droning hum of the other man's voice, instead staring out at the darkness held under the canopy of the jungle trees.

* * *

Tam woke with a start, his neck stiff from where he'd slumped in the chair. The food sat cold and congealed on the table in front of him. There was no sign of either Cilla or Simon. How long had he been asleep? Half an hour, maybe more. He got up, still a little groggy. Peering down toward the beach by the lagoon, he tried to see if there was any movement. Nothing. It was no use going to look for the other two, they could be anywhere. He headed for the sleeping hut they were all sharing tonight, hoping they'd both be soundly sleeping in there.

Three single beds all stood in a line inside the hut. All were empty, their crisp sheets still folded neat and unruffled. Where were they? And what were they up to? Dark thoughts roiled round in his mind. But there was nothing else for it, he may as well go to bed and get some sleep. He'd be damned if he was going to search for them now.

He lay in bed for another ten minutes, not able to appreciate the cool smoothness of the white sheets, or the soft cradling of the mattress beneath him, so mystified was he about what Cilla and Simon could be up to. All kinds of scenarios were running through his head, and most of them made him want to get up and hunt Simon down and crush him to within an inch of his life.

Suddenly there were voices right outside the window.

Tam turned over and feigned sleep. Through eyes open a crack, he watched as Cilla slipped in, followed very closely by Simon. Was that Simon's hand on the small of Cilla's back? It was too dark to see clearly.

'Goodnight, Simon,' she whispered.

'Goodnight, Cilla. Great chatting with you,' Simon said, making a pretence of whispering, but it came out more like a dull roar. Tam remained perfectly still.

Cilla hopped into bed and slid under the bedclothes, quiet as a mouse. But Tam saw the quick, guilty glance she cast in his direction. A thin slice of ice slithered into his heart. That look told him everything he needed to know.

CHAPTER THIRTEEN

How could Tam have done that to her? Cilla tried to swallow the lump in her throat. Her stomach twisted, making her feel sick.

It was no use wishing she'd never gone on that prize reward with Simon; that she could go back in time two days previous. If she hadn't found out about Tam's duplicity, she'd still be looking at him through those stupid rose-colored glasses.

'You alright? You look a little green.' Tam turned that amber gaze toward her, his face softening as he smiled. She wanted to hit him, scream at him.

'Must be all the food I ate last night.' She showed her teeth in what she hoped represented a smile, even though it felt more like a grimace.

'We'll be on the beach in a few minutes, you'll feel better when you get off this boat.' He leaned in to pat her shoulder, and it was all she could do not to flinch away from his touch.

'Can't wait,' she replied, crossing her arms tight across her chest and staring straight at the oncoming beach. They were on their way home from the lagoon, but because it could only be reached from the other side of the island, they'd taken the boat to get home. Cilla couldn't wait to get back in amongst the other team members. It'd be easier to hide her grief once she could mingle with them.

Simon gave her a knowing glance from the other side of the boat. If only he wasn't so smug about the whole thing. She didn't like him any better just because he'd been the one to tell her the truth. She still found him insufferable. After all, he'd been in on it too. He'd been there, and he'd seen her naked. And probably taken advantage of the situation to ogle her while he'd the chance, even though he protested his innocence. The thought made the bile rise in her throat again. But at least he'd been honest enough to admit to his part in their dirty little trick. She owed him something for showing her the reality of her position.

Simon had enticed her down to the lagoon last night after dinner. Tam had fallen asleep at the table, stuffed so full of food he couldn't stay awake, and she didn't see the harm in leaving him. He'd looked so innocent with his head in his hands, like a child.

Once down at the lagoon, Simon sat down on the sand and patted a spot beside him in a gesture for her to sit. There was a harvest moon slanting its lustrous rays over Emerald Lagoon. The edges of the water shimmered, reminding her of liquid silver. The sound of the cicada symphony was almost deafening. It was a perfect evening. If only it could be Tam sitting beside her on the sand instead of Simon. She might've brushed his arm with her hand. A fleeting touch, to see what he'd do. Would he turn those passion-dark eyes on her and push her down in the sand so he could kiss her until she could no longer breathe? Goose bumps raised all over her skin at the intoxicating thought.

'Are you going to sit, or what?' Simon's demanding voice was nothing like the honeyed rasp of Tam's in the throes of desire, and it jolted her back to reality. She sat down.

'I need to tell you something, Cilla. Something I should've told you days ago.' The goose bumps returned at Simon's words, but for all the wrong reasons this time. It sounded oddly similar to the words Tam had said to her on the beach the other night, before she'd interrupted him by stripping off her clothes. She shook her head, suddenly not wanting to hear what Simon had to say.

He didn't notice her lack of consent, however, instead he started talking in a fast monotone as if he wanted to get this over with as quickly as possible.

'A couple of weeks ago, when we were still part of Dawnbreakers, I was grabbing the snorkel and goggles to try some crabbing when Tam came over to me.'

That sounded harmless enough. Cilla released the breath she'd been holding.

'Tam said something very strange. He asked me if I'd like to get a look at the best view on the island.' Again, fairly harmless stuff. A bit odd for Tam to say something like that, but she couldn't see any mischief in it.

'There was something a bit... I don't know... underhanded about Tam's attitude, but at the time I ignored my gut instinct telling me not to go, and tagged along after him into the jungle.' Now that sounded strange, but also not too surprising, coming from Simon. He'd probably undermine Tam any chance he got. She nodded for him to continue.

'He led me to this gorgeous little bay about fifteen minutes north of the Dawnbreakers beach. Do you remember it? There was a wide sandy shelf that dropped off over the reef and lots of large boulders at the rear. The one where we found all those enormous crabs.'

Cilla's heart stilled in her chest. She couldn't move or breathe. Yes, she remembered it.

'Well, you were there…in the water…nude.' She broke out in a cold sweat. Simon rushed on, saying the words so quickly she almost didn't catch them. 'I said we should leave immediately and what was he thinking, to come here and gawp at you like some kind of perverted lecher. It was disgusting. But Tam wouldn't listen. He hid behind the boulders and kept staring at you. I pleaded with him to leave you alone and eventually he agreed to return to camp, but only after he'd seen his fill of you. Stark naked.'

Simon kept going on and on about how sorry he was, and how he should've told her that very day, but Tam made him swear not to tell her, because he knew it'd ruin any chances he might have with her. And how the guilt had eaten away at him. That's why he'd chosen her to come on the prize with him, so he could tell her.

Cilla didn't remember what she said in reply.

In a daze she hardly even remembered walking to the cabin, she was so lost in the depth of Tam's deceit. The idea was so preposterous, she almost didn't believe Simon, but he'd been very convincing.

In the end, Simon had pleaded so hard for his innocence, Cilla begrudgingly gave him absolution.

Tam was another matter altogether. How could he have been such a creep? And how could she have fallen for that amiable persona, taken in by him so completely that she'd actually had sex with him? She felt dirty and betrayed. No wonder he'd jumped on her the first chance she gave him. He was fulfilling some kind of sick fantasy after seeing her naked. And she'd led him on, she'd instigated it. The thought had made her want to vomit.

Why hadn't Tam told her? The fact he'd kept it a secret for so long was the sickest part of the whole thing.

Of course it'd be just her luck, yet again the one man she thought she could depend on had turned out to be an arsehole. Tam had proved beyond a doubt that men were all the same. Not to be trusted.

Should she confront him? Every fibre in her being wanted to have it out with him right this instant. But she had to be logical about this, she needed time to think through all the ramifications and decide how it might affect their alliance. And Alisha; she had to talk to Alisha.

The bow of the boat scrunched into the sand with a lurch, and she found herself caught in Tam's arms as she toppled sideways.

'Sorry,' she muttered, disentangling herself and backing away as fast as was humanly possible. The grin on Tam's face faded, replaced by lowered eyebrows and a furrowed brow.

* * *

'It's called the spiderweb knockout,' said JJ in his gravelly voice. He watched them all tilt their heads to stare up into the trees, and a wicked smile broke his features. 'Take a good look, because you don't want to be falling from up there.'

Tam swiveled his head around to follow the web of ropes strung between the great trunks of many large jungle trees and groaned quietly. It reminded him of some confusing military rope course. They'd all have to be part monkey to complete this knockout.

'This one's not for the faint-hearted, hey, big fella?' Simon punched him in the arm and gave a friendly grin. Tam clenched his jaw, trying to keep his breathing even. Simon was taking all sorts of liberties since they'd come back from the lagoon this morning. As if they were now best mates or something. It was annoying the hell out of him, more than usual. Tam couldn't put his finger on exactly why, but there was a self-righteousness to Simon's smile that unnerved him.

And Cilla was definitely avoiding him since they got back from the reward. She'd barely make eye contact with him now. What had she and Simon said to each other last night? For the hundredth time today, Tam cursed the fact he'd let his concentration drift and fallen asleep. Had Simon tried to ingratiate himself with Cilla? Or even worse, had he tried to kiss her? The mere idea got Tam's blood boiling. Enough was enough. He needed to get to the bottom of it. He'd confront Cilla as soon as this knockout was over, whether she liked it or not.

After fifteen minutes of fighting the confounded spiderweb course, Tam collapsed in a heap on the netting in the middle of the course, his chest heaving with exertion. He admitted defeat. He was completely drained. He knew he'd be safe enough at the conclave tonight, but that wasn't the point. He wanted to win.

Tam heard JJ cry, 'Hayden wins exemption,' and watched as JJ handed the rainbow colored parrot to him, while he gave a whoop of joy. Well, he might too. He was supposed to have been next on the chopping block.

They'd have to choose someone else to vote off tonight.

Tam made his way down the ladder, the muscles in his arms already protesting at their over-exertion. Cilla came down right behind him. By the look on her face, she felt just as bad as he did. He offered her a hand down the last few rungs, but she shied away from him.

He nearly swore out loud. What was wrong with the woman? She blew hot and cold so fast it made his head spin.

* * *

Cilla poked the campfire with a long stick, watching as the coals collapsed in on themselves, dying down to a tawny glow. It was straight after breakfast and everyone else was off doing their morning ablutions. She was alone at camp.

Lethargy sat on her shoulders like a great beast. How had things suddenly become so complicated? The alliance. Simon's revelations. Her feelings toward Tam. There was so much roiling through her head this morning, she'd not even had the energy to go snorkelling with Alisha and Marg. It seemed today she was getting further and further away from winning the million dollars, not closer.

There were only seven team members left. The idea didn't thrill her as much as it should. They'd voted Susan out last night at the conclave. Cilla had wanted to get rid of Rosa. No one else seemed to have noticed that she'd been coming a close second to Hayden yesterday in the spiderweb knockout. But once again, Simon had dictated the votes of all the old Dawnbreakers' members.

Heaving a vast sigh, she shifted her weight onto her hands and leant backward to survey the beach.

It was another perfect day in paradise. Small wavelets lapped the beach, crashing up the sand and then retreating, leaving fizzing bubbles of foam behind. A white-bellied sea eagle was doing lazy circles at the rear of the bay where the water broke, choppy and blue over the reef. It was still cool, although the heat was building and soon she'd have to move further up into the shelter of the jungle; as much to get away from the emerging sand-flies as to get away from the fierce sun.

Funnily enough, this beach was beginning to feel like home. Its familiar crescent curve sweeping off to the northern headland drew her gaze every time she returned to the coast. Even the debris and smashed trees littering the shore after the storm were now part of the landscape she was coming to admire.

Tam's face appeared before her mind's eye. He'd tried numerous times over the past twenty-four hours to get her alone, to talk to her. Of course he'd noticed there was something wrong, how on earth could he have missed her cold shoulder tactics. But she'd been lucky every time, and someone or something had diverted them. But she'd need to talk to him soon.

Distant yelling attracted her attention. It was coming from over on the southern rocky headland, where Alisha and Marg had gone fishing. A figure lumbered over the rocks toward the beach. It could only be Alisha from that gait. Why was she running?

Cilla stood up, shading her eyes. Yes, it was definitely Alisha, and she was upset about something. Cilla ran toward her.

'Cilla, you got to help Tam. Quick, he's over there with Marg,' Alisha gasped and flapped an arm in the directions of the rocky edge where they normally dove off into the water. Cilla could just make out someone kneeling down over a body.

'What's happened?'

'Marg's been stung,' Alisha panted out the words between breaths. 'Quick go and help Tam bring her back to camp. Where the hell are Simon and Rosa and Hayden?'

'Don't know,' Cilla replied over her shoulder as she sprinted across the sand. What could be wrong with Marg? There were poisonous sea-snakes or fire coral in the water, to name a few of the nasties she might encounter. Oh God, please let it not be a Stonefish. Cilla didn't want to think about that. She ran as hard as she could.

Tam had picked Marg up and was carrying her across the rocky headland. Not an easy feat considering how sturdy and muscular Marg was and how jagged the rocks were.

Cilla could hear Marg screaming as she came closer. The hair on the back of her neck rose up at the sound.

'Tam, let me help.'

'Do you know how to do a firefighter's lift?' Tam grunted through gritted teeth. His breath was nearly as laboured as Marg's; she must be heavier than she looked. Cilla nodded, and they transferred Marg's weight between the two of them.

'Do we know what stung her?' Cilla had to raise her voice above the sound above of Marg's muffled screams of pain.

'I think it might be a Stonefish,' he grunted. 'I couldn't get much out of her after she surfaced. But there looks to be a spine or something in her foot, and from the amount of pain she's in, it'd be a good guess.'

'Shit. Shit. Shit.' This was bad. Marg needed medical help. Immediately.

Simon burst from the edge of the jungle and ran toward

them. He shoved Cilla out of the way and took Marg's weight. The two men were quicker at carrying her.

'I'll get some water on the boil,' said Cilla, racing off ahead of them. As she approached the campsite, she saw Alisha talking to one of the camera crew, arms waving in desperation. He had his two-way out and was pushing buttons even as he listened to her.

Cilla sped over to the shelter and pulled out the big iron cook pot and half-filled it with water, then dragged it over to the fire. Rosa ambled into the camp, unaware of the emergency.

Cilla yelled, 'Rosa, quick, we need more firewood to build this fire up. We think Marg's been stung by a stonefish.' Rosa's eyes widened with shock, but she didn't need to be told twice. She hurried back into the jungle. They'd all learned at survival training the treatment for stonefish sting was hot water. As hot as the patient could stand. It helped neutralise the toxin and took away some of the pain.

Cilla used what little firewood was still lying on the beach to build up the fire as much as she could and knelt down to blow on it.

Tam and Simon arrived with Marg slung between them. They put her down as gently as possible in the shelter, but she still screamed every time they moved or bumped her. Cilla ran over.

'It'll be okay, Marg. Alisha has got the medics on their way and I've got some hot water to help with the pain.' Marg didn't answer, and Cilla wasn't even sure she heard her. She'd curled into a ball and was cradling her foot. Her skin was pale and sweat streamed off her body, her face drawn into a rictus of pain. She moaned constantly, tremors of agony racking her frame. Cilla had never been so scared. Not even the night of the storm.

Stroking the other woman's head, she whispered words of encouragement, sending a frightened glance in Tam's direction. He looked up from where he was bent nearly double from the effort of hauling Marg back to camp. His honey eyes were wide with worry as well.

'Tam, can you check the water in the pot, it might be hot enough now,' Cilla commanded in clipped tones.

By the time two boats sped into the bay with JJ and the medic team on board fifteen minutes later, they'd managed to get Marg up to a sitting position between Tam and Cilla with her injured foot in the hot water. She'd stopped moaning, but her head lolled backward and her eyes remained closed.

More than happy to hand Marg over to the capable hands of the medics, Helen and James, Cilla stepped back to watch.

JJ hovered near the tight circle of medics, his handsome face showing signs of uncharacteristic worry.

Cilla's hands shook. It was delayed shock; she knew that, but it did nothing to stop the trembles. Her knees felt weak, and she had a sudden urge to sit down. Tears pricked behind her eyelids. *Please let Marg be all right.* The words went round in a desperate loop in her head.

Tam came up and stood next to her, the dejection evident in the strained lines around his eyes. He took one look at her and without speaking or asking; he enfolded her in his arms.

He stood rock-solid, his chest sturdy and warm. She hated him. She hated herself for needing him. But right this second, his muscular arms around her were the only thing holding her up. Accepting her moment of weakness, she let him comfort her.

'She'll be fine,' he whispered into her hair. 'Helen will fix her, just like she fixed you.'

If only he were right.

Drawing in the last shreds of security she could before the inevitable, she drew away.

'I know,' she mumbled in reply. The rest of the team stood around the shelter in an awkward semi-circle, unsure what to do or say, watching the nightmare scene unfold before them.

At last JJ stepped away from the huddle surrounding Marg and came over to them.

'Marg needs to go to hospital, straight away,' he said without preamble. Cilla felt her chest tighten and had to suppress the urge to reach for Tam's hand. 'But the medics think that after a shot of antivenin she'll make a full recovery.'

Thank God. The tightness in her chest eased a little. Alisha and Rosa let out exclamations of relief.

'That means she'll be leaving the game, though, and won't be returning. She'll need a good couple of days in hospital to recover from this one.' JJ paused to allow his words to sink in. 'You guys did an outstanding job. If you hadn't acted so quickly, who knows how badly off Marg might be now. You should all be congratulated.' JJ's praise felt somehow hollow; Marg would be leaving the game. Nothing could save her from that now.

There was a flurry of activity at the shelter, and a stretcher was brought up from the boat.

Helen called out to them, 'Hey guys, Marg wants to say goodbye.'

They all crowded around the sick woman. Cilla held her hand, which was cold and clammy. They all tried to talk at once, finally letting Alisha say what they were all feeling. Alisha patted Marg's arm and spoke with tears in her eyes. Cilla would miss the Canadian woman's whacky sense of humour, and her constant conversations about sexuality and how men frequently got it wrong. And the way she thought everything was *awesome*. Marg would've been a huge chance to win the million with her athletic ability, competitive streak and sheer likability.

Now they were six.

* * *

'We need to talk.' Tam stood over Cilla as she sat at the edge of the water. It was now or never. They'd all gotten over the shock of Marg's departure this morning, and it was time for him to confront Cilla. After their brief consoling hug, she'd gone back to being distant and aloof.

'I don't want to talk.'

'Come for a walk with me?' he said, not quite able to keep the edge of entreaty out of his voice. She didn't move. 'Unless you'd rather do it in front of an audience.' He tilted his head toward Rosa and Alisha, who were sitting at the cook fire readying rice for dinner. They were within range if they cared to listen.

With a heavy groan, she stood up. They walked in silence side by side at the water's edge, their feet making soft sucking sounds as they left wet footprints in the sand.

Tam glanced behind him. They were out of earshot. He wanted to touch Cilla, to ask her how she was, look at her head to make sure for himself that her wound was healing fine.

He let out a loud sigh. Where to begin?

Before he could frame the words to ask the question that'd been bothering him for two days, Cilla said, 'What do you want, Tam? The last thing I need at the moment are your problems. I'm not sure I can take much more today after Marg's leaving this morning.' Her face remained averted and her green eyes cold.

He almost lost his nerve. She was right. He shouldn't be cornering her. Perhaps he'd made it all up. She'd certainly accepted his comfort as Marg had lain sick and injured. When he'd held her in his arms, he almost believed things were okay between them again.

Her reaction to him now told him otherwise. A huge wall had gone up between them and he didn't know why. He shouldn't care, but he did.

'What did you and Simon talk about the night of the prize?' There'd be no dancing around the issue; he went straight for the jugular. This conversation would either make or break them as friends...or whatever it was they'd become to each other.

'What? Why?' Her surprise at his direct question was obvious.

'Because ever since then you've looked at me as if I'm the devil incarnate, and to touch me seems to cause you physical pain.' He was surprised at the depth of emotion in his voice. He'd thought to remain calm and impartial, at least to start with, but the truth of his statement couldn't be denied. 'What have I done to deserve that?'

Cilla stopped in her tracks and turned to face him. Her hands were clenched at her sides and her face like a thunderous black cloud.

'What have you done?' The way her eyes glittered, dark and dangerous, rang warning bells in his head. 'You men, you're all the same. You're all just like my father.' Rage and something else—was it regret—flashed in her eyes.

Where had that outburst come from? Why such an intense reaction? And what'd her father done to get her so riled up and anti-men?

'I'm sorry, what—'

'Don't you dare act all innocent and wholesome, Tam Connor.' Her words hit him like a dash of cold ice.

'I know what you and Simon got up to when you thought I wasn't looking. He told me every sordid detail. How you snuck up on me while I was swimming—how you saw me naked.'

Oh God, she knew. Just as he'd feared, the incident had come back to hurt him. Big time.

'I wanted to tell you, Cilla. I tried to tell you—'

She cut him off with a harsh laugh. 'At least you don't deny it.' Her laughter didn't hide the fact that her face had drained of all color. Her voice was raw, painful to listen to as she continued, 'So then don't deny the fact you enjoyed seeing me naked that day either. You're a pervert and a liar.'

He took a step backward, staring at her in disbelief pierced. It was true; he had tried to tell her, but something always stopped him. Now he knew he should've tried harder. Much harder. Heat flamed in his cheeks. Shame and mortification cut through him with razor sharp clarity.

'And then you had the audacity to seduce me on the beach. To let me have sex with you.'

That's not exactly how he remembered it, but he'd take that one on the chin. He'd been about to tell her when she'd started stripping her clothes off. The sight of her beautiful body had driven all other thoughts away.

Looking back, it was a stupid thing to do. He wasn't an immature kid anymore. He should've been able to control his primal urges. If only he could tame this allure she cast, so that his senses weren't turned upside-down and inside out every time she came near. Even when she was hissing like an angry cat, ready to claw his eyes out, it only made her seem more spectacular to him.

Tam lifted his hands, palms up, beseeching. 'Cilla, I can't begin to tell you how sorry I am for not telling you straight away. I wanted to, but I couldn't. You see—'

'You men are all such…liars. You can't be trusted. But don't worry, I won't be gullible enough to trust you ever again.'

She turned on her heel and headed toward camp.

'Cilla, wait. You need to give me a chance to explain.'

She spun around, a feral grimace on her face. 'You've got nothing to tell me that Simon hasn't already filled me in on. I don't want to talk to you anymore. Leave me alone.'

He watched her stomp away from him, rooted to the spot with astonishment. She wouldn't listen to him. She'd come in guns blazing, fired accusations at him, not given him a chance to defend himself, leaving him battered and bleeding, then turned and walked away.

He sat on the sand, head down and fists clenched.

For someone who prided himself on his self-control and his empathy for the human condition, he'd hurt her deeply. Racking his brain, he tried to remember if Cilla had ever mentioned her father. She hadn't. It made a horrible kind of sense. Her father had wounded her emotionally, and whatever it was he'd done to Cilla, Tam had just proven himself equally unworthy.

Tam knew he deserved the label of *liar*, but *pervert*? That was a powerful indictment. A niggling voice at the back of his brain wondered exactly what Simon had said to her. Sub-consciously Tam knew following Simon's wishes not to tell Cilla would backfire somehow. He'd just not imagined that it'd happen this spectacularly.

Tam raked a hand through his hair. He wanted to go after her, to force her to listen; to run up the beach and turn her around. Tell her how much he really cared, and how he never meant to cause her pain. But nothing he could say to her would be believed right now. She'd made that crystal clear.

He needed to confront Simon as well, call him out for all the half-truths he'd said. He slammed a frustrated fist into the sand, wishing that it was Simon's face.

It wouldn't help his cause to do either of those things tonight, but God, he wanted to. It took all his self-control to hold himself back, to stay seated here on the cold sand.

He stared out to the horizon, his eyes not even registering the setting sun, painting the sky with streaks of orange and pink.

CHAPTER FOURTEEN

'It's time to vote,' said JJ. His voice tolled in Cilla's head like the ringing of a death knell. She watched Alisha get up and walk over the bridge to the crow's nest platform. Nothing felt real, as if she was in some slow-motion replay of an old black and white movie; as if her muscles had suddenly seized up and she was frozen, unable to move or speak.

Paralyzed by the choice in front of her.

Simon sat next to her, preening like a peacock, the exemption parrot sitting on his shoulder. She couldn't vote for him.

A tremendous gust of wind shook the platform, and Cilla shivered. There was another big tropical storm coming.

'Wow, Tam, your firebrand blew out.' JJ pointed to the row of firebrands behind them. Cilla turned to look. Tam's firebrand had gone out.

'I hope that isn't an omen, JJ,' Tam replied with a grin. Cilla could see he wasn't really worried, he didn't believe in portents. In general she didn't either, but tonight the sight of the gutted firebrand shook her to the core.

She hadn't spoken to Tam in two days, had barely glanced in his direction since their fight on the beach.

He'd tried to talk to her more than once, but she wouldn't let him. She'd lived up to Marco's nickname of the ice queen very nicely indeed over the past few days. All she had to do was put those walls up around her heart, reside safe and secure in her cocoon of self-righteousness, buoyed by her justifiable anger, and she knew she could stay that way indefinitely.

Were those walls high enough to protect her from what she was about to do?

As soon as they got back to camp after Simon had won individual exemption this afternoon, Simon had sought Cilla out. She'd followed him into the jungle, her feet dragging at every step. Simon had won the knockout, *know your sailor mates*, which was a series of questions about all of team Moonrakers. Cilla knew she'd seriously underestimated how good Simon was at this game.

'What's the matter, Cilla?' Simon could turn on the charm when the whim took him, and he hit her with the full force of it today, showing his straight-edged smile, with just the right amount of tender concern evident in the solicitous way he touched her arm. 'Is there anything I can do to help?'

Anything he could do to help? Simon was at the root of her problems. And he knew it. However, she didn't want to let him see how much she was actually hurting, how much Tam's betrayal had cost her. Cost her soul.

'I'm fine, Simon, but thanks for your concern.' She turned on one of her best fake smiles for his benefit.

'Oh, that's good, I'd hate to think I caused a rift between

you and Tam. It wasn't what I intended, I thought I owed you the truth, that's all.'

Bullshit. It took some effort not to say the word out loud. Simon's little ploy had gained him exactly the outcome he'd hoped for. The problem was, even though she knew Simon had manipulated her, she couldn't bring herself to forgive Tam. If she were going to survive out here, she needed a potent ally. And if Tam wasn't it, then maybe Simon might be the next best thing.

She knew she was going to listen to what he had to say. Even though every fibre of her being screamed to get away from him—that he was poison—the logical part of her brain was overriding it, telling her Simon was a strong contender. Ever since her trust in Tam had been broken into a million pieces, that compelling voice was becoming louder and louder. It was getting easier to ignore the irrational voice that told her it wasn't right to give up on Tam, that she should stick to her agreed alliance, no matter what.

Perhaps, given better circumstances and timing, something might well have flourished between her and Tam, but it was the nature of the game they were playing. Sea-Quest always ended up stripping away all excess emotions, exposing human qualities for all their naked corruption. Breaking down both weak and strong relationships. There'd been a connection with Tam, she'd felt it growing. But it would've taken a superhuman effort to maintain that connection on the outside. It was better this way, to end it now, quick and clean.

'What do you want really, Simon?' She dropped all pretence at pleasantness. Her temper was wearing thin. This game was wearing thin.

His smarmy smile disappeared.

'As you can see, I won exemption today.' He expanded his chest toward her and dangled the parody of a parrot in her face. 'So you won't be voting for me tonight, no matter how much you might've wanted to.'

'What makes you think I was going to?' she said with a sneer.

'Oh, I'm pretty sure you and Alisha and Tam would've been gunning for me. That's why it was so important I win today.'

Simon was right on target. Or he would've been three days ago. It was true, she and Alisha and Tam *had* been desperate to get him out and get themselves to the top three.

Oh, how quickly things changed.

'So what are you suggesting, Simon?'

'I have a plan. You and me, Cilla. We'd make quite the team. We could definitely make it to top three together. You're a strong woman, capable of winning almost any physical knockout. You have a sharp mind, but keep it carefully hidden, flying under the radar if you like. And best of all, people *like* you. Hell, even I like you.'

'All those traits you've listed could also make me a solid threat for the million. A good excuse for you to keep me close. Let me be quite frank, Simon. I *don't* like you. So stop trying to butter me up with your flattery, because it won't work.'

Simon took a step backward as if she'd physically slapped him.

'I see the real Cilla is finally making an appearance.' He raised his arm in a mock salute. 'And shooting from the hip too. Well, let me tell you something. You don't have to like me, Cilla, to form an alliance with me.' He enunciated every syllable of the last sentence, driving the words into her head.

She didn't answer, afraid of what she might say or do. All she really wanted was to turn on her heel and march out of the jungle. Away from Simon and all his backstabbing and conniving. Away from this game and the emotions it was dredging up. Emotions she'd tried to bury deep. Dark, twisting emotions, too much like her father's manipulative ways. How could she ever have known coming onto this island would be so fraught with emotional land-mines? She almost wished she could change her mind, be whisked away, back to the safety of her life on her yacht.

But she was too much of a realist to let that wish linger more than a second. She was here now, and she needed to save her boat if she ever wanted that lifestyle back, so she'd have to deal with the repercussions of what she was about to do.

Simon spoke into the silence, 'Tam has already showed he's untrustworthy. You can't possibly be thinking of keeping the alliance with him now?'

Instead of answering his question, she asked one of her own. 'What about Alisha, where does she fit into all this?'

'That's up to you, Cilla. But remember one thing. I'm not asking her to come to final with me. I'm asking you.'

So Alisha would have to be discarded too. Cilla knew it was an inevitable outcome, after all, there could only ever be one winner. But Simon would want someone weak in the top three with him. Someone like Rosa.

Their dream had been for all of them, Alisha, Tam and her, to be in the top three.

And they could still do it, if Cilla didn't waver.

'I'll need to think about it first, Simon. I'll let you know before we go to the conclave, don't worry.'

'Just so you know, if you don't agree, I'll be talking to Rosa. She'll be more than happy to help me vote Tam out.' Cilla knew Rosa would be eager to vote anyone out as long as it wasn't herself on the chopping block. 'But I'd rather be sitting next to you in the top three.'

The part that neither of them mentioned, the issue they skirted around the edges of, was what would happen if and when they made to the final three. Simon, with all of his testosterone fuelled ego, obviously thought he'd played a stronger game and people were more likely to vote for him than Cilla. She wasn't so sure of that.

She needed time to figure out why Simon was so determined to form an alliance with her. Rosa was as equally good a choice; perhaps better, shy and retiring, definitely someone who was flying under the radar. People might be less likely to vote for her as the winner if they thought she'd only ridden on other people's coat tails, instead of playing her own game. Simon, on the other hand, had been a very strong and visible player, treading on lots of people's toes on his path to the top.

And that led to the other burning question she needed an answer to. What if they voted Tam off and he came back from Deception Cove? They didn't know when—or even if—someone would be returned. If it were him who returned, he'd hate her guts. She'd have an enemy for life.

She'd gotten no closer to figuring that question out yet, and now here she was sitting at the conclave, still unsure of what she should do. She glanced down the line of seated team members, trying to gauge everyone's moods.

Alisha was sitting at the furthest end, but she caught Cilla's eye and gave a conspiratorial wink.

She and Alisha had gone off to do some snorkelling after the challenge. It'd become their thing to go together and sit on the rock ledge and gossip. Enjoying each other's company. Cilla had spilled the whole sordid story out to Alisha, while she sat there, chubby hands clasped in her lap, and listened. The story of how Tam and Simon had seen her naked and how they'd kept it a secret for so long. How Simon had finally confided in her on the prize and plunder knockout.

There was one part she kept secret, the fact Simon wanted to take her to the final three, expanding her tale to make it sound like Simon wanted to join their alliance instead.

After Cilla had finally wound to a halt, out of words to explain Tam's betrayal and out of breath from speaking so fast, Alisha only had one question for her. She said, 'Do you want to vote Tam out tonight? Do you want to break our alliance?'

Cilla hadn't been able to find the words to form an answer then.

Now, sitting at the conclave, Cilla knew what she had to do. It was for her own self-preservation, for her own sanity. She hoped she'd have the strength to write his name down on that piece of parchment. She gave a slow nod to Alisha, who twitched her mouth up in a wry grimace of acknowledgment.

* * *

'It's time to vote.' At the sound of JJ's voice, Tam broke his contemplation. Alisha stirred next to him and got up from her seat, making her way over the spindly bridge to cast her ballot.

'Wow, Tam, your firebrand just blew out.' He turned around to look. His firebrand had gone out. It felt like an ice blade had been drawn down his spine. The hair on the back of his neck stood up. He didn't believe in black cats or walking under ladders or any other such signs.

Then why did his guts feel as if they were twisting into a thousand knots?

He put on his best phoney smile and gave a nonchalant shrug. 'I hope that isn't an omen, JJ.'

He saw Cilla turn around and glance at the dark firebrand. She flinched when she saw it. Her reaction hit Tam like a punch to the solar plexus.

She wouldn't look at him. It'd been two days now. He wanted to grab her by the arms and shake her, force her gaze to his so he could tell her over and over again how sorry he was. But every time he'd approached her, that cold, unflinching stare stopped him in his tracks. Why had he let Simon talk him into keeping that secret? And why had it mattered so much to her? She'd blown it all out of proportion, as if she were using it as an excuse to break their friendship.

That strange prickling sensation at the back of his neck wouldn't go away. Alisha had assured him their alliance was strong, that they were voting for Hayden tonight. Of course he couldn't ask Cilla to reassure him, but she'd stick to their plan. Right? There was no reason to doubt either Cilla or Alisha.

Why then was there a niggling doubt at the back of his mind? Was it his imagination, or had Alisha's smile been a little too bright as she made her declaration that it'd be Hayden tonight?

Simon had agreed the old team Dawnbreakers should stay together to get rid of all the old Nightrebels first. But Tam didn't trust Simon one bit. Could Simon be out to get him tonight? Tam couldn't see how Simon would manage to pull off a coup like that, even if he'd been able to make an alliance with Hayden and Rosa. Tam would be protected by Alisha and Cilla.

He hoped it wouldn't come down to a tied vote.

'Tam, your turn.' He nodded at JJ and made the treacherous crossing over the bridge.

As he sat down again, he shot his gaze skywards, thankful it wasn't raining yet. Dark thunderheads were rolling across the sky, obscuring the moon with their agitated fury. The rising wind tore at his clothing. It was no wonder his firebrand had flamed out, the gusts were reaching fever pitch. Why had no one else's firebrand been extinguished, though?

'Let's tally the votes,' said JJ, placing the wooden chest on the table with reverence.

'The first vote is for… Tam.' JJ's face showed little emotion as he held out the parchment for them all to see. It had his name on it. A weight like a heavy stone settled in the middle of Tam's stomach.

'The second vote is for… Hayden.' Whew. Tam threw him a glance laden with solidarity. They were brothers in arms now, both on the chopping block. He liked Hayden, he really did. The whippet-like man had a quick smile and a straightforward manner that put everyone at ease. This vote was nothing personal.

'The third vote is for… Tam.' Uh oh. Not good. It looked as if Simon might be playing his cards after all. Tam made himself take a calming breath, trying to quieten the pulsing throb that had suddenly started in his veins.

'That's two votes for Tam and one for Hayden,' said JJ. Tam watched as he reached in and pulled out another folded parchment. JJ turned it around so they could all see. 'That makes three votes for Tam and one for Hayden.'

Now it wasn't merely a stone sitting in Tam's stomach, it felt as though his guts had been removed and flipped inside out. He could feel sweat beading his upper lip. Simon had got Rosa and Hayden on his side, that much was obvious. He'd be okay, the next two votes would be for Hayden. It'd be a tie. A tie he could handle. He could beat Hayden in just about any knockout JJ might throw their way. Except a tight-rope walk, perhaps.

'The thirteenth person voted off Sea-Quest is... Tam.' Lack of understanding made Tam slow to react. What had JJ said? 'Bring over your firebrand, Tam.' He stood, legs moving stiff and jerky, like a robot. How could this have happened?

'The team has voted,' JJ intoned as he went through the motions of putting out Tam's already snuffed firebrand. 'You'll be going to Deception Cove, where you'll have a chance to get back into this game.' JJ pointed to the exit that led away and down, toward the left of the stage. Tam moved mechanically through the noose doorway and down the stairs.

It was only then it dawned on him. Alisha and Cilla had deceived him. Let him down. Thrown him into the lion's den.

He turned around. Both women watched him. Alisha stared back at him, plump face emotionless, hands folded neatly in her lap. Cilla's green eyes were glazed with tears, but her mouth was set in a stubborn tilt. Who was it?

Who'd double-crossed him? Blindsided him? Was it Cilla or Alisha? Or both of them?

How could he not have seen this coming? He should've realized how deeply he'd hurt Cilla. So deeply she felt the need to wound him, to take the ultimate revenge. He'd cared more about his own feelings than hers, and that'd made him blind. Blind to his own downfall.

'It's time to go, Tam.' JJ gave a light touch to his shoulder, urging him to head off the stage.

A magnificent rage built in Tam's gut as he descended the stairs. It burned and fizzed through his veins, so he almost believed his vision had been overlaid with a red tinge. He let his fury build, let it carry him outside on a flood of agony. His anger would help him fight his way home from Deception. Because that's what he meant to do. He'd be back.

Try as he might, however, his resentment wouldn't completely obliterate the sorrow that tempered his wrath. Tightness clutched at his throat. There'd be no chance to redeem himself with Cilla now.

He'd lost something priceless.

CHAPTER FIFTEEN

Little wavelets lapped gently around Cilla's ribs. She sat alone in the shallow azure water, staring out into the Gulf of Thailand. Absent-mindedly she picked at the scabs on her knees. Bug bites she'd scratched that had turned into sores. The bites covered her whole body, but she'd just about learned to ignore the itching by now.

She must look a sight. Hair unwashed and bedraggled, so dry it was like straw when she ran her hands through it. Skin blotchy and red, pockmarked with angry welts and insect bites. And if the other team members were anything to go by, she must smell pretty bad too. Thirty-three days with only one proper shower and the grime was becoming so ingrained it'd take her days of cleansing to get rid of it. Scrubbing with sand was no alternative to a good old-fashioned piece of soap. Her clothes were just about falling off her. Apart from the fact she'd lost quite a bit of weight from her already thin frame, her clothing was ripped and torn and soiled.

Running a hand gingerly over the scar on her forehead, she wondered what it looked like. They didn't have the luxury of a mirror in camp, and while it didn't bother her out here, she pondered if the scar would remain obvious. A permanent reminder of her time on the island. It might be the only outward scar she received from her time on Sea-Quest, but there would be many more, equally deep scars, remaining hidden inside.

Her musings returned to the conclave last night. The night she'd helped vote Tam off. She'd made the right decision, the logical voice kept confirming in her head. Why then did her heart feel as if it'd been dragged through the mud? She felt as dirty on the inside as she was on the outside.

It'd been a struggle to get out of the shelter this morning. Everyone else was already up and off, doing their own morning ablutions by the time she roused, which was unusual. Cilla was nearly always the first person out of bed, often before the sun had turned the horizon from indigo to pink.

She hadn't slept well, tossing and turning all night, much to the ire of her fellow team members. Her dreams had been filled with the look on Tam's face as he heard his name being called last night. She knew he'd be angry and thought she'd shored up those walls around her soul high enough to withstand any onslaught. But she'd not been ready for his mute, unqualified disbelief. Then he'd turned around and the recognition in his eyes he'd been betrayed speared right through her.

Simon's unrivaled delight as they walked back to camp hadn't helped one bit, either.

This morning she tried to recall the terrible rage that'd taken hold for Tam the night he fought with her. Tried to reinstate the fierce justification she'd known when she voted him out. Somehow today, though, her indignation felt hollow, and...tainted.

She wouldn't let her mind admit that she missed Tam, because that'd be conceding defeat. Her body, however, was a different matter. When Tam had been around, he was a constant distraction, his presence a beacon for her awareness. Her body was so finely attuned to his, it'd react instantly to the slightest brush of his arm or the bump of a shoulder, igniting immediately into a flash-fire of heat and desire.

Now he was gone, there was no chance of the fire being ignited anymore. In its place was left a bone-rending ache, a resonating sense of loss she'd never felt before.

She told herself she'd endure this, these feelings would pass sooner rather than later. It was better this way, to survive on her own. She didn't need a man. Certainly not when they all turned out to be heartless betrayers. Even the best of them turned out to be just like her father in the long run, and she was better off without any of them.

She'd needed to vote Tam out, so she could go on and win the money. That was what was important to her now. Her grandmother's future, not some vague chance at a love affair that was destined to fizzle out as soon as she got back to reality.

Slamming the palm of her hand down on the surface of the water, she punctuated her determination to continue playing this game to the best of her ability.

And she'd do it minus Tam.

* * *

Tam awoke and stretched, the unfamiliar hardness of the bamboo poles beneath his body making him sit straight up in alarm. It took a few seconds to remember where he was.

Deception Cove.

A grey shape lying next to him grew arms and legs, rolled over and yawned. It was Cho. The two of them were sharing a rather small shelter in a very basic campsite, with none of the luxuries Tam was used to at the Moonrakers' camp. There were no pillows or mosquito nets or hammocks here, just a blanket each. He should be used to it by now; this was his third night out here. For some reason, his brain didn't want to accept its fate. He'd been sent to Deception Cove. His alliance was shattered, and he'd have to fight with every ounce of his remaining strength to get back into the game. If he didn't make it, he'd become the fourth member of the panel. But that was no compensation as far as he was concerned. It might even be worse than having to leave the game altogether, having to vote for one of those people who'd betrayed him would be more than he could handle.

The night he'd arrived at Deception in complete and utter blackness, he'd been more than pleased to find it was Cho asleep in the shelter. Cho had greeted him with a sleepy grunt, moving over only marginally to let him in and then falling asleep again within a few breaths.

The following morning Cho more than made up for his apathy, giving Tam a sincere hug of welcome and then grilling him for every little detail of the goings on at Moonrakers' beach. He'd been as shocked as Tam at Alisha and Cilla's backstabbing tactics.

Tam had been very careful not to mention how deep his connection with Cilla had become. How his hands still trembled when he thought about how easy it'd been for her to deceive him. She'd returned from the voting table cool as a cucumber, nothing in her demeanour led him to suspect she'd just written his name on that piece of paper. But he knew as soon as he let down his guard, let despair creep in, his carefully schooled guise would crumble. He had to keep fighting the urge to bury his head in his hands, to smash his fist into the nearest tree, to walk down that beach and never come back. To give in. Somehow he'd have to learn to bottle up his despair, his devastation. He'd use those emotions, turn them around to make him tougher and more dogged in his determination to win this game. Just to show her he could.

So Tam had listened with seeming rapture as Cho reciprocated, filling him in on how life was at Deception Cove, and how he'd beat the other four team members who'd been sent to Deception.

Staring out over the small beach this morning, Tam watched the breakers as they rolled across the reef and into the protection of the lagoon. Puffs of white clouds sat on the horizon, looking like so many scattered balls of cotton wool. The ocean was still dark cobalt blue, not yet touched by the sun's rays. It'd be a good day, hot and dry, with no sign of the torrential tropical rain that often came to turn their lives into a living hell.

The thought brought him up sharp. He'd been out here so long now it was becoming second nature to forecast the weather. Funny, he'd never cared much for the meteorological conditions living in LA. But on the island, every nuance in temperature, every slight wind change could mean a great day, or an unbearable one.

Life was a lot simpler here on Deception. The knockouts happened on the same day as the exemption knockouts on the main island. The only difference was, on Deception the castaways knew who'd been voted off in the last tribal.

The others at camp had no idea who was going to come back and haunt them in the end.

'It's knockout day,' said Cho, his muffled voice coming from beneath his armpit.

'That it is my friend.' Tam stepped down onto the sand, letting the coolness surround his toes.

'It's going to be a perfect day.'

'Mmm hmm,' replied Cho.

That was typical of a conversation between the two of them. Neither of them was really much for long drawn out chats, and it suited them both fine if they only said a few words to each other all day. Tam remembered Cho had been so full of self-importance and a desperate need to win when he'd first arrived on the island. Cho had been at Deception for two weeks now, fought and won in four other knockouts. His time out in the wilderness had pared away those more abrasive traits, to reveal Cho's innate intelligence and a calmer, more likable person. They'd developed an easy friendship. Companionship didn't always require a barrage of words to work well. Together they sat in silence and surveyed the scene from the shelter. The show's motto came back to Tam, *between deception and survival lies redemption.* Well today, he was definitely praying for redemption.

* * *

Cilla's gaze was fixed on the crackling orange blaze of the dying campfire, but she didn't see the flames flickering in front of her, such was her turmoil over the night's events. She could hear the murmurs of the other three talking amongst themselves. She tuned them out, their voices becoming a blur of white noise in her head.

Alisha was gone.

Simon had conspired to vote her off and now he and Hayden and Rosa were all sitting there congratulating themselves. Her stomach churned, and she thought she might be physically sick. Since Tam's ousting, the Moonrakers had splintered, no one trusted anyone else anymore. The game was taking too many wrong turns, spiralling out of Cilla's control, and she didn't like it one bit.

Alisha's loss hit Cilla like a fist smashing her to the ground. She'd not seen it coming. They'd been too worried Simon might be going to turn on Cilla, and not really considered any other option.

The chilly night pressed against her back, the fading embers only lending subtle warmth to her feet and knees. Suddenly she felt so alone. Alisha's exit brought home Tam's loss even more. It brought home how much Tam had been her mainstay, her confidant, someone to watch over her. But more than that, he'd been a friend, and then ultimately, a lover. She yearned for his body next to hers, to feel his strong heartbeat beneath her fingers. It'd been three days since he'd gone and the lost feeling, the idea there was a gaping hole inside her chest was becoming worse with the passing of time, not better, as she'd hoped.

'Alisha should take it as a compliment,' Cilla heard Simon say.

'What did you say?' she snarled at him.

'You heard me.' Cilla caught the gleam of Simon's teeth in the firelight. 'She should take it as a compliment. Alisha was the prime threat, so she was the one who had to go tonight. You can't be that upset, Cilla. It was either her, or you.' Simon had whispered something identical to her on the walk back from the conclave. She guessed that in his own twisted way he was trying to tell her he was still sticking to their agreement, that they'd make it to the final together, without letting on to either Hayden or Rosa. It was obvious he'd spun them all a story along similar lines to keep them voting with him.

He made her sick. This whole game was making her sick.

'Look at it this way, we should all be celebrating. We made it to the top four. That has to be an achievement in itself.'

'Whatever.' Cilla didn't want to listen to any more of his rhetoric. She turned her back on the other three and the fire. It was possibly the wrong thing to do, she might get Hayden and Rosa offside with her cold aloofness, but right now she didn't care.

Hayden was being more than a little sanctimonious at the moment anyway, unable to stop bragging about winning this latest exemption knockout. It was out of character for the Hayden she'd gotten to know in the past few days. She'd come to enjoy Hayden's company. They seemed to click somehow. He'd always been likable and easy-going, but with less team members around, she'd come to understand him better. Out of the four of them, she had the most in common with Hayden. Rosa was friendly, if slightly reserved, and now they were the only two women left, there was a definite bond of girls-only camaraderie. But the friendship was still hesitant and newly minted. And Simon. Well, she was staying as far away from Simon as she could.

Yep, Hayden really was a genuinely nice guy—when he wasn't bragging about winning exemption that was. If he'd been a little too overattentive toward her once or twice, Cilla had ignored it. Perhaps she'd even welcomed his friendly flirtations, in an inadvertent way. Because she missed Tam so much, it was nice to feel wanted. But after this last win at exemption, Cilla decided she might have to re-evaluate how she viewed Hayden.

For today's knockout, the five of them had been led to a clearing many miles inland, right in the centre of very dense jungle, to a pit of black mud. Gluggy, oozing volcanic mud. The knockout was to see who could carry the most mud from the pit to a large wooden barrel twenty-five metres away, using only their bodies in the space of five minutes. The mud was then weighed at the end. JJ had called this knockout, *pay the ferryman*, and he'd told them they should think of their bodies as the ferry and the mud as their cargo.

She had to laugh once they were all slathered with the black goo. They resembled some kind of demented mud monster conjured from the depths of a sci-fi movie, all lumpy and misshapen, with eyes and teeth the only recognisable features. She'd not seen such a silly knockout in her total time on the island.

But at the end, somehow Hayden just managed to tip the scales with a mere one hundred and three grams of mud more than the rest of them.

The conversation she'd had with Alisha after the knockout kept repeating itself in Cilla's mind. Cilla had popped up onto the rocks to take a rest after catching fish after fish, sitting next to the other woman whose black skin shone with droplets where Cilla had splashed her as she got out of the water.

'Do you think we made a mistake voting off Tam?' Alisha's frank question caught her unawares.

'I really hope not.'

'So do I. I know he hurt you and I know we would've needed to get rid of him, eventually.' Alisha fixed Cilla with one of her sharp stares, meant to skewer her to the spot, intent on speaking her mind. 'He was too much of a strong player to keep around forever. But it rankles me that we had to break our alliance. I would've liked for all of us to go to top three.'

Cilla knew she owed Alisha. And it was only now that Cilla would admit when she'd asked Alisha to choose her over Tam, it probably hadn't been fair. But then again, who was to say what was fair or not in this game.

What would Alisha say to Tam if he was still at Deception Cove when she got there? Would she tell him she was sorry? That they shouldn't have voted him out. Or would she tell him the truth? That it was Cilla's idea to get rid of him. The thought hadn't struck her before, and she spent many minutes rolling that one over and over in her mind. If it were her going to Deception, would she be ready to apologize to Tam? The answer would be a resounding yes. She knew she regretted sending him to Deception. She might even tell him it was by far the stupidest move she'd made throughout the whole game. But would he believe her?

CHAPTER SIXTEEN

The dense jungle closed in around him, claustrophobic and cloying. It was as hot as Hades in here, not a murmur of a breeze to stir the mid-afternoon air. Sweat soaked Tam's shirt and formed great dark patches under his arms and down his front. His newly grown beard itched like crazy, but it did have one saving grace, it kept the bugs away from his face. Hordes of tiny gnats swirled around his head and no matter how much he swished them away, they floated back again to torture him with their faint buzzing. It almost made him miss the barren little cove of Deception. At least it didn't close in on a person, trying to drown them in the compressed tropical humidity.

He was nearly there. Soon he'd be able to dive into the cool azure water and sluice off all this damned sweat. A tunnel of light beckoned him onwards, promising an end to his jungle ordeal. He frowned. They wouldn't be expecting him. How would they react?

JJ had made him trek to the campsite the long way round, through the jungle trails, rather than sending him on a swifter—and much cooler—boat. He said he wanted the rest of the team to be caught unawares.

Clamping his teeth together, Tam trudged on. The people on the beach wouldn't welcome him with open arms, of that much he was sure. He didn't care. What other people thought of him no longer factored into his plan, their reactions to him wouldn't even cause a blip on his radar anymore. It was a solemn promise he'd made himself this morning, after he beat Alisha at the last knockout. He was here for one reason only, and that was to win.

It'd been a shock to see Alisha arrive last night.

A tiny pinprick of light had heralded her arrival, accompanied by the hum and clunk of a boat's engine impinging on the night's silence. He'd been trying to fall asleep in the shelter, with little success. Cho had gone earlier in the day, and it was odd not to have a familiar presence nearby.

Tam had beaten Cho at the knockout and then spent the afternoon in solitary contemplation.

Alisha bumbled her way up to the camp, with only one tiny torch to light her way. He'd embraced her with an affectionate hug. But it was clouded with bittersweet emotions; pleasure at having a friend back, sorrow that she'd been voted out, and a growing anger. Anger directed at Cilla. She must've orchestrated Alisha's departure in much the same way as his own.

It didn't matter how hard Alisha tried to convince him that Cilla had nothing to do with her demise; he was sure it wasn't true. Cilla had become public enemy number one, and nothing anyone said would change his mind. He didn't even care enough to ask the question as to whether Alisha had voted for him on that fateful night as well. It no longer mattered.

The second Alisha had left Deception after he'd beaten her in the knockout, he'd made his resolution; to win at all costs, and everyone else could bloody well go to hell.

In front of him the tunnel of dark glossy leaves opened up, revealing the beach. Light rebounded from the white sand, almost blinding him after the dimness of the jungle. Slowing his pace, he allowed his eyes to adjust for a few seconds. He didn't want to be at any kind of disadvantage when he appeared.

With quiet footsteps, he walked onto the rear of the beach, coming into sight of the Moonrakers' campsite.

Rosa was sitting by the fire, stirring the pot with a stick, cooking up rice for lunch. Simon was sitting next to her, his back to Tam. He could hear the murmur of voices, but couldn't discern what they were saying. Rosa didn't notice him at first, so engrossed was she with her conversation. Perhaps a movement caught her eye as he started forward again, because she looked up sharply, her discussion cut short when she stopped mid-sentence, to stare at him.

'Tam! What...' Simon twisted around at her exclamation.

Both of them gaped at him, open-mouthed.

Simon recovered first. 'Tam. Welcome back, buddy.' He stood up and came toward him, hand extended. Tam ignored it, striding past him toward the fire. No more false platitudes for him.

'Surprise,' he said, his tone mocking and cold. 'I'm sure you weren't expecting *me*, huh?'

'Well, we weren't sure who... I mean we didn't—'

'No, I know you didn't,' Tam replied curtly, as his gaze swept the rest of the campsite. He wouldn't relax until everyone knew he'd returned. Until he'd shown everyone he meant business.

'Hayden and Cilla have gone to the little bay to catch some crabs. They should be back soon,' Rosa said, still wary. She hadn't offered him her hand or a hug to welcome him home, catching his mood better than Simon.

'Great.' Tam shrugged and sat down next to the fire, hiding the flash of white-hot emotion that burned through him. Why did his blood boil at the thought of Cilla alone with Hayden? *I don't care anymore.* He repeated the mantra in his head a dozen times before the fizz of jealousy dissipated.

Both Rosa and Simon shared an indecipherable look before Rosa said, 'I guess I'd better add some more rice for lunch then.' Tam just nodded. He wouldn't admit he was starving, that he'd had less food at Deception than they received here. He wasn't going to reveal anything about Deception that he didn't have to. Less information given meant more power to him.

After a few bumbling attempts at trying to include Tam in small-talk, which Tam ignored, Rosa and Simon rebounded to their previous conversation, leaving him to stare at the fire in contemplation.

After half an hour, as Rosa was just about to serve the rice into coconut shells, voices could be heard drifting over the sand. Hayden and Cilla were coming. All three of them stood up to await the other pair's arrival. Simon couldn't hide a slight smirk.

At first the pair didn't register there was a third person standing by the fire, so deep in conversation were they. He allowed himself one swift glance to drink in Cilla as she walked and talked. She wore her orange sports bikini with an unbuttoned long sleeve shirt draped over her shoulders, looking as fresh and sunny and stunning as if she'd just stepped out of a fashion swimwear magazine. Her limbs had gone even more golden in the tropical sun, her hair pulled back in a jaunty ponytail that flicked across her shoulders. And she was smiling and laughing along with Hayden. She looked happy. For him the effect was immediate; a tightness in his chest radiated to a low pull from somewhere down in his abdomen—his body recognizing her presence.

Tam's glance shot over to Hayden and he noticed he was bare-chested with a hessian bag slung over his shoulder, flashing his convivial smile toward Cilla often as they talked. He moved with cat-like grace, his body hard and athletic. He was obviously suited to this castaway lifestyle. Their banter was relaxed and sociable, two friends at ease in each other's company. How things had changed since he'd gone. Hayden had barely registered on Cilla's radar four days ago when he'd been voted out. Now look at them. A person would almost think they were best of buddies. The thought burned like a hot iron had been placed inside Tam's ribcage.

Hayden looked up first and stopped dead in his tracks. Tam hardly registered Hayden's reaction, his gaze was fixed on Cilla. Waiting.

It was with a stubborn sort of gratitude he watched her eyes widen when she saw him.

'Tam!' She took a few faltering steps toward him and then paused, unsure. 'You made it back.'

'Yes, I did.' It took every ounce of willpower not to go up and take her in his arms. He wanted to. So badly. A flicker of acknowledgement passed, shadow-like, through her eyes. Her hands fluttered upwards as if of their own accord. Reaching for him? Regret, or was it contrition, showed in the downturn of her mouth, the squeeze of the lines above her eyebrows. Then the emotion was gone as she lowered her palms and closed her eyelids.

'So, Alisha's gone then?' She re-opened her eyes and stared at him. Of course. That was the emotion he'd seen flick over her face. Sorrow at Alisha's loss. It'd nothing to do with him returning. It wasn't sorrow for what she'd done to him. She was the enemy, he must keep reminding himself of that fact.

'We knew someone must be coming back soon,' said Hayden, breaking their mute, glaring stalemate.

'And there was a good chance it was going to be you,' he added, very matter of fact. 'Welcome, Tam. I'm glad to see you.' Hayden strode over and offered his hand. This time Tam took it and was rewarded with an absolutely sincere handshake. 'This should make the game even more interesting.' He gave Tam one of the genial smiles he'd been bestowing on Cilla only a minute before.

'Come on then, let's get these crabs in the pot, I'm starving. We caught plenty, more than enough to go around.' Tam watched as Hayden chivvied Rosa to get some seawater to boil the crabs. The man was pretty much an open book. He'd undeniably meant what he said, Tam could feel it through the warmth of his handshake. Goddammit, why was Hayden so bloody…likable.

Tam sat down next to the fire. His manifestation in the camp had set the air buzzing with tension. It'd set them all into deep thought, he could see it in their distracted faces, weighing up old friendships, broken promises.

Good. It was good they were unbalanced. Maybe he

could use it to his advantage.

He watched Cilla waver as she stood first on one foot and then the other, finally heading over to the shelter to stow the snorkeling gear, awkward and stilted in her movements, glancing backward at him more than a few times as she went. He gave a grim smile. Let her be on edge, chary of him. That's the way it should be from now on.

* * *

Another knockout day was upon them. Cilla rubbed the sleep from her eyes. Dawn had long since broken the grey sky, revolving through purple, then pink, and then daylight had intruded with its dazzling glare. She'd stayed in bed, pretending to remain asleep underneath the warmth of the blanket. In truth, not wanting to face Tam over the morning campfire. Would he even acknowledge her presence today? With a grunt, she sat up, wrapping the blanket around her shoulders. She was about to find out.

'We've got mail from Davy.' Rosa appeared out of the jungle.

'Great. Let's hope it gives us a clue to our next knockout,' said Hayden. 'Cilla, are you gonna get up anytime soon? We want to read this now.'

'Yep, coming,' she replied, hauling her bottom over the lumpy bamboo floor. Tiny goose bumps raised on her arms and legs as she left the warmth of the blanket. The morning air was cooler than usual.

Tam was already there, standing next to Rosa, looking with interest at the parchment she held in her hand. Cilla kept her head down, not daring to make eye contact, unprepared for his imperturbable scrutiny yet. Simon was wending a course back from the shoreline. Rosa waited until they were all huddled next to the fire before she unrolled the paper and read it aloud.

Cilla tried hard to listen to the words, but her gaze kept sliding sideways toward Tam. Because she dared not look up at his face, her scrutiny slid to his feet instead. Tanned on top from the tropical sun, toes dug slightly into the sand, wide enough to keep his lofty frame standing tall and straight, broad shoulders squared. They were nice looking feet, generous and strong, just like Tam.

'Sounds as if it's going to be about knots and puzzles,' said Simon, dragging her away from the edge of distraction.

'We need to have some breakfast. The boats will come soon.' Tam was practical, as always.

'I'll get some water,' Cilla volunteered. Anything to keep her away from the camp.

Trudging along the path to the well, her thoughts kept returning to Tam. She'd wanted him to return, had wished for it. And here he was. But he wasn't the same Tam who had left four nights ago. This Tam was altered. Cold and grey as steel, unsmiling and unforgiving. Did she blame him? Not really. She shouldn't have expected anything different.

There was so much she wanted to, needed to, tell him. How sorry she was for a start. After three days, she'd finally concluded he hadn't deserved to be voted out. The ferocious anger she'd felt at his disloyalty had faded. Enough for her to realize she'd made a big mistake in breaking their alliance.

Simon was still hinting he'd like to take her to the top and she'd not disavowed him of that possibility, but somewhere deep inside there was a growing resistance to his sick little alliance. It wasn't a decision she'd intentionally made, rather a perception her unconscious moral compass had formed without her permission. She kept trying to justify the fact she'd do anything for a million dollars, but the certainty that this wasn't strictly true wouldn't leave her.

She'd never really thought of herself as a particularly ethical person before; she did what needed to be done to survive, nothing more, nothing less. This was a new idea, one that wanted to move the goalposts of how she was supposed to live her life, and she wasn't sure how to deal with it.

Tam was right, the boat arrived for them within the hour, as they were tidying up from breakfast. Cilla stood right in the bow of the narrow wooden craft watching their island slide by on the left, the water blue and perfect on her right, enjoying the motion of the ship as it dipped over the small swell. Oh, how she missed her yacht. She imagined herself alone in the cockpit, tiller in hand, mainsail and jib bulging with a strong northerly. The feel of the power of wind and waves thrumming through the boat's hull as if it were a living thing. The vibration feeding into her body, setting her mouth to laughing and her heart thudding in her chest. That was what it was to be free.

A quiet introspection had settled over the boat. The others were scattered at the edges of the deck, all lost in their own thoughts, using this as a time of contemplation. JJ, perched on the wooden bench that ran the width of the stern, watched them all with his paternal gaze.

Too quickly they rounded the rocky point of land and there was the beach where most of the knockouts were held. JJ was first out of the boat, leading them all up the slope of the white sand. As he walked, he let them take their initial look at the course they'd be negotiating today. Cilla viewed the five wooden towers, interlaced with a spiderweb of ropes and the small table at the bottom of each tower. It didn't look too complicated today.

'Don't be fooled by appearances,' said JJ, as if reading her mind. 'This is going to be a tricky knockout, requiring your mind to be at its peak.' He waited until they all stood on the mat before he said, 'For this knockout you'll need all your mental faculties, but as you all know this experience out here isn't only brutal on your body physically, but mentally as well. The lack of food and clean water will have dulled your deduction skills.'

There were murmurings of agreement within the small team.

'You're down to the final five. Single exemption is vitally important. Whoever wins today is guaranteed a spot in the final four.'

'You said it, JJ,' Simon spoke from his spot at the rear of the mat. 'This is going to make or break someone today.' Even though Simon was right, Cilla couldn't look at him; couldn't look at the arrogant twist to his mouth or how he stood with legs apart as if he owned the whole beach. Funny, but for some reason she'd not been able to raise any enthusiasm for the knockout today. She hadn't wanted to get on that boat and her feet had dragged up the sandy spit. Now, with Simon's self-important statement thrust in her face, a sudden fierce desire to beat him swept through her. He wouldn't win exemption if she had anything to do with it.

'Today you'll need to weave your way through a rope

maze, untying knots as you go and collecting bags of puzzle pieces. When you get to the end of the rope with all your bags, you need to put together the words in your puzzle to make a well-known phrase. The first to complete the puzzle correctly wins exemption.' Cilla listened to JJ's speech, a thrill of excitement buzzing through her. Of course, Hayden had mentioned it on the beach this morning, but she'd been too interested in Tam's feet. This knockout was all about knots.

And she knew a lot about knots.

On JJ's command, everyone raced to their allotted tower and worked through the maze of ropes. There was a definite order to be followed, a start and a finish to the tangle of ropes and knots, and that was the hardest part to sort out. Once she worked out the direction she needed to go, the rest came as second nature.

The first couple of knots were easy, a bowline and then a double bowline. She undid those quickly and moved on. So did everyone else; they were simple knots, after all. She stopped checking on everyone else's progress after that and became lost in her own little world as a strange kind of calm descended; a gauze netting of cool logic that separated her from the rest of reality.

The next one was an ashley stopper knot, used to stop the end of a rope from slipping through a ring. It was a lot harder to undo than it looked. Unless you knew the trick. She released it with a flick of her thumb and forefinger.

There were other knots she recognized as she progressed through the course. An alpine butterfly loop. And the hardest of all, a chain splice with its myriad of intertwined loops. She disengaged them all with relative ease.

When Cilla reached the last knot and looked up, she was streaks ahead of everyone else. JJ urged her to take her bags to the table and start working on her puzzle. The bubble of calm remained with her, shielding her from the raucous grunts and yells of frustration from the other contestants.

The puzzle was tricky. Made up of perhaps fifty wooden pieces, it took her a while to fathom out the theme. Suddenly it hit her. The phrase she was trying to spell out. Yes, it had to be.

Between deception and survival lies redemption. The show's motto.

She raised her hand to beckon JJ over to check her puzzle.

He read the words on the puzzle out loud. 'You're a step closer to the million,' JJ pronounced, each word clear and concise, so the other contestants could hear. 'Cilla wins exemption.' Those were the sweetest words she'd ever thought to hear.

At last she lifted her head and looked around. Only Hayden had made it to the table with his puzzle pieces, the other three were still struggling with the knots. Not only had she beaten them, but she'd done it with comprehensive skill.

Her gaze skimmed over the others. Simon hit one of the wooden struts with his hand and muttered something inaudible as he made his ungainly way out of the maze. He was infuriated, probably madder at his own lack of progress than because she'd won, however. Hayden's forehead was creased with a deep frown, but when he caught Cilla's gaze she saw him sweep the sentiment away, replacing his frown with a wink in her direction.

He'd be annoyed at himself too, but much more gallant and self-effacing in defeat than Simon. Rosa was still trying to disentangle herself from the cobweb, so Cilla couldn't see her face. From the tense set of her jawline and her rigid backbone, she foretold the pixie-faced woman would be wearing a scowl as well.

Tam stood in the middle of his maze rope tower, unmoving, legs set wide apart, broad shoulders squared and tall. Staring at her. His normally kind mouth was set into a thin line, tawny eyes wide and focussed. On her. And only her. Not a single emotion was evident on his face. What was he thinking? Why was he staring at her? Then he gave an almost imperceptible nod in her direction, as if he were tipping his hat in recognition of a job well done. A corner of his mouth lifted for just a second in a half smile. Her heart fluttered like a trapped bird in her chest. It was the first hint of any other sentiment besides abhorrence he'd showed toward her since he'd returned. Was it a sign—albeit a very small one—he was softening? Even if it was her imagination running wild, she was going to take it, anyway.

'What a brilliant victory, Cilla,' said JJ. 'Come over here and claim your figurine.' A grin appeared of its own volition on her face, and for once she didn't seek to quash it. This was her first win. She deserved it.

The parrot was heavy as JJ handed it to her. She let her fingers come up to feel the smoothness of the feathers. Turning the stuffed bird, she took in its bright staring eyes and sharp black beak. It was possibly the ugliest thing she'd ever seen, but it wasn't what it looked like that meant so much; rather, it was what the sad looking rainbow bird represented. It infused Cilla with a daring sense of buoyancy. She was untouchable now.

As she walked toward the other four people standing on the mat, Hayden came out and gave her a pat on the back, smile broad and delighted.

'Well done, Cilla. You deserved that.'

'Thanks, Hayden.' She'd have to gain control over this silly grin that refused to leave her face, or they'd all start to think her quite mad.

Rosa touched her arm as they went to gather their belongings and get back on the boat. 'Congratulations. Those knots were so hard, I don't know how you did it so quick,' she said in her discreet manner. Simon added his praise in a voice gruff with self-recrimination. Only one person didn't raise his voice in compliment. But she knew. She'd seen it in his face for that split second. He was proud of her too. Her stomach tightened at the thought.

The boat trip to their beach was a blur of blue to Cilla. This bird changed everything. It put her in a position of power. How would she use that power?

'See you all at the conclave tonight.' JJ's words seemed to have an ominous quality as he spoke to them from the stern of the boat while it was pushed backward into the surf by one of the deckhands. 'Use your time this afternoon well. It'll be an interesting night.'

As she watched his boat get smaller and smaller on the spreading blue ocean, his words echoed in her head, and Cilla knew she had to get away. So she could think.

Simon pounced on her before she'd made it half-way to the camp.

'Cilla, I need to talk to you.' It'd started already. The mad scramble of everyone trying to re-align their votes; find the weakest link. Some people would go further than others to secure themselves a spot in the top four. It was odd to hear the note of uncertainty, of pleading in his voice. Odd, and just a bit satisfying. Simon wasn't used to being the one who had to ingratiate himself. Powerless.

'Yep. Give me a minute, Simon.' Cilla made a beeline for the perch that'd been set up over the roof of the shelter, where everyone sat the exemption figurine for all to see after they won. There it'd remain, as a reminder, until Cilla reclaimed it again for the walk to the conclave. There was only one person she really wanted to talk to. And he wouldn't seek her out, of that much she could be certain. She'd have to go find him, and she wasn't ready yet to start that conversation. First she needed some time to herself, to get everything straight in her head.

Simon hovered at the campfire, pretending to reignite it, but keeping an eagle eye on her. She let out a heavy sigh. How was she going to avoid him? She knew exactly what he was going to say, anyway. Tam had to be voted off for good this time. How dare he think he could come back from Deception Cove and usurp the rest of them! They'd worked hard to get where they were, and they didn't need someone who'd already been voted off once to return and put it all in jeopardy. Yep, it'd be Tam that Simon was gunning for tonight, of that she was certain. And he probably thought because she'd voted him off the first time, she'd be as responsive the second time round.

Hayden came up to stow his bag underneath the shelter. He draped an affectionate arm over her shoulder.

'You're going to be the centre of attention today, girl, you know.'

'Yes, I know,' she replied heavily. She didn't resent his light touch, it wasn't meant to be invasive or even persuasive. It was just Hayden. He was a charmer, that's for sure. But he also had a truly sincere heart. She was acutely aware of Tam's gaze falling hot and thick on her back. What did he think of her sudden closeness with Hayden?

'I'd like to know what you're thinking too.' He cast a sideways glance at the impatient Simon. 'But don't worry, I won't push you. If you don't want to talk, that's okay with me.'

'Thanks, Hayden. Soon. I'll come and talk to you shortly. I need a little time to myself first.'

'Understood.'

He let her go, and she headed toward the little track out the rear of the camp, miming to Simon that she needed to use the lavatory and she'd be back in a minute. Once in the cover of the jungle, though, she veered off on a tiny animal trail leading deeper into the island. Eventually Cilla came out onto the edge of a riverbed. Mostly it was dry and sandy, pale rounded rocks strewn in a haphazard manner. A thin river of water meandered its way through the middle, sometimes stopping to fill a small pool, at other times diving around rock piles or swishing through a bend.

Finding a large rock to perch on in the dappled shade of a tropical walnut, she rested her head on her knees and stared into the shallows of a wide puddle of murky water. As soon as she sat, a plume of little gnat-like flies descended and did slow circles around her head. She tried to ignore them.

What was she to do? Winning the exemption knockout was an unexpected boon, she'd never factored it into her plans before because she'd thought it unattainable. Until an hour ago her hold on Sea-Quest had been tenuous at best, reliant on how much she was prepared to abase herself to Simon. The thought of being deferential to Simon, to stroke his ego so he'd contemplate not getting rid of her had made her feel physically sick. Exemption meant she no longer needed to do that. She held the power now. But what to do with it? Should she use it to get rid of Simon, as she so desperately wanted to do? Or should she keep him there and get rid of Hayden?

The different permutations and consequences fought for their right to be heard in her mind and became so loud and bewildering she wanted to scream to release the tension. She leapt off the rock and walked. The direction wasn't important, all she needed was movement. The act of doing something helped calm the harsh voices in her head. She knew what she really wanted to do.

She needed to talk to Tam.

Tam. Every time she thought about him, a pain formed deep inside. The pain—a question, really—which clawed and tore, trying to shred her from the inside out. So far she'd kept that pain at bay, shoved it behind a reinforced wall in her mind and locked the door. She thought she'd thrown away the key too, but that question kept battering and battering, wanting to crash through her barriers. She knew if she let it out, explored her feelings for Tam, all her accustomed, solid beliefs might be altered. She'd held that question in limbo for the past few days, nursing it, letting it prowl through the peripheries of her consciousness, not ready to learn the consequences of it.

But it was time. Time to let the question out.

What did Tam mean to her? How far did her feelings go for him? Was she in love with him? And what did that mean for the choice in front of her today?

CHAPTER SEVENTEEN

The golden orb melted into the ocean, turning the waves to shimmering metallic blue. A lonely seabird sailed across the sky, flying home to roost before the dark of night claimed the island. The drone of cicadas, loud at Tam's back, emanated from the thick blanket of jungle leaves. A low thrum vibrated through his body, as the waves smashed themselves against the rock face, lulling him with the familiar sounds of the evening.

Tam drank it all in so he'd remember this peace, this tranquillity, this feeling of aliveness, when he returned to the city. If this was to be his last night here, then he wanted to make the most of it.

He'd accepted his fate. He'd lost at the exemption knockout today; his only genuine hope of staying on any longer. Without doubt, the other four would conspire to send him home. He was an intruder returned from Deception, to be got rid of as soon as possible.

At one stage earlier this afternoon, Tam had approached Rosa when she'd gone to collect firewood. She'd smiled and simpered and pretended to agree to his suggestion, saying she'd think about the ramifications of voting Simon off instead of him. But Tam knew. She wasn't about to turn, no matter how good his proposal sounded.

And Hayden had cemented that idea when he'd turned up, inadvertently interrupting their tête-à-tête, saying, 'Look, mate, it's nothing personal, but we'll be sticking to our original plan. We have too much to lose if we don't.' At least the man was straight to the point, no mucking around or keeping him on tenterhooks.

He was going to be voted out tonight.

So he'd decided to come out to the headland one last time. To enjoy the solitude and think back to when he and Alisha and Cilla had all sat at the edge of the Dawnbreakers beach, laughing and gossiping.

A sound caught his attention, and he turned to look behind him. Cilla was walking toward him, picking a path over the uneven rocks.

He felt the muscles in his face tighten, even as his heartbeat kicked up a few notches. What could she possibly want from him?

'Do you mind?' she said as she drew up alongside him. He shook his head, but didn't look up. Her feet appeared, dangling in the cool water next to his. Tam followed the line of her legs, up her well-defined calves to her taught, tanned thighs resting so near to his.

A silence stretched between them.

Tam wouldn't be the first to break it. His guts were knotted tight, every nerve on edge.

It wasn't fair, what she did to him. The chemistry between them still crackled. It was there in the way he longed to reach out and stroke her shoulders, run his tongue over her collarbone and taste her sun-kissed skin.

He let out an unsteady breath. She was so quiet and still next to him. He wanted to nonchalantly drape his arm around her shoulders the way Hayden had earlier today. Four days ago he'd have been able to do that, now the wall between them was so high he wasn't sure he'd ever scale it again.

He could feel the trepidation oozing from her and knew she was as tightly wound as he was. What did she want? Surely, she hadn't come to ask him back into an alliance? Surely, she knew him better than that.

The silence hovered, and finally he had to know. He forced his gaze up. Emerald eyes darkened as she met his stare. He lifted an eyebrow in query and she bit her bottom lip.

'Tam, I...' she faltered and stopped, casting her gaze out to waves breaking over the reef, as if to gain some much needed fortitude. 'I want to apologize,' she said, her voice low, speaking as if talking to the ocean.

He knew how much it must've cost her to say those words. Her pride kept her strong, kept her independent; to swallow that pride must've been a bitter pill indeed. Something in him softened, the lump of cold hard rancour, which had sustained him over these past few days thawed a little, the edges blurring. Not enough to make him ready to give in to her needs. He stared at her profile but remained mute, waiting for more.

When he didn't reply, she went on, 'You probably have every right not to accept my apology, but I want to give it, anyway.' This time she turned her face toward him, allowing him to search her gaze for any form of deceit. There was none. It seemed her confession was heartfelt and sincere, not merely a ploy to get him back on her side.

The tiny diamond in her nose-piercing glinted in the dying rays of sunlight. That same light caught her eyes, turning the dark flecks in her irises to gold.

'I'm sorry I voted you out the other night.'

'You did what you thought you had to, Cilla.' He knew he was being obtuse, but he was unwilling to make this easy for her. It was her fault he'd been sent to Deception, and it was only by sheer luck and skill that he'd made it back into the game. Three long days and nights he'd spent at Deception, turning her change in loyalty over and over in his head. No matter how he looked at it, he could find no plausible reason for her to have turned on him so cruelly. Sure, he'd been wrong not to tell her of his voyeuristic viewing while she was naked at the little bay. But the more he thought about it, the more he knew she'd overreacted. Any normal person would've been embarrassed and angry, but she'd twisted his fairly minor deceit into a major betrayal. Blown it all out of proportion. Something much more was at play here, and unless she gave him more, a lot more, he would not be involved in her little game. He wasn't nearly ready to absolve her yet.

'I did what I thought was right,' she replied, her voice small. 'I know you're probably furious at me, but…' He could tell by the manner in which a muscle pulsed in her jaw she was working to find the right words. 'I was hoping we might be friends. That's all. You know, after this is all over.'

'Friends? You want to be friends?' The last word came out in a menacing growl. He couldn't keep up with her drastic changes in direction. Even as little as an hour ago she'd still been studiously ignoring him, letting him believe she regarded him with distaste and abhorrence.

Now she wanted to be *friends*. This wasn't what he'd expected, and it wasn't good enough.

A thought interrupted, whispering to him that perhaps she was angling to get him back on her side, to help her overthrow Simon. That she was still trying to use him, to manipulate him, to play to his weakness. His anger flared and her duplicity pierced his gut, making him clench his hands into fists at his side.

'You think I'm vulgar, that I can't be trusted.' He shook his head to clear the memory of their fight on the beach. Her accusation burned hot in his chest. 'How did you put it…us men are all the same? All a pack of liars,' he said, voice rough and hoarse. He could see he'd hit the mark when she flinched and dropped her chin.

'I know I said that in the heat of the moment, but I've had a lot of time to think about it over the last few days.' Lifting her head again, she braced both hands on the rocks beside her. 'I have trouble trusting men sometimes.'

That was an understatement if ever he heard one. But the look on her face—of the terror of exposing such a confidence—made him check his heated answer before it left his lips. It seemed as if she'd just taken a big step, admitting even that much to him.

'It's a long story, and not one I like to tell many people. Actually, I've never told anybody else.' She closed her eyes for the briefest of moments, as if steeling herself. 'My father is the antithesis of everything a good father should be. He is a liar and a cheat, with a dirty gambling addiction. He's the reason I'm out here on this island.' Releasing a breath, she gave a self-deprecating laugh. 'How about I just say, I have daddy issues? You should understand that, being a shrink and all.'

He felt a quiver of defensiveness at her mockery of his profession, but he knew it wasn't meant in malice, more of a way to make light of her own predicament.

'Anyway, I shouldn't have projected my prejudices onto you, it was unfair. I know that now.'

It was all making a little more sense. He wanted to kick himself. No psychologist worth their salt should have missed the signs, they were obvious if anyone cared to look. The lack of self-esteem, the fact she was adamant she could cope with everything on her own. She was finally opening up to him, and God knows how he'd love to delve into the mysteries that made up Cilla Parsons. Should he take what she was saying at face value? Was this really the truth, the heart of Cilla?

Part of him wanted to believe her; that she'd changed, that she was ready to accept him as he was. To forgive her.

But the question remained. Should he trust his heart? Or his head?

He almost laughed out loud at the irony of it all. Four days ago he'd been ready to tell her about his past, about his months spent in juvenile detention. About his family and where he came from. Face it, they both had monumental trust issues. The question was, could they get past them? It'd take time and fortitude to work through their problems together, but they could do it, if they'd just allow themselves to fall.

Did he want to explore this further, this thing with Cilla? Was the magnetism, the strongest physical attraction he'd ever encountered, this strange feeling of joy when he was near her, enough?

One thing he knew, he didn't regret one minute he'd spent with her. And suddenly it dawned on him. He'd never be happy unless he possessed her body and soul.

With unexpected clarity, he realized he couldn't do what she was asking of him.

'I forgive you, Cilla, for voting me out.' He raised his hand to forestall her quick smile. He wasn't finished yet. 'But I'm sorry, I can't do just *friends*. My feelings toward you are…complicated, but I need more than that.' She gave a start, his answer not what she was expecting. In the dimming light he could see her face cloud with distress, but he ploughed on. 'If we were merely friends, seeing you, being near you and not being able to touch you. That would rip me to shreds, piece by tiny piece. I want to be with you, but if you don't want to *be* with me, then it's better we stop this.'

He'd finally said it, there was no recalling those words. But instead of the self-recrimination he'd thought the admission would bring, he felt as if a great weight had lifted from his shoulders. Somehow, confessing his feelings to her had released him. It was an odd sensation, strangely enlightening. How would she react? He watched her face, letting his eyes rove over her cheekbones, follow the smooth curve of her jaw. Savouring her face one last time, so he'd remember this moment.

They sat for uncounted seconds, gazing at each other while she digested what he'd said. A pink flush crept up her neck, tinging her cheeks with an enticing rosy glow.

Keeping her gaze fixed on him, she finally said, 'I think I…that is, I know…I feel the same way, Tam.'

Her quiet words overwhelmed him.

She felt it too. He ran a shaky hand through his hair. Could he really believe she had such a change of heart in less than a day? Disbelief shrouded his mind, clung to his insides like a black veil.

'Prove it.'

'What?' She gave a convulsive swallow.

'Give me some kind of sign. Show me what you're willing to do to prove you feel the same as me.' His pulse began to race, wondering how she'd answer his dare. Cilla wet her lips with the tip of her tongue, her fingers fidgeted up and down on her thigh.

She hesitated.

The flare of hope in his heart died.

'Don't worry about it, Cilla.' He turned away from her, ready to lever himself up off the rocks.

Her hand on his arm stopped him. 'It's not that I don't want to, Tam,' she repudiated. 'I'm confused. Afraid of what I might discover.'

'Discover about me?'

'No. About me.' Her words were so quiet he almost missed them.

A shout from behind made them both turn simultaneously. Simon waved at them as he made his way over the rocks, and Tam noticed the grey light of dusk had descended, smudging the edges of his vision with growing darkness.

Damn Simon. Damn him to hell.

Their chance for reconciliation was gone.

'It's time to go to conclave,' Cilla said, resigned, the flush on her cheeks dying with Simon's arrival.

They had so much left to discuss, so much left unsaid. But at least she'd forgiven him, and he her. He'd be going home tonight with the great burden of that all-consuming anger lifted from his soul. His heart would bear the brunt of the scars earned on this island. He'd be leaving as a changed man, and it was all because of her.

The least he could do was let her know it was all right, that he could forgive her now.

'You do what you need to do tonight, Cilla. I'll understand, no matter what you decide.'

The look she gave him was full of such raw confusion he almost wished he hadn't said it.

* * *

Cilla took her seat on the upturned log at the conclave, along with the other four contestants. Shadows from the flames in the fire pit flickered with the wind, causing the wooden statue of some kind of sea monster in the corner of the platform to seem as if it was giving her the evil eye. It was breezy, but still warm and humid. Thankfully, the rain held off tonight. The last thing she needed was a soaking, not for what she was about to do. Her decision had been remarkably easy to make after all, and she was impatient to get on with it.

Her gaze settled on the panel who were sitting in the bleachers on the opposite corner of the platform. It had shocked her to see them all file in, just after the contestants had taken their places. Every castaway had stopped whatever he or she had been doing to stare. JJ told them now Deception was finally finished, the secret as to who was part of the panel was out, so they needed to lay all the cards on the table. The next two people voted off the island would go straight onto the panel as well. A shiver chafed down her spine at the thought.

Cilla surveyed them, all people she'd played the game with. It was hard watching them file in, knowing she'd had a part of some in their downfalls. Cho came first, then Jason. They both looked clean and relaxed and happy.

Susan and Marg came next and Cilla found her hand lifting of its own violation to give them a wave. She let it flop back into her lap. JJ told them they weren't allowed any kind of interaction with the panel whatsoever. It was great to see Marg looking healthy and fit again, she'd obviously recovered well from the stonefish poison. And it was even better to see they'd allowed Marg to take her rightful spot on the panel. Cilla had been worried they might exclude her because of the way she'd left the island.

Alisha was the last to come up the stairs, and Cilla had to hold in a gasp of surprise. She looked beautiful, her hair brushed and pulled back into a chignon, and wearing a blue dress which emphasized her shinning dark skin. Alisha gave a secret smile, meant only for Cilla to see. Her spirits lifted.

'So, Cilla.' Her attention snapped back at the mention of her name. 'You have the exemption talisman, well done.'

'Thank you, JJ.'

'I assume you'll be keeping it, but I have to ask, anyway. Did you want to pass on your figurine to anyone else before we start the vote?' JJ's gaze had already flickered away from her, presuming she was going to shake her head, the same way everyone else who'd held the talisman this season had done.

Cilla stood up. JJ stalled, half way to raising his arm to point at Simon.

'Actually, JJ, I'm going to give up my parrot.' There was complete silence. She couldn't remember when she'd last commanded such attention. Everyone on the panel leant forward, watching her, some with their hands over their mouths to stop the intake of breath. 'I want to give it to Tam.'

Rosa gave an audible gasp at exactly the same time as Simon stood up and yelled, 'You can't!'

'What? Really?' JJ asked. Cilla could see him trying to pull his face into a semblance of poise, but the way his dimple was twitching told of the effort it took.

'You can't do that, Cilla,' Simon repeated.

'Yes, I can, and I will,' she said, glaring at Simon. He had no authority over her. Simon's frown turned into a grimace and he made as if to take a step toward her.

Tam was on his feet in a second, coming between her and Simon.

'Leave her alone,' Tam snarled, and Cilla wondered at the surge of intensity in his gaze. Fists clenched so firmly she could see his knuckles turning white, shoulders tight and controlled, ready for anything. She was left in no doubt he'd do whatever it took to protect her. So this was what Tam was capable of when roused. It was impressive, and at any other stage Cilla would've been grateful. Both men glared at each other like two rabid dogs wanting to tear each other apart, hackles raised and teeth bared.

'Sit down, all of you,' JJ roared. The shock of his raised voice drew Cilla's gaze away from the two threatening men. JJ never raised his voice. Ever. He was the ultimate professional. Looking at JJ, his stance and the way he was tipped forward on his toes, she realized he was ready to stride in and break Simon and Tam apart if he had to. JJ was definitely big enough—nearly as tall as Tam—and muscular enough to take on either of the two men behind her. She sat, but Tam and Simon still stood, glowering at each other from opposite ends of the log.

'This conclave won't continue until you both sit down.'

'Fine,' Simon spat, but started to lower himself onto the

bench. Once Tam was sure he was down, he also lowered his backside down. They continued to stare at each other, adding to the air of tension already swirling around the platform. Whispers could be heard flitting backward and forward, people shocked and amazed at the turn of events.

'And there will be no more noise from the panel either, unless you want to be exiled from this conclave.' JJ glared at the members, dark brows drawn into a fearsome frown.

'Cilla. Did you say you wanted to give up your exemption?'

'Yes, JJ.'

'And you want to give it to Tam.'

'Yes—'

'Well, I don't want it,' Tam's voice cut through hers. 'I won't accept it.' He shifted his fiery gaze away from Simon, penetrating her with a fierce purpose. She hadn't really expected him to make this easy for her and her heart leapt at his courage; he was showing her the truth of his convictions. He wouldn't take her exemption away from her. He cared about her too much. He was a good man, compassionate and resilient and brave. She knew that now, had always known it, but hadn't wanted to acknowledge it before. He was everything Simon wasn't. Simon would've taken the talisman at her very first offer.

Cilla kept her tone measured. 'Well, I don't want it either. So if you don't take it, I'll give it to Simon instead.' There were loud gasps from everyone at tribal.

'You can't be serious?' Tam stood up again.

'I'm deadly serious, Tam. I don't want this exemption, and if you don't take it, I'll give it to someone else.' He'd asked her to prove herself to him down at the beach, so she was doing just that.

'But why?' There was such yearning in his face, a weary hopelessness, and she wanted to go up and touch his cheek, stroke away the deep lines and tell him everything would be okay.

'Yes, why, Cilla?' JJ repeated.

'Because it's the right thing to do.' And that was the truth. Well, the partial truth. The rest she couldn't reveal, not to everyone here and not on prime-time television. She couldn't say it was because she was falling in love with Tam. Because the million dollars was worth less to her than keeping her morality intact. She didn't want to end up like her father, and if she kept this exemption, that's exactly what'd happen.

A slow smile spread over Simon's face. 'I'll have it, Cilla. Give it to me if that dropkick won't take it.'

'What's it to be, Tam?' JJ asked, ignoring Simon, his features once again serious and in control.

'You can't make me do this, Cilla. You can't make me choose.' Tam came over and knelt down next to her, capturing her hands in his. Cilla couldn't stop the spike of heat that ran through her at his touch, warming her from the inside out. He held her gaze, and it was as if they were fused together by their line of sight, as if a gossamer web of warmth and light and awareness passed between them. Everything else was forgotten. Only the two of them existed in this place. 'Please don't.' It was almost a murmur.

'The choice isn't yours to make. It's mine,' she said softly. 'I need to do this, Tam. It's the only thing that'll make it right again.' She tried not to sound like she was pleading with him. 'This game has been in control of me long enough. It's time I took back that control.' He had to do this for her. She needed him to take the bloody parrot, couldn't he understand that? She watched him, waiting for his reply. She saw it in his eyes even before he spoke the words.

'I'll take it then.'

Yes! Joy coursed through her. With a thick grunt he stood up, pulling her up with him.

'Bring it over here, Cilla,' said JJ.

Amid an air of solemn ceremony, JJ transferred the bird talisman and placed it in Tam's hands. The weight seemed to drag him down, his shoulders sagged beneath the burden, and on instinct she grasped his hand. Holding on tight, she gave him one of her best smiles.

'Thanks, Tam.' He squeezed her hand in answer, but the scowl didn't leave his face.

'If you two will return to your places, then I think we can get on with this conclave.' JJ waited as they both took their seats. Cilla endured the stares of the other three while she got comfortable. Simon was shooting her daggers, he'd never forgive her for this. Rosa was also stern and unforgiving. Of course, she'd never think to break her alliance with Simon, so she couldn't fathom why Cilla chose to. Hayden regarded her with equanimity, a slight quirk to his mouth telling her that while he didn't understand what she'd done, he was okay with it. She didn't care, she'd made her decision, and she was bound to stand by any of the repercussions that came her way.

'Tam has the exemption figurine, so you cannot vote for him. Okay, Hayden, your turn to vote, off you go.' JJ jumped straight into the ballot, not giving the others any chance to try to realign their votes.

She'd told no one of her plan to give up the talisman

tonight, and therefore she had no way of knowing how the vote was going to pan out. A small flicker of hope lived in her mind that maybe Hayden and Rosa might be so impressed by her self-sacrifice, they'd vote against Simon.

It was a slim hope and one that died a quick death as JJ read out the votes.

'The fourteenth person voted off the island and the sixth person to join the panel is... Cilla,' JJ said as he turned the last voting parchment around for them all to see. 'Bring me your firebrand, Cilla.' The familiar words rolled off Cilla's back as she retrieved her firebrand.

'Cilla, wait.' Tam leapt up and pulled her into his embrace. 'I still can't believe you did that for me.' She let him hold her for a moment, enjoying the safety, the honesty and the relevance of his arms wrapped around her. She kept the knowledge this might be the last time he ever held her in his arms, stuffed way down in the pit of her stomach. There'd be plenty of occasions to cry later, but not now.

'Do good, Tam. I expect you to win.' They both knew he'd have an enormous battle ahead of him. But her exemption had given him the change in fortune he needed tonight. And tomorrow was another day. Anything could happen in twenty-four hours. 'I'll see you from the other side tomorrow night,' she said. 'Right now I can hear a very long, very hot shower calling me.' He laughed, and it was good to hear the release of tension in his voice. A smile she didn't feel arranged itself on her face. She had to let him go, that dam of emotion inside her waiting to burst was rising higher and higher the longer she held him. Placing a hand on his chest, she pushed them apart. She could feel his heartbeat through the fabric of his T-shirt under her fingers, strong and sure.

'The team has spoken,' JJ intoned as he snuffed out her firebrand.

'Good luck guys,' she called over her shoulder as she walked through the hangman's noose toward the exit. The steep steps down from the platform blurred beneath her feet, and when she got to the bottom, she could no longer see for the tears flooding down her cheeks.

CHAPTER EIGHTEEN

It was so strange to be sleeping in a proper bed again. Crisp white sheets rasped lightly against her bare skin, and a feather-down pillow cushioned her head. But no matter how hard she tried, Cilla couldn't get comfortable. It didn't feel right. A fan whirled above her head, cooling her body, but not her mind. She couldn't stop replaying those last few minutes of the conclave over in her mind. Tears threatened anew even as she thought about Tam's words, his touch. So she jumped up, grabbing some clothes and pulling them on. A walk under the stars would cure her.

Opening the door, she let the heat and humidity rush in. This was more like it. Out in the elements and not caged in some tiny room, it was somehow easier to breathe. Bare feet making no sound on the paved walkways, she headed toward the sound of crashing waves coming from beyond the pool. The straight lines of pathways and hedges and manicured lawns of the resort gave way to the softer shapes of sand and water and dark sky as she moved toward the beach.

Lying down on the cool shore, with her hands supporting her head, she stared up at the stars. So bright and sparkling and infinitesimal, as if an artist had swept their paintbrush loaded with fairy dust across the sky in a heavenly arc. Her mind floated upwards, to mingle with the millions of shimmering pinpricks of light.

What would Tam be thinking right at this moment? It was past midnight, so he should be tucked up in the shelter fast asleep. She should be asleep too, God only knew she was tired enough. It'd been a rough night, after all.

The boat trip to the mainland had only taken twenty minutes, but much of it was still a blur. As soon as they'd boarded, Alisha slipped her arms around Cilla and hugged her like a mother would hug a child. It'd set Cilla to crying so hard she never thought she'd stop. Marg came and added her arms in support, and the three of them stood in the bow of the boat for many minutes, Alisha crooning, 'Poor baby. It's okay,' over and over.

When the flood of tears ebbed to a trickle and Cilla looked up, she felt washed out, exhausted, but also clean somehow. Jason, Susan and Cho joined them and they'd all talked about what it was going to be like for her on the mainland, easing her back into reality.

They talked for hours over dinner, remaining at the table long after the servers cleared the remnants away. Gorged on food, relaxed in a comfortable chair and sipping gin and tonic, Cilla found some added perspective on the night's activities, allowing her to finally expose her heart and talk to the others freely. She told them the complete truth as to why she'd needed the prize money. It felt good to open herself up to the burdens of the secrets she'd carried on the island. Secrets she'd carried all the way through the better part of her adult life.

Everyone could hardly believe her story when she first told them how her father had mortgaged her grandmother's house, and her boat, to support his gambling debts. Saying it out loud, Cilla still hardly believed it herself. The notion belonged in some second-rate movie, not in the reality of her life. Jason proposed he'd go around and sort out her father. And Marg seconded him, much to Cilla's undisclosed delight. She politely declined their offer. It'd be fruitless anyway, nothing and nobody would ever change her father. He was a cold-hearted bastard, and that was that.

There were two things she didn't divulge to the other four around the table that night, though. The first was how deeply she hated her father for what he'd done. She didn't want to admit, even to herself, how great his hold had been.

The second was the fact she'd fallen in love with Tam. She'd only just figured it out today. It was an irrational love. One she wasn't sure would ever be returned. Even if he went on to win this game, she knew he owed her nothing, and she expected nothing. Telling anyone else might tarnish the memory of him.

She'd see Tam tomorrow night, at the penultimate conclave, and then she'd return to her normal life. It was over now. She'd have to confront her grandmother, admit she hadn't won the million dollars. Would her grandmother understand why she'd given up her exemption?

Had she made the wrong decision? Maybe people looking into her life from the outside, when they viewed her on the television series, might think her stupid and reckless and irresponsible. It'd been the right thing for her to do, however. There were no more recriminations, no nagging doubts eating away at the fabric of her soul. She hadn't become her father, and that was the most important lesson she could learn from the island.

The soothing sound of the waves settled over her, and her eyelids drooped. Standing, she knew it was time to head back to her room, where sleep might ultimately claim her. She'd face all her other problems tomorrow. For tonight she felt at peace, free and vindicated, and that was enough.

* * *

One more night. He'd been given one more night's reprieve. It was unexpected and an immense shock. Tam lay awake, staring at the shapes the pandanus leaves formed against the stars in the midnight sky. Would Cilla be asleep? Probably snoring her head off in the comfort of a king-size bed at the resort. He wished he could do the same. There'd be another exemption knockout tomorrow, and he needed all the sleep he could get, so he was alert and ready for whatever they might throw at him.

Simon snored like a steam train from the other side of the shelter, the noise in no way conducive to sleep. The man hadn't been happy with how things turned out at conclave tonight and had expressed his anger once they got to camp. He'd bellowed and flexed those enormous biceps of his, throwing pieces of driftwood into the jungle and kicking the sand up in great sprays. But once his displeasure had been vented, he'd calmed down, becoming rational again. He was still rude and vain, but Tam could deal with that.

Tam knew the island was in part to blame for Simon's outburst. The island changed a person, skewed their values and beliefs, turned everything you thought to be correct on its head. Even without the constant mind games going on in the background, making everybody paranoid, most people would become cranky and prickly after only one day without food. They'd been out here for thirty-five days. It was hard to maintain equilibrium when you were starving all the time. No, Tam didn't really blame Simon for his tantrum. There'd been a few times lately where he'd wanted to do the same thing.

Why had Cilla done it? Why had she sacrificed herself for him?

Her actions had been so unexpected, so shocking. He'd been resigned to going home tonight, looking forward to it in a twisted sort of sense. It'd be a relief to get off this island. Instead, he got to stay and play another day.

She deserved to stay as much as he did. They'd both broken promises to other people and to themselves to remain in the game. That was part of the island's allure, part of the maladjusted temptation of it all. It was obvious she felt she had to atone for something she'd done on the island. But to whom? To him? Because she'd voted him off? Whatever her moral compass had found so repugnant made her give up her grasp on the million dollars. She'd wanted that money badly. They all did, but she more than most. Call it his shrink's intuition, but he knew she'd been holding back on all the truths. You only had to look at the desperation behind how she cried when she lost the first chicken-eating knockout, how she fished so hard for the team as a way to be accepted, how she took it so silently to heart when it became clear Madison hated her. Yes, she needed the money to buy a better house and by the sounds of it a stable home would do her the world of good after living on a boat for the last few years. But the wound went deeper than that, he was sure of it. And it'd something to do with her father, that much she'd intimated before Simon interrupted them.

If he was being completely truthful, he knew the money meant more to him than it might for others as well. Of course, he was going to give most of it away to improve the lives of the kids he treated. His donation would allow for another psychologist to be brought on board, their clinic could expand and more kids reached; their lives changed. Saved.

There was more to it than helping the underprivileged children of LA, though. A million dollars also afforded a person power. It'd keep him safe, lend him gravitas. He need never worry about falling back down to the bottom of the pit of humanity with that money in his pocket. Poverty wouldn't cling to him anymore, the money would give him a shiny new coat, protect him.

He just wished they'd been able to finish their conversation out on the point this evening and not been interrupted by Simon. Cilla was about to reveal her genuine feelings, he'd been sure of it. If they'd been able to work out their differences, then maybe this night wouldn't have taken such a drastic turn.

Of course he could have stood firm, refused to take the talisman. Let her hand it over to Simon. What would that have achieved, though? Now he'd never know.

* * *

JJ welcomed them into the arena with a wave, right as the midday sun hit its zenith. 'Come on in to your last ever exemption knockout guys.' JJ stood there looking as fresh as a daisy with his starched black shirt and fedora hat pulled down to shade his eyes. 'The winner of today's knockout guarantees themselves a spot in the final three. What do you think of that, Rosa?'

Caught off-guard by JJ's question, Rosa stared at him with wide eyes, a rabbit ensnared in the headlamps of an oncoming car.

'I can't really talk for Rosa,' said Hayden, jumping in, 'but I want to win this one real bad. Matter of fact, there isn't a lot I wouldn't give up for a chance to triumph today.'

'I think I'm pretty safe in saying you probably speak for the other people standing next to you, Hayden,' replied JJ, nodding at them all in turn. 'Tam, bring your parrot over here and I'll return it to the stand.'

Tam heard Simon mutter under his breath, 'It's not his bloody talisman,' but didn't bother to return comment.

'Righto guys, exemption is back up for grabs. Let's get this thing started. Your knockout today consists of all of you moving along a beam of wood, which gets progressively thinner. The last one left standing wins exemption. Pretty simple, really. It's called *walking the plank.*'

The first beam was nice and wide, and Tam positioned his feet in the middle of the plank as JJ counted them down to the start. He balanced easily, one foot behind the other.

It was windy today. There was probably another storm on the way. A gust of wind hit Tam, and he wobbled a little. That was all it took to make him lose his balance. He corrected, but a little too much, and he nearly went off the other side. Goddammit, he would not let a stupid gust of wind beat him to one million dollars. He tightened his focus on the plank, slowed his heart's frantic beating and re-settled himself, vowing the wind wouldn't catch him off guard again.

The next gust was more ferocious, but he was ready this time, concentration honed to that single plank of wood.

Rosa wasn't so lucky and she overbalanced a tiny bit, but it was enough to make her lose her footing and she teetered on one foot for a second until she dropped with a plop onto the sand.

A small part of Tam's consciousness registered Rosa's little scream of defiance, but he didn't lift his gaze. The only thing that mattered was that wooden plank in front of him.

After fifteen minutes JJ got them to move onto an adjoining, thinner plank. The sides of his feet hung over each edge of this one, and he had to concentrate much harder just to keep a steady position on the wooden beam. But he kept his stare straight ahead and slowed his breathing. All he had to do was stand here. It didn't matter his left calf was cramping, or sweat was running into his eyes. He ignored all physical distractions.

It was up to the trio of men now. A fight to the death. It seemed a little innocuous they should be reduced to a battle of balance skills to see who'd be in the final three. Another flurry of breeze whipped at Tam's ankles and he clamped down on his mind's wanderings.

After ten more minutes elapsed, Tam could feel the sweat running down between his shoulder blades, but he refused to let the strain get to him. The wind had picked up even more, starting to howl through the trees at the edge of the clearing. They were all tired, the intense concentration taking its toll. In one fell swoop, another gust of wind buffeted them and Hayden overbalanced and landed on the ground. Perhaps it was the distraction of Hayden falling next to him, but Simon started to lose balance as well. Tam dared not watch, keeping his eyes directed straight ahead. He heard Simon swear and then the thump as his feet hit the ground.

He'd won.

Let the chips fall where they may.

A sense of grim achievement settled on Tam's shoulders. The exemption parrot was his again for another night, and this time he'd won it fair and square. Simon might've hated him last night when Cilla had given him her talisman, but his hate would multiply tenfold today. Now that he'd won it back on his own terms.

Two hours later, sitting in the shade at the rear of the beach, it was the sand-flies biting his ankles that eventually forced him to move. Little blighters. Tam had learned to detest them with a vengeance the very first day they landed on this island, and his hatred had only grown over the ensuing weeks. They were so tiny they were almost invisible. They were silent; they were insidious, and they left red welts on every inch of exposed skin, which itched like hell for weeks afterwards.

Standing, he reached his arms above his head and stretched his spine. Sitting on the cooling sand had cramped up his muscles. But at least he had a plan. Would Simon go for it, though? He needed to talk to him before the conclave, less than an hour away.

His task was made easier when he spotted Simon swinging in the hammock at the back of the campsite.

Squaring his shoulders, Tam marched toward him. This wouldn't be a straightforward conversation.

'I need to discuss something with you.' Simon's eyes remained shut, but a slight twitch of a cheek muscle betrayed him.

'Not interested.'

'Really?' Tam kept his amusement well hidden, the man's colossal ego wouldn't brook anything that remotely resembled condescension.

'Yeah, really.'

'Even if it involves you not being voted out tonight?'

Simon's eyes flew open, revealing the naked animosity Tam knew had been brewing since last night. 'Just because you won exemption today, you think you're bloody king dick, don't you? Well, I won't get down on my knees and lick your bloody ass, no matter what you're offering.' Tam wanted to turn around and walk away. The man was insufferable. He wished he didn't need to be having this conversation, but after hours of looking at his own predicament in every possible light, it was the only thing that made sense.

Grinding his teeth together, Tam said, 'I didn't come here to be *king dick*, Simon. I need to have a chat. If you aren't man enough to see this might be in your own interest, then that's fine by me.'

Spinning on his heel, he'd taken two steps away when Simon called out, 'Wait.' Tam could hear the strain in the other man's voice, the effort it cost him to say that one little word. 'You can talk, but I'm not promising anything.'

'Good.' Tam returned, stiff and formal, perching himself on a vacant piece of driftwood. Out of the other man's line of sight as he glared with unseeing eyes into the jungle, but near enough for him to hear every word clearly.

'Where are Hayden and Rosa?' asked Simon, his words controlled and quiet. Too quiet.

'Not sure. I think they might've headed off down the north end of the beach together. Probably strategizing.' Tam had watched them disappear in that direction a quarter of an hour ago. No one else needed to overhear what he had to say.

'So you took your opportunity to pounce, huh?' There was an undercurrent of malice running through Simon's voice, even as he made his tone sound perfectly light and cordial.

'Whatever, Simon.' Tam wasn't about to pander to his attempts to drag him into a slanging match. 'I want to vote Hayden off tonight, and I want you to help me.' For the first time in their conversation, Simon's gaze slid over to him. Tam could see him assessing the validity of his remark.

'Why?' The word was like a gunshot leaving Simon's lips.

'Because he's a nice guy. Everybody likes him. He's played the game successfully, with more moral fibre than the rest of us. And he'll be almost impossible to beat. The panel will vote for him if he gets into the top three.'

'And they won't vote for me, is that what you're implying?' A flush crept up Simon's neck; a warning.

Tam ignored it and ploughed on. 'In a nutshell, yes. I want to take you to the final three because I think you've made more enemies than me. I think I can beat you.' It was the simple truth, one that Tam had battled with for over an hour down by the water. If he wanted any chance at winning the million, he'd have to do it with his enemy sitting by his side. Oh, the irony of it. If Tam had any moral fibre at all, he'd take Hayden with him. It'd be the right thing to do. Hayden was the good guy, he deserved to be there at the end. Cilla would've taken Hayden with her. Well, the new and improved Cilla would've. But it was partly for Cilla's sake he made this decision. She'd offered him her trust, had passed her mantle over to him with the talisman. He had to win for her, as much as for himself.

'What if I don't want to?'

'What other choice do you have? You could try to vote Rosa out, but then you'd be in the same predicament when it came to the final three, only worse off because you'd definitely lose to Hayden in the end. Besides, I'm sure Hayden and Rosa are gunning to get you out. I'm sure that's what they're off planning right now.'

'Let's say I vote with you, how're you going to get a third vote? How're you going to guarantee there isn't a tie? Us two against Hayden and Rosa.' Good, Simon was considering his offer.

'There're no real guarantees in this world, Simon. But I was hoping you'd whisper in Rosa's ear, tell her that Hayden is secretly aiming to get her out, and if she votes with us, she'll definitely be in the top three. You're no rookie at this game, you'll know what to say to make her turn, I'm sure of it.'

'So, not only are you trying to recruit me to your dodgy plan, but you want me to do your ass-licking for you as well,' Simon said in an annoyed growl.

'She'll listen to you, Simon, and you know it.' There was silence for what seemed like unending seconds.

'It's an interesting theory. I'll think about it. Now leave

me the hell alone.'

'Yeah, you do that, Simon. Let me know what you decide.' Tam got up and strode away, fists clenched, only vaguely interested in Simon's answer. He'd laid out the bait, he'd just have to wait and watch to see if he took it. If Simon was as sharp as Tam gave him credit for he'd overcome his loathing for Tam and vote with him. And if Simon chose to be childish and vote off Rosa instead, then Tam could live with that choice too. After all, he was guaranteed a spot in the grand finale. Top three. The million dollars was that little bit closer.

CHAPTER NINETEEN

Butterflies tumbled inside her stomach. She was about to face the remaining contestants, walk past them to the panel benches and pretend she wasn't affected by the things she'd done on the island. She'd also have to endure Simon's animosity after what she'd accomplished at the conclave last night. But that was only part of it.

There was Tam. It'd only been twenty-four hours since she'd set eyes on him; had his arms folded around her, saying goodbye.

They hadn't been able to finish their conversation yesterday out on the headland, and the implications of what the outcome could've been churned in her head all day. He'd admitted he could never be *just friends* with her, and they'd both agreed that things were complicated between them.

It was irrelevant how Tam felt about her; she reminded herself. It wasn't why she'd given him the talisman.

At least she looked one hundred percent better than yesterday. Clean and showered, with shiny hair and new clothes. She'd use her cleanliness as a shield from their scorn. They were dirty, hungry, with matted hair and shrunken eyes.

'Righto, the castaways are in place, up you go,' she heard a crew member whisper from the sidelines. It was time to make their way up the stairs and onto the conclave platform. As the first person voted onto the panel, Jason was first in line. Then came Cho and she was right at the end, after Alisha. One more person would join them tonight, to make up a panel of seven. Seven people who'd decide the winner of the one million dollars.

Holding her breath, she steeled herself for her first glance in their direction.

Tam had the talisman!

She almost let out a whoop of delight, but stopped herself. They weren't allowed to have any contact whatsoever with the castaways. If she were caught doing anything that looked remotely dodgy, she could be banned from the conclave. And that's the last thing Cilla wanted.

So she did a little dance inside her head instead. Tam had won exemption. He was safe for tonight and into the final three. Things couldn't have worked out better if she'd planned them that way. A smile crept onto her face. She could sit and watch this conclave unfold and enjoy the scene. Her shoulders seemed elevated somehow, as if a cleansing breeze had blown through and swept all the heaviness away.

JJ nodded to each member of the panel as they took their seats and then fired questions at the contestants. It was no good, she couldn't concentrate on what JJ was saying, all she wanted to do was look at Tam. He sat, serene and solid, showing no signs of the inner turmoil that must be churning through him. Trying to etch the lines of his face into her memory, she drank in every detail of his features. She'd allow herself this final indulgence.

The dark cropped hair he'd started out with a month ago was growing out nicely. Long enough to run her fingers through. There was also a month's worth of stubble on his jaw, not quite a beard yet, but still scruffy and unkempt. How would it feel to kiss him right now? Would the beard be scratchy or soft? It looked soft from here, if only she could rub her palm over his cheek and down his chin to find out. That mouth was set into a hard line, listening to JJ's questions, but she knew it could be so forgiving and yielding beneath her own. A shiver ran down her spine as she remembered how his lips had tasted kissing her.

But it was in his eyes she found herself getting waylaid. A soft amber color, so reminiscent of butterscotch candy; intense and iridescent, as if lit from inside by some internal fire burning bright.

Suddenly, his gaze switched to her, caught her staring. She couldn't look away; daren't look away, even as a flush crept up her neck. A smile, ever so slightly crinkled the corners of his eyes.

That smile tore shreds out of her already battered heart. In that smile, she could see how much he cared about her. Even after she'd treated him so abominably.

His eyes never left hers, and suddenly she knew all her efforts over the past month to keep emotionally detached had failed. Her attraction to Tam—which was far more than merely physical—couldn't be denied. The power of this attraction terrified her. She knew her feelings must've shown on her face, as clear as day for Tam to see.

Did it terrify him too?

JJ's voice penetrated her consciousness as he asked Tam a question, and their connection was shattered as he tore his gaze away.

'Sorry, what did you say?' Tam dragged in a lungful of air, as if he'd momentarily stopped breathing. 'I wasn't really listening.'

'I said, do you feel vindicated now you've claimed exemption fair and square? Do you believe Cilla's faith in you was well placed?'

'Yes. Yes, I do,' he replied.

She hadn't meant to place the yoke of expectation upon him when she'd offered him the parrot. He seemed to have accepted it though, with a sense of clarity and destiny that surprised her. She didn't want him to win it for her, but with a growing awareness she realized their fortunes were intertwined.

Alisha, who was sitting next to her, gave her a swift glance, full of concern. 'Are you okay?' she mouthed silently. Out of all the people here tonight, Alisha was the one person who realized how hard this was to watch. To be so close to him, but not be able to give him her support. To let him know how desperately she wanted him to win.

Cilla gave Alisha's hand a squeeze and nodded. She had to pull herself together. Tam needed to concentrate on his strategies, not on her neurotic problems.

'And I assume you won't be giving your talisman away tonight, Tam?' JJ's question hung in the air, thick with innuendo, before Tam answered with an abrupt shake of his head.

'Good. Then it's time to vote. Hayden, you're first up.'

Cilla watched him make his nimble way over the shaky bridge. It'd be the last time he took that trek. The last time any of them would see this platform.

All the contestants would be shuttled off the island tonight as soon as the conclave was over. They'd all go back to their normal lives for the next two months until they were dragged into a studio in Hollywood for the big reveal of the winner of Sea-Quest.

She'd miss the island. There'd been a few poignant moments during her stay where she'd realized this was indeed a special place. Being part of the game of Sea-Quest had given her an extraordinary opportunity, one most people never got to experience. She'd remember those times, store them like precious jewels in her memory forever. Like the times she and Alisha had spent sitting on the rock ledge gossiping in the sun. Or soaking up the natural wonder and beauty of Emerald Lagoon in the middle of the island.

The wind whipped her hair around her face and she grabbed handfuls of it, trying to smooth it into a semblance of neatness. That gale had been growing in intensity all day, and it was still howling around the platform, making the trees hammer and moan. Cilla gave an unconscious touch to her nearly healed scar. Whenever the wind blew like this, it reminded her of the storm that'd brought the tree down on her head. Yes, there'd been dangerous times as well, but looking back she knew she'd loved every second.

JJ had garnered the wooden chest containing the votes, while she'd been ruminating on her memories, and his voice brought her back to the present as he read out the votes.

'The fifteenth person voted off the island, and the seventh and final person on the panel is…' There was utter silence as everyone waited. 'Hayden.'

Cilla was stunned. Watching Hayden gather up his firebrand and take it to JJ, she wondered why it hadn't been Simon voted off, or at the very least Rosa. Simon would've been her choice, and Tam detested him as much, if not more, than she did.

'It's the hangman's noose for you,' JJ intoned as he put out Hayden's firebrand. 'You may take your place on the bench with the other panel members.'

Hayden looked shell-shocked; he hadn't been expecting this tonight. Cilla suspected Rosa may have betrayed Hayden, sided with Simon instead. The more Cilla thought about it, the more it made sense. Rosa would have more of a chance of winning if she was up against Simon in the final three. Hayden was too likable. Rosa had broken her alliance right at the ultimate second. Poor Hayden. He'd been blindsided. But at least he was in good company.

She stood up with the rest of the panel members to welcome him into their midst. He managed to raise one of his endearing smiles as he walked over, and she clasped him in an earnest hug. He smelt bad, but she didn't let that deter her, patting him on the back as he took his seat just in front of her. Funny, she'd never noticed it when she'd smelt as bad as the rest of them. Nothing that a good long shower wouldn't fix.

'Now comes the really interesting part of the night. The whole reason the seven of you are sitting over there tonight,' said JJ, once Hayden had taken his seat. 'You'll get to decide who you think is ultimately deserving of the right to dig for the treasure.'

Yes, this was the part Cilla had been waiting for, her

chance to get even, to vote for the person she thought should win the million. They were allowed to ask the final three any questions they deemed fit in order to help them make up their mind. Nothing was out of bounds.

Cilla didn't need to ask questions. There could be no doubt who she'd vote for. If she couldn't win the million, then it had to be Tam. Alisha would vote the same way, of that she was sure.

'Cho, do you have questions?' asked JJ. He smiled as he made the enquiry and Cilla wondered at the slight predatory gleam in his eyes. But of course he'd be relishing this part. To him this was as much about the real people as it was about the television spectacle. Cilla would do well to remember the same thing. It'd pay not to get too emotionally involved in tonight's proceedings, this wasn't reality after all. But how could she not get caught up in the melodrama of it all? Her guts twisted in anger whenever she looked at Simon, and her lungs expanded with elation when Tam cast his gaze over to her. Pursing her lips together, she composed her hands in her lap and sat as immobile as possible, waiting for Cho to speak.

'I don't really want to vote for any of you three sitting up there today,' said Cho, standing with arms crossed and legs akimbo. 'But the rules say I have to choose one of you.' Cho seemed to have chilled out some since Deception. He'd spent a lot of time out there, sometimes completely on his own, waiting for the next person to be voted off the main island. The arrogance she remembered from their first day on the island was gone, replaced by a calm surety of who he was. Of them all, Cho was the one who'd perhaps benefited most on a personal level from his days out here.

'Tam, I like you. We spent time out at Deception together, but I'm not sure you deserve to win the million, bro.' Tam seemed dazed at Cho's statement, perhaps wondering whether he was supposed to give an answer. Cho let him off the hook, when instead of waiting for a reply, he directed his next question toward Simon. 'You, on the other hand, are another matter. After all that self-indulgent bullshit you made me listen to around the campfire, about how many kilos you could bench-press, and how many girls were drooling over you back at the gym at home, the Mustang convertible you drive around town and how much your earn. With all that self-importance, I need to know if there's more inside you than just your ego.'

Wow, that must've hit Simon where it hurt. But Cho didn't stop there. He went on and on in what could only be described as a long rant about how vain Simon was. Everyone's island experience was going to be different, and Cho was all about purging himself of those pent-up emotions. She tuned out most of the rest of his rant, wondering what she'd say to them when it came to her turn. Would she be brave enough to say what she really felt?

Next up was Jason. He stood up in front of the remaining contestants.

'Hi guys.' He cleared his throat nervously. 'First, I want to say congratulations to you all. You made it to the final three. You beat fifteen other people and you deserve to be where you are tonight.' Trust Jason to start off with a fair-minded and benevolent opening statement, lauding their prowess. 'You've achieved what I couldn't. And while I admit I'm jealous, I'll also admit you all played a better game than me.' Jason stood tall and proud as he delivered his speech, and Cilla couldn't help but notice how good he looked now. When he'd first landed on Ko Mae Ko Island he'd been in not bad physical condition, especially for a man in his early sixties, but four weeks on an island enduring physical hardships and lack of food had actually been kinder to Jason than most. He'd lost that extra layer of padding he'd been carrying, and the new beard—neatly trimmed—complemented his handlebar mustache well. Cilla enjoyed a warm glow of solidarity for this man.

'But I have a question for Rosa, if I may?' He cast a quizzical glance toward JJ, who indicated he proceed with a nod of his head. 'As the last surviving member of team Nightrebels, I'd like to know what skills you showed throughout the game which you think might've brought you to where you are now, and also what'll you do with the money if you win?'

'Well, that sounds like two questions to me, Jason, but answer as best you can, Rosa,' said JJ. Rosa stood up slowly, looking a little intimidated. Cilla didn't really care what the pixie woman had to say, her mind was already made up. Would Rosa's speech sway anyone else to vote for her? Maybe. There were three old Nightrebels team members on the panel, Jason, Hayden and Susan, and they might possibly still want to vote along those lines for loyalty alone. Cilla hoped it wasn't true. Jason might give her his vote, but he'd be the only one. The main fight would be between the two opposing strong personalities, Simon and Tam.

* * *

Tam clenched the gunwale with both hands. The boat pitched and rolled beneath his feet, and his stomach lurched in sympathy. Oh God, he was going to be sick. Again. It felt as if this journey would never end, the rough seas adding an extra twenty minutes to the normal half-hour trip. Tam kept his eyes glued to the horizon, where a flotilla of twinkling lights were slowly emerging out of the dark. The mainland was only a few miles away.

What a complete reversal from the euphoria he'd felt less than two hours before when the last conclave had come to an end. It was over. Time to leave the island and never return. He'd survived, and triumphed, making it to the final three. True, they had to wait another two months to find out who was the winner, but it was such a relief to finally have this part over and done.

The boat listed savagely to the right, and Tam tightened his grip even further. To get his mind off the fact that he was in a tiny wooden boat being tossed about in a very large, very dark ocean, Tam let his memory slide back to relive the painful experience of being questioned by the panel.

Sweat had soaked the back of his shirt and the palms of his hands were so clammy he had to keep wiping them on his shorts. Every time someone stood up to take their place directly in front of him, he had to breathe in deeply to quell the rising panic beating a tattoo on the inside of his rib cage. This was a lot more nerve-racking than he'd ever imagined. He needed these people to like him, to pick him over the other two. It was like being back at school waiting to see who'd be chosen for the basketball team, only one hundred times worse.

And none of them had shied away from the hard questions either. Jason asked him why he thought he deserved to be sitting there instead of him. Susan asked him point-blank if it'd been him who helped vote her out. He'd answered both people truthfully and just hoped to God they believed him. It was like trying to walk through a minefield with a blindfold on. Almost impossible.

Then Cilla stood up and his gut clenched so hard he had to force himself not to double over with the pain. She looked fantastic. With her hair left long to hang in soft chestnut waves over her bare shoulders, she wore an aqua colored top, which brought out the green in her eyes so they were almost luminescent. He could see she was still the feisty, determined, gorgeous Cilla he'd become so familiar with on the island, but he could also see a veneer of classiness that made her completely irresistible. Jealousy flared, hot and dangerous in his chest when he watched Hayden take her in a welcoming hug as he'd moved over to be with the panel. God, he'd wanted it to be him holding her right then.

The problem was, he didn't know if she wanted the same in return.

He could see by the way she was fidgeting with her hands, she was nervous.

'I don't actually want to ask anyone a question,' she said. 'I just needed to say something, if that's okay?' She glanced at JJ.

'Of course you can, Cilla. This is a forum where anything goes. Go on, get it off your chest.' He pointed at the three of them sitting on their stools. Vulnerability flared in her eyes. Just for a second and then it was gone, replaced by the blunt determination Tam knew so well.

'I want to tell you...' She hesitated, her eyes linking with Tam's for uncounted seconds in time. She was trying to convey something, but what? Clearing her throat, she started again. 'I want to tell you all, that I'm incredibly sorry.' Turning in a slow circle, she took everyone in with her green gaze. 'I've learnt a valuable lesson on this island. A hard lesson, but one that will stay with me forever. I'm sorry for not staying true to myself and I'm sorry for the abominable way I've treated some of you.' Tam was stunned to see the shine of tears welling in her eyes. Was this remarkable woman about to break in front of everyone?

'When I first came to the island, I was consumed by my need to get my hands on that million dollar prize.' Tam felt the hot gall of guilt rise in his face, for that's exactly what all of them had come for. Especially him. That money meant everything to him. Was she putting all of their motivations under the spotlight? Trying to unnerve them by calling them all out on some of the despicable things they'd done to each other. Things they wouldn't have done under normal circumstances.

No, he could see she wasn't directing her condemnation at them, her focus was turned inwards, naming her own demons. This wasn't about anyone else but herself.

'I'd have done anything to get my hands on that money, and because of that I changed without even knowing it. But something happened to make me realize I was about to turn into someone...do something that'd make me despise myself for the rest of my life. I didn't want to turn into...' She stopped again, her bottom lip trembling. The tears spilled, leaving wet trails down her cheeks. Tam realized he was holding onto the stool with both hands, fingers digging painfully into the wood to stop himself from standing up. From going over to her. From taking her in his arms. But it wasn't up to him to save her. She was doing that for herself.

With a shake of her head, Cilla dashed the tears away and gave a weak smile. She'd regained control.

'That's all I wanted to say, really.' JJ took an involuntary step forward, his gaze fixed on Cilla. Tam recognized the angst in JJ's face. He was reacting to Cilla's pain in the same manner every other red-blooded male on this platform was. Tam's heart battered in his chest, willing him to jump to his feet, trail his fingers over her cheek and let her know he understood, he cared.

JJ controlled his reaction quickly and stepped into his allotted space on the dais.

'Thank you, Cilla. I'm sure everyone accepts your apology, as unwarranted as it may have been.' There was much nodding of heads and murmurs of, *yes*. 'You can take a seat now.'

Alisha patted Cilla's knee and held her hand as she sat down, comforting her.

Tam couldn't take his eyes off her after that. Even when Hayden stood up and asked him a question. He answered robotically, not caring anymore, the thrill of the vote gone. In baring her soul, Cilla had raised questions about his own conduct. He'd always thought of himself as a man of high moral standards. What personal integrities had he given up to be where he was right now?

Then the panel all cast their vote. But instead of being read out straight away, JJ whisked the chest away, leaving the rest of them on the platform nursing a huge feeling of anti-climax. Tam found himself herded onto a boat immediately afterwards, with no chance to talk to the panel. The crew were keeping them separate on purpose it seemed, the three finalists stayed at the front of the boat, while the panel huddled together at the rear. He caught a couple of glimpses of Cilla as they boarded, but she wouldn't meet his gaze, and then once the boat had taken to the ocean, it was too dark to make out her face in the knot of shadowy forms amongst the other panel members.

The notions Cilla brought up consumed him, tumbling around in his head like many rocks plunging down a mountain landslide, even while the boat was pitching and rolling and he was emptying his stomach contents into the sea.

Later that night at the resort, after the best shower he'd ever had in his life, he went to meet up with everyone for drinks and a meal. Tomorrow morning they'd all be flown home, returned to their respective lives and families. To try to pretend that everything was normal again and not give away the fact he'd made it into the final three. How he'd keep that a secret, especially from his mother, he wasn't sure, but he'd signed a contract and somehow he'd have to stick to it.

Tam chose a seat at the end of the large table where everyone else already gathered, talking noisily. He scanned their faces, looking for her. Cilla wasn't at the table yet. Alisha got up from her spot between Marg and Cho and moved to sit next to him, placing a beer on the table in front of him.

As if she could read his mind, she said, 'Leave her be, Tam.' Pushing the open beer closer to him, she took a swig of her own, condensation running down the bottle and dripping from her portly fingers. 'I'm not really sure what's going on in that girl's head, but it seems to me she's mighty mixed up about something.'

'But I have to talk to her, Alisha.'

She rested her ample bosom on the tabletop, leant across and took his hand in hers.

'She doesn't want to see you, Tam. I can't put it any plainer than that.'

Pain ignited in his chest, like a knife being slowly twisted around and around. She didn't want to see him?

She hated him after all.

He got up and left the table, headed toward his room. He couldn't stay there any longer. Couldn't let anyone see him fall apart.

Chapter Twenty

'Are you absolutely sure this is what you want to do, Grandma?'

'Yes, I'm sure.' When her grandmother, Barbara, used those clipped tones, Cilla knew it was time to stop arguing.

'Alright. I'll organize it first thing tomorrow.'

'Good girl. Thank you.' Her grandmother's frail shoulders sagged a little. 'I think I might get my first good night's sleep in a long while, now we've finally made a decision.' Cilla reached for her grandmother's hand, her fingers knobbly with arthritis and cool to the touch, more fragile somehow than she remembered.

'I agree with you, Grandma. At least we're doing something proactive about this, instead of letting the bank take it all. I hate the fact we even have to consider this option at all.' Cilla let go of her grandmother's hand so the old woman wouldn't feel the wrath quivering through her body. 'Most of all, I hate him.'

'Now, now, dear, he's still your father.'

Cilla let out an exasperated sigh. Why did her

grandmother insist on defending that man? Cilla would disown him in an instant. And if he ever dared show his face near her again, God help her, she wouldn't be responsible for her actions.

'I'll talk to Leon down at the real estate office in the morning. He should be capable of getting us a good price.'

'Okay, dear. Can you give the soup a stir, and I'll put the toast on.' Her grandmother bustled around the small kitchen and Cilla stood next to the stovetop, watching the vegetables swirl in the pan as she stirred.

It'd been three weeks since she'd flown back into Buffalo. Three very long, very tense weeks.

The hardest part had been forcing herself to sit down at her grandmother's kitchen table and admit she hadn't won the million dollars. Technically, she shouldn't have revealed that information, but she couldn't very well not tell her, they needed to do something quickly, before they lost the house. She'd imagined there would be copious tears and possibly hysterics—her grandmother was prone to melodramatic moments—and was ready for just about any kind of reaction. Except the one she got.

'Oh well, dear, never mind. We'll think of something.' Where'd her grandmother's pragmatism come from all of a sudden? It was a shock, but not completely unwelcome. The bigger shock came when her grandmother started talking about selling her house. At first Cilla wouldn't hear of it, saying they were going to fight this thing tooth and nail. Her father would not win this one.

Eventually her grandmother talked her around. It seemed she'd spent the last two months, while Cilla was marooned on the island, sorting through all their options. She didn't want to spend years fighting court battles with the bank, never knowing if she might be evicted the very next day, arguing that even if they did ultimately win the fight, all their accounts would be frozen until then. It would be living a life in limbo.

'At least we could sell the house on our terms, and we may indeed make a small profit from it,' she'd said in her bird-like voice. And she was right. If they sold now, before the bank evicted them and flogged the house at the lowest price possible so they could recoup their losses, then they stood a good chance of coming out with a little money to spare, perhaps to put toward a new house. That'd been the other shock her grandmother had in store for Cilla when she arrived home.

'I'd like to move to Miami. What do you think?'

Cilla was speechless.

'Miami?' she'd finally asked in a small voice.

'Yes, I've always wanted to move there. All that warm weather and beaches and young boys to ogle.'

'Barbara Parsons!' Cilla said in mock dismay.

'And you could get a job there, working on one of those cruising boats, couldn't you?'

'You really have thought of everything, haven't you?'

'Yes, dear, I have.' A little self-satisfied smile had settled on her grandmother's lips.

So they decided. They were moving to Miami.

Cilla would stay with her grandmother now. There was no way she could support herself financially alone. Cilla owed her that much. Besides, her boat had already been repossessed.

Her beautiful boat. Her freedom.

Brad had broken the awful news as soon as she'd phoned him to tell him she'd returned from the island.

'Oh no, Cilla, I have something dreadful to tell you,' he'd groaned over the phone. 'Your ketch, your precious ketch.' Even though she was thousands of miles away, she could picture Brad, standing in his messy office, Chicago Bulls cap on backward, rubbing his hand over his face, knocking off his hat and mussing his hair. He always did that when he was anxious.

So it was gone. She hadn't been given one last chance to run her hands over the smooth wooden deck, or to winch the ropes in tight so she could feel the power of the thrumming sails as they hummed with the wind at their back.

'You don't need to say anymore, Brad. I can guess what happened.'

'I'm so sorry, Cilla. I tried to stop them taking it, I really did.'

'It's okay, there would've been nothing you could've done anyway, but thanks for looking out for me, Brad.' Then she'd steered the conversation to her time on the island, distracting him with all the titbits of information she knew he'd love to hear. Even though Brad knew she'd been sworn to secrecy, he asked if she'd tell him who'd made it to the final three.

'You know I can't tell you that. You'll have to watch the show like all the rest of the Sea-Quest fans.' She'd rung off the phone promising Brad she'd fly to the Whitsundays to see him as soon as she was able.

But the conversation had rattled her in more ways than one. The program was due to start in less than a week, and would run its course so it coincided with the big finale when they all congregated together in the studio in Hollywood in a month or so. Cilla didn't want to think about that. It meant she'd have to come face to face with Tam one last time.

One thing Cilla made sure Brad didn't know, was how she'd let herself fall in love with one of the other contestants. She'd barely come to terms with it herself. How would they portray her relationship with Tam on the show?

It was the question which had kept her awake almost every night for the past three weeks. The reality show's editing team probably watched her and Tam's fight on the beach and rubbed their hands with glee. It'd be a great turning point in the game, a juicy bit of real-life drama so they could market their production.

Cilla stopped stirring the soup, staring off into space. For the hundredth time she wished she'd played it out differently, wished she hadn't been so naïve as to air her dirty laundry on national television. But they'd all become so accustomed to the television crews by the end, as if they were part of the scenery, they'd say anything, act completely natural in front of them. Playing straight into the director's hands. It was what the crew lived for after all; to capture those moments of complete abandon, where people let their true feelings out.

Dropping the spoon into the soup, Cilla let out a frustrated groan.

'Are you okay, dear?' Barbara's watchful stare caught her from across the room. What was her grandmother going to think of all this? Cilla wasn't going to be able to persuade her not to watch the show. She cringed at the thought.

'Yep, fine, Grandma,' she said, keeping her voice light. 'I'm going to freshen up a little before dinner. Okay?' Cilla headed toward her bedroom. Shutting the door, she flopped onto the bed and covered her face with her hands. She was regretting ever going on this bloody show.

The hardest part was going to be watching Tam on that screen. To see his face again, to stare into those honey-colored eyes and not touch him. Watch him be gentle and kind to her. Watch that tenderness dissolve and his face crumble as she screamed at him, destroying his faith and trust in her, pushing him away, forever. And then to try to pretend to everyone it meant nothing. It was just a holiday fling; her means of cementing an alliance to get her further in the game.

If only he were lying next to her right now, his body cradling hers, his warm heart beating under her cheek. He'd tell her it'd all be okay.

If only it were true.

She missed him terribly. Missed the look in his eyes when she'd turn unexpectedly and find him staring at her; hunger and yearning, tinged with an empathy she hadn't understood at the time. Missed the knowledge that in an unspoken pact, he had her back, even if she never needed his protection. Missed his honesty and integrity and the way he demanded the same from her. He wouldn't have betrayed her in anger. Not like she'd done to him.

She'd made an abysmal mess of the whole thing. Not only had she not won the money, but she'd screwed up something that should've been precious to her, thrown it away in pursuit of her own greed. It'd been easy to justify her actions by saying she needed the money to save her grandmother, but she knew that was false. Her grandmother was fine, they'd survive, carve out another life for themselves. Deep down, she'd probably always known they'd be okay.

What'd Tam be doing right now? LA was two hours behind Buffalo, he was presumably leaving work. Perhaps saying goodbye to the latest group of kids under his care, giving them a carefree wave, long legs striding down the pathway, head held high, looking everyone in the eye as he passed with his direct, unflinching gaze.

God, how she ached for him.

* * *

The traffic light turned red and Tam smothered a curse. The line of cars hadn't moved in the last five minutes. He was officially stuck in a traffic jam. He should've taken the Santa-Ana freeway, but he'd let the urgent need for a coffee see him stop off at the Ember Cafe on his way home from work, and he was well and truly caught on Lincoln Avenue.

He texted his mother to let her know he'd be late for dinner, then sat sipping his coffee thoughtfully. At least the traffic jam gave him time to drink his espresso in peace. He rubbed his neck, trying to ease out the kinks that'd worked into the muscles. Today had been stressful, and the caffeine was a much-needed boost to his flagging spirits. It also lent him fortification for the upcoming dinner with his parents. They probably weren't going to be pleased with the news he had to tell them tonight.

Coffee still tasted extraordinarily good to him, even now, three weeks after he'd left the island. Actually, everything tasted good. After having been deprived of anything but plain rice, beans and fish for thirty-nine days, he had a healthy regard of all things he'd once taken for granted.

His thoughts turned to the contemplation of the

upcoming Sea-Quest finale and how his attitude toward the outcome had changed. It was over a month away, but he no longer dreaded the conclusion and he was no longer distracted by the important need to be the one to dig up the chest. Now he looked forward to the night because he'd see Cilla again.

His whole outlook on the million dollars had changed. That night at the resort, straight after the final conclave had been the beginning of his change of heart. But it'd been the talk with his mother a few days after returning from the island which had really cemented his feelings on the subject. His mind drifted back to their discussion a couple of weeks ago.

'Why on earth would you think that, Tam?' His mother's eyes, a shade or two darker than his own, had widened in surprise. 'Of course, we'd never think any less of you if you didn't win.' Sitting at the small kitchen table, Tam had avoided his mum's gaze by tucking into the plate of pancakes she'd made him, aiming to fatten him up after his ordeal on the island. He wasn't allowed to mention how the show had ended, it was all top secret. He'd signed contracts to make sure he kept his mouth shut, but he was nevertheless trying to winkle out how his family would react to the idea of him winning. Or not. Casting a sideways glance at his mum, he took in her fading blonde hair tied back in a bun, face devoid of make-up, her trim figure swathed with an apron. She hadn't aged a day, at least not to him.

'You have to admit, the money would be a help though, Mum.'

'Please tell me you didn't enter that castaway show just to help me and your dad? We're happy here, fine just the way we are, darling.' She stopped bustling around the kitchen long enough to throw a tea-towel at him. 'I'm not sure, even if you won, that we'd take one red cent from you.'

'No, of course I didn't enter just for you.' Well, that was almost the truth. He'd done it as much for the kids' clinic as for himself and his family. But things had changed for him since that last, fateful night on Ko Mae Ko. He was realizing he wanted something much more precious than wealth. A pair of emerald green eyes, for instance.

His mother didn't notice his distraction and went on talking, strangely enough, sounding as if she'd just read his mind. 'Money isn't worth a spit if you don't have someone to share it with. Family is what makes a man, Tam, not riches. If you've never known that feeling of coming home to the refuge of someone who adores you at the end of the day, the joy of holding your own little baby in your arms for the first time, or the satisfaction of watching your kids grow into gorgeous, good men, then you would've missed out on so much. Money will never buy you that.'

He stopped eating and stared. He'd never heard his mother talk like this before. It was both refreshing and daunting. She'd always been one to keep her feelings low-key. Serious and capable, she'd busied herself around his father and the household. But when he thought about it, her actions had always been carried out with great affection. Perhaps he hadn't been able to see past his own sense of teenage dissatisfaction at how they'd struggled, never having enough, to the core of the love that kept his family going.

Yes, he'd suffered through poverty in his early

adolescence, and yes, he'd taken to crime as his manner of helping. But if he was completely honest with himself, a lot of his ill-gotten gains had been directed straight into his own pocket. Cash to buy those Nike shoes he'd coveted or that packet of cigarettes so he'd look cool at school. Maybe, through his own selfishness, he'd missed the fact it wasn't the materialistic things which held his family together after all.

Sitting down at the table with him, she said with a sigh, 'I know we did it hard when you were younger, after your father got hurt, and I'm truly sorry you were deprived of so many things.'

He started to dispute her words, but she waved him to silence with the tea-towel.

'I hope you know your dad and I still love each other, even after all these years, and I never resented him for what happened to us. It wasn't his fault. It's no obligation to take care of someone you love. I thought we'd brought you up to understand how much we cared for you and your brothers.'

'You did, Mum. You did.' And he could see it now. Money wouldn't save him.

His mum might've helped him see the error of his ways, but she still wasn't going to like what he had to say tonight. How'd they take the fact he was thinking about moving away from LA? Would they understand?

* * *

Cilla stood at the bow of the boat, watching the jetty slide closer. Holding a plastic fender in each hand, she judged the timing perfectly, swinging them down into place right before the yacht bumped gently up against the wooden pylon. Crystal, one of the other MiamiZ Boat Charter employees waiting on the jetty, grabbed the railing, caught the rope Cilla threw to her and tied the front end of the yacht off to the bollard. Cilla made her way quickly down to the stern and dropped another two fenders over the side to protect the rear end and helped Crystal tie off that end as well. Between the two of them, they manoeuvred a small gangplank into place for the passengers to disembark.

'See ya, Cilla. Thanks for the great day,' Christina yelled as she tripped lightly over the gangplank. She'd been the youngest daughter in the family they'd taken out today, and the most entertaining of the bunch.

'Here, let me give you a hand.' Cilla rushed forward to help the mother disembark. She was more unsteady on her feet than her daughter, especially after those few glasses of wine, and Cilla made sure she had a strong grip on the lady's arm as she helped her over, passing her off into Crystal's capable hands on the other side.

This family was a nice change from some other passengers she'd crewed for in the past three weeks. They were friendly and talkative, and treated Cilla as an equal, asking her questions and joking as if she were a long-lost friend. Their day trip around the Florida Keys had been a happy, fun-filled time.

'Thank you, Cilla. It's been a very pleasant day. We'll be back here soon,' a deep male voice said from behind, and she turned and beamed her best professional smile.

'Thank you, Mr Malooney. We're very glad to have you on board.'

'I'm in love with this boat, I have to say. Maybe I'll buy myself one, one of these days.' He patted the side of the cabin and gave the yacht a last admiring glance before heading off.

Cilla didn't agree with him, but she could see the allure this craft might have for many. It was a sleek and luxurious eighty-one foot Firretti yacht called *The Cat's Whiskers*. It had a large entertainment deck with a second story fly-bridge above it, where people could sit in complete extravagance on leather lounges and sip champagne and eat oysters with the wind whipping through their hair.

Give her an old wooden sailboat with plenty of character and stories hidden in the planks any day.

But she was lucky to have this job, and she wouldn't begrudge it one little bit. This was a good crew, young and full of energy and a love for what they were doing. Brad had written her a glowing recommendation as soon as he heard she was moving to Miami, making her a shoo-in with his mate who owned the luxury charter company.

'What a great day!' The captain, Doug's, loud bellow returned her from her musings. 'I wish we had more jobs like that one. Hey, Cilla?' He gave her a wink and a pat on the shoulder as he passed. 'I'll lock up the helm, are you right to tidy up the rest?'

'Will do,' she said, giving him a mock salute on her route into the lounge area. Piling the empty glasses and plates onto a tray, she took them into the galley to wash. There wasn't much to do. Today hadn't included any wild parties or drinking orgies, only a quiet family get-together.

She heard Doug clatter over the gangplank and knew she was alone. Leaving the dishes to drain on the sink, she went forward to sit in the bow. The boat was docked in Sunset Harbour, one of the ritziest harbours in one of the ritziest areas of Miami. She could see the high rises of

South Beach peeking over the rooftops of the houses in the art déco district. The playground for the rich and famous. A lifestyle she could never hope to join and didn't really want to. She and Barbara were happy in their little three-bedroom place in Cutler Bay.

Her grandmother seemed to have taken to living in Miami like a duck to water. She'd already met quite a few of their neighbours and even joined a walking club, and had started a jazz dancing class one night a week down at the local Senior Citizens Club with Mabel from next door. It almost put Cilla's social life to shame. Apart from going to work and back every day, Cilla hardly left the house.

Staring at the skyline without really seeing it, Cilla let the cool of the encroaching dusk enfold her. The air still dripped with humidity, as it always did here in summer, but her body was quickly acclimatising, especially after her month spent on the island in Thailand. Greeting-card clouds floated like white fuzzy bunnies out over The Bay, slowly turning salmon pink as the sun disappeared. The sound of waves lapping along the yacht's water-line drifted up to where she sat. She loved sitting here at the end of the day. It was peaceful, her calm little bubble in the midst of a madly rushing humanity.

Tomorrow was the Sea-Quest finale. She was heading out on a plane in the morning for Hollywood. Her stomach tightened at the thought.

'Hey, Cilla, is that you?' a familiar voice floated to her over the water. Casting her gaze out to the rear, she tried to pinpoint the direction of the hail.

And there was her ketch, *Halcyon*, sailing up The Bay, with Brad at the tiller.

'Brad! What... How?' She was lost for words.

'I wasn't sure I'd be able to find you, but Doug's directions were pretty good. Where can I moor this great hulk of a yacht?'

'How... Who?' She was still trying to get her mind around what she was seeing.

'Stop stuttering girl and point me to somewhere I can tie this thing up.'

'Take it over there.' Cilla pointed to another pier tucked in at the side of the main marina. 'They have a few berths set aside for visitors. I'll meet you round there.'

Quickly stowing the gangplank away, she locked up the cabin and leapt onto the jetty. The wooden planks rattled beneath her feet as she zigzagged her way through the maze of docks to the far side of the harbor.

Arriving out of breath, she was just in time to guide Brad and her boat into an empty berth. Tying off the bow rope to a bollard, she couldn't help herself, she had to run her hand over the wooden bowsprit, to make certain it was real. Her boat was here. Her beautiful yacht. The white hull gleamed in the soft dusk light, set off by the dark green stripe around the top and the timber finish on the decking. Cilla knew right then that Halcyon was the prettiest craft she'd ever seen. Just looking at her ketch made her soul lift like it hadn't done in months. She hadn't known how much this boat meant to her until right this very second.

Hurriedly tying off the tail end of the ketch, Cilla stepped on board and rushed to embrace Brad.

'I don't know how you did it, but thank you.' Her throat felt thick, and it was hard to get the words out.

Brad chuckled as he replied, 'Aww, it was nothing. Those stupid men from the bank didn't have a clue what she was worth. So when I heard they were flogging her off down in Brisbane for next to nothing, well, I stepped right in and gave them an offer they couldn't refuse.' He tried to extricate himself from Cilla's embrace, but she wasn't willing to let him go yet.

'I'm going to repay every cent.' Unbelievably, she was almost sobbing.

'Well, let's just see about that shall we.' This time he managed to loosen Cilla's arms from around his waist and guide her to a seat in the cockpit.

'No, no, I mean it, Brad.' She was so adamant that she jumped up again.

'Okay, we'll talk about it later,' he soothed. 'Now come on, sit down and tell me what you've been up to.' Cilla was still trying to compose herself, sniffing and dashing away the tears that threatened to overwhelm her. 'Is there anywhere I can get a beer in this town? It's been quite a while since I had a quenching ale.'

'Yes, yes, of course you can,' she said. 'There's a great little English pub down the street. Come on, I'll buy you dinner. It's the least I can do.'

'Sounds good to me.'

Resuming their conversation once they'd ordered a large dinner and Brad was sipping on a delicious cold beer, Cilla asked, 'You didn't sail my boat all the way over here, did you?'

'Don't be silly, that would've taken me too long. And scared the bejesus out of me. All those enormous waves and deep ocean currents. I put it on a cargo ship.'

'Of course you did,' Cilla replied softly.

'Of course I did, and it's only a half hour sail up The Bay from that big old port. Mind you, I'd have been here two days ago, but they took their sweet time getting your boat off that ginormous cargo ship and into the water.'

'I still can't find the words to thank you enough, Brad.' He was a great friend indeed and she counted herself as one of the luckiest girls in Miami at this particular moment. She gave him a fond glance, taking in the dishevelled clothes draped over those broad shoulders and the weeks' worth of stubble on his face from his time spent on the cramped cargo ship and felt the urge to walk around the table and embrace him once more.

As if he read her mind, he said, 'Now don't go getting all mushy on me again. Don't worry about it for one more minute. I needed a couple weeks off and I'm glad I could put right at least part of that travesty of your dad selling everything you own out from underneath you.'

'I meant what I said before, though. I'm paying you back.'

'If that's what you want, Cilla, that's fine by me.' Their meals arrived and there was a drawn out silence as they both tucked into their food.

'You know the other reason I'm here, don't you?' Brad said through a mouthful of food a few minutes later.

'No. Why?' Too busy chasing a baked potato around her plate, she didn't look up.

'I have to find out how it ends.'

Uh oh, alarm bells started ringing in her head.

'How what ends?'

'Your love story. Everyone at home in the Whitsundays made me promise to find out. We're all intrigued by the romance.' Suddenly her food went to ash in her mouth and she laid her fork down on the table, her appetite gone.

'There's no romance, Brad. Sorry to burst your bubble.'

She wouldn't meet his gaze, staring out the window at the people hurrying by on the street. Brad put down his fork as well and she could see from the corner of her eye he was staring at her.

'Really? It sure looked that way on the show.'

A piece of food wedged in her throat. So it'd been obvious to everyone who watched the spectacle. Something had blossomed between herself and Tam, and it seemed she was the only one dumb enough not to have seen it.

'Didn't you see how it ended, Brad? I voted him off, he hates me.'

'Yeah, but they always make it seem worse than it is on the show, to keep the ratings up. That's not how it ended. Is it?' Forcing herself to look at him, she nearly flinched when she saw the open curiosity and hope in his eyes.

'Yes, it is. I haven't seen or heard from Tam since we left the island.' Her grandmother was the only other person who knew the whole truth, and being here, saying these words to Brad made it seem very final indeed.

'I'm sorry, Cilla.' But for some reason he didn't sound as contrite as he should, and she watched him with suspicion while he tucked into his steak with gusto.

'Anyway, I'm off to the finale tomorrow,' she said.

'Well ain't that lucky, I got here just in time. I'd love to come with you.'

'What? You can't.'

'Why not?'

'Because…'

'Thought so,' he said with a smug grin and continued eating his meal.

Great, one more person to be a witness to her

humiliation tomorrow night.

CHAPTER TWENTY-ONE

Studio lights blazed down from every angle, and Tam was jostled by warm bodies as people rushed past like scurrying mice. Loud voices barked out commands and someone tried to stop him and put makeup on his face. Confusion reigned. Pacing to and fro, aimless and apprehensive, he looked to the front of the stage where a sea of faces were scrutinizing him. Ducking his head, he tried to disappear into the throng of humanity. It was daunting being watched by that many people. And he was about to be the absolute centre of attention. The idea sent shivers of anxiety down his spine. Why had it never been this obvious his face was being beamed into millions of homes all across the world when he'd been on the island?

He wasn't sure what he'd been expecting of the Sea-Quest television studio, but this wasn't it. They were on a very large outdoor set, open to the night sky. The TV crew tried their best to make the area look like an authentic beach scene straight from Ko Mae Ko Island. Tam was standing on a slightly raised wooden platform, where some large cast-iron pots had been transported from the original conclave platform and glowed with fires burning deep in their bellies. Even some of the brightly colored rugs, wooden treasure chests, and Jolly Roger flags that'd been scattered on the island were now sitting in pride of place around the stage. There was also a large fire-pit right in front of a set of bleachers for all the contestants to sit next to. And if his eyes didn't deceive him, there were actual trees growing in the surrounding piles of sand. Coconut palms and a small tropical almond, the same as the one they'd built their shelter beneath.

But this facade wasn't close to the real thing.

Gone was the hum of cicadas singing in the background, replaced by the jabbering of an excited studio audience sitting in neat rows of folding chairs down upon the sand. Gone, too, was the bright winking blanket of tropical stars overhead. Now the starkness of the spotlights hid all but the very brightest stars from view. Tam had a sudden nostalgic wish to be transported back to the island, just for one more night. So he could listen to the sound of the waves dashing against the beach, the wind sighing through the leaves and feel the warm humid air envelope him.

A technician carrying an enormous microphone bumped into him and the fantasy was shattered.

Snap out of it. There was something he needed to do before the show started and he was running out of time. Using his height to full advantage, he craned his neck so he could see above the scuttling crowd.

'Hey, Tam, how's it going?' A hand clasped his. Hayden gave Tam one of his winning smiles turned up to maximum wattage as he pumped his hand up and down.

'Hi, Hayden, great to see you. Hey you haven't seen

Cilla have you?' Hayden chuckled and pointed over toward the rear of a low series of bleachers. The seats were set up for all eighteen castaways to sit on as JJ interviewed them in front of the live audience.

'Yeah, I saw her over there, talking to Marg a couple of minutes ago.'

'Thanks. We should catch up after the show for a drink,' Tam replied, his focus already shifting.

She was here.

'Sure, sure. I'll see you at the after-party,' called Hayden, moving on toward the next group of people.

Tam's palms sweat.

There was no way he was going to back out now. He hoped like hell she didn't just turn her back on him and walk away. But if she rejected him, then so be it. He had to find out. Squaring his shoulders, he strode across the stage.

There she was. God, she looked good. Wearing a dark brown tank top, the earthy color accenting her golden tan, and a pair of denim shorts with high heels, it was difficult to take his eyes off her. The shoes made her legs look impossibly long, showing off tight, firm thighs and a pert backside. At the sight of her, a hot surge of desire swept through him and he realized he'd stopped dead in his tracks.

Switching his gaze over to Marg, he steadied himself. He didn't want to have to explain away a raging bulge in his pants when he greeted Cilla for the first time in two months.

Marg looked wonderful too. She was wearing a tight singlet top and a short black mini-skirt, all the better to show off her pumped-up muscles. And they were impressive. Good for her, she obviously worked hard to keep her body looking great. Even if that kind of physique on a woman wasn't for him. Cilla's willowy curves on the other hand…

'Hello, Cilla.' Emerald eyes fixed on him as he spoke.

'Hi, Tam.' The emerald eyes didn't flick away from his face as he'd feared they might, instead fixing him with a steady gaze, a slight inquiring tilt to her left eyebrow. Then she smiled and the entire room lit up.

'How have you been?' *Dumb ass.* He could've kicked himself for the lame question. It didn't even encompass what he really wanted to say.

'You know. Surviving.' The cheeky smile he'd grown to love played across her lips. 'No pun intended, of course.'

He returned her grin, the muscles in his neck relaxing.

'Do I get a hello as well, or am I just the invisible woman here?' Marg sounded more amused than angry.

'Great to see you too, Marg. Fully recovered from the stonefish sting, I see.'

'Yep, I'm awesome.' She fluffed her short blond hair, so it stood out in a halo around her head.

'Perfect.'

There was an awkward pause. Into the silence a voice boomed over a loudspeaker, 'Going live in five, places please everyone.'

Quick, he had to say something, before it was too late.

'Cilla, I need to ask you a question.'

'Righto, I know when I'm not wanted.' Marg gave an exaggerated wink to Tam. 'I'll leave you two and locate my seat.' She gave them both a last excited hug before skipping off. Tam wished he had half her enthusiasm. He was about to discover if he'd won one million dollars, and all he could think about was whether Cilla would talk to him or not. Cilla's gaze followed Marg as she headed toward the bleachers.

'We should go find our seats too.' Tiny frown lines appeared on her forehead. He noticed the scar was looking much better; no longer red and angry. Given time, it'd fade into the hairline and become a distant memory.

'Ahh, Cilla...' Dammit, he'd rehearsed the words so carefully, but his tongue was feeling thick and unwieldy, his mind a complete blank.

'Will you promise me something?' he said in a rush.

'Depends.' Her answer was slow to come, her hands fiddling with the fringe of her suede handbag. She looked unsure. He wanted to kick himself. They'd parted on uncertain terms, not seen each other for two months, and here he was almost jumping down her throat at their first encounter. He ploughed on anyway, relentless. If he didn't, he might lose her forever.

'Will you meet me for dinner after the show is over? Or a drink, at the very least?'

She raised her shoulders in a delicate shrug.

'Please.' He was practically begging, but no longer cared.

After another moment's hesitation, where she measured him with calculating eyes, she finally said, 'Sure.'

But he needed her absolute assurance. Once she gave her word, he knew she'd keep it. 'Do you promise, no matter what happens tonight?' The unsaid words hovered between them. *No matter who wins?*

'Yes, I promise,' she replied with a touch of exasperation.

'Great. There's a funky little Mexican place down the

road, they do wonderful vegetarian tostadas.'

'I love Mexican.'

He hoped the relief wasn't showing too much in the goofy smile he offered her. This wasn't how he'd intended this conversation to go, but it was something, a start.

He felt a hand on his shoulder and a firm voice saying, 'You have to take your seat now, sir. We're about to start our live feed.' Tam let himself be led by the production assistant to the front of the bleachers, following Cilla, who was being steered in the same direction by a woman with an ear attachment and a large clipboard.

Taking his seat in the front row, Tam noticed JJ already perched on his high stool next to them. The man looked resplendent in a casual dark green shirt and long, white chinos. The famous dimple was still in place and his teeth just as pearly as ever as he beamed down at them magnanimously. Sitting next to Tam were Rosa and Simon, the final three up front for everyone to see. Rosa gave him a tentative smile, but Simon didn't even glance his way. And that was fine by Tam.

'We've less than a minute before we go to air. Can the studio audience please be quiet,' a voice reverberated over a loudspeaker again. The crowd fell silent. People with clipboards and earpieces hovered in the shadows, all watching someone whom Tam assumed was the director wave the contestants to silence and then point at JJ and start counting down for the moment they went to air. Tam noticed two very large cameras circling the stage, pointed straight at him.

It was time.

He almost laughed to realize although he was nervous, it was nothing to how he'd felt confronting Cilla only moments ago. He stole a glance down the line of people in the front row. She was there, tucked in between Alisha and Hayden. She and Alisha had their heads together, arms linked, whispering in conspiratorial tones. As she listened, Cilla began biting her lower lip and looking decidedly uneasy.

And maybe she had a right to look apprehensive. They both knew one of JJ's questions would be, *Why did you do it, Cilla? Why did you give Tam the talisman?* He'd been asked the same thing at least ten times today already. It was the question on everyone's lips. He'd love to know the answer as well. People in this show weren't supposed to be selfless or noble. They were there to win the money.

There was a light tap on his shoulder and looking around he saw Marg sitting behind him.

'Good luck,' she mouthed. Jason was beside her on the second tier and he added a wink of encouragement. Casting his gaze further backward, he could see Glen and Cho, and even Madison right up on the third row. They were all here. All eighteen of them had returned for this one night. It'd be good to catch up with everyone afterwards, to see how their lives had changed—or not— after their time on Sea-Quest. Hell, he might go talk to Madison. His feelings of antagonism toward her had mellowed nicely over the past couple of months.

But first he needed to talk to Cilla. The rest could wait.

'Hello, everyone, welcome to the finale of Sea-Quest.' JJ's voice cut through the expectant silence. 'In just a few brief minutes, we'll find out who is the winner. Who *will* dig up the treasure and go home with one million dollars in their pockets?'

Tam was about to know once and for all if that money

was going to alter his life. Second prize would be good too, if he won that he'd still be able to help his clinic out, but it wasn't a life-changer, not like the million.

It was all a little surreal. His mind wouldn't focus properly on what JJ was saying. He had a one in three chance at winning, and his heart should have been beating like a drum with anticipation. But for some reason he couldn't summon the requisite enthusiasm. Even if he won tonight, he knew it'd be a hollow victory. The realization had dawned on him slowly over the past two months. He'd fallen in love with Cilla. And no amount of money would make his life any happier if she wasn't in it.

* * *

'Rosa wins the million dollar prize,' JJ yelled above the deafening cheer of the crowd. Cilla's chest felt hollow. Tam hadn't won. He'd come second. Her head reeled with the shock of JJ's announcement. Tam should've had the numbers, Cilla was so sure he'd win. But the game of Sea-Quest played its last ironic trick. Cilla's gaze fixed on Tam's face, wanting desperately to change the outcome. He deserved to be the hero in this story. Instead she watched him, gallant in defeat, being the first to congratulate Rosa, picking her up and spinning the excited woman around in a bear-hug. Cilla knew that such was the character of this man, his delight for Rosa was completely genuine. There was no malice or discontent in Tam Connor, he was kind and unaffected in his happiness for her. The thought made the breath catch in her throat.

The only good outcome from the whole vote was the fact that Simon had come away with nothing. Simon didn't even try to look gracious when JJ announced Rosa as the winner of Sea-Quest season twenty-two. His mouth screwed up like he'd eaten a whole lemon, and his eyes narrowed dangerously. He'd left the stage immediately, pushing people out of his road as he stomped down the stairs, and she could even hear him swearing at the producer above the noise of the crowd congratulating Rosa. He'd been one of the most manipulative and destructive players in the game, but now he was a sore loser with nothing to show for his vanity.

Before Cilla could gather her thoughts, she was pushed into line with the rest of the contestants to dutifully watch Rosa use the map JJ gave her to pace out lengths and find the landmarks on the make-believe beach of the TV set, until she at last started to dig through the sand to where she thought the treasure was buried. But Cilla's mind was whirling with notions of Tam, wondering who in hell had actually voted for Rosa. It must've been Hayden, Jason, Susan and perhaps Cho? Cilla had been sure that at least either Jason or Hayden would have enough sense to realize that Rosa had coasted through on other people's coat tails. That Tam had been the stronger player. But it wasn't to be.

Returning her thoughts to the scene in front of her, she was just in time to hear the thud of the metal spade against wood. Rosa had found her treasure. One million dollars in gold bullion.

Then came Tam's turn to dig for the much smaller second prize of two hundred thousand. A snarl of emotions tangled in her gut as she stared at him digging, and she fought to unravel what she was feeling. Frustration, anger, betrayal—they were uppermost in the swirl of her sentiments. But as she regarded Tam's strong back bend and straighten while he shoveled sand, other, softer emotions surfaced. Pity—he so deserved this money to help his kids. Warm affection for the way he winked as Marg cheered him on. Respect for how he was handling himself with such humble humor. Desire as she observed those long legs, encased in butt-hugging jeans, flex and bulge each time he bent down. He looked so handsome, his light grey sweater stretching nicely over his chiselled pecs. Clean-shaven, with hair stylishly tousled, he was the picture of health once again. Love. Yep, there was no doubt, she'd fallen inextricably for this man. The answer as to what she was going to do with those feelings, however, remained a mystery.

Half an hour later Cilla squeezed her handbag tightly in front of her, trying to quell the awkwardness threatening to take over. Tam was heading straight for their little group from across the other side of the reception lobby, where they were all waiting for the after-party to start. Those hazel eyes were fixed right on her. Other women cast covetous glances as he approached through the crowd and Cilla caught herself frowning at those women, even though she knew she had no right. Tam didn't belong to her.

And now she was wishing she hadn't agreed to go to dinner with him so readily. What would she say to him? What was he going to say to her? In all the scenarios she'd run through her head tonight, it always ended inevitably —with a goodbye.

She'd betrayed him abominably, used him deplorably, and he'd never forgive her for that. She certainly wouldn't if she were in his shoes. If he'd ever had any feelings for her, she'd well and truly killed them by voting him off the island. Besides, they lived on opposite sides of the continent. Even geography was conspiring against them. Add to that, Tam hadn't tried to contact her in the past two months. Not once. It all added up to the fact that Tam didn't feel the same things about her. She would conquer these feelings. Not let them show. If she kept shoving them deep down inside where no one else could see them, then it'd get easier and easier to act as if she didn't care. Eventually. One day. Maybe.

But going to dinner with him was definitely not a good idea. She had to come up with some kind of excuse. But what? She'd promised him, after all.

Raising her chin a little, Cilla watched Tam walk toward them. Standing next to her talking to Brad, Alisha lifted her head and noticed Tam's approach as well. Her black eyes twinkled with amusement and she gave Cilla a knowing glance. The two of them had taken up their great friendship exactly where they'd left off. Cilla had been ecstatic to see Alisha again, and they'd organised for Cilla to visit her family in New Orleans. She couldn't wait to meet Humphrey, Alisha's husband, or her three kids, all grown and left home, but still living in the neighbourhood. Would they live up to the image Cilla had in her head from the hours they'd spent discussing their families while snorkelling for fish on the island? They sounded like such a close-knit, loving family, she couldn't wait to find out.

'I saw Rosa over there, I need to talk to her,' Alisha whispered into Cilla's ear. 'I think I'll leave you to it. It was great to meet your grandmother. Meet you at the wind-up party.' Before Cilla had time to protest, Alisha gave a little wave, the twinkle still evident in her eye as she headed off toward the group gathered around Rosa.

Plastering a smile on her face, she closed her eyes for the

briefest of seconds and then touched her grandmother lightly on the elbow when she felt Tam's presence behind her. 'Grandma, I'd like you to meet Tam.' The old woman's arm tensed under her fingers. Fiercely protective of her granddaughter, Barbara had made a pre-emptive decision after watching the television show that Tam was to blame for Cilla's downfall on Sea-Quest. Or at the very least Cilla was Tam's scorned lover. Her granddaughter deserved better than a traitor. No amount of cajoling from Cilla's side would get her to see it otherwise. 'Tam, this is my grandmother, Barbara.'

'Very pleased to meet you.' Tam held out his hand in welcome.

'Hmm.' Barbara pursed her lips and Cilla was afraid she wouldn't return his handshake. But even her grandmother wouldn't leave a man dangling out there like a fish hung out to dry, and she did eventually give his hand a quick shake before glaring openly at him again.

'Hi, my name's Brad.' Brad offered his hand into the awkward silence. 'I'm Cilla's old boss,' he said when Tam threw him a quizzical grin. 'I just happened to be in town when this finale thing came up and I couldn't pass up a chance to study the whole spectacle for myself.' Brad gave one of his trademark belly laughs and Cilla was thankful for her boss' impeccable sense of humour.

'I have to admit, I'm a bit of a Sea-Quest addict. I watch every season,' Brad enthused. 'But this time it was extra special, with Cilla being part of it and all. It's a pity she didn't win.' Brad took off his Chicago Bulls cap and fixed her with an unswerving gaze. 'You were definitely in there with a good chance. But I guess congratulations are in order for you, Tam.' Brad reached out and slapped Tam on the shoulder. 'Second place ain't too bad. I bet that two hundred thousand will come in mighty handy, huh?'

Tam smiled and was about to reply when Barbara said in a very loud voice, 'Yes, and we all know who he has to thank for that opportunity, don't we?' She gave Tam one of her sour looks, eyes narrowed to squinty pinpricks, lips puckered up like a dried prune.

Uh oh. Cilla didn't want to answer the question of why she'd thrown away her exemption for the hundredth time today. Quick, she needed to change the subject and fast, before her grandmother launched into an unjustified tirade.

Then she saw him.

Her father.

She'd not seen him in over six years, but she'd know that hunched stance, that pinched, haunted face anywhere. He hadn't seen her yet, and he staggered forward a few steps and then stopped, swaying on the spot as he scanned the groups of people in the reception area. He was tipsy. Her stomach lurched violently at the thought. What was he doing here?

An angry sneer lit up his face as he spotted them, and he almost fell in his haste to get to them. Cilla stood transfixed, suddenly unable to move.

'You stupid little bitch,' her father snarled, loud enough so that other people standing nearby stopped their conversations to stare. 'What the fuck were you thinking, giving away that talisman? You threw away one million dollars, do you realize that?' There was no familiar greeting, no *how-do-you-do*. He launched straight into his bitter tirade, raging about the only thing that mattered to him anymore. Money.

He didn't care one whit what happened to either her or her grandmother; his mother. Didn't care if they ended up on the street, Barbara living out the rest of her life in some horrible public aged-care facility, and her, penniless. All he cared about was himself. The notion leant an edge of steel to her resolve. He would not hurt them again.

'Oh no,' Cilla heard her grandmother gasp as she took an instinctive step backward. Anger rose vicious and sudden, burning hot through Cilla's veins. How dare he frighten his own mother! How dare he speak to her in that way!

'Brad, can you look after Barbara for me?' Cilla ground out between clenched teeth. 'Whatever happens, don't let this…him, near her.'

'Sure thing, Cilla.' She saw Brad wrap a protective arm around her grandmother and lead her away to the edge of the room, the look on his face one of set determination. She knew he'd be back at her side in an instant if she needed him.

'Well come on, girl, do tell. I'd love to hear the story of why you thought you needed to give away that money.' Now he was closer, Cilla saw drops of spittle fly from his mouth as he spoke. 'We could've been rich, if you hadn't been such a little slut.' Not only was he drunk, but he was as mean as she'd ever seen him before. Her fists came up in front of her, an instinctive move, surprising her. Would she really go as far as actually hitting her father?

'Hold on a minute,' said Tam, stepping in between Cilla and her father, his shoulder bumping with hers. 'I don't know exactly what's going on here, but you shouldn't be speaking to Cilla like that. You need to back off.' If she'd not been so full of rage, Cilla would've felt a warm glow of gratitude creep into her body. Tam was protecting her. Putting his body on the line for her.

'It's okay, Tam, I've got this one,' she said quietly.

'Yeah, boy, get the fuck outta my face. I'll talk to my daughter any fucking way I please.'

'Excuse me?' Tam couldn't hide the incredulity in his voice. Cilla put a hand on his bicep and moved to stand beside him.

'I'm sorry you had to find out like this, Tam, but this is my wonderful, loving father.' Her voice dripped with resentment. 'Get out of here, Wayde. You're drunk and making a scene.' Her whole body was shaking with the effort of keeping her tone civil.

'I'm not leaving until I'm good and ready. Until I get my fair share.' Wayde was slurring his words badly, and a crowd had gathered, enjoying the spectacle, completing her humiliation.

'Fair share of what, exactly, Wayde? You already stole your mother's house and my boat from us. When will you be happy? When we're both living on the streets, as destitute and desperate as you are?' An enormous well of abhorrence, pent up for over ten years, boiled inside her. She knew her face was warped into a snarling grimace, but she no longer cared.

'Don't give me that crap, girl. You've got money to spare, I know it. You just don't want me to have it. Money is as important to you as it is to me. I'd never have given that talisman away, and you shouldn't have either.'

'And that is the exact reason I did it. You disgust me, and I'll never, ever, be like you.'

'Don't be such a stupid little ingrate. You've got my blood running through you. Of course you're the same as me. You're exactly like me.' Her father stepped closer, looming menacingly. She felt Tam push up against her shoulder, ready to react instantly. But she didn't need him. She'd settle this one on her own.

'Get away from me,' she snarled.

'Make me,' he snarled in reply.

Then she hit him. Full in the face. He fell backward and landed hard on his backside. Blood spurted from his nose. She felt a sick sense of elation at the sight.

'I don't ever want to look at you again. Ever. Do you hear me?' Her father looked up, his expression dazed, blood running down his face. Two security guards arrived. They picked him up, one under each arm.

'Take this guy out of here.' Cilla was glad when Tam took control, she was too angry to speak. 'I'll tell you what happened on the way out.' Tam steered the three of them toward the nearest exit, the two guards practically dragging Wayde between them.

She watched her father's unceremonious exit. He was a sad sight, all shrunken and dishevelled, stooped and small between the large guards. She should've felt pity for her father, or grief, something. But she didn't. All she felt was relief and a fierce hope that he heeded her words and never set foot near her again.

Remembering her grandmother, Cilla whirled around and headed straight for Barbara and Brad. He still had a protective hand under her elbow, a concerned look crowding his face.

'Oh my God, Cilla, you hit him,' Barbara gasped. 'I can't believe you hit him.' She was practically hyperventilating.

'Let's go over here and sit down.' Cilla led them over to a couch and eased her grandmother down onto it.

'Is he going to come back?'

'Calm down, Grandma. The guards will make sure he doesn't return.'

'Yeah, and after Cilla punched him, he won't want to show his face in here again,' Brad chuckled. Cilla threw him a look that told him he wasn't helping. 'I'll get a glass of water, hey?'

'That'd be great.'

Tam strode into the room. He was so tall he towered over most of the other guests. For a millisecond the mere sight of him made the room seem brighter, made her want to smile. Until she remembered what he'd witnessed.

'I'm so sorry, Tam, I can't go out with you tonight. I can't leave my grandmother in such a state.' It was true, Barbara had worked herself up so much, she dare not leave her tonight.

'Of course, you can't,' Tam said, his tone sympathetic. But there was a tightness to his eyes that spoke to how disappointed he was.

'Tomorrow perhaps?'

'Sorry, we fly home first thing in the morning,' Cilla said, patting her grandmother's hand absentmindedly.

'Oh, I understand.' He was no longer hiding his disappointment.

'I'm sorry you had to watch that, Tam. But now you know the truth about me. I came onto this show to win back money that my no-good gambling father stole from me.' Her dirty laundry was out for everyone to see. He'd never want to be with her now he'd seen what a dysfunctional family she came from. She'd just punched her own father in the face, for Christ's sake.

'It explains a lot about you, Cilla.' Tam fixed her with a

serious gaze, eyes a dark treacle.

What did that cryptic remark mean?

'Yes, well, the truth always comes out in the end, doesn't it?' She didn't want to see those eyes fill with pity, as she knew they would any second. She didn't deserve his pity, anyway.

'I have to look after my grandmother. I guess I'll catch you sometime.' She turned her back on him and pretended to fuss over Barbara on the couch, not daring to look at Tam any longer. This was for the best. It'd do her no good for him to see how much she wanted him to stay. She was a lost cause, and Tam was too decent a man to want any part of her. Not after she'd acted so unforgivably on the island, and certainly not after she'd showed him exactly what kind of person she was by brawling with her own father.

'If that's the way you want it, Cilla. Then goodbye and good luck.'

Seconds ticked by and she finally dared to glance up. Tam was halfway across the room, steadily retreating as he made for the doorway.

She hadn't gotten the chance to tell him how much she wished he'd won the million dollars instead of Rosa. Or ask him how the kids in his clinic were all doing. Did they think he was a hero for becoming a castaway on an island for thirty-eight days?

And how he was a hero in her eyes.

That she'd fallen in love with him.

All of these things rolled through her head as she watched him walk away. A lump of something cold and unnameable formed in her chest. It was hard to breathe.

She wanted him to turn around, to flash that captivating

smile and tell her this was all a joke, he wasn't going to let her push him away this easily. Wanted him to drag her into his embrace and hold her safe and treasured against his chest. Stoke her hair and whisper words of adoration. But this wasn't a TV show, this was reality. And in reality, Tam would never return her love.

Inside she wanted to scream, to cry and wail and throw a tantrum on the floor. On the outside her eyes remained dry, her face fixed into a mask of unqualified indifference. There'd be time for tears later, but not here, and not now.

'Would you take me up to our room please, dear? I need a cup of tea and a lie down,' her grandmother said in a tremulous voice, and it made Cilla jump guiltily. For a second she'd forgotten where she was; had forgotten everything but watching those broad shoulders walk away from her. Forever.

'Of course, Grandma.' She helped her up and as she took one elbow, Brad lifted the other and they walked slowly toward the hotel lifts, in the opposite direction to which Tam had gone.

CHAPTER TWENTY-TWO

Head down in the forward rope locker, Cilla didn't notice the figure standing on the jetty at first. Settling the last coil of rope neatly in place, she came up onto her knees and closed the locker hatch with a flourish. Finally, the last rope was stowed properly. She was ready to take the ketch for a sail; the first occasion since Brad brought her to Miami nearly a month ago.

'Permission to come aboard.'

Startled, Cilla looked up. She could only make out a dark outline of a man on the jetty, with the early morning sun blazing directly into her eyes. The voice was familiar, however. The figure moved a step closer.

Tam.

'What... What are you doing here?'

He was standing there, a black bag resting at his feet, looking as nonchalant as you please. As if his presence in Sunset Harbour was an everyday occurrence. Confusion swirled in her head. Heart pounding, she took an involuntary step backward.

'I brought Jelly Babies,' he said, holding up an opened

bag and popping one into his mouth. He'd remembered. They were her favourites. She was still at a loss for words, his presence here, on her jetty, had completely undone her. What the hell was going on?

Noting her complete lack of coherence, he prompted gently, 'Will you let me come aboard?'

His mouth turned up in one of his stunning smiles. Oh God, she'd missed that smile. For a split second she allowed her gaze to roam over his familiar face, the aquiline nose, sumptuous lips, dark hair—longer these days but still curling temptingly on top, those honey-colored eyes which remained fixed on her. He looked so good, exactly as she'd remembered him. Exactly as he'd appeared in her dreams. Dreams, which had been haunting her these past few months. Which hadn't subsided over time as she hoped, but had instead intensified to the point where she almost dreaded going to sleep.

Why was he here? She'd been so sure it was the last moment she'd ever see him, that day at the Sea-Quest finale. His presence here threatened to undo all the hard slog she'd endured trying to rid her body of the effect he had on her. And now she recognized why it'd been so painful to banish him from her mind. All it took was one smile and her spirit soared. *Goddamn the man to hell!*

'Doug told me I might find you here,' he added, pointing toward the MiamiZ Boat Charter office. 'He said Monday was your day off, but if you weren't at work, then the only other place to find you was tinkering on your damn yacht. I think he might've also mentioned that you love this boat more than any human being, as far as he could tell.'

'That's not strictly true,' she replied, finding her voice at last. It wouldn't do to show how much he rattled her. She could do this. She could act normal around him.

'I can see why you love her though, she truly is as beautiful as you described.' Tam gave the ketch an appreciative once over.

'Why don't you come aboard and have a closer look then.' The cost of those words was almost too much, the thought of Tam on her boat something she'd fantasised about, but never, ever, thought would truly happen. Keeping her face blank, she indicated he pass her his bag, watching as he climbed on board. He did an admirable job for a city slicker. His height helped, making it easier to lift those long, jean-clad legs over the safety line in one fluid movement. Holding onto the rigging, he stood on the foredeck, a pleased grin lighting up his face.

'I've often wondered what it'd be like to be standing on this deck. When you were telling us about your boat on the island, I promised myself I'd come and see her one day. And here I am.'

'Yes, here you are,' she replied, impressed by the fact he'd actually wondered about her boat. Then she caught his gaze travelling down the length of her body and she was suddenly aware of her very short cut-offs and the button-up shirt she'd tied in a knot, revealing too much midriff. He was also standing much too close for comfort. Needing to put some space between them, she moved, barefoot, down the narrow strip of deck, toward the cockpit.

'I was just about to have some breakfast, before I went out for a sail. Would you like some? It's only toast and Vegemite.'

'Yes, please. I've come straight from the airport. I haven't had anything to eat yet.' Tam made his way forward, a little slower than her, holding on to any piece of available rigging as he came.

'What's Vegemite?'

'It's an Australian thing. It's kind of an acquired taste. It's very salty and very black, but I love it.' Most Americans hated it at first sight, but she'd learned, if spread thinly, with lots of butter, it was delicious on toast.

'Sounds disgusting, but I'll try it.'

Ducking down the companionway, she implied he take a seat in the cockpit.

'Stay up here, I'll be back with the toast in a jiffy.' She didn't want him following her down into the close quarters of the cabin. It'd be too much for her to take, at least until the shock of seeing him had worn off a little.

She had to rest her palm against the galley bench-top to light the little gas stove, her hand was trembling so much. Tam's presence here had completely thrown her, it was so unexpected. She took a deep breath, and then another, before gingerly placing the toasting implement over the naked flame and then popping in a piece of bread. By the time she bent down to grab the butter and Vegemite out of the small refrigerator, the shakes had subsided to mere tremors. But keeping her hands busy didn't stop her mind buzzing with a million questions. What could he possibly want?

Sliding her bare feet over the polished wooden floorboards, she let the familiar aura of the cabin sooth her. She'd re-done the whole inside of the ketch when she'd first bought it. Painstakingly sanding all the old, misused cedar, slowly bringing it back to life, making it gleam and shine once more. It smelled like home to Cilla, much more than the little villa she and her grandmother shared ever would. Musky and salty with the spicy scent of varnished wood.

At last, the toast was cooked, and she dropped it onto a waiting plate sitting on the compact wooden dining table that doubled as a map desk as well as a workbench. With knife in hand she went to spread it, but the butter never reached the toast. Her hand stayed poised in mid-air as her whirling mind finally took over and she was lost in a fantasy of memories. Tam and her in the surf at midnight. Making love in the ocean. The image came so fast and clear Cilla gasped. His wet hands sliding over her body, the feel of his muscled chest beneath her breasts.

'Wow, it's just as gorgeous down here as it is upstairs.' She hadn't even heard him come down the companionway, and now he was standing directly behind her, mere inches away. Her body reacted immediately, the lingering images of Tam in the surf only helping to accentuate her response.

Not daring to turn around, knowing if she did she'd want to touch him, to take him in her arms, she asked the question that'd been begging to be asked the second she saw him standing on the jetty, 'Why are you here, Tam?'

'To see you. I couldn't leave things in the state they were between us.' His voice was husky, running like smooth treacle down her back.

'Why not? We said goodbye, didn't we? Surely that's the end of it. I know it was for me.'

Actually, it was nowhere near the end for her. She'd spent the past month unable to drag herself out of a deep funk. Even Doug commented on how desultory she'd become and told her to get it together for the sake of her job. She'd put on a brave face at work, but she still lay awake most nights, the vast hole in her chest making sleep impossible. And when sleep did finally come, her dreams were full of him. Drops of seawater sparkling, like flashes of starlight in his dark hair after he emerged from the ocean. Or the straight line of his jaw as she'd studied him, face in profile while he listened to something JJ was saying.

'Perhaps it's over for you, Cilla, but I need more. I need to know, once and for all.' His hands landed on her shoulders, compelling her to turn around to meet his gaze.

'Know what?' Her voice was suddenly as husky as his.

'How you really feel about me.' His face remained impassive, the only giveaway a twitch at the corner of his mouth. 'Do you truly hate me?'

'Hate you? Why would you… God no, I don't hate you!'

'You certainly seemed to when you voted me off the island.' She squirmed, wanting to turn away, to avoid that piercing gaze. His firm hands denied her, keeping her eyes centered straight on him.

'Did I?' She tried to think back to that day, over three months ago, but any impressions of animosity had faded. Maybe she had hated him for a fleeting second, but not anymore. They were such powerful emotions, hate and love. Perhaps she'd been using hate to conceal her true feelings.

'I responded very badly to your anger, and I guess a part of me knew you'd every right to act the way you did. You felt betrayed, and I didn't want to see that at first. I should've known better. It's part of my job, after all, to help people understand what they're feeling. But I was too close to the whole thing. I want you to know how sorry I am. Things should've been so different between us.'

'Different how?' If only things could've ended differently. But they didn't and she couldn't see how any of this was going to help. Her gaze flittered around the cabin, looking for a way out, answers to an unsolvable question.

'Cilla.' His finger caressed beneath her chin and then with a firm yet gentle touch he forced her to look at him. 'Put your hand on my heart.' Taking his finger from under her chin, he guided her hand, pushing it hard onto his chest, their eyes never breaking contact. The beat was strong and true and solid beneath her fingertips. A tiny spark of hope flared within her. The honey in Tam's eyes darkened to molasses, his gaze becoming hungry, a wicked grin suffusing his face.

'You feel it too, don't you? Hearts don't lie.'

His mouth collided with hers, fiery and indulgent. She should've stopped him. But the low groan he made when her tongue darted out to taste his drove her on. The desire, which had flared the second he'd stepped onto the boat next to her, was burning so hot she could no longer think straight. She wanted him. So badly.

Tam had come because he wanted closure. There was no future for them. He lived on the other side of the country and she couldn't leave her grandmother. But maybe she could give him a fitting farewell before they said their final goodbye. For good this time. If they were going to do this, then it had to be different to that wild, hasty sex they'd had in the ocean, rutting as if they'd been dogs on heat. If she was going to let herself give in one final time before Tam left her life forever, then she was going to make the most of it. Slow and sensuous, she was going to enjoy every second of this.

Yes. She'd take this one irrevocable thing from Tam and savour it for the rest of her life.

Taking him by the hand, she led him forward to the main double bunk crammed into the V-shape at the bow of the boat. She pushed him down onto the bed and then climbed on top, straddling him. Dipping her head, she brushed her lips against his neck, tasting the slightly salty hint, inhaling his masculine scent. Using the sharp edges of her teeth, she nipped at the curve of his collarbone, enjoying the rush of craving when his pulse became erratic beneath her mouth.

'Bloody hell, Cilla,' he moaned. 'Wait, I need to see more of you. All of you.'

Sitting up, his deft fingers attacked the buttons on her shirt and she soon found it discarded onto the floor. His hand worked around her back and unfastened her bra. Impatient, she helped him by slipping each strap off her shoulders.

'You're just as beautiful as I remember,' he said, eyes roving over her breasts and down her abdomen. Lifting a lock of auburn hair, he inhaled through the silken tresses as he threaded them through his hand. 'At least this has healed,' he said, touching the scar on her forehead lightly. A slight frown crossed his brow, as if he might suddenly be having second thoughts.

Standing up, she stripped off her shorts and panties. Tam got the hint, unbuckling his blue jeans and kicking them from his legs while she pulled the white T-shirt over his head in one quick maneuver. Laying there completely naked in front of her, she reveled in his perfect physique.

Lean, but still strong and well-muscled. Resting her entire length down next to him, she gloried in the feel of their legs entwining together, skin on skin. She shivered. For the past few months she'd dreamed of this and nothing else, but the reality of it was bittersweet. Tears filled her eyes, and she closed them as he skimmed his tongue over her lips. She couldn't let him see how much this moment meant to her. If she couldn't have him in her life, then at least she'd be able to hold this instant in her soul forever.

'I've thought about doing this ever since we left the island.'

She stilled beneath him. Was he reading her mind?

'I'm all yours, Cilla.' Tam's voice was so low and throaty it was like a carnal stroke to her body.

With a quick flick, Tam had her lying under him, the unexpected dominance electrifying, the delicious weight of him on top of her sending a sizzling curl of heat through her abdomen. Drawing in a gasping breath, she was again taken by surprise when his lips descended over her nipple. He sucked, taking it deeper into his mouth, neither overly gentle nor too rough, but completely demanding. Her fingernails were leaving score marks in his skin, but she no longer cared.

'Do you still have the implant?' he asked, pupils dilated and eyes dark.

She nodded in reply. It was all she was capable of.

Taking the weight of his body on his hands, Tam slowly lowered himself over her. She felt his erection rubbing against her inner thighs. Capturing her mouth, he tasted her with his tongue. Then his lips left hers and he trailed kisses down her neck, her collarbone and over her shoulder, his mouth feather light.

The look in his eyes hid nothing, his kisses so tender she knew he wanted her. With a passion that was deep and fierce. The feeling was mutual. Tam groaned, a primitive, deep sound from within his chest. She melted inside.

'You take my breath away, Cilla.'

With that, he nudged her legs apart and slid inside her. Her body responded to the intimate contact with a rush of red-hot desire.

The spectacle of Tam's defined muscles strained tight as he held himself back, the heat in his eyes burning bright, the feel of him hard inside her proved to be Cilla's undoing. She swallowed hard. It was no good, slow and sensuous be damned, she was going to explode any second. Her core contracted around him and she felt him jerk irresistibly. She let herself go, rocking her hips to and fro. Tam joined the rhythm, driving harder and harder into her, sensing exactly what she needed. His incredible perception of what she desired affected her soul, and the rapid thumping of her heart—matching the pounding of his heart—lifted the flames of desire to unfathomed heights. She was so close to release.

'I love you, Cilla.'

What?

Words she'd never thought to hear.

Then she heard him give a guttural cry, and it sent her over the edge, the white-hot pleasure tearing her into tiny pieces as wave after wave washed over her, and she cried out with him. He shuddered, overpowered, then collapsed on top of her.

The only sound inside the boat's cabin was that of their rough panting.

This time had been just as quick and hot as the moment

in the surf. But something fundamental had changed between them, a connection that hadn't been there before. Tam had said those words. He was indeed in love with her. Cilla was filled with the feel of Tam touching her skin; heart and her soul. It was so right. She was surrounded by an incredible sense of completion and peace as she lay here with him.

'I love you too, Tam,' she whispered into the silent morning. Her announcement shocked her for a second. Had she actually said that aloud? But the relief she felt in saying those words was worth the effort they took. So was the look in Tam's eyes as he stared down at her. He caressed the side of her cheek.

'I know.'

'What do you mean?' She pulled him down next to her, where they lay in each other's arms, legs tangled together on the disheveled bed.

'Well, I guessed anyway. It was pretty obvious. Why else would you have given me the talisman?'

'Because…' She halted while she tried to find the right answer. It'd been plain as day then, why she'd given up the talisman, but how did she explain it. 'If I couldn't win, then I wanted you to.'

'But you could've won, if you'd only stayed in the game.'

'No.' She shook her head. 'That would've meant I had to give in to my greed, to trample on those I cared about to get the money.' A frown hovered on her brow and she pursed her lips as she thought about her next words. 'That'd be too much like my father.'

'Oh, I see.' His reply was quiet, but filled with the weight of understanding. One hand stroked her bare shoulder absentmindedly. The gesture sent shivers racking through her body. It was so casual, yet so intimate.

'Can I just say, you're absolutely nothing like your father.' He continued to caress her bare skin, but the other arm gathered her in closer. 'You're a strong and capable woman, devoted and passionate. And that's what I love about you.' Silence fell between them as she digested his words, the only sound was of gently lapping wavelets against the outside of the hull. It was such a reassuring sound, Cilla began to relax, letting the lethargy of the afterglow engulf her.

Tam wasn't going to judge her for her actions. He'd seen her punch her father in the face, but there was no censor in his tone. It seemed he'd seen through her smokescreen of independence and indifference, put there by a fierce need to protect herself from what she perceived to be all men's avarice. Now she understood not all men were the same. He appreciated why she'd acted the way she had. Maybe, as much as she still squirmed to think about it, it'd been a good thing Tam had been there that night. To see just how much her father's self-indulgence and disregard for his family had shaped her life. It'd been so hard to admit to people how badly her father had let her down, but she knew if she was finally going to let others into her life, she'd need to stop worrying about how they might perceive her.

Tam's compassion had unchained her.

'Cilla, I have something to tell you and I hope it doesn't scare you.' The stroking stopped, and he got up on one elbow so he could stare down at her. The look on his face so earnest and sweet made her heart swell yet again.

Running her fingers through the soft curling hair on his

chest, she said, 'Nothing you say will scare me, Tam. Go on, out with it.'

'I'm moving to Orlando.'

Her fingers stopped their investigation as she stared up at him.

'I've taken a job at Disney World in Orlando.' For the second time that day, hope flared. Could it be true? If it was, this might change everything. It meant he was an easy three-hour drive away. The fact she'd trusted him enough to divulge that she loved him took on a whole new meaning now. She might actually have to follow through on her avowal. And that thought didn't scare her nearly as much as it once might've. In fact, it made her feel as light as air. Deliriously happy, as if her heart would beat right out of her chest. Then it hit her. He'd known all along this encounter might not be their last. And he'd told her he loved her, anyway.

'What about the children's clinic in LA? I thought you lived for that.'

His smile was warm and indulgent. 'You're not wrong, but it's going great and my partner is taking over the reins. I'm using the money I won in Sea-Quest to help start a new clinic over here. God knows, there's just as big a need in Orlando for dispossessed kids.'

She digested his statement. It must've been a hard decision for him to make, but he'd done it, anyway. Would she have been able to do the same thing? Taken a leap of faith. Moved interstate, not knowing what kind of reception he was going to receive.

'That isn't the only thing that brought me to Florida,' he said.

'Really?' She gave him a sassy smile, but his face

remained serious.

'I came here to be with you. If you'll have me.' Her heart fluttered beneath her ribcage. He was here. He was going to stay. With her. For her. At last, she realized not all men were the same. Some men were good. Dependable. His eyes lingered on her face, waiting for her answer.

'You could come down on the weekends and I could teach you to sail.'

A delighted smile split his lips. 'I'd love that.' He bent his head and kissed her, deep and sensuous. Pulling her in toward him, so that her breasts brushed against his chest, he nuzzled her hair. Then she heard his deep voice rumble, as he asked, 'Are you truly okay with me being here?'

'Yes, I believe I am.'

'Well, that's saying something,' he said with a laugh. He lowered his head so that his face hovered an inch away from her own, his eyes fixed on hers. 'I love you, Cilla Parsons.'

Laying her hand on his chest, right above his heart, she felt his lips press into hers and her soul soared up into the heavens.

'I love you, Tam Connor.'

Turning her arm over, she studied the words inked into the soft skin beneath her elbow. FREEDOM.

And now at last she knew. This was what freedom truly meant.

Connect with the Author

I really hope you enjoyed reading Island Redemption. For more action romance info, upcoming release dates, and access to free books join the exclusive Suzanne Cass reader club. As an added bonus, you'll get a copy of my FREE STORY.

Island Souls

http://www.suzannecass.com/contact/

Or you can stay in touch via my website
www.suzannecass.com

Facebook: www.facebook.com/suzannecassauthor/
Instagram: www.instagram.com/suzanne.cass/
Pintrest: www.pinterest.com.au/suzanne_cass/
Twitter: twitter.com/SusieCass1

Also by Suzanne Cass
NEW
Stargazer Ranch Mystery Romance Series
Combustion: Prequel Novella
Wildfire
Firelight
Snowbound: A Christmas Novella
Snowfall

Island Bound Series
Books can be read as stand-alone
Bound by Truth
Bound by Silence
Bound by the Stars

Colors of the Earth Series
Books can be read as stand-alone
Shadows in the Dust
Shadows in Deep Blue
Shadows of Red Earth

Romantic Suspense
Single Title
Island Redemption
Glass Clouds
Chasing Bullets

Love in the Mountains Novella Series
Books can be read as stand-alone
Rain on a Tin Roof
Lost and Found
Rescue his Heart

Please Leave a Review
The greatest gift you could ever give an author is to leave a review. You will be helping other people to discover this book and making a difference to me as an Independently Published Author. If you liked this book and want

other people to read it too, please leave a review.

About the Author

Suzanne Cass is an Australian author who writes rural romance and romantic suspense abounding with passion and danger.

Her debut novel, Island Redemption, won the Romance Writers of Australia Emerald Award in 2016. Suzanne was also a finalist in the 2019 Romance Writers of Australia RUBY award.

She had always had a fascination with the tough resilience of people who live in our amazing red-dirt outback country. When not writing about the characters that inhabit her head, Suzanne can be found roaming the Perth beaches with her border collie, or encouraging from the sidelines as her two sons play sport.

Visit her website www.suzannecass.com or subscribe to her newsletter via: www.suzannecass.com/contact

Acknowledgements

This journey has been a long and winding one, and I'd never have completed it without the help and support of so many.

To Gary, for believing in me and encouraging me to follow my dreams. Without you beside me, I'd never have achieved this goal.

To my sensational family and friends, fans right from the start, who've read (and re-read, and re-read) my never-ending drafts. Thank you for embracing my characters, celebrating my Australian settings and helping put my feet on the path to becoming a true-blue Aussie author.

To Rachel, thank you for all your friendship and patience in helping me shape this grey lump of clay into a vibrant story full of romance and adventure.

And to the amazing organisation, Romance Writers of Australia, whose volunteers give up their time for the love of books and writing. I've learned so much through my association with them over the past three years.

www.ingramcontent.com/pod-product-compliance
Lightning Source LLC
Chambersburg PA
CBHW020657110726
47901CB00001B/220